Books by Alex Willis

Non-Fiction

Step by Step Guitar Making 1st and 2nd editions

Standalone fiction

The Penitent Heart

The Falcon, The Search for Horus.

Crichtons End

The Road Home

DCI Buchanan Series

Book 1	The Bodies in the Marina
Book 2	The Laminated man
Book 3	The Mystery of Cabin 312
Book 4	The Reluctant Jockey
Book 5	The Missing Heiress
Book 6	The Jockey's Wife
Book 7	Death on the Cart
Book 8	Death Stalks at Night

O Lord, *how manifold are thy works*
In wisdom hast thou made them all?
The earth is full of thy riches
So is this great and wide sea
Wherein are things creeping innumerable
Both small and great beasts
There go the ships
There is that Leviathan
Whom thou hast made to play therein.

Psalm 104 Vs 24-26

THE PENITENT HEART

One Man's Journey from Despair to Hope

Alex Willis

First published in Great Britain by Mount Pleasant Press 2014.
This edition published with new cover by Mount Pleasant Publishing 2020

The story contained between the covers of this book is a work of fiction, sweat, and perseverance over many years. Characters, place names, locations, and incidents are either the product of the author's imagination or are used fictitiously. Any resemblance to actual persons, living or dead, or locals is entirely coincidental.

ISBN 978-1-913471-02-6

All rights reserved
Copyright © ALEX WILLIS October 2014

No part of this book may be reproduced, stored in a retrieval system, or transmitted in any form or by any means without the prior written permission of the copyright holder.

Text set in Garamond 11 point.

Cover photo https://pxhere.com

The image is released free of copyrights under Creative commons CC0.

This book is dedicated to my lovely children who say, 'My dad can do anything,' and to my lovely wife who calls me, 'Alexander the Great.'

1
A close shave

'Edward William Drysdale, you have been found guilty of the lesser charge of dangerous driving, aggravated by being under the influence of alcohol; a conviction which is clearly serious enough to reach the custody threshold.

'In the process of deciding your sentence I have taken into consideration the fact that Mr Ambrose contravened the Motorway Highway Code by walking back down the carriageway to remonstrate with you and was subsequently struck and killed by a passing vehicle.

'Edward William Drysdale, I sentence you to a term of two years in custody, wholly suspended for four years, and you are disqualified from driving for a period of three years, plus costs of £400. During this time, you are required to complete the alcohol awareness programme and before you can reapply for your licence you are required to sit an advanced, enhanced driving test.'

♦

'*A househusband* – is that all I am to you, Ruth? Someone you picked up to keep house and take care of your children?'

'Of course not, I married you because I loved you, and still do. And besides, in case you forgot, they're *our* children – you adopted them, remember?'

'But you called me a househusband, and in front of all those people in court.'

'What's wrong with being called a househusband, that's what you are?'

'Well, since you raised the subject, what's wrong with my name, why do you have to use his?'

'Listen Bill, when I'm in court I'm a QC. I have to act completely impartially and within the constraints of court procedures. I go by my previous married name because that's the name everyone in court circles knows me by.'

'But a househusband?'

'Bill, for goodness sake, stop going on about it; just remember that, instead of going to jail, you're going home. You might show a little gratitude for what I did for you.'

'I suppose you're right. Thanks.'

'Accepted. Now, since you're no longer able to drive, I suppose it's up to me to drive us home. Your case has cost me a lot of valuable time I can't afford to lose. What we're going to do about getting the girls to school during your ban I don't know. A taxi I suppose; more expense.'

'Sorry.'

'In the meantime, as soon as I can, I'll file an appeal against your suspension. We've got 21 days to file, but no guarantees though. Don't get your hopes up.'

'I'll ask my mum to help with the driving; she's always asking if she can help.'

'Bill, sometimes you're the limit. Anyhow, thankfully your Mum is collecting the children today so that's not an issue. In the mean time, I've got to get back to the office.'

'You're not going to be home this evening?'

'No, of course not, I told you yesterday, my advice is still sought on legal issues to do with the party manifesto. The general election is less than a year away and Boris says till we get it right I'm still needed at party headquarters.'

Ruth parked in the driveway and went into the house. Bill looked forlornly at his car, shrugged, and followed Ruth into the house to order a taxi to take him into town for the shopping. The busy life of a househusband must go on regardless he supposed.

♦

He returned from shopping and saw Ruth's car still sitting beside his old Volvo. What was it doing there? What was wrong? Why hadn't Ruth gone to London?

'Pizza's arrived,' said Ruth's eldest daughter, Abigail, as Bill walked into the kitchen, his arms festooned with dry cleaning and shopping. 'We've had ours. I've put yours on a plate, Bill; it's in the microwave.'

'Where are the twins?'

'You mean, where's Hannah and Rachael?'

'Sorry, I meant to say Hannah and Rachael, had a lot on my mind lately, if you hadn't noticed.'

'Rachael and Hannah are in their room packing. Apparently were off to Finland tomorrow to see Aunt Doris.'

Bill was stunned by this news.

'Where's your mother?'

'She's in her study. I think she's on the phone to Aunt Doris.'

'That's just great – Abigail, will you take these clothes upstairs, please? Put them on the bed in the spare room then come back down. I have some other tasks for you. In the meantime, I'm going to see what chaos your Aunt Doris is causing.'

Bill walked down the hallway to Ruth's study. He stopped by the hall mirror, looked at his reflection, gritted his teeth, and reached into his pocket. His hands shook as he took out a hip flask and took a swig of its contents. He waited for the shaking to stop, and then returned the flask to his pocket.

He stood in the study doorway, illuminated by the glare from Ruth's computer screen.

'– honestly Doris, it's no problem, really. I booked the flights as soon as I heard the news – yes, we'll be there tomorrow evening – Doris, Bill's just walked in. He looks – he wants to talk to me. I'll give you a call as soon as we land – Yes, I'll text you a picture of the girls. Bye.'

'Text a picture of the girls, why?' asked Bill, holding on to the doorknob to steady his hand.

'She hasn't seen them in months – that's all.'

'And what's this about us going to Lapland?'

'You remember. Aunt Doris fell and broke her hip while skiing in Finland. She's got no one to visit her in hospital, especially since my parents have gone overseas. You do remember me telling you, don't you?'

He shook his head.

'I told you, last week.'

'You only said she'd fallen while skiing, nothing about us going to see her.'

'Ah – well, I thought since its Christmas.'

'You thought – what about me?'

'Bill, if you'd paid attention, you'd remember I'd said we might have to go see her.'

'Oh, stupid me, I forgot. If you remember I had something rather pressing on my mind.'

'No need for sarcasm, of course I remember, I was your defence counsel. I thought you'd be glad to get away for a couple of days.'

'That's not the point; do you have any idea how much I'll have to do to get us ready to leave in the morning, or what this wild adventure idea of yours will cost? I have mountains of ironing to do, and the packing to complete; Abigail will help, I suppose. The twins probably won't want to go to bed and the thought of the two of them moaning all the way to the airport is enough to make me want to stay home.'

'That's why I suggested pizza for dinner, no cooking or cleaning up – what do I not understand?'

'What you do not understand is that you hadn't bothered to ask me before you booked this trip to see your Aunt Doris. Have you any idea how long I've been preparing for this, our first Christmas in our new house? My parents are coming to spend some of the holidays with us and on top of that I've managed to get tickets for *The Lion King*. Do you have any idea how *difficult* that was?'

'Sorry, I had no idea. You did such a wonderful job of keeping it all so secret,' she said, turning up her hands in a conciliatory gesture. 'I thought you would love to have a holiday away, especially with the accident and your trial being so stressful.'

'And what am I supposed to do with all the presents and games I've bought? The garage freezer is full with the biggest turkey I could find and the butcher has sent over a huge ham. The larder is full of vegetables and Mrs Parker is booked to come over Christmas Eve to help prepare Christmas dinner.'

'I'm so sorry. I'll call Aunt Doris and say something has come up and we can't make it.'

'What – and disappoint the girls? That would be cruel.'

Ruth sat back down and sighed. 'I am sorry. I should have discussed it with you first.'

Bill walked over to Ruth and stood beside her. He leaned over, wrapped his arms round her, and as he stroked her hair said, 'What's done is done. I'll call my mum and tell her they can help themselves to the food.'

'Thanks,' she said. 'I am truly sorry.'

'But tell me, counsellor,' he said, standing up, 'pray tell the court, why do we need to leave at three-thirty in the morning? The flight isn't till half-past seven.'

'M 'lord, if you've ever tried to drive up the M3 past Bracknell to the M25 during the early morning rush, you'd know why. Those few miles can take over an hour when the motorway is busy. Just look at the early start as part of our adventure. Here, I've printed off our boarding passes, it will save time when we check in tomorrow morning,' she said, a smile growing on her face.

He looked at the tickets and passes and groaned. London Heathrow to Helsinki, departing LHR 07:30, arriving HEL 12:25; a shiver ran up his spine.

He turned and headed back to the kitchen deciding that during the holiday, no matter what, he would carve out some time for himself. He'd have his own adventure.

2
Adventure in Rovaniemi

The drive to Heathrow at three-thirty in the morning was just as uneventful as Ruth said it would be. The M3 was almost empty. Hannah and Rachael slept; Abigail updated her Facebook, and Bill stared out the passenger-side window at the rain streaking across the glass in little curved rivulets.

The flight to Helsinki was as good as business-class could be. While Ruth read, Bill caught up on his lost sleep. Due to the high demand for seats, business class wasn't available on the second flight to Rovaniemi, so Bill spent the flight looking down at the snow-covered forests and at the flight magazine. The holidays in warmer climes caught his interest. He wished they were on their way to somewhere nice, like the Caribbean, instead.

'Wait here in the arrival hall for me,' said Ruth. 'I'll go collect the car, drive round to the front and come in and get you. I've got a surprise for you.'

'What's the matter with you two?' Bill asked the twins.

'Nothing really,' said Rachael.

'We thought we would be riding in a sled with huskies,' said Hannah.

'That's tomorrow. Tonight, it's dinner then bed for all of us; it's been a long day.'

Fifteen minutes later Ruth reappeared and announced that the car was waiting outside for them.

'Recognise it?' she asked, as they stood on the snow-packed pavement, illuminated by the streetlights.

'No, why should I?'

'It's the same model we were looking at in the showroom a couple of weeks ago, a Mercedes 4x4. Different colour but the same model – the one you said you liked. When I booked it, I thought, knowing how fond you are of my aunt, while here you could take it for a quiet meander round the town on your own. But since you've managed to lose your licence, I guess it will be me who drives it.'

Bill looked at the car for a moment then shrugged his shoulders. 'So it is, how *smart* of you.'

Ruth ignored the jibe and did the best she could to smile.

♦

The early night did Bill good and by the next morning the stress that had been part of his daily life had faded and he felt he could take on the world.

Bill breakfasted with the girls in the dining room while Ruth went off to organise a taxi to the hospital. She'd said after the previous day's flight and with the looming snowstorm she was too tired to navigate through the snow-covered streets.

'Are you coming with us, Bill?' asked Abigail.

'No. After all the running around I did getting us ready I think I'll just take the day as it comes and sit in the lounge in front of the fire and read.'

Ruth returned half an hour later with someone she had met in reception.

'Bill, this is Major Thornton, he says he knows your father.'

'Major,' said Bill, nodding his head.

'Ah, just a passing acquaintance, Mr Drysdale. We met at Twickenham at a charity event last year. We shared second prize in the raffle.'

'Small world Major. Um, Ruth, if you don't mind, I'm going to sit in front of the fire in the lounge and read till you get back. You know what your aunt thinks of me, better not to cause a fuss.'

'That's fine; we'll meet back here at dinner time.'

'I have to go as well,' said Thornton, 'pressing business matter to attend to. Been nice meeting you Mrs Drysdale, Mr Drysdale.'

Thornton headed off to the lobby while Ruth and the girls went to their rooms for their coats.

Finally, alone, Bill went into the lounge accompanied by his book and a large whiskey. He relaxed into a huge armchair in front of the crackling fire. He took a break for lunch then resumed his place. By mid-afternoon, he had finished his book and got up and looked around. The lounge was empty except for a waiter loitering by the service door. Bill nodded and smiled at the waiter, then wandered into the lobby. Through the hotel front doors, he could see a blanket of snow covering the car park and a lead-grey sky suggesting more snow was imminent.

'Hello, Mr Drysdale,' said Thornton.

'Oh, hello Major.'

'Excuse me if I startled you. Did you finish your book?'

'Yes, I did, thanks.'

'Enjoy your lunch?'

'Yes, it was brilliant, especially the lamb.'

'I had a bear steak – the flavour took a bit of getting used to, but other than that it was fine.'

'You wouldn't catch me eating bear,' said Bill, wrinkling his nose in disgust. 'Venison I might try, but definitely not bear.'

'Anyway, the hotel's menu certainly lives up to its reputation. And it's just plain John Thornton now – I retired a few years ago. Just do a little private consultancy work now and again.'

'Oh, I see.'

'I expect you'll be off out to play in the snow with your family?'

'I wish – my wife has taken the girls to see their aunt in hospital, and then out for a sleigh ride. She's as excitable as a six-year-old; no way will you catch me riding around in the snow on a sleigh. I doubt they'll be back much before dinner time, so I have the rest of the day to myself.'

'Oh – sorry, didn't mean to intrude on your quiet time.'

'That's OK. I'm quite refreshed now. I was thinking how nice it would have been to go out for a spin in the hire-car, get some fresh air.'

'Mr Drysdale, in that case, I wonder if you would do me a favour? I have missed my ride to the airport, and I have to catch a flight to Hamburg.'

'And you'd like me to give you a lift?'

'If you don't mind.'

'Ah, there could be a problem.'

'Why?'

'Slight problem with my driving licence, I–er–misplaced it.'

'Got banned?'

'Sort of, can't drive for a while till I take a re-test.'

'Can't see that being a problem, you were banned in the UK?'

'Yes.'

'This is Finland. Your licence is good here, believe me. I used to work for the government, had a friend who worked in the DVLA. He told me that you could lose your licence in the UK but still drive in other countries.'

'Well then, if you're sure.'

'Of course, I am.'

'You'll have to give me directions though; with all the fresh snow that's fallen I couldn't find my way.'

'Your wish is my command.'

'I'll get the keys and bring the car round.'

'Great – thanks! I'll just get my case and meet you outside.'

Bill pulled up at the front of the hotel just as the snow started to fall again. How odd life was, he thought; two weeks ago he'd been in the supermarket car park in Alresford watching the rain fall. Now he was watching snow billow in dusty clouds across a car park in Lapland.

Thornton appeared with his case, climbed in beside him, and said, 'If the forecast is correct, you won't be using your car during the next few days.'

'That's OK, it's got four-wheel drive. Getting around shouldn't be a problem.'

Thornton opened his case and looked inside. 'Damn.'

'What's the matter?'

'I've left some very important papers in my customer's office. I don't suppose we could make a slight detour, could we? It's almost on the way.'

'Won't they have gone home for the day?'

'No, they always have someone who works late, due to the time difference between Rovaniemi and London.'

'OK, let's go,' said Bill. 'Just give me directions as we drive.'

'Stay on this road, I'll tell you when to turn off.'

♦

'Doesn't look like anyone's here,' said Bill as they drove into an empty car park. A sign over the door read 'Zhukovski Limousines.'

'Turn round and park over by that gate. I'll go in and see.'

Bill kept the engine running with the heater on full and stared through the windscreen. He could see Thornton through the blustery snow in his rear-view mirror; he seemed to be having trouble opening the office door. Finally, after a hefty shove, it opened, and he went in.

He'd been gone about ten minutes when two black BMWs entered the car park and stopped outside the building. A passenger got out of one of the cars and went into the office.

Bill turned back to watch the snow. It was falling very heavily now, completely obliterating their tracks.

'Can I help you?'

He jumped as his car door was opened by a mountain of a man dressed head to toe in black.

'Hey, close the door – it's freezing outside! I'm waiting for someone.'

'Come with me, you can wait inside,' the bruit said, reaching into the car and turning off the engine.

He grabbed Bill's arm and tried to pull him out before realising he still had his seatbelt on. In the struggle, Bill tried to pull the door closed but gave up as the brute reached down, released his seatbelt and wrenched him, still struggling, out of the car. He was half-dragged through the snow and into the office reception. Seven faces, all male, turned to stare at him. No sign of Thornton.

'Found him sitting in his car, Boss.'

'Good work, Yuri,' said the tallest one. 'What were you doing?'

'I was waiting for someone.'

'Who?'

'A friend. Who are you?'

'Zhukovski.'

Bill looked at Zhukovski. He could imagine him dressed head to foot in black leather, black fur hat, a Kalashnikov over his shoulder and a smoking pistol in his hand. He was never a chauffeur, he thought to himself.

'What's your friend's name?' Zhukovski persisted.

'John Thornton. Is he here?'

'He's in the back room. He–er, had an accident.'

The others laughed.

'Can I see him?'

'Sure. He won't make much sense though – he's been given something to ease the pain.'

Yuri grabbed Bill's arm again, oblivious of the bruises from their previous encounter, and forcibly shoved him down a corridor and into a small room.

Thornton was lying on a settee, rivulets of water running down his face from the wet cloth he was holding to his forehead, a half-empty bottle of vodka grasped in his other hand.

Bill heard the door close and the lock click behind him.

'Mr Thornton! What have they done to you? What's going on? Who are these people, and why are we locked in?'

'Hold on,' he said rolling on to his side and slowly sitting up. 'Give me a minute – my head feels like mush. I'm sorry I've got you involved, Mr Drysdale. We must get out of here – they're going to kill us.'

'Why? I've never seen them before in my life.'

'It's a long story – I'll tell you later. First, we need to escape.'

'How are we going to get out? The door's locked and there is a room full of desperate men at the end of the corridor.' He glanced frantically from Thornton's livid face to the door and back, still struggling to digest what had just happened.

'Relax,' Thornton said, 'I've already thought of that. I fixed the window before they arrived, just in case I had to escape that way.'

Bill stared at him. How could he be so calm? Who was he, and what was he up to?

'Undo the catch and slide the window up.'

Showing no sign of the agitation he felt, Bill did as instructed. The window opened onto a vista of white snow-covered fields edged by a thick forest of tall spruce trees. He took in a deep breath of the cold, fresh, spruce-scented air and looked down.

'We're on the first floor with a twelve-foot drop to the ground. Now, what do you propose?'

'Look, it's not that bad, climb out and hang by your hands. You're a tall lad; you'll only have to fall a few feet; the snow should break your fall.'

He was about to remonstrate with Thornton about calling him a lad, when the urgency of the situation took over. Pushing the window as high as it would go, Bill lifted his leg over the windowsill, ducked under the top sash and sat for a moment catching his breath. It had been years since he had played climbing games. He half-smiled, recognising the blend of fear and excitement, but this was no game. Holding on to the top sash he lifted his other leg over the sill and adjusted his position till both legs hung over the edge. Should he just jump? The snow looked deep enough to break his fall; then quickly he changed his mind and turned onto his stomach, carefully sliding over the window-ledge till he was hanging by his fingertips. His toes rattled the window directly below. He held his breath, waiting for the sound of the door being opened and their attempt at escape thwarted.

'Go on,' urged Thornton, 'no one's noticed.' Bill pushed off with his hands as he let go and landed about two feet away from the wall in a snow-drift up to his waist. He stood up and watched the bulk of Thornton ease through the window and dangle. Although he was quite agile for a man of his size, he landed heavily with a muffled cry.

'Are you hurt?'

'Not sure, don't think I've broken anything.'

'Your ankle?'

'It's nothing, just a scratch.'

'But you're bleeding. Your trouser leg is wet with blood.'

'Let's get to the car. I'll bandage it later. You do have the keys, don't you?'

'There should be a spare in the glove box if they took mine.'

They managed to cross the car park unobserved and scrambled into the car. From the driver's seat Bill glanced in the rear-view mirror and saw Zhukovski and his henchmen emerging from the building. They stood in a huddle beside their cars, unaware that their captives were fleeing. He started the engine and eased the transmission into drive.

Zhukovski shouted something, ran to his BMW and jumped in.

'Damn the man, he's seen us,' said Bill, stamping on the throttle. A red mist washed over him; all he could think about was getting away from Zhukovski.

'Turn left through the gate,' shouted Thornton.

Bill wrenched the wheel over and just managed to miss the gatepost. The road sloped up and trailed into the forest then swung to the left and down into an icy stream. Sheets of muddy water flew up as the car ploughed its way through then bounced up the rutted track on the far side.

As they crested the hill he glanced in the mirror. Zhukovski's headlights glowed orange in the falling snow. Bill missed a left-hand corner and the car ploughed straight into a snowbank. They burst through, bounced over a ditch then slithered sideways.

He turned to look at Thornton. 'How are you feeling?'

Thornton shook his head, grimaced, closed his eyes, and fell back into his vodka-induced slumber. Bill smiled. The red mist cleared. Memories of his teenage years, steeplechasing on his granddad's retired racehorse and a string of first place cups sitting on his parents' mantelpiece came to mind. Poor old Rifleman, what a way to go. He'd escaped from the stable when the door was accidentally left open, gone for one last gallop and never returned.

The left rear wheel bounced off a tree stump and spun the car violently to the right. Turning into the skid and with a light touch on the accelerator, Bill motored gently out of the slide then accelerated. The car shot out of the trees and leapt three feet down onto the track. He was back on Rifleman, balancing his body for the next jump.

Zhukovski was nowhere in sight. With all the fresh snow on the road, Bill didn't know whether Zhukovski had passed him or given up the chase while he was off-road. Either way he wasn't going to hang around to find out.

He put the wipers on full and accelerated through the drifting snow. Halfway round the next bend he slammed on the brakes and skidded to a halt.

They were standing line-abreast, all eight of them, Kalashnikovs at the ready, every barrel pointing directly at him. He was back in Zhukovski's car park with nowhere to go and access to the road blocked by Zhukovski's car.

He switched off the engine, got out and looked at the car. Hertz wasn't going to be pleased.

Zhukovski strode through the fresh snow and stopped in front of him. He smelled of expensive cologne. Zhukovski stared intently at him for a moment then shouted, 'Yuri, take these two back to the base and lock them up – securely this time.' Thornton collapsed, the snow underneath him turning crimson where the blood oozed from his leg wound.

'Boss, this one's bleeding,' said Yuri.

Zhukovski looked down at the prostrate Thornton. 'Take him to the cell and get Karl to have a look at the wound.' He turned back to Bill. 'I'll talk to you later. You have a lot of questions to answer.'

A basement cell this time; no hope of escape. The walls were solid brick, with no windows, continuing up into a vaulted ceiling. A single light bulb behind protective wire-reinforced glass dimly illuminated the cell and a battered bucket in the corner.

Bill watched as Karl ripped open Thornton's trouser leg, surveyed the damage then cleaned and bandaged the wound. He looked at his handiwork, grunted at Bill then left, locking the cell door behind him.

Forty minutes later Yuri reappeared and beckoned Bill to follow him.

'Good luck,' croaked Thornton.

He was shown into a small empty room; it smelt of – of something he hadn't smelled since childhood. It was fear. The memory of the time his dog Bear was hit by a car, breaking his leg at the shoulder, flooded back into his mind. He'd carried the trembling animal from the house to his dad's car and then all the way to the vet's surgery. Afterwards Bill's coat smelled so bad his mother threw it out.

There was a small table and two chairs in the middle of the room. In the far wall was a barred window, the glass opaque with dirt and ice. He shivered and pulled his coat tight.

'Sit,' said Yuri as he left the room, locking the door behind him. Ignoring the order Bill stood up and walked over to the window. He pulled his hand up into his sleeve and scrubbed at the years of accumulated filth and ice on the glass. Leaning forward he tried to peer through, but his breath kept freezing on the glass. Between scrapings he spied a small snow-covered courtyard. Directly opposite he could just make out a stout post sticking out of the ground, like a cut down telephone pole. Thoughts of a firing squad at dawn flashed into his mind. He quickly returned to his seat when he heard footsteps in the corridor.

He stiffened at the sound of the key in the lock. The door swung open and Zhukovski entered, followed by Yuri. 'Sorry to keep you waiting. We've been talking to Thornton.'

Bill shrugged his shoulders, looked away and stared at the wall, puzzled by a faded poster of Lenin, then looked back at Zhukovski.

'Coffee?'

'Could I have a large cappuccino, with a dash of brandy, a slice of chocolate cake and after that, a nice hot bath?'

'It's black coffee or nothing.'

'Gosh – I'm spoiled for choice.'

Zhukovski turned to Yuri and nodded. Yuri returned a few minutes later with two cups of steaming coffee. He placed them on the table and without a word turned and left.

Bill picked up his coffee, noted the fragrance of brandy and gratefully took a sip of the hot liquid.

'Tell me, Mr Edward William Drysdale, why are you here in Finland? And why was Thornton in your car?'

'I'm here with my family. My wife's aunt had a skiing accident and is in hospital.'

'And Thornton – are you working together?'

'Certainly not, we only met this afternoon. He asked me for a lift to the airport. As we were leaving, he said he'd left an important document here and could we collect it first.'

'And?'

'He made me park – look, what's this all about? I offer to give someone a lift to the airport, and now I'm being treated as a criminal!'

'Why did you run away?'

'Thornton said you were going to kill us.'

'What gave him that idea?'

'Something to do with the way you treated him. I don't know – it's what he said and how do you know my name? I haven't said who I am. Are you the police?'

'Hmm, you're smart, I like that, and to answer your question, your wallet – and Yuri's wife works for Hertz at the airport.'

'You're not really a chauffeur either, are you?'

Zhukovski shrugged.

'Look I'm sure there's been a big mistake. Take me back to the hotel; my wife will tell you who I am.'

'Nobody is going anywhere just now,' said Zhukovski, glancing at the window. 'There's a blizzard blowing outside.'

'Well, at least let me out of this – this – damn prison.'

'I need something stronger than coffee, what about you?'

'What are you offering?'

'I keep vodka for visitors.'

'Hmm – do you have any whisky?'

'Jack Daniels Bourbon?'

'Straight glass with ice, and make sure the ice is floating high.'

Zhukovski smiled. 'Let's go to my quarters, we'll be more comfortable there.'

Zhukovski took out his mobile and pressed a number on his speed dial. 'Yuri, you can turn in for the night. Just make sure Thornton's secure, and tell the others they can go home.'

Zhukovski's quarters were plush. Bill chose an armchair in front of the blazing log fire while Zhukovski opened the drinks cabinet, took out a bottle and poured Bill a tall drink.

'Why *is* Thornton a prisoner?'

Zhukovski handed Bill the Bourbon and stood with his back to the fire. Drawing himself up straight, he announced, 'My full title is Colonel Vladimir Sergei Zhukovski, retired. I am a security consultant and this building is my Finnish office.' He smiled to himself and went on, 'I advise governments on certain areas of national security and as such sometimes have confidential papers kept here.

'Thornton is a disgraced former English spy. He steals, and then sells his secrets to the highest bidder. Apparently, he has become quite an embarrassment for his people – I understand they wish he would disappear, like one of your Cheshire cats.'

He smiled at his own joke then continued, 'Thornton tried to steal some papers from us last week. He was disturbed while doing this and apparently returned today for those he had missed. We believe it was his intention to sell the information to the Chinese intelligence service. We tried to apprehend him at the hotel earlier today but we just missed him.'

'That was my fault. I gave him the lift.'

'So, I have subsequently found out.'

'Have you got the information back?'

'He photographed the documents with his mobile phone then swallowed the SIM card. We are waiting for it to work its way through his system.'

'How was he planning to get away?'

'Well, as you probably know from your arrival yesterday, Rovaniemi has good connections with Helsinki and the rest of the world. Thornton was indeed booked on a flight this evening – not to Hamburg as he said to you, but to Hong Kong.'

'What will you do with him? Will you kill him?'

'No, that would serve no purpose.'

'What, then?'

'We will just scramble his mind.'

'How will you do that?'

'Our scientists have developed a very appropriate drug, it's genetically modified methamphetamine. It doesn't kill, it just causes permanent confusion.'

'Serves him right I suppose, who knows what he had in mind for me? So, tell me, how did you get involved in the security business?'

'I had just joined the army when the Soviet Union disintegrated. The Mafia moved in and took over, and the KGB was disbanded. I spent some time in the FSB before retiring. That's when I set up my consultancy. This driving school and limousine service is a way of working without attracting too much attention to my real business – the gentlemen you met earlier are my drivers.'

'You do lead an interesting life.'

At that Zhukovski put down his glass and said, 'I need to check on Thornton.'

'Can I come along?'

'Please, be my guest.'

Zhukovski opened the cell door and turned on the light. Yuri was lying on the floor, moaning. Bill entered and instinctively crouched down to have a look at Yuri's injury while Zhukovski swore, glanced round, then came to help.

'What happened, my friend? Where's Thornton?' said Zhukovski.

'It was the pillow-under-the-blanket trick – I came in thinking he was sleeping, and he hit me from behind.'

'He can't have got very far. It's blowing a blizzard and I have all the car keys locked up,' said Zhukovski.

'What about the troika?' asked Yuri.

'He won't have had time to harness the horses.'

'The snowmobile,' said Yuri. 'We hang its key on the wall by the garage door.'

'Damn the man,' said Zhukovski. 'He won't have gone by road I'm sure. Just in case, Yuri, call the team. I want half of you to cover the station and the rest to go to the airport. We can't assume that he doesn't have more passports stashed somewhere.'

'What will you do, Boss?'

'I'll take the troika and follow his tracks through the woods. I imagine he's making for the airport.'

'And him?' said Yuri, nodding at Bill, 'Shall I lock him up?'

Zhukovski turned and looked at Bill, then smiled mischievously. 'Well, what's it to be, a cold night in a cell, or a wild moonlight sleigh ride through the forest with a mad Russian?'

'Steeplechasing was my thing, never ridden in a sleigh. But I'll freeze to death in this coat.'

Zhukovski left the room and returned a few minutes later with a fur coat and hat and handed them to Bill. 'These will keep you warm.'

He put them on, pulled the coat collar up, sniffed at the fur, and smiled at Zhukovski. Zhukovski stared at him for a moment, shook his head, and then said, 'Hurry, this way, we waste time.'

Bill was at home again. The familiar sounds and warm muggy smells of Zhukovski's stable invaded his senses. Any minute now he expected to hear the welcoming whinny of Rifleman.

Working at a feverish pace they harnessed the horses to the troika.

'Get in, we don't have all night,' said Zhukovski.

Bill stepped on board and sat down on the rugs. Zhukovski picked up a bundle of furs and tossed them at Bill.

'Wrap yourself up, tight; it's well below freezing out there.'

Bill watched while Zhukovski walked round to the horses and scratched their foreheads while blowing gently into their nostrils. He spoke soothingly to each in turn, encouraging them thought Bill, just as he used to do with Rifleman before a really tough competition.

Zhukovski climbed on to the back of the troika, picked up the reins, and snapped the cold air once with the whip. The horses responded with a lunge then slowed to a swift trot as the weight of the troika came on to their traces.

The last wisps of snow were falling as they turned out of the car park. The moonlight sparkled on the snow-covered bushes reminding Bill of the snowman he had made for the girls last year, except these were everywhere and didn't have buttons on their fronts or carrots for noses.

Thornton's crude snowmobile track was easy to follow where clumps of trees had blocked the drifting snow.

'He must've rehearsed this escape route before he roped you in to his plan,' said Zhukovski. 'He's following your car tracks from earlier, and he would have succeeded if you hadn't gone off the track, even I had difficulty keeping up with you.'

Bill smiled.

'Why are we slowing?' Bill asked when they were deep in the forest.

'The tracks are getting fresher. Thornton has slowed. He's possibly concerned that he's being followed and has stopped to set a trap for us.'

They stopped at the edge of a clearing. Thornton was lying on the snow beside the upturned snowmobile.

'Wait here, I'll check him,' said Zhukovski, stepping out of the troika. He pulled out a gun, cocked it, and walked over to the prostrate Thornton. 'He's run into a branch: the broken end has stabbed him in his chest.'

Bill climbed out of the troika and walked round to the front of the horses. He gathered the reigns and brought the troika over.

Zhukovski picked up the unconscious Thornton and laid him on the pile of furs. He rummaged in the bottom of the troika, found a cushion, ripped the material from the bottom, and using it as a makeshift bandage, wrapped it round Thornton's bleeding wound.

First it was one, then a response, followed by the whole forest erupting in a cacophony of howls.

Bill looked nervously over his shoulder while covering the injured man.

'Wolves,' said Zhukovski, 'they've caught the scent of horses, or of Thornton's blood. We must be on our way.'

'Are we in danger? I didn't think there were any wolves left in Finland.'

'Only a few hundred in the wild, this bunch must have escaped from a captive breeding programme.'

'Will they attack us?'

'Not as long as the horses keep going. Wolves rarely attack humans – unless they are really hungry. They mainly attack animals that have been weakened by illness or are injured.'

It was Bill who first saw the dark, swirling shadows. He watched, fascinated, yet petrified, as the wolves darted in and out of the trees, keeping pace with the frightened horses.

'Are those wolves hungry?'

'What do you think?' Zhukovski gathered the reins and cracked the whip; the horses surged forward.

Bill counted seven wolves; the lead wolf was systematically leading the pack closer. Within minutes of appearing from the trees they were less than twenty feet from the troika. He watched, horrified, as the pack slowly made ground, then split in two and ran abreast of the troika.

Zhukovski fired his pistol into the wolves on the left. They dissolved into a mêlée of fur and teeth as the injured beast was devoured. 'That will keep them busy for a few minutes.'

'You mean they'll be after us again?'

'Afraid so, there's not enough meat on that one to satisfy them all.'

Zhukovski let the reins go slack. The troika shuddered and bounced as the horses ran scared, flecks of snot flying from their nostrils. For what seemed ages they ran flat out, dodging the trees while slowly pulling away from the wolf pack. Eventually, when the last wolf had loped off into the woods, Zhukovski reined in the horses and slowed their pace.

Thornton groaned and tried to stand up.

'Sit down, you fool,' shouted Zhukovski. 'You'll fall out.'

Thornton stared at Zhukovski and said, 'I'll take my chances,' then leapt off and made for the trees.

His injured right leg now stiff from sitting in the troika, and his left arm in a sling, Thornton made heavy work of wading through the knee-high snow. He'd gone thirty feet when Bill saw the first wolf. It was a large one with the torn ear he'd noticed earlier.

'That's the alpha male,' said Zhukovski, 'leader of the pack.'

Thornton stood his ground, raised his good arm, and shouted at the wolf. It threw back its head and howled. Within minutes the rest of the pack appeared.

It was all over in seconds. Before Zhukovski could shoot, the wolves piled in and began ripping Thornton to pieces.

Bill shouted at Zhukovski, 'Don't just stand there, do something, shoot them!'

'There's nothing we can do for him now.'

Bill looked on in horror. 'At least you won't have to recover the SIM card.'

Zhukovski looked at Bill, smiled, and shook his head.

'What will you do now?'

'Get you back to your hotel.'

'My car, I can't leave it at your office, it's hired.'

'I'll drive you back in your car. Yuri can follow in the troika and bring me home.'

'No, let Yuri drive the car, you can take me in the troika,' he said not looking forward to what Ruth would say about the car and its damage caused by the tree stump.

As they approached the hotel car park Bill saw Ruth and the girls standing by the car. She was waving her arms and obviously shouting at Yuri.

'What's going on?' asked Bill.

'Standard procedure,' said Zhukovski, 'part of the training. When you don't know what to say, say nothing. Yuri is just pretending he doesn't speak any English.'

'Vladimir, do you know how to make an entrance?'

Zhukovski smiled, nodded in understanding, cracked the whip, and yelled at the horses. Tired as they were, they immediately shot forward and into the car park. He pulled up four feet from Ruth.

Bill stood up and climbed out of the troika.

'Bill!'

'Of course, it's me. Who did you expect, Santa Claus?'

'I was so worried. This oaf drives up in the car, looking like it's been hit by a train and doesn't say a word. What do you expect me to think? And while we're at it, who's this idiot in the fur coat?'

'The car went off the road in the forest while I was taking Major Thornton to the airport and this idiot, as you so rudely call him, arranged for the car to be recovered while he returned me to the hotel.'

'But you've been gone for hours! What have you been doing and just what the hell do you mean by driving the car when you know you shouldn't?'

'Major Thornton said it would be alright. He said my ban isn't valid in Finland. Also, look at the car. Remember the blizzard this afternoon? I was sheltering from the storm, that's all.'

'Honestly Bill, you are so gullible. Your driving ban is world-wide. Don't you realise when the court takes your licence away, you have no licence? This is going to take a lot of explaining, not sure what I'm going to say to Hertz.'

'You'll think of something, you always do.'

'Thanks.'

Bill turned round and looked at the girls and saw tears in their eyes. 'Oh Ruth, it was awful, Major Thornton.'

'What about Major Thornton?'

'Mrs Drysdale,' interrupted Zhukovski extending his hand, 'Vladimir Zhukovski. Major Thornton was in the process of stealing confidential information from our office. Your husband was unwittingly giving him a lift to the airport when the blizzard started and caused his car to crash. We looked after your husband in our office till the blizzard blew over. Major Thornton foolishly ran off into the blizzard and was attacked by a pack of wolves, your husband – unfortunately – witnessed Thornton's demise.'

'And you saw that?' said Ruth.

Bill nodded.

'How awful for you,' she said.

'I love you, Ruth,' he said reaching out and gripping her tight.

'Mr Zhukovski,' said Ruth as she looked up, 'how will we ever be able to thank you?'

'Just doing my job, Mrs Drysdale, goodbye, enjoy your holiday.'

♦

Later that evening as Ruth and Bill were going up the stairs to their room, Bill said, 'Ruth, after today I can't wait to go somewhere warm for our next holiday. I've had enough snow for a lifetime.'

'How about the Caribbean, for the Easter half-term break?' she said smiling.

3
Back to basics

The Rovaniemi holiday now a distant memory, Bill woke to a chilly bedroom. He sat up for a moment and looked out the window; the countryside was shrouded in mist, the only sound a solitary blackbird defending its territory. Why couldn't life be more exciting?

He lay back down, closed his eyes, and not for the first time, relived the wild chase through the Finnish forest with Zhukovski. Now there was someone who led an exciting life. No-one's fool, a man who commanded all about him; bet he never had to do the dishes or ironing. For a fleeting moment, Bill imagined being one of Zhukovski's drivers, delivering some important dignitary to a secret rendezvous. And what was to be Bill's excitement for today? He was going to have to tell the children they weren't going to the Caribbean for the half-term break.

Ruth had broken the news to him the previous evening while they were eating dinner at the golf club. Boris had insisted that Ruth be present at the presentation of the party's manifesto at headquarters, the same week they had booked for the Caribbean holiday. As a sweetener, Boris had told her that, after the election, a cabinet position for her was being considered, possibly that of Home Secretary.

Sighing in resignation Bill rolled over and raised his head a little to look over Ruth's slumbering form. It was Monday morning; the alarm clock said five-fifty, plenty of time. He cuddled up close to her. Reaching over her sleeping body with his right arm he started to trace figure eights on her cheek. She stirred slightly and sighed as he nuzzled his lips against her neck.

'And good morning,' announced the radio. 'It is six o'clock, the temperature is three degrees, and there are possibilities of some scattered snow showers, clearing later in the day. But now the news, read this morning by the inimitable Fred Walker.'

As Fred droned on, Ruth stirred and got out of bed.

'Ruth, why are you up so early? Come back to bed for a minute.'

'I'm sorry, you know I have to be at the Party HQ early this morning for the manifesto read-through.'

'You're a QC, make them wait.'

'I may be a QC, but I still have an example to set.'

'And what about me?'

'You should have thought about it last night, before you had that last drink.'

'The last drink you refer to is the only one I had at the table.'

'And what about the drinks you had at Marcie's table? You spent most of the night there.'

'What's that supposed to mean, I was talking to her brother. He's off to Saudi Arabia to look at some horses she wants to buy. If you spent more time with me instead of with your Party friends I wouldn't have had to sit at other tables for company.'

He scowled, rolled over, and pulled the covers up over his head, ignoring Ruth's protestations.

Ruth continued to dress in silence then went downstairs to make her breakfast. Twenty minutes later she returned to the bedroom to say goodbye, but Bill ignored her and pretended to be sleeping.

He dozed fitfully, his anger slowly abating till a radio time-check told him it was seven-thirty. Throwing off the blankets he climbed out of bed and slid his feet into his slippers. His formerly clear head was now starting to throb. Standing up and stretching, he caught sight of his figure in the wardrobe mirror. Not bad for a thirty-eight-year-old, pity about the expanding waistline, maybe a trip to the gym would help. He shrugged and thought, or maybe not.

He pulled on his dressing gown and went down the corridor to the girls' bedrooms. The beds were made in both rooms and the school uniforms missing from the chairs. What had got them up so early? Then he remembered the new demonstrator car, the Mercedes 4x4. The dealer had delivered it on Saturday, and they were to have it for the week. Ruth had taken them out for a short drive to the club on Sunday. With trepidation, she had let Bill go for a drive round the club grounds, although he thought it had been a tame drive compared to the run in the hired car at Christmas. Today was supposed to have been the demonstrator's first trip in earnest – the school run. He shrugged in resignation and picked up the phone to call his mother to say that they would be ready to leave in about forty minutes. He got a busy signal; his mother was on the phone. He replaced the receiver meaning to call again in a few minutes, then thought, why not? Nothing could go wrong, and besides, they would be driving on country roads. Who would know?

He went into the kitchen to write a note for the housekeeper and saw Abigail had left him a slice of buttered toast with jam and a cup of coffee. While he ate, he wrote:

> *Mrs Parker, please don't forget the engineer is due this morning to service the boiler. Also, the gardener will be here to tidy the garden, as it is desperately needed after the recent storms. Mrs Drysdale said her whiskey is evaporating. While you are in town getting the shopping can you get another bottle for her? I think she likes Laphroaig; it's cheaper if you go to the cash and carry, also…*

He was interrupted by the sound of the car horn. Oh, those girls, so impatient. Finishing the note, he caught sight of the kitchen clock and realised he would have to rush if he was to make his hair appointment, collect Ruth's dry-cleaning and be at the club for lunch. Why was life so complicated? He definitely couldn't be late for the lunch meeting. Although Elizabeth and Marcie would understand, the childless Nigella wouldn't.

Leaving the note on the kitchen counter he dashed back upstairs to shave and dress.

◆

He pulled the front door closed and made sure it had locked behind him. He walked briskly over the gravelled path to the car, grateful for his jacket as it kept out the cold and the sleety drizzle which had just begun. Looking skywards he saw the earlier promise of sunshine receding behind dark inky clouds.

The little minxes, as he often called them, were waiting patiently in the car, singing along with the radio. He got in, checked the mirrors, turn signals, gear stick and finally his seat position. It wasn't that he was such a careful driver; it was just the children liked to play practical jokes and move things. Since it was a new car and he was running late he could do without the game this morning.

'Where's Grandma?' asked Hannah. 'I thought she was going to drive us to school today.'

'She's late and you need to get to school,' he replied, not saying he'd deliberately not called her. He had let his mother assume they were taking a taxi. Besides this might be the only time he got to drive the new car.

'Are you sure you should be driving, Bill?' asked Abigail.

'Of course, I haven't forgotten.'

'We have a name for the car,' announced Hannah.

'Oh, what is it?' said Bill, glad of the interruption.

'Chelsea,' came the chorus from the back seat.

'That's nice,' said Bill, getting ready to drive off.

'Sounds more like a football club than a car,' muttered Abigail.

'It's not,' said Rachael with a smirk. 'We call it Chelsea after Chelsea Tractor, that's what the nice man Jeremy on TV calls them.'

As he stared at the information on the dashboard, Hannah said, 'Bill, are we still going to the Caribbean for our half-term break, like Mum promised?'

No time like the present thought Bill. 'I am sorry, girls. Your mum has a very important project on at the moment, so we won't be able to go. But we will get some time away. Your mum has arranged for us to go and stay at your Uncle George's flat. The four of us will be there during the week and your mum will join us at the weekend.'

Two sad faces appeared in the rear-view mirror. Bill glanced to the left at Abigail and saw the disappointment in her face reflected in the window. Tony Bennett finished singing he had left his heart in San Francisco.

'Where's Uncle George's flat?' asked Hannah.

'In a minute,' said Bill.

Yellow Submarine came on the radio; the twins joined in the chorus.

He accelerated onto the main road and just as quickly slammed on the brakes, just missing the ubiquitous white van man racing to his next delivery.

'Damn fool, driving like that – someone could have been killed!' he yelled at the disappearing taillights of the van. 'Girls, how many times have I told you to be quiet while I am driving? You could have caused an accident.'

There commenced a silence that lasted till they caught up with a line of stationary vehicles a mile down the road.

'Sorry,' he said as they pulled up behind the line of cars. 'I should have looked; it was my fault.' He glanced in the rear view mirror and could see tears in the twins' eyes.

'It's all right, Bill, we shouldn't have distracted you,' said Hannah, sniffing.

Abigail pressed the button to lower her window and looked out to see what the hold-up was. 'There is justice in this world after all.'

'What?' said Bill.

'You'll see.'

A few moments later they passed the cause of Abigail's smugness. Sticking tail-up out of the ditch was the white van. The driver, ignoring the sounds of passing car horns, was talking on his phone.

The mood in the car changed. Bill said, 'Who knows where Bournemouth is?'

'I do,' was the chorus from the back seat.

'Will they ever learn proper manners?' mumbled Abigail.

'It's next to Poole,' said Rachael.

'That's good,' said Bill. 'Your Uncle George's flat is in a town called Canford Cliffs. It sits on top of a sandstone cliff looking out to the sea. There is a pathway leading down to the beach. You will need to be careful as there's a road directly in front of the flat. Something really interesting though: people sit in their parked cars, have picnics, and take naps.'

The back seat thought this was strange and looked forward to investigating the phenomenon.

'Will we have to share bedrooms?' a worried-looking Abigail asked, remembering her sisters' habits of picking each other's noses, and snoring.

'No. Your mum and I will have the large double bedroom and the three of you can choose which of the remaining two bedrooms you want.'

Being a few minutes late allowed him to find a parking spot up on the grassy embankment beside the school gates.

As the girls got out of the car Abigail said, 'you won't be late Bill, will you?'

He looked at her; she was frowning, lips pursed in anger. 'No, of course not, why would I?'

'Never mind,' she shook her head and walked off.

♦

After dropping the girls at school, Bill was soon looking for a parking space near the hairdressers. He was proud of his long black wavy hair and had studiously avoided the traditional men's barber shops all his adult life.

Most of the parking slots were taken and all the free places were too narrow for the new car. In frustration, he pushed his way back out into Station Road. A few yards later he did a U-turn and slid into a vacant slot in front of the hotel.

'Good morning Mr Drysdale,' said Debbie, the receptionist. Picking up the phone she said, 'hi Anne, it's Debbie. Can you tell Marcel that Mr Drysdale is here – thanks.' She put the phone down and taking

Bill's coat hung it up on the rack behind the reception desk. 'If you'll follow me, Mr Drysdale.'

Sitting down beside the salon window Bill said, 'Where's Isabel?'

'She hasn't been to work for a few days; no one seems to know where she's got to. I've asked Marcel to look after you today. He's new but don't worry, he really knows what he's doing. Would you like a cup of coffee?'

'Yes, please.'

Bill opened the magazine Debbie had handed him and turned to the article on holidays in South America. He was sailing up the Amazon when the coffee arrived.

Bill looked out at the rain now being driven hard against the window, and the mini-Amazons running down the gutters in the street. He shivered and turned to see if anyone was looking his way. No one was, so reaching into his pocket he took out his hip flask and poured a good measure into his coffee. It took three sips before he felt the warmth of the highlands coursing through his veins.

Bill had just finished his fortified coffee when Marcel walked over to his chair.

'Good morning Mr Drysdale. I'm Marcel; I'll be looking after your hair this morning.'

Bill was more than a little surprised when he saw Marcel, a muscled giant at six foot plus, with thick black hair tied back in a ponytail. He was wearing dark tailored slacks and crocodile skin shoes. On top, he wore a tight fitting short-sleeved barber's smock over a pale blue silk shirt with the sleeves rolled up, exposing his well-toned biceps.

Bill was used to the gentle smile and the innocent banter he had with Isabel each time she worked on his hair. Looking at Marcel brought back memories of his days in the Royal Navy and the illicit haircuts in the aft mess. This was a different situation altogether and he could not help but notice the ripple of Marcel's biceps as he the combed his hair.

'Do you know what happened to Isabel?' Bill asked.

'No, why do you ask?'

'No reason in particular, just that she was bringing me a gift back from her holiday.'

'Something nice, I hope.'

'It was something personal.'

They fell silent until Debbie came over.

'Marcel, there's phone call, something about your mother. I told them you are with a client.'

'Go get the call,' said Bill. 'I can wait.'
'Would you like another coffee Mr Drysdale?' asked Debbie.
'Yes please.'
When he felt no one was watching, Bill retrieved his hip flask and poured a good measure of the Scottish ingredient into his cup. He picked up the magazine and once again turned to the holiday section. How unfair life was. Why couldn't he be going somewhere – somewhere exotic like the Amazon?

Marcel returned and said, 'my mother fainted last week and was taken to hospital, That, was my father to let me know that she is now home, and resting, panic over.'

Relaxing even more to Marcel's ministrations Bill asked, 'Have you always been a hairdresser?'

'No – I have just left the Spanish Navy and am looking for a career in the family business. We manufacture hair care products. My father said that if I wanted to take my place in the business, I should gain unbiased experience by working in the industry away from the family influence, so here I am.'

'Are you married?'

Marcel grinned, and said, 'Unfortunately no, spending time in the Navy precluded any long-term relationships.'

'Know what you mean,' said Bill. 'I spent three years in the Royal Navy.'

Marcel looked at Bill in the mirror and said, 'only three years?'

'Ah, that's another story for another time. The Navy and I didn't get on so we decided to part company. Sorry I interrupted you, you were saying about relationships.'

Marcel continued, 'I hope someday I'll find the right person and settle down, in the meantime I work.'

'Any hobbies?'

'No, not unless you call golfing a hobby.'

'Play much?'

'No. Not as often as I wish, although I've just heard from my home club in Spain that I've been given reciprocal membership in a local golf club over here.'

'Oh, which one is that?'

'Hamsworth, have you heard of it?'

'Of course I have, it's my father's club. Are you going to play in the tournament?'

'Didn't realise there was one.'

'Oh, you must. I know the club secretary. I'll ask him to send you an invitation.'

'I'd be delighted, as long as it's not going to cause trouble.'

'Of course, it won't. And besides I can introduce you to my wife's friends, some of whom are single.'

'Thank you, Mr Drysdale, I'd be delighted. I'll write down my address for you.'

On his way over to the till Marcel intercepted Bill and handed him a salon business card with his home address handwritten on the reverse.

'I told you would be pleased with Marcel,' said Debbie picking up Bill's credit card.

♦

It had just started to rain and turning up his coat collar, Bill headed off to his car. He wandered up and down the street looking for the Volvo before remembering it was at home in the garage and he should be looking for the Mercedes. Dodging dripping umbrellas, he passed the bakery. There was an empty table beside the open fireplace. He felt a pang of hunger but ignored it. He knew lunch would be waiting at the club.

Further down the pavement he saw a large poster in the travel agents': a family relaxing on a beach in the Caribbean. It was no good wishing things could be different. They would just have to enjoy Canford Cliffs, although he hadn't a clue what there was to do there.

He found the car and jumped into the driver's seat. The road to the club took him back up through Station Road, which at this time of day was full of people trying to shuffle cars into the limited number of parking spaces. All of this would have to be repeated again in two hours' time and all through the day, week, month, and year. Why didn't these people just use public transport?

Next was to collect Ruth's dry cleaning from the cleaners. No parking spaces there either, so he double-parked and ran in for the clothes. When he returned there was a parking ticket under the windscreen wiper. He drove off ignoring the ticket until he was forced to stop and deal with it wafting past his face. Unfortunately, he had not turned off the engine and trying to grab the moving ticket brought audible laughter from a nearby bus queue.

Back in his seat he turned on the radio and settled down to drive to the club. Once on the dual carriageway he was finally able to see what the car could do. He jammed his foot on the accelerator and as the

Mercedes reached 105 mph, a roadside traffic camera flashed, he eased off to a comfortable 80 mph.

His heart still racing with excitement he exited into the quiet country road to Chinechester, only to be brought to a near standstill behind a convoy of drivers crawling past an accident at the entrance to the country club.

At the impressive cast-iron gates of the Hamsworth Country Club he said a mental goodbye to the queue of slow-moving cars.

The driveway was lined on both sides with immaculately manicured beech hedges, now turned brown with the winter frosts. Soon great drifts of daffodils and tulips would dazzle visitors with their welcoming show.

He partially lowered the windows and let the car walk along, gently stepping over the speed bumps. Further along, the driveway opened out into the private woods of the estate, a forest of ancient oak, ash, and beeches. The smell of wet leaves brought back happy childhood memories of times spent with his grandparents in Yorkshire. The engine was so quiet he could hear the sounds of the birds in the trees. Off in the distance, in a copse, he saw a deer with its fawn.

The road wound its way down a hill to a little humped-back bridge over a stream, which acted as a dividing point between the two lakes in front of the impressive clubhouse. He stopped close to the edge of the parapet on top of the bridge, wound the window all the way down and leaned out as far as he could.

Looking straight down he could see water cascading over the larger rocks, creating small streams of bubbles that were carried away by the swift-moving water. At the edges of the stream the water gurgled in and out of the reeds. Occasionally a small fish would meander through the stiller parts, it was so peaceful.

> *Clear and cool, clear and cool,*
> *By laughing shallow and dreaming pool,*
> *Cool and clear, cool and clear,*
> *By shining shingle, and foaming weir.*

Where did that come from? Then he remembered. It was from *The Water-Babies* by *Charles Kingsley*, a story he'd read when he was a teenager. Why couldn't life be this simple? Why was he always so busy? He envied young Tom; if only he could slip into the water and join him.

4
Hamsworth Country Club

Bill parked beside Nigella's Porsche 924. It was not a real Porsche of course Marcie had said, but then that was Nigella: grand champagne gestures of elegance on a beer budget.

As Bill ascended the steps to the club, the magnificent varnished, stained glass panelled, oak door was opened to him from the inside by Harry Greyson, also known to the children as Uncle Harry. Detective Chief Inspector Harry Greyson, to give him his full title, smiled as Bill passed through. 'Bill, good to see you. How are Ruth and the children?'

'They are all fine. Ruth is really looking forward to the weekend; she is leading off the woman's tournament on the Sunday morning. Will you be playing?'

'Yes, providing work doesn't get in the way.'

'That's what Ruth says.'

'Have Ruth's parents left the country yet?'

'Yes, they left last week. They are helping to dig wells and build schools in Malawi; they won't be back for several months.'

'Must call them when they get back, love to hear about their work. We just don't know how fortunate we are in this country. Here for lunch?'

'Yes. Thanks to Ruth I've been volunteered to be part of the dinner arrangements committee. Elizabeth, Marcie, Nigella and I, are going over the arrangements for the evening events of the tournament. Not sure what I can contribute though, I'm just a househusband. Are you here for lunch as well?'

'Yes, I'm meeting some colleagues – in fact there they are now. Will you excuse me?'

Bill handed his coat to Dan, the cloakroom attendant. 'The ladies are in the main dining room. The men have commandeered the committee room.'

'Only in the world of golf are men and women *equal*,' said Bill over his shoulder as he walked away and into the dining room.

The ladies were already at a table drinking coffee. They were sitting by one of the big sliding picture windows overlooking the veranda and

18th hole. They turned as he walked over, but before they could say anything, Bill said, 'And why are we not in the committee room? I thought it was booked weeks ago.'

'The men have it,' said the chorus of voices resignedly.

Bill looked around the large dining room while the ladies argued the merits of giving way to the demands of the male members.

'Sorry I am late,' said Bill, once the comments died down.

'Did that old Volvo break down again?' asked Nigella.

'No – new car.'

'Well, it's time you replaced it – it looks so out of place in the car park,' continued Nigella.

'Ruth is going to buy a Mercedes,' Bill said, 'it's outside in the car park – at least the demonstrator is.'

'Oh,' said Nigella. 'I thought you were.'

'Banned from driving, not on private property and the club road is private property.'

'Well that must be all right then,' said Elizabeth.

'We have it for the week to decide whether we like it.'

'Just perfect for the M25,' said Nigella.

'Bill,' interrupted Elizabeth, deftly defusing an awkward moment, 'you've had your hair done. It looks different – what have you changed; do you still go to the same salon?'

'Thank you,' said Bill. 'No change really, except a new hairdresser He's Spanish. I think I'll ask for him again.'

He relaxed, grateful to Elizabeth for putting a stop to Nigella's questioning. All the same, he still liked Nigella, even felt sorry for her because she was childless, something they had in common. Apparently, her husband had flatly refused to adopt.

Once he was seated the waiter came over and asked, 'Would you like something to drink, Mr Drysdale?'

'Could I have a coffee, please? You know the one I like—the one with the froth on top.'

'One cappuccino coming up.'

'Oh, I was just reading something about a hairdresser in the local newspaper. I wonder if it is the same person?' said Elizabeth, picking the paper out of her bag and turning the pages. 'Let me see now.' She read out:

> *A Spanish national, Isabel Hernandez, was apprehended at Bilbao airport yesterday while attempting to smuggle cocaine into the UK.*

'Do you think that's your hairdresser?' Marcie asked.

Bill shrugged his shoulders as the waiter delivered his coffee. It was just the way he liked it, froth on top and the secret Scottish ingredient inside. Sipping the coffee, he thought about Isabel, trapped by her circumstances; someone else he had something in common with.

At the table the conversation returned to the subject of Bill's hair and subsequently Marcel. At the mention of his name, Marcie, the only single and unattached person at the table, sat up.

'What's he like?' she asked, a flush of excitement showing on her face.

'Well, let me see,' said Bill with deliberate slowness, 'he's tall – dark – and handsome.'

'Bill, stop teasing,' said Marcie, laughing excitedly.

'No, really, he is tall dark and handsome. He's from Spain and is just out of the Navy.

'Everyone loves a sailor, sounds right up your street, Marcie,' said Nigella.

'Stop, enough already!' said Marcie.

♦

As they were finishing their meal with coffee and brandy, Elizabeth sighed contentedly and said, 'If you ladies will excuse me, I have a meeting booked with my husband. There are some details of the upcoming event that need to be completed.'

Marcie announced, 'Nigella and I are off to the driving range, then it's back to work for me. I have a class of children waiting for their dressage lessons at five.'

They all turned and looked at Bill.

'Me, I have to go and collect the children, busy life of being a househusband. Will you excuse me?'

'Oh dear,' said Dan, as he returned Bill's jacket, 'I just heard from the computer tech that the main road to town is closed, something about an overturned tanker.'

'Do you know of another way back into town? I just can't be late for the girls.'

'You could try the delivery entrance. The club management don't encourage its use by members, full of potholes this time of the year, but it brings you out on the main road about a mile past the accident.'

'Sounds fine, should give me an opportunity to try out my new 4x4.'

Bill took out his mobile phone to call the school then changed his mind and stuffed the phone deep into his jacket pocket. He wouldn't be late; Chelsea would get him there on time.

The service road turned out to be just two rutted wheel tracks covered with crushed rocks. The recent rain had settled into the potholes dotted along its length. Not quite the wild ride in the snow through the forest last Christmas being chased by Zhukovski he thought as he drifted around the first corner.

He tore up the road past an old, weathered, leafless oak tree. A flock of rooks made their protests known by flying in circles and cawing angrily. The road went straight for a quarter of a mile then turned gently to the right. Reluctantly, he backed off for the corner and swept through it as though he had been doing this for years.

Off to the right he could see a farmer driving a tractor across the field towards a gate about fifty yards ahead. The last thing he wanted was to be stuck behind a tractor.

He glanced back at the road and was confronted by the sight of a leopard-sized black cat crossing the road in front of him. He panicked; pushing his right foot down hard on what he thought was the brake pedal and hit the accelerator instead.

The car changed down a gear; shot forward, smashed through a low stone wall, became airborne, and came to rest piniond between two trees at the river's edge. As he tried to release his seat belt and open the door a large branch from the centre tree broke off and fell full length over the car, crushing the roof and knocking him unconscious.

He heard the sound of voices, two young children playing on the far side of the river; they looked like brothers. Bill watched while the younger of the two, wandered off towards the river. Bill tried to call out to the older brother, but his voice was just a squeak. He watched with growing apprehension as the boy toddled unsteadily towards the swift-flowing river. Bill waved a warning to attract the older brother's attention.

'Do something,' he tried to shout.

The lad looked at Bill and waved back.

Bill watched in horror as the little boy fell into the river and was carried away with the swift-flowing current. As he floated by he raised his arm and appeared to wave goodbye to Bill.

5
Hospital for one

Andy Jackson saw the Mercedes racing along the service road. Stupid bugger, he mouthed, someone will get killed driving like that.

He stopped his tractor and hurried over to the gap in the wall. The car must have been airborne for at least the first twenty feet. The tire marks didn't start till halfway down the embankment. Only the tail end of the car was visible, sticking out from under the branches.

It took him a few minutes to reach the car. He pushed his way through the broken branches and worked his way round to the front of the car. When he looked in through the crazed windscreen all he could see was a blood-covered face.

The trees were blocking access to the doors and the heavy branch at the front was pushing the remains of the broken windscreen into the driver's face. He called out that he was going to call the rescue services, and without waiting for a response stumbled up the hill to the tractor and his mobile phone.

Harry Greyson was just leaving the club after a most enjoyable meal. Getting into his car he turned on his police radio and heard the call to the traffic car in the vicinity to respond to an RTA on the club's service road.

'Control, DCI Greyson, I'll respond and assist with the RTA,' he radioed.

Harry made his way through the broken wall down to the scene of the accident. At the bottom of the slope the fire chief stood involved in an intense conversation with the farmer.

Harry went over to introduce himself.

'How's the rescue progressing?'

'It's difficult to get to the victim, both sides of the car are trapped between those two trees,' said the fireman. 'And having that large branch from the middle tree across the top doesn't help either.'

'Can't you cut it up with a chain saw?' asked Harry.

'We don't carry chainsaws on the rig and the saw we do have will never get through that branch, it is just too big.'

The rest of the discussion was lost in the sound of an air ambulance landing on the field beside the road.

Immediately the helicopter touched down, a doctor and a paramedic loped, crouching, under the helicopter's still spinning rotors, down to the scene of the accident. The fire chief met them and explained the problem.

'The only way we can get the driver out is to get the roof off,' he said. 'On top of that the driver keeps moaning about a missing child, we've looked but there's no sign of a car seat, let alone a child.'

'Can you use your truck ladder to lift the branch off?' asked Harry.

The foreman shook his head. 'The farmer's going to see if he can get his tractor down here. If he can we'll sling one of our ropes over that large upper branch and use the tractor to lift the branch,' he said, pointing. 'Then we'll cut off the roof of the car and extricate the driver.'

'OK, but before that,' said the doctor, 'let me see if I can crawl in from the back and stabilise the driver.'

'We'll have to clear some of the metalwork first,' said the chief. 'Dave, Jim, bring the jaws, spring the back door. See if we can clear a passage for the doctor.'

♦

The firemen worked calmly and a short while later Bill was released from the wreck.

Harry stepped back as the driver, strapped to the stretcher, head supported by neck blocks, was carried up to the waiting helicopter. All Harry could see of the face was blood, dark red, oozing out in a line from under the scalp.

He returned to the wreck to see if he could discover the identity of the driver. He found a wallet and was saddened to realise his worst fears. It was Bill who he had just seen taken off to hospital. Harry climbed back up the hill to his car and called Ruth's London office number.

'Mrs Drysdale's chamber,' said Ruth's secretary. 'How may I help you?'

'It's Harry Greyson, Ruth Drysdale please, it's personal.'

'I'm sorry Mr Greyson, but Mrs Drysdale is in conference and can't be disturbed. Would you like to leave a message?'

Keeping a hold on his temper, Harry said, 'Mrs Drysdale's husband is currently en route in an air ambulance to the hospital; would that do for a message?'

'Please wait, I'll get her for you,' he said putting the call on hold.

Harry drummed his fingers on the dashboard while listening to Michelle Bublé sing *Come Fly with Me.*

'Harry, its Ruth; what's happened?'

'Ruth, Bill has been in a road traffic accident; he's being airlifted to the A&E unit at Mount Pleasant Hospital. The doctor says he is stable and in no immediate danger.'

'But the air ambulance?' interrupted Ruth.

'Just happened to be in the area.'

'Who else was involved?' asked Ruth wondering if Bill's mother had been driving.

'No one else, he was driving on the club road and hit a tree.'

'What the hell was he doing driving; he's just started a three-year ban.'

'I didn't know.'

'We weren't advertising the fact.'

♦

Immediately hanging up, Ruth called Bill's mother.

'Agnes, can you collect the children from school? Bill's been in a car accident and he's on his way to the hospital, not sure how serious it is.'

'I thought when he didn't call this morning, he was taking a taxi.'

'That's what we'd arranged, but the silly sod drove the girls to school in the new car. Another fine mess he's created, who knows what this stupid act of his will cost. Sorry Agnes; forgot he's your son.'

'That's all right; I've done the same myself at times. Don't worry, I'll call the school and let them know.'

Ruth only got flashed by one camera as she sped out of London. At the hospital, she parked her car and went straight into A&E. She would argue both the driving and parking tickets later.

'How can I help?' asked the receptionist.

'I'm Ruth Drysdale; my husband was brought in by air ambulance a short while ago.'

'One moment and I will find out for you.'

Ruth could hear a phone ringing somewhere behind the screens.

The ringing stopped and the receptionist spoke into the phone.

'Janice, can Mr Drysdale see visitors? It's his wife – all right, I'll tell her.' She turned to Ruth, 'Mrs Drysdale, your husband is being assessed. As soon as the doctor is finished, he'll come out and talk with you.'

Ruth just had time to get a cup of coffee from the vending machine and sit down before a nurse came over to her.

'Mrs Drysdale, the doctor is finished, if you would like to follow me.'

Ruth got up and threw what was left of her coffee in the waste bin.

Bill was resting on a gurney, an IV drip plugged into the back of his hand, a green-faced monitor beeping in time with his heart rate.

'He's sleeping, it's quite normal after a head injury,' said the nurse, seeing the look of consternation on Ruth's face.

'But where are the bandages and why is his face still covered with blood?' she asked.

'The doctor will be with you shortly to explain.'

Ruth looked at the Bill's ravaged face. If it wasn't for the sound of the monitor and the steady rise and fall of his chest, she would have assumed he was dead.

She pulled up a chair and sat down beside him. She wanted to hold his hand but the IV tubes were in the way, so she had to settle for his fingers.

The curtain at the end of the cubicle rustled and the doctor came in. Ruth relaxed. 'Ed! I thought you worked at Barts.'

'Moved down at the end of last month. A senior consultancy came up, I applied, and here I am.'

'Can't tell you how relieved I am to see a familiar face. How is Bill doing?'

'I've checked him and I have to say he is a very lucky man. It appears that most of the injuries are superficial and confined to the face, but he will require plastic surgery. We did a brain scan a few minutes ago and I am letting him sleep while I wait for the results to come back.'

'What about the injuries to his face? You surely can't leave them like that?'

'When I am satisfied that there are no other problems, I will have one of the specialists from plastic surgery look at the injuries, then we'll get him cleaned up and the dressings applied. As soon as I have the results of the scan I'll come and see you.'

'Thanks, Ed,' Ruth said, slowly letting out her breath, 'now to call Bill's mother.

'Agnes, its Ruth,' said Ruth exhaling, 'The doctor says that most of his injuries are superficial – not sure what he means by superficial – sorry my mind's a muddle at the moment. I'll ask him when I see him next – yes, please bring the girls, even if Bill's sleeping it will reassure them.'

Ruth returned to the waiting room and another cup of machine-brewed coffee. She was halfway through a copy of *Surrey Life* when Agnes arrived with the girls.

She looked down at the three worried faces and said, 'Bill will be all right, he has no broken bones, he's only shaken up.'

'Shaken not stirred,' said the twins in unison with just a hint of a nervous giggle in their voices.

'Can we see him?' said Hannah.

Agnes looked at Ruth.

'Yes, of course you can. 'His face is—will be bandaged, so he might look more like a mummy than a daddy.'

'Mum, that's a howler,' said Hannah.

'Sorry, you will need to be quiet though. I think he's sleeping.'

Ruth didn't need to wait long for Ed.

'Ruth,' said Agnes, 'I'll watch the children while you and the doctor talk in private.'

'Thanks Agnes.'

'This way Ruth, we won't be disturbed in here,' he said leading Ruth into a small consultation room.

'How's politics?' Ed asked.

'We're still working on the new manifesto. Boris is being pedantic about transport issues.'

'Nothing new there then. Ruth, I'm sorry we are meeting under these circumstances.'

'Just glad it's not worse – it isn't is it?'

'No. Bill will be fine,' began Ed. 'He has some fairly deep facial lacerations. We'll put some temporary stitching in to start the healing, but he will require specialist surgery if he is not to have permanent scars.'

Ruth sighed.

'The initial diagnosis was a possible traumatic brain injury, the result of the CT scan is negative, although.'

'Although what?' said Ruth, the colour draining from her face.

'Relax Ruth; I was going to say that in Bill's situation, it's possible he may display some, temporary, emotional symptoms.'

'What do you mean; temporary emotional symptoms?'

'Teary and feeling sorry for himself. Sometimes he may act very childlike.'

'Great, another child in the house; just what I don't need.'

'I said temporary, Ruth, they won't last.'

'That's a relief.'

'Bill has no broken bones,' Ed continued, 'though I see from the doctor at the scene's report Bill was suffering from hallucinations. The doctor's report says that on the way to the hospital Bill became coherent for a moment and said, *It's all right, the police can stop looking for the baby, he's dead.*'

Ed looked at Ruth, 'Any idea what he meant by that?'

She looked away at the curtained window, shook her head slowly, and said, 'we've tried for children, but nothing seems to work?'

Ed continued, 'Bill was given a tetanus booster and prescribed Co-codamol, Co-amoxiclav and Valium.'

'What are they for?'

'The tetanus booster is a precaution for rabies, the Co-codamol is for pain relief, the Co-amoxiclav is to prevent infection developing and the Valium is to provide emotional stability during this stressful time.'

'How long will he need the Valium?'

'His doctor will review his situation in three weeks.'

Ed looked back at the notes and continued with the review.

'The blood test showed a blood alcohol content at 0.15. Ruth, I'm sure I don't need to tell you the legal limit in the UK for drinking and driving is currently 80 milligrams of alcohol per 100 millilitres of blood. Bill was at almost twice the limit for drinking and driving—and I'm sorry to say the police requested a blood sample.'

'I'd thought he'd given up drinking; he promised.'

'When was this?'

'First time was last February. He'd been in town to meet up with friends. On the way home, he said he'd stopped in a lay-by to check something on the car. Unfortunately, or maybe it was fortunate, there was a police car in the lay-by. When they talked to him they found he'd been drinking. He was breathalysed and taken to the police station to be re-tested. Fortunately, the re-test showed just under the limit. He was given a warning – he said he'd learned his lesson, I – I just don't understand. Then last week – Ed he was given a suspended jail sentence for dangerous driving while under the influence.'

Ed handed Ruth a well-thumbed small paperback book.

Ruth looked at the title: *Getting them Sober.* 'Do I give this to Bill?'

'No, it is for you to read. It will help you to understand better where you fit into this situation.'

Ruth slid it into her purse and said, 'I'll read it later, thanks.'

♦

'Agnes, I'm going to stay on here for a while. I would like to sit with Bill, just in case he wakes up,' said Ruth.

'I understand. Stay as long as you wish. I'll take the girls home and feed them dinner.'

'Thanks.'

At half past eight she got up and said goodbye to her husband and thought and wished all that was needed was a kiss to wake them from this nightmare.

The journey home from the hospital was one of the longest Ruth had ever experienced in her life. What a mess this was; she felt as drained as the whiskey bottle she'd found at the back of the kitchen cabinet. They'd had a couple of drinks after dinner Saturday and one with lunch on Sunday; now it was empty.

Ruth parked the car in the driveway, went in the front door, and walked through to the kitchen.

'Hello Ruth,' said Agnes, 'I've fed the girls. They're in bed waiting for news. I can come round in the morning and help with getting them ready for school if you want?'

'Thanks for the offer, Agnes. I'm not sure what we would've done without you today. I'm sure we'll manage and besides I could do with their chatter more than going into chambers. I'll work from home tomorrow. Boris will just have to understand that family comes first.'

She said goodbye to Agnes and wearily climbed the stairs. She looked into Abigail's room and said, 'Abigail, would you join me in the twins' room, please?'

Three pairs of tear-stained eyes looked expectantly at her.

'I talked with the doctor before leaving the hospital and he said that Bill will be fine, he'll be coming home on Thursday. The doctor says he will need to spend a few days in bed, then when he has rested he will need some minor surgery for the scars on his face.'

Three faces relaxed and smiled back at her.

Later that evening she read the booklet from Ed. She read about how the alcoholic goes from one crisis to another.

They now had a housekeeper and even a part-time gardener, so what did Bill do all day? The clock on the mantelpiece struck midnight and she realised she needed to be up early to make the girls' lunches and get them to school on time.

She remembered to put out the empty milk bottles, checked the doors, and went upstairs to bed.

'Good morning,' it was Fred again with the news about wars and rumours of wars. 'Why can't people get along?' Ruth said to her image in the mirror while she applied her makeup. She dressed and went down to make breakfast for the girls, wondering what they would like. She couldn't remember the last time she made them breakfast.

She wasn't prepared for what she saw when she went into the kitchen. There they were, her three princesses eating breakfast.

'I've made you bacon and eggs, Mum,' said Abigail, 'and I fried your tomatoes instead of grilling them. Do you want brown toast or white?'

'Er, brown is fine, thanks. When did you learn to make such a wonderful breakfast, Abigail?'

Shrugging her shoulders Abigail said,' I have always been able to. I make breakfast and lunches most mornings while Bill gets ready. Oh, we have a final rehearsal for the school concert this evening, I've told the twins to get their homework finished early so we won't be late. I've also told Gran that I'll make dinner.'

Ruth remembered the bit in the book about how the family balance shifts to prevent chaos while others in the family group take over certain responsibilities. Stress levels go up; children usually suffer, with the bright ones not doing as well as they should at school. She made another mental note to find out how they were doing at school, after all she should know, she was their mother. She had missed the last parents' evening, busy with the Brent bi-election. She wished she could be more part of the girls' lives.

'I will be calling the hospital this morning to find out about Bill. Suppose I stop by Burger King?'

'School rules, Mum. No junk food allowed at school. Only food prepared at home or in the school kitchen,' said Rachael, with Hannah nodding sagely in agreement.

'That's all right, Mum, not to worry. I've already made our lunches,' said Abigail 'Would you like one as well?'

'No thanks, I'll probably have lunch out today.'

'Oh Mum, Mr Willis called to say he's finished repairing my guitar.'

'OK, I'll collect it this afternoon.'

'Please don't forget, I need it for the school concert rehearsal.'

'I won't forget.'

'Hannah, can you clear the table while I put the dishes in the dishwasher? Rachael, will you help me please?' said Abigail, turning to the twins.

The three of them worked well as a team, Ruth observed.

'Can I be of any help?' she said.

'No thanks, Mum. We'll be finished in a minute,' said Hannah.

'Right then, I'll get my jacket and briefcase and meet you in the car.'

Disentangling herself from the morning school run she took the shortcut through to the A3, London and her chambers.

She busied herself with phone calls and correspondence until it was ten o'clock and time to call the hospital.

'Ah yes, Mrs Drysdale, can you wait a moment and I will see if the doctor is still here.'

'Ruth, its Ed Vincent. How are you this morning? Sleep well?'

'I'm fine Ed, thanks for asking. How's Bill?'

'I looked in on him about ten minutes ago and he was still sleeping. He had a quiet night. The night staff reported he woke during the night slightly confused and wanting to know if the child had been found yet. I will look in again on him later this morning. Why don't you call just before twelve?'

Next on the list was the car dealer.

'Good morning, Falke Mercedes. How may I help?' answered the receptionist.

'Yes, good morning. It's Mrs Drysdale, can I speak to Justin Harrison in sales, please?'

'Just a minute, I'll transfer you.'

Schubert on hold; a trout swimming up the river.

'Mrs Drysdale; good morning, how are you, and how is Mr Drysdale?' boomed Harrison.

'I'm fine, but I'm afraid Mr Drysdale has had a slight accident with the car.'

'Not to worry,' said Harrison. 'Is Mr Drysdale all right?'

'Mr Drysdale is in hospital. The doctor says his injuries are only superficial.'

'That's good to hear. When can you bring the car in, or would you like us to come and collect it?'

'There lies the problem; the rescue services had to cut the roof off to get Mr Drysdale out of the car.'

There was the sound of a sharp intake of breath. 'Can you hold on for a minute Mrs Drysdale?'

After a while the trout swam on down the river and was replaced with a lark ascending into a cloudless sky.

'Sorry for keeping you waiting, Mrs Drysdale. Can you tell me where the car is?'

'Ah, good question number two. I don't think I can. I went straight to the hospital to be with my husband.'

'Not to worry Mrs Drysdale. I will contact the police and find out where the car is being stored.'

Ruth was relieved to find out how well the report of the accident was received and pleased that they had taken out the insurance. And since the accident had been on private property, she hoped the insurance would cover the costs.

At five to twelve she called Ed Vincent.

'Ed, its Ruth, how's Bill?'

'He was awake when I looked in on him five minutes ago; he ate a light breakfast and is chatting to the nurses.'

'That's wonderful news, thanks, Ed.'

Ruth picked up her briefcase and stopped at her clerk's desk.

'Andrew, I am off to the hospital to see my husband, I probably won't be back in chambers today. I will be in for a short time tomorrow morning then I will be at the hospital Thursday to collect my husband. On Friday I will work from home.'

◆

Ruth had to wait a few minutes while the receptionist found which ward Bill was in.

The room was tidy and functional. Just big enough to accommodate the bed being swung round ninety degrees and being wheeled out through the door. A monitor sat on a trolley beside the head of the bed and a large picture window took up the wall opposite the door. The remaining wall at the foot of the bed had a doorway into the en-suite toilet.

Bill was lying with his head and shoulders slightly elevated, sleeping quietly. Even with the bandage on his head he looked ten years younger. She sat down on the chair beside the bed.

Looking at his sleeping face she couldn't stop her eyes from watering. She sniffed and reached into her purse for her handkerchief.

Bill stirred, opened his eyes and without saying a word looked at her. Ruth said nothing but watched his face as he struggled to focus his eyes, then she saw his confusion turn to fear.

◆

Ruth unwrapped the flowers she had brought with her and placed them in a vase found in the bedside cupboard. Bill turned his head to see what she was doing, looked at the flowers for a moment then burst into tears.

His knuckles turned white as he gripped the blanket. Ruth reached over, gently released them and took his trembling hands into hers and kissed them. He pulled them away and gripped the blanket again.

'It's all right, Bill, everything is going to be fine. The doctor says you will be able to come home Thursday.'

'Will I have to go to jail?'

'Why on earth would you think that?'

'I was driving when I shouldn't, you remember what the judge said. Two years in jail. I just keep thinking, what would have happened if your girls were in the car, what would you have said then?'

'But they weren't, though you were stupid to go driving when you shouldn't have. I'm sure we can work this out. I'll see what I can do, remember I've already filed an appeal.'

'A fat lot of good that will do. As soon as the police put in their report, the judge will send me down for two years, or more. Oh shit, suppose he gives me a longer sentence, what's going to happen to me? I wish you had never got me the car, there was nothing wrong with the Volvo.'

'So now it's the car's fault, who was the stupid arse who was driving it? It didn't drive itself.

'That's right; kick me when I'm down.'

'No body's kicking you, except yourself. Bill, when are you going to realise you can't go on living like this; one day someone is going to get seriously hurt.' Then she remembered someone had. Mr Ambrose on the motorway had died when he walked back to remonstrate with Bill, and Major Thornton, if Bill hadn't given him a lift to the airport he might be alive today, what a bloody mess.

It had resumed raining; rain ran down the glass creating waterfalls at the base of the window frame.

Still looking out the window Bill said, 'Will the police come to the house and arrest me? Who will look after the girls while I am in jail? You won't be able to; you're always too busy at work. You have an example to set. I suppose you'll get Andrew to help out at home, like he does at the office.'

'I need a drink of water; I'll be right back.'

Ruth ignored the jug of water on the bedside table and instead walked down to the nursing station.

'Hello, Mrs Drysdale.'

'Mr Drysdale, he's – he's being emotional, he is not like himself at all.'

The nurse picked up Bill's chart. 'He's due for his medication.'

She returned a few minutes later and said, 'I have given your husband his medication, he's resting now.

Ruth returned to the ward and the chair. Bill was sleeping, his hands no longer clutching the blankets.

After a few minutes he opened his eyes. He looked at her, smiled, and said. 'I'm sorry Ruth; I don't know what came over me.'

'That's all right, you've had quite a shock with the accident and – and.'

Tears started to trickle down his face again. Ruth pulled a tissue from the box on the bedside table and handed it to Bill. He reached up and squeezed her hand, sniffed a few times and said, 'I don't deserve you. How will I explain it to the girls?'

'You don't need to. These things do happen. There's not always a reason, that's why it is called an accident.'

Bill lowered his hand, relaxed and closed his eyes. A minute later he was fast asleep. Ruth sat there for a few minutes, emotionally numb. She felt confused. Bill was the patient who needed help, not her. Then a thought came to her, a dreadful thought. What would happen if he went to jail? Who would look after the girls, worse still what about her reputation? A QC with a husband in jail for causing a car accident while under the influence, with a death as well. There would go any chance of getting into the cabinet. The end of her political career before it had begun.

The door opened behind her as an orderly came to collect Bill's tray. Ruth stood for a minute beside the bed staring at her husband's face. The bruising around the eyes was darkening. She leaned down and kissed him on the cheek. 'See you tomorrow,' she whispered.

Ruth parked in the driveway in front of the house and went in. She was met in the hall by three sets of expectant eyes. Agnes was standing behind the girls by the kitchen door.

'How's Bill?' voiced an anxious chorus.

'He ate most of his dinner and looked very peaceful. When I left he was sleeping. I'm sure a good night's sleep will do him the world of good.'

'How is he really?' asked Agnes, after the girls had left the room.

'He looks worse than he is, but I'm sure he'll be fine, except.'

'Except for what,' asked Agnes?

'The fact that the silly idiot had an accident while driving after the judge had warned him he mustn't. He's worried he will have to go to jail.'

'Will he?'

'Who knows, it will depend on the police report to the CPS.'

That evening after dinner Ruth read to the girls then went downstairs to read again from the book Ed had given her.

♦

Bill was awake and sitting up in bed reading when Ruth walked into the room.

'Good morning young man, how are you?' she said, bending down to kiss his cheek.

'The doctor says I am doing fine,' he said putting the magazine down on the bedside table.

'Were you able to sleep?'

'Best I've had in ages.'

'Oh, your Mum and Dad are coming to see you this afternoon.'

'Lovely, I look forward to that. How are the girls? Have they been behaving themselves?'

'They have been perfect angels. The doctor says you can come home tomorrow. His instructions are, you should take it easy for the first few days, stay in bed till you feel rested.'

'I am so looking forward to getting home – what's happening about the car, the Mercedes?'

Ruth smiled and said, 'I called the dealer yesterday. They're going to collect the car, or what is left of it.'

'It was a very nice car and the girls did like it.'

'I liked it too, better than my BMW, should we get another one?'

Bill thought for a moment and then like a child nodded his head. 'Please, could we have a silver one?'

'OK, silver it shall be. I wasn't sure you would want another, but I suppose since I'll be the one driving, it won't matter that much.'

'It saved my life. It is, or rather was, a good car.' He yawned and said, 'I'm sorry, Ruth. I keep getting these feelings of just wanting to close my eyes and sleep.'

A large black crow landed on the window ledge. Ruth watched as it shook off the rain then looked in the window and stared at Bill. A cold shiver went down Ruth's back.

'Probably exhaustion from stress after the accident,' she said continuing to stare at the crow. 'It will be good for you to get home. We all miss you.'

When he didn't respond, she looked back and saw he had dozed off. She bent over and kissed him again.

She left the hospital and drove home. Her first call was the car dealer and the order for the family's new car.

'What time will Bill be home?' said Hannah at breakfast next morning.

'I'm not sure, it will depend on the hospital routine, I suppose. There's something I need to tell you about Bill,' she said. 'Due to the accident, Bill is having illusions that he has lost a baby.'

'Baby? You weren't,'

'No, of course not; I wasn't having a baby. Bill hurt his head and he is having slight problems with his memory making him quite emotional, that's all. The doctor says he will get better with time.'

'Oh Mum, how horrible for Bill,' said Hannah.

Abigail put her arms round the twins and gave them a hug. Ruth put her arms around all three and tried not to cry.

♦

Ruth went straight up to Bill's hospital room and was surprised to see him, not in bed, but fully dressed and in a wheelchair.

Bill saw the look of concern on her face and explained. 'The nurse said that since I was a little unsteady on my feet, I could use a wheelchair to go down to the car.'

'That's a relief, when I saw you in the chair I almost panicked. Do you have everything?'

'Yes,' he said, pulling his case up on to his lap. 'Oh, we need to stop at the chemists for my prescription.'

'Fine. How about we get you home and into bed and when I go for the girls, I'll get your prescription filled?'

'OK. Now can we go? As lovely as everyone has been, I can't wait to get home.'

'It will be wonderful to have you home.'

♦

Agnes was waiting for them at the front door.

'Mum,' said Bill, tears welling up in his eyes.

'I've turned down the bed for you and aired the room.'

As Bill got into bed, Ruth puffed up his pillows, pulled up the blankets and fussed over him as much as Agnes.

'I will be sleeping in the guest room for a few nights, Doctor's orders,' she said, smiling.

Bill smiled in return, shrugged his shoulders, and squirmed deeper into the blankets. He yawned, closed his eyes, and within minutes was fast asleep.

6
Isn't life wonderful

Next morning Ruth rose early and, for the first time in days, felt life was returning to normal.

'Morning, Mum.'

'Abigail, I didn't expect you to be up this early.'

'Is Bill awake? Do you think he will want breakfast?'

'I checked a few minutes ago and he was still sleeping, and.'

The remainder of Ruth's reply was lost in the din of the twins charging into the kitchen.

'Hannah, Rachael, shush, you'll wake Bill.'

'Oops,' said Rachael, 'forgot.'

Ruth continued, 'I'll pick up Bill's prescription after I drop you off at school.'

'Good.' Abigail turned to the twins and said, 'Hannah, Rachael, breakfast is on the table, please eat it before it gets cold. 'Mum,' she continued, 'Bill's toast and coffee. Do want me to take it up?'

'No, that's OK, you have your breakfast, I'll take it up.'

When Ruth went into the bedroom, Bill was lying on his back staring up at the ceiling; he turned his head to look at her.

'What's wrong?'

'Absolutely nothing, isn't life wonderful? It seems like years since I slept in this bed.'

Ruth thought about the last time and of the ensuing argument.

'I know what you mean. One night in the guest room and I feel like I have been away for ages.'

'You don't have to,' he said, with a smile on his face.

She returned the smile and said, 'Give it a few days, till you are properly rested.'

'I am so fortunate to have such a wonderful family who love me so much. I don't deserve you lot.'

'And you're nuts.'

This was the Bill she remembered from years ago. Inspired by his jubilant mood, she decided to broach the subject of his drinking.

'Bill, we need to talk.'

'In a minute,' he said. 'Ruth, I have given this a lot of thought and I've decided to give up drinking alcohol. I am tired of being picked on about my drinking. The guys at the club, they don't actually come out and say it, but I can see it in their faces when we meet. Now, with the accident and trying to avoid that panther on the farm road, they will say that I was drunk. I certainly don't want to give them ammunition for any future gossip.'

This statement stunned her; he had actually come to the conclusion she wanted without her having to say anything.

She thought for a moment, and then said, 'While you were in the hospital, I had a discussion with Ed Vincent. He suggested that you might like to try attending a group such as Alcoholics Anonymous.'

Bill's cheeks filled with colour and, raising his voice, he almost shouted, 'I am *not* an alcoholic and I certainly don't have a drink problem! Have you ever seen me drunk? Of course not, I only drink occasionally to be social.' He leaned back into his pillows, breathing hard and staring at the ceiling. 'Besides, I'm already going to an alcohol awareness programme, and you know how I don't like going to your club. The people there don't really like me. They're only polite to me because I am your husband. I just don't fit in. I wish you wouldn't make me go there. In fact, if I hadn't gone last week, I wouldn't have had the accident.'

'Bill,' she said, holding the pill bottle, 'we do need to talk. There should be enough pills in here to last through till next week and now the bottle's empty.'

'I know the bottle is empty. I was going to throw the pills out; they're on the counter by the sink in the bathroom.'

Ruth went into the bathroom and picked up the tiny white pills with the V-shaped hole in the middle. She returned and offered one to Bill. Reluctantly he took it from her hand and swallowed it with a gulp of his coffee.

'Bill,' she said, recovering her composure, 'Ed Vincent prescribed them for you to take. They are part of your treatment.'

'Hah, another one of your London friends, trying to keep me drugged and under control.'

Ruth sighed and stood up. 'I have to leave now, or the girls will be late for school. Your mother will be here by ten. I will be collecting your prescription from the chemist's, should be back before lunch. The girls would like to say goodbye before going to school. Shall I send them up?'

'Are they up already? I hadn't realised what time it was.'

'Not only are they up, they are dressed, fed and ready to go to school.'

'Abigail, what a strength she is. I don't know what I would do without her.'

'Would you like me to send them up?' she said.

'Of course, send them up. I want to see them,' he said, laughing, then. adding sheepishly, 'Sorry, I will take my medicine like a good boy.'

Ruth smiled and turned away to get the girls. She wondered how she would ever be able to keep him happy. It would be a lot of work for her, but she would find a way. He was her responsibility, he just had to stay out of jail.

She left the bedroom to find three faces staring at her.

'Mum, you're crying,' said Hannah. 'Is Bill all right?'

'Yes, he's fine. I'm just happy to have him home. You can go in now; he's waiting for you.'

Ruth stood back and saw the smile on Bill's face as the girls approached the bed.

'Good morning girls, ready for school?'

Abigail nodded yes; Rachael whispered something to Hannah.

'What's got your attention, Rachael?' asked Bill.

'It's your stitches; they look like a bunch of hairy caterpillars out for a morning stroll.'

'That's just what I thought,' Bill said laughing, with the girls joining in.

'Good, that's better. I want to hear all about your day when you get home. Grandma will still be here and, if the sun is still shining, we can have a picnic in the conservatory.'

'You're getting out of bed?' said Rachael. 'I thought you were unwell.'

Bill smiled. 'Of course, I am getting out of bed; I only had a bump on the head. I will be fine in a couple of days.'

'Bye Bill, see you later,' they shouted as they ran down the stairs and out to the car.

After dropping the girls at school Ruth drove into the town and the chemists.

'Can I have this prescription filled, please?'

'Just a minute and I will ask the pharmacist.' The girl was back in a few minutes explaining, 'We are out of stock of one of the items. We have our delivery at one-thirty this afternoon. If you come back after two it should be ready for you.'

Next on her list was the doctor's surgery to make an appointment for Bill.

'Dr Crookshank is not in today – he's at our other surgery. Dr Aswan is available at ten forty-five – what's your husband's name?' asked the receptionist, while staring at the computer screen.

'Dr Crookshank is our GP and I want to make an appointment with him for my husband.'

The receptionist turned back to the screen, typed some details and, continuing to stare at the screen, said, 'I'm sorry, but he doesn't have any time today. His schedule is full, and he is then off, till next Tuesday.'

Keeping her temper in check, Ruth explained slowly and deliberately, 'My husband was in a very bad car accident, suffered serious head injuries.' Continuing, she said, 'The attending doctor at the hospital has written to Dr Crookshank making recommendations for further treatment for my husband Now, can we start again? I would like to make an appointment for my husband with Dr Crookshank.'

The receptionist turned back to her computer, 'Dr Crookshank has time next Tuesday morning at ten for a consultation, will that do?'

Ruth nodded. 'Yes. There now, that wasn't so difficult, was it?'

As she drove home, the previous feelings of disorientation grew into feelings of foreboding. A great sense of loss came over her. There was something wrong with Bill, but she didn't know how to help him. For once in her life, her position as a QC, her connections with the party, and her wealth counted for nothing.

Her hands were shaking as she opened the front door. The whole house was quiet; the smell of freshly baked chocolate chip cookies filled the hall. She ascended the stairs with trepidation and stood by the open door. Bill was lying on his back completely still. She crept into the room, sat on the bed and stared at his face. The dark fuzz of his returning hair was becoming quite prominent. She looked at his long wavy hair and wondered why he grew it so long.

He stirred, took a deep breath, and opened his eyes. He looked at the bedside clock and then back at Ruth.

Ruth saw the puzzlement on his face and said,' I had to drop off the prescription and go to the doctors to make an appointment for you. And I've got good news for you.'

'What is it? Good news is scarce around here these days.'

'I've just been informed that your driving ban has been suspended pending your appeal—you are serious about giving up drinking?'

'Of course, I am, I never want to go through that experience again.'

'Good, though I don't know what will happen when the CPS gets the police report on your accident, probably have the suspension rescinded and you will – '

'I will what – go to jail?' he said sitting up straight, the colour draining from his face.

'Relax, were not there yet. I've still got a few rounds in the chamber.'

'I'll take the good news for now, I'll deal with – with the accident later.'

He relaxed, smiled then closed his eyes and within a few moments was sleeping again.

Ruth left him and went downstairs to work till it was time to go and collect the prescription and the girls from school.

♦

'Hello girls,' said Agnes, when they returned, 'I've made some sandwiches for the picnic, there's some cold juice in the refrigerator and as a special treat I've baked you some chocolate chip cookies, they're in the cupboard by the glasses.'

'Thanks, Gran,' they chorused.

'Bill's up!' shouted Rachael, running off into the conservatory, followed by her sisters.

'I've prepared a chicken dish for you all,' said Agnes. 'It's in the oven along with some potatoes. Bake at 300 for about thirty minutes, take the foil off, and bake for another thirty minutes. Any questions, ask Abigail.'

'Thanks, Agnes,' said Ruth. 'I don't know what we would have done without you.'

'That's all right, that's what families are for. Oh, Bill has planned a picnic in the conservatory for the girls, care to join us?'

'I'll come through and say hello, then I have some phone calls to make.'

Ruth followed the girls into the conservatory, kissed Bill and stood back to listen to the chatter.

'Hello girls; how was school?' asked Bill.

'Fine,' said Hannah, as Agnes brought in the sandwiches and set them out on a side table.

'Later that evening after dinner Ruth brought up the subject of the car.

'The salesman from Falk's called this morning. He said that our car has arrived, and they asked which silver we wanted.'

'It was the darker one,' said Bill.

'Fine, I'll give them a call. They have both in stock and said they can have it ready this week. Plenty of time before the holidays; it's not too late to cancel the order if you wanted.'

'What about my ban, do you really think you can get it lifted, permanently?'

'As I said earlier, it's not up to me. But I think we have a good chance. I had a word with old McKern yesterday and he said there is a precedent that covers your situation and we stand a good chance of winning the appeal.'

Bill thought for a moment, then said, 'Good. They are nice cars. No, my mind's made up, I'll take it. I am sorry about the other car and promise I won't break this one.'

♦

On Tuesday Ruth drove the girls to school, then returned home to take Bill to the doctor's.

'I have read the letter from Dr Vincent and he appears to be very happy with your recovery,' said the doctor, smiling. 'He has suggested that you may need help with getting over your dependence on alcohol.'

'Not anymore,' said Bill, his cheeks flushing red, 'I have completely given up drinking, alcohol that is, so I won't need any treatment, and besides I'm already on an alcohol awareness course.'

'I can only recommend. I will renew the prescription for your Valium and would like to see you in four weeks' time,' he said, handing the prescription to Ruth.

♦

As they entered the house the phone rang.

'Just a minute,' said Ruth, answering it, 'I'll transfer you to my study. Now Andrew, what's up?'

As Ruth listened, Bill wandered into the study.

'This evening?' Ruth exhaled between her teeth. 'OK, where does he want to meet, then?'

Bill could barely make out what Andrew was saying, but he did hear the words Crockfords.

'OK then, nine o'clock at Crockfords.'

Bill's colour was rising as he asked, 'Who are you meeting tonight at Crockfords? And what *is* Crockfords?'

'Boris wants to discuss the manifesto and has called a meeting at his club in London.'

'*His club*? I suppose that's another bloody expense the taxpayer will get stuck with?'

'Bill, it's all above board, an allowable expense when working in government.'

'Who else will be at the meeting?'

Ruth shrugged, 'I'm not sure.'

'Will you be having dinner?'

'Yes.'

'When will you be home?'

'I'm not sure, depends when the meeting ends. I think there's a half hourly train service up till midnight from Waterloo. I'll get a taxi from the station.'

'Haven't you forgotten something?'

Ruth looked blank for a moment, then said. 'Damn, I forgot; the girls' performances at the school concert. What time are they on?'

'Must you swear?' he said mimicking one of her mannerisms.

'Sorry.'

'It's bad enough you forgetting their concert. And for your information the concert starts at seven. Don't worry, I will explain it to your girls; after all they are used to you not being home.'

♦

On Thursday morning Ruth was awakened by the sound of footsteps in the hall. She looked at the alarm clock: it was ten-thirty.

'Good morning, sleepy-head,' said Bill, 'I've brought you some breakfast.'

'Thanks. After last night's dinner, I'm starving.'

'I thought you were going for a proper dinner meeting?'

'I thought so too. Turned out Boris had work on his mind, so we had sandwiches and coffee instead.'

'But not what you were expecting.'

Ruth shook her head, 'how did the girls do last night?'

'Abigail was very good. The twins on the other hand, well they were the twins. I told everyone they took after their grandfather.'

'What do you mean?'

'I videoed the concert, you can watch it and decide for yourself; most of the parents laughed. Will you be home today?'

'Yes, I'll work in the study this morning. Blast, just remembered, I think I have a meeting in chambers this afternoon. I'll have to skip the rest of breakfast and get up to London.' She leapt out of bed then stood and laughed.

'It's not a laughing matter. Abigail has a dental appointment at two this afternoon and the dealer will be delivering the car today.'

'I'm sorry, forgive me? I forgot – that meeting was last week.'

His face relaxed. 'We really do need a holiday, Ruth. I don't know if I can handle any more stress.'

Ruth reached out and pulled him to her. Hugging him tight, she said. 'It will be all right, you'll see. Life *will* return to normal.'

'I hope so,' said Bill.

'Tell you what,' said Ruth. 'How about we go out for dinner this evening, give us a chance to talk and not be interrupted?'

'Brilliant idea, I've spent enough time indoors, be good to get out and stretch my legs.'

'And, since it's our anniversary,'

'Oops, sorry, I forgot.'

'That's all right, you've got a good excuse,' she said grinning. 'Why don't we walk down to the White Hart? We can get a taxi home if you don't fancy the walk.'

'Sounds perfect.'

That night, Bill didn't sleep alone.

7
Reminisces

'Who was that?' asked Bill, as he walked into Ruth's study.

'Oh, you're up. No-one, at least no-one spoke; it was just another one of those silent calls. How are you today?'

'I'm fine, especially after last night,' he said smiling and drawing her to him. 'Are you going to be home today? I thought I would go for a drive.'

'Yes. Thought I'd catch up on some paperwork, then go over to the club and check on the arrangements for the tournament tomorrow. Going shopping?'

'No. Just want to go for a drive. I think I'll go have a coffee with Marcie's brother. I heard he's just back from Saudi Arabia; apparently, he's been out there teaching some of the princes how to ride European and looking at some new horses for Marcie. I will drive carefully.'

The equestrian centre car park was almost empty when he arrived. The only two cars he could see were a tired-looking Volvo estate and a shiny black Ferrari parked in front of the restaurant; Bill parked beside the Ferrari.

He was disappointed to see no-one at the tables but was captivated by the smell of freshly brewed coffee coming from a large Americano sitting on the counter.

'Hello, is anyone there?'

A fresh-faced teenager came out from the kitchen. 'Sorry to keep you waiting, we've only just opened. Can I get you something?'

'A large cappuccino and I think I will have something to eat, please.'

'We have carrot, walnut and date, iced orange or lemon cakes and double chocolate with dark chocolate fudge icing. We also have a selection of muffins, scones, flapjacks and biscuits; I was just about to bring them out.'

'Hmm, I am spoiled for choice.' Bill thought for a moment then said, 'I think I'll have a slice of the chocolate cake, please.'

'If you would like to take a seat, I'll bring it over to you.'

'Thanks. Oh, is Marcie's brother here, I think that's his car in the car park?'

'Not sure, I'll call the study. Can I have your name, please?'

'Bill Drysdale.'

Bill went over to a window seat, sat down and stared out at his car. It really was quite a nice car.

'Penny for your thoughts,' said a voice, waking him from his reverie.

He turned and looked up into the smiling face of Marcie.

'Oh, Marcie, you startled me! A penny might be too much.'

'Sorry, you looked so much at peace looking out of the window. I didn't know if I should disturb you. Is Ruth with you?'

'No – she's working, as usual. And looking out the window is becoming a pastime for me these days, is Dean around.'

'No, he's gone up to London for the day. I just got back from taking him to the station.'

'Pity, would have liked to hear about his time in Saudi.'

'I'll tell him you were here. Mind if I join you?'

'Be my guest.'

'So, Bill, how are you and the family?'

'They're all fine. Ruth is still working from home and the girls are getting ready for the half-term break.'

'And you?'

'I suppose I am fine as well. At least that's what the doctor says.'

'And what do *you* say?'

'I'm sleeping better, not so tired at the end of the day.'

'Taking lots of medication?'

'Oh no, not you as well!'

'Oops! Sorry.'

'That's all right, I'm used to it.'

'Nuff said, I won't mention it again.'

'Good, I can do without any more helpfulness.' Bill said picking up his coffee. 'This is quite some place you've got here, wasn't expecting such a choice of cakes at riding stables.'

'One must take advantage of all the opportunities that are presented.'

'What'd you mean?'

'See the covered dressage ring across the parking lot?'

'Yes.'

'It's where the young darlings exercise their ponies. Mum's and Gran's sit here sipping their cappuccino's and eating their way through plate-fulls of those cakes you were just mentioning, makes the stables a nice profit.'

'That makes sense.'

'Now then, what were you and Dean going to talk about?'

'I heard you had some new horses.'

'Not yet, they're due next month.'

'Pity, I could do with something to think about.'

'That all?'

'No, I just needed to get out of the house for a while and talk to someone who's not family.'

'OK. But I do need to mention I have a large group of bankers arriving shortly.'

'Really? Is that usual – the bankers, I mean?'

'Ah, the price of being successful, it makes for a very busy life. Everyone wants things done *now*. For instance, yesterday, as we were closing, the phone rang, it was the woman from the London bankers I just mentioned. It's her group that will be here shortly. She said she wanted to book the dressage ring for a staff team-building exercise today.'

'That's good for business. Bankers have lots of money to spend.'

'It's not good,' Marcie said, shaking her head, 'history might show that this country will never be defeated by an invading army, but mark my words Bill, one day capitalism will devour itself with its own greed.'

'Marcie, you're a contradiction,' said Bill. 'You make lots of money at what you do, then criticise those who make you rich. Has running your own business made you a champagne socialist?'

'Ha ha, there is a difference. I work for my money; they steal theirs. Is that your new car over there? I don't care what Nigella says, I think it is quite smart, wouldn't mind one myself.'

'I'll take that as a compliment.'

'Would you like to go for a ride while you are here? I am sure we could find some suitable size riding clothes for you.'

'No thanks, no riding today. I just came to chat with Dean and hear about your new horses.'

'Pity, Deerstalker could do with a good gallop.'

'I've never heard how you got involved in running an equestrian centre?'

'I was a trainer for one of the UK Olympic riders and when he didn't get picked for the team I was at a loose end. Then one of my American friends heard I was available and offered me a job in her stables in New England. I jumped at the opportunity and as soon as my visa came through, off I went. After living in the USA for a few years I got homesick and returned to the UK and set up on my own.'

'You have had a productive life,' said Bill. 'Not like mine – all I ever do is run around picking up after Ruth's children.'

'Ah, but you have a family to run around after. The only family I have are my four-legged friends,' said Marcie, looking closely at Bill's face. 'Those are nasty bruises.'

'That's what happens when you are in a car crash like I was.'

Bill pulled up the edge of his fringe to reveal the shaved area and the angry pink scars nestling in the fuzz of his returning hair. 'I will be going for plastic surgery in a couple of weeks to sort out the scars on my face.'

'Sounds like it was a serious accident, were you on your own?'

'Yes. But it wasn't my fault – I swerved to avoid a black panther.'

Marcie thought for a moment, picked up her coffee and said, 'The American truck drivers who drove the horse transporters said that truckers always blame a black dog running out in front of them for causing an accident.'

Bill looked straight at Marcie, his eyes tearing, 'You don't believe me, do you?'

Marcie shrugged her shoulders, while tilting her head to one side. 'Things happen, life happens, accidents happen, what is there not to believe?'

'I almost died in that crash, when the CPS finds out I was driving while banned I will be going to jail.'

'Bill, it was an accident. Ruth told me yesterday your ban was temporarily rescinded, technically you weren't driving while banned.'

'That's what I keep telling myself—it still doesn't take away the feelings of foreboding. Do you have any idea what happens to a man in jail when the old lags get him alone? Or what it's like to live with the thought that if the girls were in the car they could have been killed in that crash? At any moment the police could knock at the door and arrest me.'

'In life, one must cross many bridges and we don't always get to choose our bridges.'

'Marcie, enough of the philosophy for one day, please.'

'Sorry, I was just thinking of something.'

Bill caught a fleeting glint of sadness in Marcie's eyes. 'You do know what I feel, don't you?'

Marcie shrugged her shoulders and was about to speak when they were interrupted by the noisy arrival of what Bill assumed was the group of bankers.

'Please excuse me,' Marcie said, getting up to greet her guests. 'I have to attend to business. Will you be all right?'

'Thanks, I'll be fine. It's time for me to go home anyway,' said Bill, standing to go.

They stood together in awkward silence for a moment, then Marcie said, 'I'll let Dean know you were looking for him, goodbye.'

♦

There was no one in when he got home. Ruth had left a note for him.
Gone to the club with the girls, back by teatime, love Ruth.

♦

Next morning, he woke to find another note from Ruth.

> *Didn't want to wake you, I am off for an early round of golf. I said I would help Elizabeth with the setting up after my game. I've brought my dinner clothes with me so I can change at the club. See you this evening, love Ruth.*

As he read the note the phone rang.

'Bill, its Ruth, did you get my note? I forgot to mention, could you please bring my shoes? I left them on the bed.'

'Is that all?' he shouted.

'What's wrong?'

'You leave me to get the girls ready while you enjoy yourself, that's what's wrong. And what about Monday, who's going to help me get everything ready for the holiday? Not you, you'll be off at work.'

'Sorry—I forgot; I'll give you a hand Sunday afternoon.'

'That's all right, you don't need to bother yourself. I'll get Abigail to help.'

♦

'Girls, wait for me,' shouted Bill as he got out of the car and handed the keys to the valet.

'Mr Drysdale, good to see you,' said Dan, taking their coats.

'Thanks Dan, it's good to be back. Have you seen Mrs Drysdale?'

'I saw her go into the bar with the men a few minutes ago.'

'Thanks,' said Bill, then turning to the girls, 'let's go find our table.'

The restaurant had been rearranged with the tables spread around the edge to leave room in front of the low stage for dancing. Their table was to the right of the stage in the front row. Nigella and Elizabeth were already seated.

'Hello ladies, I suppose our partners are in the bar?'

'You guess correctly,' they replied in unison.

'Bill, Marcie was looking for you, something about a Spaniard,' said Elizabeth.

'Oh, I'd completely forgotten I'd invited him, I hope he turns up—for Marcie's sake.'

'We do as well,' said Elizabeth. 'Marcie has been acting like a child on Christmas Eve since she got here. Oh, there she is, Bill, over by the bar talking to Jack Palance, the golf pro.'

'She's not trying to pick up golfing tips, is she?' said Bill.

'Are you kidding? The only things she picks up are men,' said Nigella.

'Nigella, Bill's girls are here.' said Elizabeth.

'Oops, sorry kids; didn't see you there.'

'Let's sit down. Maybe the men will get the hint and join us,' said Elizabeth. 'How are you feeling, Bill? You look well.'

'I feel fine now, especially since the bruising around my eyes has mostly gone.'

'You've changed your hair, it suits you,' said Nigella.

'Thanks, I had the barber style it to cover the bald patches at the front. I am scheduled to go into hospital in two weeks for plastic surgery for the scars.'

'Hello Bill,' said Marcie, I like what you've done with your hair.'

'Thanks, are you going to join us, or are you out to snare that nice Mr Palance?'

'No, of course not, he knows Eric from years back and was bringing me up to date on what he's doing.'

'And what *is* Eric doing these days?' said Nigella.

'Five years for embezzlement. Glad I got rid of the bum.'

'Who is Eric?' queried Bill.

'My ex.'

'Oh.'

'Then who are you looking for?' said Nigella.

'If you must know, Nigella, I am looking for Bill's tall dark handsome stranger. Has anyone seen him yet?'

Just then the microphone on the stage crackled and the master of ceremonies announced, 'Ladies and gentlemen, would everyone please take your seats for dinner. For your entertainment this evening we have a surprise. Just back from a success packed tour of Europe, please welcome Dave Bennett, and his Benny Goodman Tribute Band.'

With the silky-smooth strains of *Moonglow* circulating around the room the men joined their partners and became immersed in their menus.

As the band finished playing, a still hush descended. Bill turned to see what everyone was looking at.

Standing in the doorway to the restaurant was Marcie's tall dark handsome stranger.

Bill stood up and said, 'please excuse me Ruth, our guest has arrived.'

Marcie grabbed Bill's wrist. 'Is that him?'

'The very same, what do you think?'

'Don't bother wrapping him; I'll take him as he is.'

Bill smiled and waved to Marcel; he waved back and headed in their direction. Bill began to walk towards him, but was intercepted by Marcie.

'You've got a partner, this one's mine.'

Everyone at the table watched as Marcie walked out to the middle of the dance floor and stopped in front of Marcel. He took her hand, bowed and kissed it. She made a little squirming motion of delight, linked her arm with his and as they walked slowly back to the table as the band started playing *It had to be you*.

'Mr Drysdale, thank you again for the invitation,' said Marcel.

'Thank you for sorting my hair. Everyone, I would like to introduce you to Señor Marcel Galan.'

'Marcie, you struck oil – he's a doll,' mouthed Nigella.

'Wow! What a dish, Rachael,' said Hannah, 'He's Bill's barber!'

'Back off girls, he's mine,' said Marcie. 'You can sit by me Marcel,' she giggled.

'I would be delighted to, Señorita.'

Bill could see he had chosen well. Marcie and Marcel giggled and made innuendos at each other all through the meal.

♦

The band came back on for their final session. Bill looked around for the twins and said, 'Abigail, have you seen your sisters?'

'Not since the interval. Do you want me to see if I can find them?'

'Please. Your Mum and I are going to dance some more then we must go home.'

'Mum, I've found them,' said Abigail, when Ruth and Bill returned to their table.

'Where are they?'

Abigail motioned with her head to under the table.

Bill lifted the tablecloth and gently helped the sleepy twins out from amongst the empty champagne bottles.

'Girls, what shall we do with you?' exclaimed Ruth.

'We only sipped the empties.'

'That's not the only thing they have been up to this evening,' said Abigail.

'Oh? So, what else have you two been up to?' asked Ruth.

The twins made a rude gesture at Abigail.

'Remember earlier this evening when there was a big queue outside the ladies' toilet? Well, these two locked the cubicle doors from the inside then climbed out under the doors.'

Bill turned away so that no one would see him stifle a laugh.

8
Holiday in Poole

'What have you got planned today?' Bill asked Ruth, as she prepared for work.

'I'm in court all morning, then a committee meeting in Parliament. When are you planning to leave for Poole?'

'I had hoped to have breakfast then be gone by ten. The girls have asked to sleep in so it will probably be closer to midday before we leave. It's not far to Poole so we'll have plenty of time to get settled before bedtime.'

'Wish I was going with you. I remember going to Poole as a young girl. We made a huge whale out of the sand on the beach, took ages.'

'We'll build one in your honour,' he said, smiling.

'Thanks, now I must be going.'

They stood by the front door and hugged for a moment. 'I wish you were coming with us,' he said, 'nothing has been right since my accident. It feels like we are two strangers who just happen to occupy the same house.'

'We have been through all this before. I just can't say no to the Party, especially with a general election coming up.'

'We can't go on like this Ruth. Something has to change.'

'I know, but listen, the election will be over in a few months then we can get our lives back to normal.'

'I could get a job,' said Bill, 'and you could take on regular cases, then we would have more time for each other and the girls.'

Ruth shook her head. 'Be patient please; in a few months we'll have plenty of time. Tell you what, we'll go away for a short break during the next school holiday, somewhere warm and dry, Mexico, perhaps, or how about the Caribbean? I hear that Martinique is a lovely island.'

He shrugged, kissed her, and said, 'You win. Have a good day at work.'

As he walked to the front door the post fell through the letter box. Bill bent down and picked up the single letter. It was addressed to him, it was from the court. His hands started to shake, was this, *the* summons he had been dreading. Had Ruth failed in his appeal? The memory of

Zhukovski's cell came to mind, the low brick-vaulted ceiling. A single fly splattered light behind a mesh reinforced glass cover, the battered bucket in a corner, smelling of stale urine and the steel framed bed with a yellowed, stained mattress. His hands started to shake; he crumpled the unopened letter and stuffed it in his jacket pocket, hastily took out his hip flask and took a long deep draught of its contents.

In spite of the late start Bill and the girls arrived at the flat in time for tea. Bill put his things in the large double room, Abigail chose the smaller of the rooms, and the twins took the bedroom at the far end of the hall.

'Bill, there's no food in the refrigerator and the cupboards are empty,' said Abigail

'Don't worry, we can go out for pizza and then go shopping for groceries.'

At the sound of the word pizza the twins came running in with an advertising brochure that they had found in the hall.

'Here Bill, they deliver, can we watch a movie as well.'

'I suppose so; after all we are on holiday. Tell you what, let's go out for pizza, then we can go online, choose a movie and stay up late.'

'Can we light the fire and toast marshmallows?' begged Hannah.

'There's only an electric fire,' said Abigail.

'We could use the hob in the kitchen, couldn't we?' said Hannah.

'Why not?' said Bill 'Let's get our coats and we will go get the pizza.'

It rained hard all night but by morning the storm had passed. Looking out the window towards the Old Harry rocks, Bill saw by the disappearing clouds that the day might turn out to be nice after all.

'What are we going to do today, Bill?' asked Rachael, stuffing her mouth with cereal. 'Can we go down to the beach?'

'That sounds a great idea. Tell you what, we could walk down to the chain ferry and go across to the other side for a picnic. I heard there are wonderful sandy beaches to walk on.'

The Sandbanks chain ferry was on the far side of the channel when they arrived, so they purchased their tickets and stood and watched the yachts going out to the bay.

The trip across to shell bay took only a few minutes and when they got off at the far side the twins said, 'Bill, can we walk along the beach?'

'OK, but don't get your feet wet.'

'Bill, that's like saying to a duck don't go into the pond,' said Abigail.

'I know Abigail, but we are on holiday.'

♦

Abigail ran to the ringing phone as they entered the flat.

'Bill it's for you, its Mum.'

'Hello, how are you doing, been on the beach?'

'It has been beautiful today. The sun hasn't stopped shining.'

'How are the girls, are they enjoying their holiday?'

'They are fine. At the moment the girls are climbing the walls; well the twins are. They have invented a game where they have to get from one end of the flat to the other without touching the floor. They've managed to get footprints on the ceiling; I don't know how I am going to get them off.'

'What, the twins?'

'No not them, their footprints silly, I miss you. What time will you be down Friday?'

'Well, that's why I am calling.'

'Oh no, don't tell me! You are going to have to work?'

'No, it's not that. A surprise birthday party has been arranged for my uncle; it's at the club on Thursday evening. I thought that if you drive up with the girls tomorrow, we could go to the party, then I could drive us all back down on Friday morning. It will save us the bother of driving two cars back at the end of the holiday.'

'Must we? I'm tired and the girls could do with relaxing. We walked along the promenade to Bournemouth and back today.'

'It would be a bit awkward if we didn't, especially as we are using his flat and Bill, we need to have a talk.'

'About what?'

'About your speeding ticket, it arrived in the post this morning. What possessed you to do 105 in a 70 zone? I don't know how I'm going to get you out of this mess. Don't you care about going to jail?'

'It could mean that?'

'Of course, it could. The judge clearly said if you got in trouble again it would mean an immediate imposition of your prison sentence.'

'Oh shit, I hadn't realised that, but you'll think of something, you always do.'

'Honestly Bill, sometimes I wonder what planet you live on. Listen we'll talk about this later, I'm due in court in five minutes, see you tomorrow.'

'Oh, all right, but we won't be there till late in the afternoon. I'm not getting them up early, it would spoil their holiday.'

'What did Mum want?' asked Rachael.

'We have to drive home tomorrow, there's a surprise party at the club for Uncle George.'

'Must we, Bill?' moaned Hannah, 'we're just starting to have fun.'

'Your Mum thinks it's a good idea, she'll drive us back down on Friday.'

'What about us staying up late again tonight then?' said Rachael, 'we haven't finished the marshmallows, and there's still the other movies to watch.'

'I told your mum that I wasn't going to spoil your holiday, so we will leave in the afternoon, when we're good and ready.'

'Right Hannah, marshmallows at the ready,' said Rachael.

Reluctantly the next afternoon the four of them headed homewards.

'Where have you been?' said Ruth as Bill walked into the house.

'I'm sorry Ruth, I couldn't help it. There was an accident on the M27 at Portsmouth.'

'Well, you should have left earlier. I came home from work early this afternoon to drive us to the party. I've been worried sick, why didn't you answer your phone?'

'I told you I wasn't going to wake the girls early and spoil their holiday—and I think I left my phone in the flat,' Bill said, rummaging through his backpack.'

Ruth breathed out, brushing her hair back with her hand said. 'I'm sorry; I was just worried about you and the girls. Your accident, remember?'

'How can I forget? Every time I get in the car, I have to take a deep breath,' he said, breathing hard through his nostrils. 'I'm sorry Ruth, what with the holiday being cancelled then the accident and now your uncle's party, it's all been a bit too much for me.'

'No, it's my fault, I should have been a bit more sensitive,' she said, drawing him close in an embrace. 'We'll get through this, you'll see; very soon now life will get better, things will change, I just feel it in my bones. Though I don't know why we haven't heard from the court on your appeal yet, I'll check when we get back from holiday.'

Bill fumbled with his jacket pockets wondering what he'd done with the letter.

♦

In spite of best intentions, it was past eleven before they set out for Poole.

'Mum, come and see our room,' shouted the twins with excitement as they entered the flat.

'In a minute, let me get in the door.'

'Mum, can we go out for dinner tonight, please?' asked Abigail.

'I thought you would have had enough of restaurant food by now.'

'No, we're on holiday. We went to a nice restaurant on Tuesday and Bill said we could go back when you got here.'

Bill nodded and said, 'It is extremely nice, they specialise in local caught fish and have window seats with views over the harbour.'

'You can see the windsurfers, and the big truck ferry when it leaves the harbour,' chimed in Hannah.

'OK, I'll give them a call and see if they have a table. What's it called, Bill?'

'Harbour View, their number is on the brochure by the telephone.'

'OK, eight o'clock, table for five by the window, thank you,' said Ruth, hanging up the telephone.

'Mum, look at us,' chorused the twins as they worked their way, crablike up the hall wall.

'Girls, not again; I have to clean the walls before we go home,' said Bill.

♦

'This is really nice,' said Ruth, as they sat down for dinner.

The waitress came over to their table and said, 'My name is Elise and I will be your waitress for this evening, can I get you something to drink?'

'Girls, what would you like?'

Abigail interrupted the study of the wine list and said, 'I think we will try the 7up. It has a slight taste of lemon, with just the right sweetness and this one appears to be of a particularly good vintage.'

They all laughed at her imitation of a well-known television food presenter.

'Bill, what would you like?' said Ruth, hoping he would ask for the same.

'Large white wine, whatever is chilled please.'

Ruth sighed and shook her head.

Later that evening she half carried him into the flat and put him to bed. She stood at the bedroom door and wondered when her Bill would come back. She made up a bed on the settee. The last they heard of Bill was his snoring.

9

Larsen

The train down from Waterloo had been busy, full of families headed for Poole and a short seaside weekend break. Arriving at Poole, Larsen hailed a taxi.

'Where to, mate?' said the driver.

'Can you suggest a quiet hotel? Somewhere close to the water, nothing too expensive?'

'Hmm, that'll be the Admiral Aubrey, right on the quay. It's privately owned, favourite hangout for locals, sailors, and people that want a bit of old England; will that do you?'

'Sounds fine.'

'You a sailor?'

Larsen thought of the two letters in his briefcase, snorted and said, 'Ask me tomorrow.'

Poole quay was teaming with visitors but that didn't prevent the taxi driver from parking on a solid yellow line outside the Admiral Aubrey.

Larsen went in through the double doors and walked over to the reception desk.

'Good afternoon, can I help?'

'Yes, do you have any rooms available?'

The receptionist looked at the register and said, 'I am sorry we are full, it's the time of the year.'

'The taxi driver recommended your hotel very highly.'

'Did he give you his name?'

'He said to say Terry sent me.'

'That Terry, he'll be wanting a commission next. Let me have a look on-line and see if there have been any cancellations. These days with the internet, business goes on without you putting a hand on things. Now let me see. Oh, how convenient—we have a cancellation; it's a double room at the front. I'll need a deposit, please.'

'Cash or card?'

'I'll take the card for a deposit and the first night. You can pay for the room with cash if you want when you leave. I know how awkward credit card bills can be when you travel. How long will you be staying?'

'Can I let you know tomorrow?'

'Certainly, you can have the room as long as you need.'

Larsen signed the register and as he looked up, he noticed a painting of a container ship hanging on the wall behind the reception desk. 'That looks like the MV Sargasso, that's my old ship.'

'Really? A friend of my partner painted it – Jim Robertson, did you know him?'

'Did I – he was my chief engineer! Is he around?'

'You'd have to ask Dot, she's my partner, I'm Beryl. So, you're a captain?'

'Who knows? It's the reason I'm down here. I have a meeting tomorrow that should resolve the matter.'

'Well, I hope it all goes well for you. Here's your room key. Turn left at the top of the stairs, your room is on the right at the end of the corridor.'

The room had a queen-sized double bed with an en-suite. There was a flat screen TV on the wall and a fine view of Poole harbour through the double-glazed window. Larsen stood looking out onto Poole Bay and wondered if this would be the weekend where his fortune turned for the better.

He kicked off his shoes, stretched out on the bed and promptly fell asleep. When he woke, he looked at his watch and saw it was seven-thirty. Taking the letters out of his briefcase he went down to the bar.

The only other patrons were two women seated at the far end. Larsen nodded to them, then sat down at the opposite end and waited to be served.

'Can I get you something to drink, Captain?' said Beryl.

'Ah – can I have a large black coffee, please?'

'Coming right up.'

'Will you be wanting dinner this evening, Captain?' said Beryl as she placed his coffee on the bar.

'Yes please, could I see a menu?'

'You can eat in the restaurant or here in the bar,' she said handing him a menu.

'That table in front of the fire looks perfect.'

'No problem, Captain. I'll get Dot to bring some more logs through while you decide.'

'Evening captain.'

'Evening, Dot. Can I help with the logs?'

'No thanks, I can manage.'

'Is it always this quiet, Dot?' asked Larsen as she stacked the logs by the fire.

'It's Friday night, the local youngsters are probably getting ready to go clubbing, sailing season hasn't started yet, and the other guests are all out at the theatre. Have you decided what you'd like to eat?'

'Yes, can I have the Admiral's Special, please?'

'How do you like your steak?'

'Well done, please.'

'And for dessert?'

'I'll let you know. Oh, by the way, have you seen Jim Robertson lately?'

'Not recently, did get a letter from him a couple of months back. He said he's got a job in Saudi Arabia, looking after a de-salination plant.'

'That doesn't surprise me; he always was a genius with anything mechanical.'

'Anything to drink?'

'Just water, plain tap water will do fine.'

♦

'That was one of the tastiest steaks I've ever eaten, Beryl,' said Larsen as she cleared the table, 'my compliments to the chef.'

'I'll let Dot know, she's always pleased when guests enjoy her cooking. Can I get you a nightcap? We have a fine selection of brandies.'

Larsen shook his head slowly. 'No thanks, much as I'm tempted, I'd rather have a mug of hot chocolate if that's possible?'

'I'll be right back,' said Beryl.

Beryl returned a few minutes later. 'Dot will be right out with your drink. You surprise me captain. I'd have thought a captain would be finishing off the day with at least a shot of rum.'

'It's a long story, doubt if you'd have time to listen, or find it interesting.'

'Try us,' said Dot, who'd just come out from the kitchen with Larsen's hot chocolate. 'The restaurant's closed for the night, all the guests are either out or have gone to bed and we can keep an eye on the bar from here in front of the fire.'

Larsen shrugged and said, 'Well if you're sure, I.'

'Just a minute, Captain, 'said Dot. 'You might not want a drink, but I do, Beryl – a brandy?'

'Why not, make it a large one; I believe the Captain's story will be at least a double.'

'I joined the Merchant Navy when I was seventeen,' began Larsen, 'worked my way up through the ranks, got my Captain's Ticket, and worked the container routes for several years.'

'Friend of ours had a cruise on a container ship,' said Dot, 'sailed through the Panama Canal and up the coast to San Francisco.'

'I've had guests on some of my ships,' said Larsen, 'they can be a right pain in the ar – excuse me, they can be a lot of work. Especially when they find out there's no shops or casino on board.'

'Dot, you're interrupting the Captain,' said Beryl.

'No problem,' said Larsen. 'One day while docked in Oakland, California, I met a lady. We fell in love and within six months we were married. I tried working ashore to keep Samantha happy, but I couldn't stand working in an office, so I went back to sea. This worked for us, till one day I received a letter to say Samantha had died in hospital giving birth to our daughter Stephanie – I went to pieces and hit the bottle.'

'How awful for you,' said Beryl, 'what happened to Stephanie?'

'Samantha's parents, they were living in San Francisco at the time, raised Stephanie for me.'

'Where is she now?' asked Beryl.

'At Stanford University, she's studying law.'

'Smart girl,' said Beryl.

'Typical,' said Dot. 'Some people don't deserve children.'

'Dot,' said Beryl, 'Captain Larsen's a guest.'

'My apologies, Captain, I'm just a little touchy when it comes to children.'

'Are you with anyone now, Captain?' asked Beryl.

Larsen shook his head. 'Not sure if I could trust myself in another relationship. If I did, she'd have to be someone very special to put up with me.'

'I'm sure there's someone out there just right for you, Captain. All you have to do is be patient,' said Dot. She looked at Beryl.

'Go on, you may as well tell him now,' said Beryl.

'I too was married once,' said Dot. 'When I fell pregnant with my third child I felt over the Moon. Unfortunately, I lost the child during childbirth. I wanted to kill myself. If it wasn't for Beryl and her selfless determination to see me through my hard time I might have succeeded. My husband, the rat, tried to get me committed and when that failed he left me and took the other kids with him.'

'What happened after he left? I mean, where are your children now?' asked Larsen.

'Somewhere in the USA, he was an American serviceman when we met. After my breakdown he returned to the USA, taking the children with him. He kept moving every few months, so I wasn't able to trace them.'

'How did you and Beryl meet?'

Beryl answered, 'We were school chums. I was going to a therapy group to help get over a bout of depression. My ex-husband was an alcoholic and sometimes he would come home stoned out of his mind and beat me. I finally left him after the time he tried to strangle me. I had some money set aside for an emergency and Dot had some from her pension plan, so we clubbed together and bought this place.'

'You've both certainly had a rough time. Sorry about your kids, Dot.'

'It's not so bad; life does have its compensations.'

'What do you mean?'

Dot looked at Beryl.

'We have a young girl working for us,' said Beryl. 'Michelle was having a rough time at home and needed a safe place to stay; Dot's sort of adopted her. Now we always look out for women and men that may need a safe place while they sort things out.'

'*Men, and women?*' said Larsen.

'Captain, unfortunately men get battered by their partners, just like women.'

'I never realised.'

'Most men don't,' said Dot.

'And neither of you have remarried?'

'No, running the Admiral is husband enough for both of us,' said Beryl.

'You two amaze me,' said Larsen. 'Much as I would like to sit here and reminisce with you I must say good night. I've a big day tomorrow and I need to be at my best, I'm off for an early night.'

'Breakfast starts at seven, Captain,' said Beryl. 'Good night, pleasant dreams.'

10

The Nightmare

To anyone walking past in the street below, the flat in Canford Cliffs was quiet and peaceful; to Bill, it was anything but. Trapped in another alcohol-induced nightmare he struggled to free himself from a tangle of brambles. He watched in horror as his baby was picked up from the grass by a yellow-eyed, saliva-dripping panther. Bill tried to yell '*Bring back my baby!*' but no sound came from his mouth. He woke clutching his pillow, sweat stinging his eyes.

When would these nightmares end? The doctor had said the medication should help – but he'd also said no alcohol.

Bill untangled himself from the blankets, sat up and immediately lay back down, his head throbbing. He waited till the spasms of pain subsided before easing himself out of bed. With trembling hands he pulled his bathrobe tight about his waist and looked out the window and down at the waves of morning mist washing against the chine. He glanced back at the bed, only his side had been slept on, he'd failed again.

He shivered, shuffled out of the bedroom into the hall, and stopped at the kitchen door.

'Is anyone home?' His voice echoed through the empty flat.

He pushed the kitchen door open; it banged against the wall. The throbbing in his head returned. Bill opened a cupboard and fished behind the tins of beans for the opened bottle of whiskey. He drained it in three big gulps.

With shaking hands, he picked up the cafetiér and filled a mug with cold coffee. He didn't notice the note that Ruth had left him till after some spilled coffee had soaked into it. The words, *along the beach,* were all he could make out. He placed the mug of cold coffee in the microwave and set the timer for three minutes.

He put two slices of bread in the toaster and waited until the microwave beeped. He jumped in pain and dropped the mug as the hot liquid burnt his lip. He saw smoke rising in wisps from the toaster and grabbed the toast as it popped out of the top. It was burnt, and the attempt to spread frozen butter on it broke the toast into pieces. He swore and threw what was left in the bin.

His attempt to eat cereal met with the same level of success. By the third mouthful his sleepy taste buds told him the milk tasted odd. It wasn't till he picked up the carton and read the label that he realised it was soya milk. Grabbing a glass from the draining board he rinsed out his mouth with fresh water.

Bill returned to the bedroom and got dressed. Then he went into the bathroom to brush his teeth, but his head started to spin and he vomited what little there was in his stomach.

He returned to the bedroom and put on his coat. He heard the sound of the crumpled letter from the court as he did up the zipper.

He sat back down on the bed and took the letter out of his pocket. He stared at it, unopened, afraid of its contents. Why was this happening to him? Why did he feel the way he did? The accident wasn't his fault. He should be excited, looking forward to future with a loving family.

He had everything he wanted, a lovely home, three wonderful children, a wife that says she loves him and an allowance to run the house that any self-respecting man would consider outrageously generous. Also, there was the new 4X4, membership at the golf club and plenty of friends to hang out with. With all that, why was he so unhappy? He'd become reconciled to the fact they had no children between them. Though that didn't stop him from dreaming; a son would have been nice, someone to grow up with, a friend to hang out with, but it wasn't too be.

He stuffed the unopened letter into his backpack, along with his phone and raincoat, made sure his wallet was in his trouser pocket and headed for the door.

He headed for the beach then changed his mind, he needed time to think. The last thing he needed right now was a cold walk along a wet beach. A drink in front of a log fire came to mind and he decided to head into town to find a suitable pub. As he made his way along the road the cold mist blew into his jacket making him shiver, he pulled the hood over his head and did the zipper up to his chin. At the high street he looked for a taxi. Finding none, he had to wait for the bus.

Twenty minutes later Bill was in town but not sure where to go. The idea of a town pub didn't appeal, and his stomach was telling him it was time to eat. He stopped at a cashpoint in the mall. He stuffed the cash into his wallet before returning it to his pocket.

As he walked past the marina, he wondered what it would be like to live on a boat and go travelling. But what would he do with the girls? They had school, and of course Ruth would always be too busy. He looked at several restaurants but disregarded them all until he came to the Admiral Aubrey Hotel. It was situated on a street corner across from the quayside, and of all the places to eat this looked the most interesting.

The Dickensian bowed windows of the restaurant were spotless and gave a good view of the interior. Bill looked in and saw that there were several spare tables.

He wove his way past the smokers' tables on either side of the pub entrance and went into the bar. A drink first then something to eat, he said to himself.

'What can I get you?' asked the barmaid, momentarily staring at Bill's face and the scars.

'A pint of best bitter, no wait, do you have any Jack Daniels?'

'Yes, it's on the shelf.' She said pointing to the large square bottle with the black label.

'Make it a double, with ice, please.' said Bill looking at the barmaid's name tag. 'Michelle rowed the boat ashore?'

'Not you as well?'

'Sorry. I used to get picked on and called *Billy goa*t at school,' said Bill.

'I was always being asked what's on the other side,' said Michelle.

'Children can be so hurtful.'

'Visiting?' asked Michelle, as she put the glass down on the counter.

'Yes, down with the family.'

'Must be lovely to have a family.'

'It has its moments. Right now, it is having a very big moment.'

'What's wrong?'

'My wife has taken the kids out for the day and left me behind – again.'

'Wish I had a husband, or boyfriend even,' said the Michelle.

'I've wished and dreamed for many things in my life,' said Bill. 'I'm still waiting for them.'

'Dreams are not something to wait for; they're something to work for; that's what Dot says.'

'Who's Dot?'

'One of the owners of the hotel, she's sort of like a mum to me.'

'That's nice. Can I get something to eat?'

'The bar menu is on the board over there beside the dart board,' she said pointing to a small blackboard to Bill's left.

Bill got off of his stool and walked shakily over to the board and looked down the list of salads, sandwiches, pies, and puddings.

Returning to the bar he caught his reflection in the mirror. He almost didn't recognise himself, his eyes looked drawn and lifeless, his face sad. Where had his dreams gone, what was the point in going on with life. A life on the road doing as he pleased sounded better than what he had just now, no alarm clock, no one to clean up after, no house to tidy or meals to make. He'd have to get a job. What about being a bartender, after all he knew most of the labels on the shelf and when they had parties at the house his friends always complimented him on his cocktails.

But not in England, it rained too often. France? No, didn't like frog legs. Spain, he shook his head, paella had too many unidentifiable ingredients, Portugal, yes why not, land of the barbeques, and he'd learned some Portuguese during his gap year.

'I'll have the salmon salad please.'

'Would you like another?' said Michelle, picking up Bill's empty glass.

'Why not? make it a double, I'm not driving.'

The memories of the past weeks rose to the surface and a tear ran down his cheek.

'Are you all right?' asked Michelle, pouring Bill's drink.

'Yes thanks, I'm fine.'

'I'll just pop your order through to the kitchen.'

Bill stared at the bottles on the shelf at the back of the bar. At one point or other in his life he'd tried most of them, some quite enthusiastically.

Ten minutes later an older lady came out from the kitchen with Bill's salad and put the plate on the bar in front of him.

Bill wondered if this was Dot.

'Would you like some salad dressing?'

'Yes, please.'

'I'll check in the kitchen.'

She returned a few minutes later with another lady.

'Here you are.'

'Thanks.'

'If you need anything else, just ask.'

'Could I have another bourbon please?'

The two older ladies busied themselves cleaning while Bill ate his salad in silence. At two-thirty the last of the other patrons departed and they were left alone.

As if they had been waiting for that moment the two ladies stopped what they were doing, walked over, and introduced themselves.

'Hello, I'm Beryl and this is Dot. We own this hotel and wondered if there was anything we can do for you?'

'I'm fine, thanks,' Bill sniffed, as another tear ran down his cheek.

'You sure?'

'No, really, I'm fine; just need some fresh air, back in a moment.'

He got off of the bar stool and headed for the door.

Beryl walked over to the window and watched as Bill collided with a pram. Bill looked in at the baby then jumped back. He shook his head then stepped off the pavement in front of a taxi. The driver made a rude gesture after him as he continued his unsteady walk across the road.

'I'm going to follow him,' said Beryl, 'got one of my feelings. Need to make sure he doesn't do something silly.'

As Beryl waited for a gap in the traffic, she watched Bill totter towards the edge of the quay and steady himself on a large timber bollard. As Beryl stepped off the kerb, Bill let go of the bollard and took a couple of wobbly steps towards to the edge of the quay before vomiting into the harbour.

A sailor who had just ascended the dock-side steps started towards Bill as Beryl crossed the quay-side. Neither of them was quick enough to catch Bill as he toppled into the harbour.

Dot ran out of the pub and across the road as Beryl pushed past the sailor and down the steps.

To Beryl's relief, Bill had landed feet first in the water, the top half of his body resting on the bow of a dinghy. As Dot arrived to help, Beryl began to pull the dinghy towards her. Just as Bill was within reach, he slithered off the dinghy and under the water. Dot immediately reached out, grabbed Bill's hair and pulled him to the surface. With a struggle Dot and Beryl managed to get the prostrate form of Bill out of the water and on to the foot of the steps.

'Is he breathing?' asked Dot.

'I think so; give me a hand to get him up the steps. Thankfully he's only been in a few moments, though I don't like the look of that bruise on his forehead.'

Halfway across the road Bill said, 'Where am I? What's happened?

'You've had an accident, dear, fallen in the harbour. We are taking you back to the hotel where we can get you help,' said Beryl.

With a few sly remarks about too much to drink from quayside fishermen, Dot and Beryl guided Bill across the road and into the hotel.

'Let's take him through to our lounge,' said Beryl, 'It'll be much warmer in there; the fire should still be burning.'

'Just relax, dear,' said Beryl.' You need to get those wet clothes off; you'll catch your death otherwise. Dot, pass me the blanket from the settee, please.'

They helped Bill undress and wrapped him in the blanket.

'Why don't you sit down in front of the fire for a moment?' Beryl suggested. 'We'll call an ambulance for you.'

'Please don't,' said Bill.

'Please don't what, dear?'

'Please don't call the ambulance – or the police.'

'Why? You've fallen in the harbour and by the look of that nasty bruise you banged your head when you fell in.'

'Are you wanted by the police?' asked Dot.

'I don't know. I just – I just don't want you to call anyone, at least not till my head clears.'

'If you're sure, dear, but realise this: someone's probably worried about you and needs to know you're safe,' said Beryl.

'Please,' said Bill.

'OK,' said Beryl, 'as long as you're sure.'

'I am,' said Bill. 'Can you tell me where I am?'

'You're in our hotel,' said Dot, 'the Admiral Aubrey. Beryl and I are the owners, this is our private flat. The hotel bedrooms are upstairs.'

'Oh.'.

'Dot, put the kettle on for a cup of tea,' said Beryl, 'then go through to guest services and get one of the hotel bathrobes and a couple of towels. I'll take our young friend through to our bathroom and run him a bath.'

Twenty minutes later Bill returned to the lounge in a hotel bathrobe, his wet hair hanging round his face like a bunch of seaweed after the tide's gone out.

'How do you feel now, dear?' asked Beryl.

'I'm exhausted and my head hurts,' said Bill, yawning.

'We have a room upstairs you can use, why don't you take a nap?' suggested Beryl. 'In the meantime, we'll see what we can do with your clothes. You can't put them on as they are. Are you absolutely sure you don't want us to contact the police?'

'Absolutely,' he said grimacing as he shook his head.
'Ok, if you're sure?'
'Thanks,' said Bill, yawning again.

♦

'What do you think, Dot?' asked Beryl, as they stood watching Bill sleep. 'Those stitches on his face and the bruising – do you think he's a battered husband?'

'Or worse; it would explain his reluctance to call the police.'

'What about the loss of memory? Is it for real?'

'Who knows? Let's go slowly with him; if he's been beaten up by someone, he'll want to know he's safe before he opens up and tells us what's going on. In the meantime, you run his clothes through the washing machine, and I'll call the doctor, can't have our guest snuffing it in the hotel.'

11
Gone

'Mum, where's Bill?' asked Hannah, walking back down the hallway.

'Isn't he in his bed?'

'No, and the bathroom's empty.'

'He must have gone down to the beach. I expect we passed each other somewhere while walking back up to the flat. Abigail, can you start the tea, I'm going out to see if I can find him.'

'OK Mum. Rachael, Hannah can you set the table in the front room, please?'

Twenty minutes later Ruth returned. 'The beach is deserted; he might have gone to the shops. I'll walk round and see if he's there.'

'Probably a pub more likely,' muttered Abigail. 'Did you try his mobile?'

'Yes, all it does is go to voicemail.'

'What about town and the mall?'

'I thought of that, Hannah, but the car is still in the driveway.'

'He might have taken the bus,' said Rachael.

'You should see the kitchen, Mum,' said Abigail, 'it's in a real mess.'

'Something horrible has happened,' said Hannah.

It could mean only one thing thought Ruth: Bill had gone back to drinking and this time it wasn't being done discreetly. Now what was she going to do? Call the police? But was he really missing or just drinking in one of the pubs in town? How foolish she would feel if she called the police and while the police were at the flat Bill walked in the door.

They would have to wait till later, but not till the pubs shut. But suppose he was down on the beach somewhere, hurt and not able to get help? He could have fallen over the edge of the chine and be trapped in the brambles at the bottom. It was no good; she would have to call the police.

'What did they say, Mum?' asked Rachael.

'They have taken a report and will send a patrol car round to get further details.'

♦

There were three of them: a female police constable, a male sergeant, and someone in plain clothes.

'Good evening, Mrs Drysdale. I'm Sergeant Wilson, this is police constable Chapman, she'll sit with your girls and this is –.'

'DCI Ross,' said the plain clothed visitor, 'ignore me, I'm just getting a lift to the station.'

Constable Chapman sat with the girls while Ruth, followed by the sergeant and the inspector, went into the kitchen.

'Quite stressed, are we, ma-am?' Ross nodded to the empty whiskey bottle.

Ruth shook her head. 'It's my husband; he – he.'

'Likes an occasional drink before dinner, ma-am?' suggested Ross.

Ruth looked at the mess on the floor and nodded.

'Did he take the car, ma-am?' asked Sergeant Wilson.

'No, it's still in the driveway.'

'Does he have any friends or family who live near here?'

'None, that I'm aware of.'

'Can you think of anywhere he may have gone to for a drink?'

Ruth shook her head and said, 'No, they've only been here a few days.'

'They?' asked the sergeant.

'My husband and the girls came down last Monday while I was at work. I called to invite them to a family party at home on Thursday evening and then I drove us down Friday.'

'Does your husband work?'

'No, he looks after the house.'

'What do you do, Mrs Drysdale?'

'I'm a QC. My chambers are in London.'

'Does your husband have any medical conditions that might incapacitate him?'

'He was in a bad car accident a few weeks ago, spent three days in hospital; then a few days in bed at home.'

'Did your husband take any clothes with him?'

'I don't know, I can check.'

What a weird question to ask, thought Ruth as she walked down the hall to the bedroom. Why would he want to take clothes with him?

Ruth returned a few minutes later, 'I can't really tell, all his clothes appear to be still in the bedroom. His backpack and raincoat are not here though.'

'Maybe he went for a walk ma-am.'

Ruth shook her head, 'It's just not like him.'

'What about money?'

'I looked earlier. He usually carries his wallet in his trouser pocket and his mobile phone is missing; he must have them with him.'

'Credit cards as well?'

'Probably.'

'How many?'

'Six, seven, I don't know.'

'Did you call his mobile?' asked the sergeant.

'Yes, it goes to voicemail.'

'We may need to check with the bank later,' said the sergeant. 'Also if you have a recent photograph it would be very helpful, ma-am?'

'Mrs Drysdale,' said Ross, 'you say you are a QC, have I seen your photo in the papers?'

'You may have done; I get involved in all sorts of cases.'

'No, not that, wasn't there a piece in the Telegraph about you being the new Home Secretary? that is if your party wins the next general election?'

'Inspector, I am too busy to take notice of newspaper speculation.'

'All the same, your husband going missing?'

'It won't come to that, will it? Oh crap, what will Boris think?'

'Can't help you there ma-am, I'm afraid.'

'Inspector, you just have to find him – the newspapers – what am I going to do.'

'Can we have a look around before we go ma-am?' said the sergeant. 'Sometimes it helps with a fresh pair of eyes, sometimes we see things the homeowner doesn't.'

'Yes, yes, of course, go ahead.'

Ruth went into the front room to make a phone call, while the inspector and the sergeant looked through the flat.

'Mrs Drysdale,' said the sergeant, 'I will pass your husband's details to our control centre. They will pass the information to our patrols, if he is anywhere in town they will spot him. We can't do any more at this time, oh, and if he turns up would you let us know?'

'Inspector, the newspapers?'

Ross shook his head.

'Mrs Drysdale,' said the sergeant, 'at this time it's simply a missing person report and the information you have provided is strictly confidential. At this time, there is no need to inform the press.'

Ruth saw the police to the door and realised the girls still hadn't had any dinner.

At twelve-thirty, Ruth shepherded her sleepy girls through to their bedrooms. She waited while the twins cried themselves to sleep. Unable to sleep, she slumped into an armchair and waited for the phone to ring.

12
Leviathan

Larsen finished his breakfast and headed for the waiting taxi.

'Good luck with the meeting,' called Beryl.

'Thanks, I think I'm going to need it.'

'Well, was I right?' asked Terry, as Larsen climbed into the taxi, 'The hotel to your liking?'

'Yes, it's just fine. You related to Dot and Beryl?'

'No,' Terry said, laughing, 'they looked after my Sandra when her mum was sick. So where are you off to today?'

'You know the marina?'

'Which one?'

'Sorry, I didn't mean the marina, take me to Grindley's, it's the boatyard beside the marina just past the Ship and Anchor pub.'

'Not any more it isn't.'

'What, they've closed the yard?'

'No, old man Grindley knocked the pub down two years ago, built a block of flats in its place. The yard's still there though. Newspapers said he wanted to fill in the marina and build houses, couldn't get planning permission. Apparently, the slough beside the yard is home to an endangered species.'

'What kind?'

'Weekend sailors,' said Terry, laughing at his own joke.

It had been several years since he had last laid eyes on her, but when he looked at her now, down by the water's edge, he fell in love all over again. The years of neglect had not been kind to her, though he realised her present condition was his fault. The rent and the maintenance bills, which he hadn't paid for almost five years, had mounted.

The closer he got, the more bedraggled she looked. Even so she still had that regal look to her and the power to thrill him. He shook his head, the once mighty *Leviathan* now looking more like the wreck of the Hesperus.

It wasn't the letter from the yard's solicitor that had brought him down on this damp Saturday. Rather it was another letter which contained thirty halves of fifty-pound notes, all with different serial numbers. Intrigued, he had come down to meet this mysterious benefactor.

He looked at the letter and the stack of half fifty-pound notes again. The letter was addressed to Captain Joshua P Larsen.

It read:

> *Captain Larsen, if you want the other halves to these notes and more, meet me by the yacht on Sunday at ten am. I have a proposal that you might find to be to your advantage,*
> *A Smith*

Who was Smith, wondered Larsen, and how did he know of his present situation?

His steps quickened as he walked down the dock then slowed as he got nearer. He could see movement through one of the portholes. Someone was inside – was it Smith?

He stepped on board and headed for the companionway.

'Piss off, this boat is private,' came a female voice from below.

'You're damn right this boat is private,' he replied. 'This is my yacht. What are you doing on board?'

'I live here,' said the voice.

'Like hell you do! Get your backside out of here before I throw you off.'

'Fuck you,' interjected a male voice from behind.

Larsen turned and grabbed the raised arm of his adversary, twisted it up his back and launched him into the oily water.

'That goes for you as well. I want both of you off of this boat in fifteen minutes.'

'We'll have words with Mr Grindley,' said the dripping attacker as he climbed out of the water and onto the dock.

Larsen was momentarily distracted by the arrival of a black S series Mercedes Benz with darkened windows. The headlights flashed twice and an arm waved at him from the driver's window.

He stepped off of the *Leviathan*, pushed past the dripping squatter and said, 'You now have fourteen minutes.'

As he got to the Mercedes the rear window rolled down and a cloud of expensive Cuban cigar smoke issued forth.

'Captain Larsen?' said the voice from within.

'Mr Smith, I presume?'

'Mr Smith will do for now. Get in, we need to talk.' As he spoke the passenger door opened and let out even more clouds of Cuba.

'Won't you get in trouble for doing that?' questioned Smith, as Larsen closed the door.

'Just saving the bother of getting a court order.'

Smith chuckled. 'A man after my own heart. I think you're going to do just fine, Captain. Here,' he said, handing Larsen the other halves of the fifty-pound notes. 'There's a lot more where these came from.'

They sat in silence in the back of the car while Larsen checked the serial numbers of the two bundles of fifties.

'Match all right?'

Larsen nodded in the gloom of the back of the car.

'Intrigued?' said Smith.

'You have my undivided attention.'

'Good, let's go have lunch.'

'Mr Jones,' Smith said to the uniformed driver, 'find us somewhere nice for lunch, somewhere we can talk without being disturbed, you know what I like.'

The hat in the front seat nodded sedately and the car drove off.

They travelled in silence, the heady smell of the rich Cuban cigar making Larsen light-headed.

The sign over the door read, *The Fallen Angel*, a board by the door added, 'Guest ales and fine food available all day'.

The air outside was fresh and invigorating. They must be close to the sea thought Larsen. He knew the smell of a beach at low tide anywhere.

He followed Smith into the restaurant. Although smoking was no longer allowed in pubs, one hundred and sixty years of smokers had left their mark on the atmosphere.

'Wait here,' instructed Smith, walking over to the reservation desk where he was immediately recognised. They were shown to a table at the far end of the dining room.

'Can I get you a drink while you wait?' said the waitress.

'Yes, whiskey and water,' said Smith.

'Sir?' she said to Larsen.

'I'll have an espresso, please.'

'Not drinking, Captain?'

'You may, I choose not to.'

Smith grinned and said, 'Make them doubles.'

As they waited for their drinks, Smith picked up the menu, looked it over then said. 'The fish here is excellent.'

The waitress returned with their drinks and said, 'Are you gentlemen ready to order?'

'I'll start with a salad,' said Smith.

'And your main?'

'I'll have the chef's special.'

'And for you, sir?' she said to Larsen.

'I'll start with a salad as well. Is the salmon farmed?'

'No sir, it's wild; comes down from the London marked each Friday.'

'In that case I'll have the salmon, with boiled potatoes and mixed vegetables, please.'

'Any desserts?'

'We'll let you know,' said Smith, dismissing her with a wave of his hand.

As they sipped their drinks, Smith said, 'Well, Captain, I suppose you are wondering what this is all about?'

'I had wondered.'

'UNESCO has commissioned a survey of the upper reaches of the Amazon to see what damage is being done to the indigenous people from illegal logging and low rainfall.'

'And what's my part in this grand scheme?'

'I have been engaged by a team of researchers to find suitable accommodation and transport. Your yacht, Captain, if it was in shipshape condition, would fit the bill perfectly.'

'Ah, that could be a problem.'

'You're a few quid short to get it ready to go to sea, that it?'

Larsen sighed; he could feel his dream voyage running aground on the reef of Norman's Woe.

'I've already talked to the yard manager, Grindley, nasty bit of work,' said Smith. 'Anyway, I digress. I've also had a discussion with the expedition leader, and he is prepared to advance the necessary funds for the repairs and provisioning of your vessel, the balance payable at time of departure.'

'The Amazon and back, that's going to take several months.'

'We expect to avail ourselves of your services for up to a year. You will have to be ready to depart in seven weeks' time.'

'Seven weeks! I haven't even been on board yet let alone gone below decks. Five years in that stinking slough, no telling what damage has been done.'

'Nonsense, a few licks of paint and she will be as good as new.'

The discussion was interrupted by the arrival of the salad. Larsen was surprised at how hungry and lightheaded he had become. He wasn't sure if it was the caffeine or the idea of the *Leviathan* being made ready for a sea. He mused for a moment and realised it was the latter fuelled by the former and he decided he liked the moment very much. It was as though a curtain had been drawn back in the dark room of his mind, and he could see the sun rising on a new day.

After the salad, Larsen said, 'First, even if you provide the funds, what yard has the capacity to just stop what they are doing to work on the *Leviathan*? Secondly, even if I can get the *Leviathan* ready for sea in seven weeks, I have no crew; I let them all go when we docked five years ago. Thirdly, it's the wrong time of the year to be crossing the Atlantic, it's hurricane season.'

'And fourthly?'

'All right, you put up the money and I can try and get in touch with my old crew and if we are lucky we might just manage to sail south of any hurricanes and arrive at the Amazon. Then what? Sail boats don't usually sail up rivers, even wide ones like the Amazon.'

'Captain, I'm sure when you put your mind to the problem, you'll figure it all out. Now my friend, I see the young lady approaching with our lunch; let's eat and enjoy.'

'How many in the team?' asked Larsen between mouthfuls of salmon.

'Dr Kaufmann has six members on his team.'

Larsen thought about crew numbers and Kaufmann's team; it would be tight for berths. But at least it wasn't going to be a regular charter, more of a delivery trip, should be a breeze he thought to himself.

'Captain,' said Smith, during the cheese and biscuits, 'what got you into sailing?'

'I joined the Merchant Navy when I was seventeen and worked my way up through the ranks till I got my Captain's Ticket. I was married for a while. My wife died in childbirth; her parents raised my daughter. I tried living ashore but couldn't hack it, so I went back to sea.'

'And the yacht?'

'One day, while docked in Southampton, as I was walking round one of the many marinas, I came across the *Leviathan*. Curiosity got the better of me and I went and had a look. The English climate had ruined the paintwork, but other than that she was a fine vessel. Seeing her gave me an idea. The owner wanted a quick sale, so I drew out most of my savings and after a quick refit I started chartering in the Caribbean.'

'I've been to Martinique,' said Smith, 'know it, Captain? Might even go back sometime for a visit.'

'Yes, it was one of our ports.'

'Make lots of money chartering?'

'At first I made very good money, and then 9/11 happened. The business suffered till finally it was so bad that I decided to make a change.'

'Wise move, it's good to know when to fold and when to hold.'

'I sailed the boat to England intending to refit her and charter in the Med.'

'What happened?'

'Met a woman, thought it was serious, found out she wasn't. I travelled in Europe for a while then ended up back in London working for a shipping company, till a few days ago that is. You, are you married, have kids?'

'Captain, my family is very large, so large in fact I couldn't live long enough to meet them all. We are in business worldwide, and we like to keep a low profile.'

Getting in the car Smith asked, 'Where are you staying, Captain?'

'Admiral Aubrey for one night, I hadn't planned on staying long; just came down to Poole to meet you.'

'Perfect place, know it well.'

'Part of the family business empire?'

'You might say that, Captain Larsen. Mr Jones, drive us back into town. We'll drop the Captain at the Admiral Aubrey.'

Just as they were parting, Smith gave Larsen his card and said, 'If you have any questions, just call, otherwise I will talk with you tomorrow.'

The name on the card was, *A Smith Director, International Project Management.*

Larsen watched as the Mercedes with Smith and Jones drifted off into the traffic.

Larsen went in through the double doors and walked over to the reception desk.

'Yes, Captain, can I help?'

'Beryl, I wonder if you could help with a small problem?' said Larsen placing two left hand and two right hand £50 notes on the counter. 'I accidentally cut these in half.'

'Ah the handiwork of Mr Smith, next time you see him, say Beryl says to not be a stranger.'

'I will do just that,' he said grinning, realising that Beryl must also be a member of the family.

He headed up the stairs, two at a time, to his room. He took a notebook out of his briefcase and went down to the bar. Tomorrow he would go shopping for new clothes, proper sea-going ones.

Larsen sat down at the end of the bar and waited to be served. While he waited, he called his landlord in London to say he would be away for quite some time and probably wouldn't be returning, but before he left he would collect his things and settle the bill.

'Can I get you something to drink, Captain?' said Beryl.

'Sorry, I was miles away. Beryl, I think I'll have a cappuccino with a dash of brandy, no, cancel that, I just can't take a chance. I'll just have the coffee.'

'Celebrating, are we?'

'Beryl, I'm going back to sea.'

'Wonderful. Does that mean you'll be leaving soon?'

'Unlikely, there's a shipload of work to be done first. Probably be here for at least a few weeks – that a problem?'

'As I said when you checked in, you can have the room as long as you want.'

'Thanks. Beryl, you don't know of any local boatyards that can handle a really large yacht, do you?'

'You could try Baron's yard. They've recently laid off some of their workers, they could probably do with the business.'

13
A new life

'Breakfast? What do you mean, breakfast?' asked Bill.

'You've slept right through, dear; it's eight-thirty Monday morning. You must have been really tired, not a peep from you all that time,' said Dot.

'Oh dear,' said Bill while massaging his temples, 'my head hurts, do you have any aspirins?'

'I'll get you some,' said Dot, rummaging in one of the kitchen drawers. 'There is some bacon left and I could fry you an egg to go with it if you're hungry.'

'Yes, please, I'm famished; I feel like I haven't eaten for days.'

'You haven't. Do you want brown or white toast, tea or coffee?'

'Brown toast and coffee would be fine. Is it really Monday? I slept all yesterday. I haven't slept this well since.' He grasped at a passing memory, but it was too quick for him. 'Thanks for drying my clothes, Dot.'

'That's all right, couldn't have you putting on wet and wrinkled clothes and catching a cold.'

'Where's Beryl? Is she up yet?'

'Beryl has gone into town to do some shopping. She should be back soon. She's an early riser, does all the early breakfasts. Some of our guests go out fishing early in the morning and they all want feeding before they go. I do the dinners in the evening; we help each other during the day.'

'You two run this place on your own?'

'No, not quite, we have one permanent help with the room changes and we take on seasonal help when needed.'

'Did the police come into the pub last night?' Bill asked.

'They stop in most nights.'

'But they did come into the pub, didn't they? They want to lock me up, I just know it. I'll never be safe. What will I do Dot, where can I hide?'

'Look, your breakfast is ready, go find a table in the dining room and I'll bring it through. Coffee's on the dresser and there's newspapers if you want something to read. We'll wait for Beryl; she'll know what to do.'

As Bill was trying to make sense of the newspaper, Beryl and Dot came into the dining room.

'Morning, Beryl.'

'Morning, love. How'd you sleep?'

'Fine, haven't slept so well in – in, well I don't really know how long. If it wasn't for the headache, I'd feel fine.'

'I thought we should have a little chat and see how we can help you. Have you had time to think things over?'

'Yes, I think I need to go away somewhere safe, at least till my memory returns and I can think clearly. Every time I try to remember, my head hurts. I just need to be somewhere I can think, and it needs to be somewhere no one knows me.'

'You sit here and finish your breakfast. Dot and I have to get ready for lunch; come and join us in the kitchen when you've finished.'

Beryl stopped to greet one of the guests who'd just walked in.

'Good morning, Captain. Did you sleep well?'

'Yes, thanks. Am I too late for breakfast?'

'No. We serve breakfast till ten-thirty, full English, tea and toast?'

'Sounds great,' he said, rubbing his hands in anticipation.

'If you'll take a seat, I'll get you your tea. Oh, Mr Smith called to say he was running a bit late – be here about eleven.'

'Thanks, Beryl,' said Larsen, looking at the clock, 'plenty of time to have an undisturbed breakfast.'

Bill put down his newspaper and went over to the buffet table to refill his coffee cup. He was curious as to what sort of captain, Larsen was. While he poured his coffee, he took a good look at Larsen. He was rugged, well-tanned, the sort of tan you get working out of doors. He would've looked good on a horse, riding with the hounds; broad-shouldered, long armed but with hands that belonged on a pianist. Bill didn't think it was likely Larsen was military. No military captain would let his hair look so dishevelled. Was he the captain of a sports team? Not likely, he was too tall for football, and not heavyset enough in the neck for rugby. Unlikely to be an airline pilot either, so that left the sea. Then the obvious struck him: he must be a sea captain. He was here to join his ship. Bill returned to his seat and resumed his pretence of reading the newspaper. But who was this Mr Smith that could disturb the captain's breakfast?

He was soon to find out. As the dining-room clock chimed eleven, Smith appeared at the door.

'Well, Captain Larsen, how did you sleep?' Smith asked, sitting down facing Larsen with his back to Bill.

'Very well thanks, and its yes.'

Bill peeped over the top of his paper as Smith said, 'So you've made up your mind then? Good, I'm glad to hear that.'

Bill watched Smith slide a small thin briefcase across the table.

Larsen looked at its contents, his eyebrows lifted.

'That should get you started, Captain. There's more if needed,' said Smith as he turned to head for the door. 'And, Captain, in case you are thinking of going it alone, here is a photo of your daughter leaving home yesterday morning.'

Bill saw the colour drain from the captain's face.

♦

With no other conversations to eavesdrop on, Bill retired to Beryl and Dot's lounge, sat in front of the blazing fire, and contemplated his future.

'You will need some clothes,' said Beryl, as Bill sipped his tea, 'you can't wear what you have on forever.'

'I've found some cash and I still have my wallet with my debit cards,' said Bill, 'I suppose you both saw it when you cleaned my clothes – Bill Drysdale sounds so strange, I feel I should be called something else. I also found a note with phone numbers; I think it's my way of remembering my bank account PIN numbers.'

'Unless you have an unlimited supply of cash you will need to get work sooner or later,' said Beryl. 'I suggest you take as much out of the cashpoint machine as you can, then go shopping for some simple clothes. First though, we need to do something about your hair, and at some point, the stitches.'

'What's wrong with my hair?'

'It's too distinctive. If we cut it short and restyle it to cover the bald patches, I doubt if anyone will recognise you. Dot, is Michelle in today?

'She was earlier, shall I see?'

'Yes, please.

'Who is Michelle?'

'She's Dot's unofficial daughter; she works and lives in the hotel.'

'Ah, I think we've already met, she served me when I came into the pub.'

'You wanted to see me, Beryl?' said Michelle as she wandered into the room.

'Oh, hello,' said Michelle.

'Hi,' replied Bill.

'Michelle, you're about the same size as our friend here, could he borrow one of your hoodies?'

'Yes, why?'

'He needs it for a short trip to the shops this morning.'

'No problem, I'll go get one, grey or blue?'

'Won't matter,' said Beryl, 'so long as he can cover his head.'

Bill put on the hoodie and said. 'But suppose someone recognises me and calls the police?'

'No one will recognise you, especially dressed like this,' said Beryl.

'The nearest cashpoint is two hundred yards up the road just past the White Hart Hotel,' said Dot. 'Would you like Michelle to go with you?'

'Yes, please,' said Bill, looking relieved.

'You'll be fine,' said Dot.

Bill had only gone a few steps when he caught sight of his reflection in a shop window and realised he wouldn't have recognised himself.

He tried withdrawing £500 but had to settle for £300 from his card and was dismayed to find the same for the remainder of the others. He would take more money out tomorrow, he thought.

'How did you do?' asked Beryl when they returned.

'I got as much cash as I could,' said Bill. 'We popped into Debenhams and I bought a couple of shirts, another pair of jeans, and some underwear.'

'We need to do something permanent about your hair,' said Dot.

Beryl reached out to Bill and gently pushed his hair back. 'If only my hair was this soft.'

'But I like it long,' said Bill.

'Not any more you don't,' said Beryl.

Two hours later Bill stood in front of the mirror and felt confused about his new look, at least it wasn't a short back and sides and it would grow out again. But who was he? Every time he tried to remember more than his name, his head started to throb.

'What happened to your stitches?' asked Beryl.

'I was brushing my hair and thought, why not? I used Dot's nail clippers to cut the stitches, and then pulled them out with her eyebrow tweezers.'

Beryl smiled. 'What are we going to call you, since you don't want to use your real name?'

'According to my driving licence, my full name is Edward William Drysdale,' said Bill. 'I'm sort of used to Bill though.'

'Edward's a lovely name,' said Dot. 'I had an Uncle called Edward when I was a little girl.'

'Edward it will be then,' said Beryl. 'Now, we need to go get ready for lunch.'

'Will you be all right, dear?'

'Yes thanks,' said Bill, 'I think I'll go upstairs and lie down for a while, try to shake this headache.'

♦

Bill woke at five. Feeling revived and hungry he went down to the bar for a drink and something to eat.

'What would you like to drink, Edward?' asked Michelle.

It took Bill a moment to realise Michelle was talking to him.

'Oh, that's me. Sorry, my mind was miles away. Jack Daniels with ice please.'

He picked up the food menu, looked down the list of bar snacks and settled for scampi and chips with a side salad.

'Dressing is on the counter in the basket,' said Michelle, pointing to the red plastic basket stuffed between the menus and the stack of *What's On* brochures.

A poster pinned to the end of the bar caught Bill's attention.

'Michelle,' he said, when she had finished pouring two pints of best bitter for a couple of sailors, 'what's an open mic evening?'

'We have live music on Monday nights. Usually starts at between eight and nine. There's some very good singing and guitar playing if you like folk. Not my sort of thing. I prefer going clubbing.'

'Never been one for folk either,' said Bill. 'Though with my headaches, clubbing is definitely out for me, for a while at least.'

By eight o'clock the bar had filled to near capacity, latecomers having to stand where there was room. A hush descended. A tall, languid musician with a guitar hanging from his shoulder approached the microphone and introduced himself.

Bill had never heard music performed this intimately before and he found himself moved by the young girl with the huge guitar who sang *Somewhere over the Rainbow*.

The languid musician approached the microphone and announced, 'Ladies and gentlemen, we will now take a short break. Would you show your appreciation for the performers by dropping coins and notes in the glass when it comes past? Thank you.'

'Can I buy you a drink?' said a voice to his left.

'No, thank you,' Bill said, turning to the voice, 'I'll buy my own thanks.'

A set of yellowed teeth framed in an untidy beard and moustache grinned back at him. 'No need to bite my head off, only trying to be friendly,' yellow teeth said, turning and shuffling off through the crowd.

The music ended at eleven-thirty and the bar started to empty. Bill felt queasy and headed for the side door and the alley.

It had started to rain. There was a crowd of smokers loitering in the doorway so he wandered off down the alleyway to get away from the smoke. He sheltered in a doorway for a moment hoping the world would stop spinning, then the inevitable happened and he vomited into the gutter.

'Need help?'

He looked up, shook his head, and tried to focus; it was yellow teeth and a friend.

'I'm sure we could help you, we know just what you need,' he said, grinning at Bill.

An unfortunate memory from his days in the Navy floated into his consciousness, Bill could feel the blood drain from his face, the gall rise in his throat.

'Like hell you do!' boomed a voice from behind.

Bill looked into the gloom and saw Captain Larsen grab yellow teeth and friend and toss them across the alleyway. His vision faded to black.

'What's happened to Edward?' said a worried looking Beryl, as Larsen carried him into the bar.

'Fainted, that's all,' he said, 'a little too much celebrating perhaps?'

'Bring him through here,' Beryl said leading the way to the lounge. 'Put him on the settee, I'll get him something to drink.'

'Make it water, or Alka-Seltzer might be more appropriate,' said Larsen.

'I'll get him some lemonade and plain crackers.'

Larsen sat down in the armchair by the fire while Bill sipped slowly on his lemonade.

'Thanks, Beryl,' he said.

'I've locked up,' said Dot, coming in to the room. 'Michelle said she'll finish off before she goes to bed. Would anyone like a nightcap? I've just put the kettle on.'

'I'll leave you ladies to talk,' said Larsen.

'No, please stay, Captain,' said Beryl, 'I think we could do with a man's perspective.'

'OK, in that case tea's fine,' said Larsen.

'How's the headache?' Beryl asked Bill, putting down the tray.

'It's going. I'm starting to remember who I am, thanks to you two.'

'We're only too glad to be of help,' said Dot.

'Edward,' said Beryl, 'Dot and I have been talking and we were wondering how we could help you, considering your situation?'

'You already have; you saved my life. If you hadn't pulled me from the harbour I would have drowned.'

'We'd have done that for anyone,' said Dot. 'What we mean is about you. Are you going to try and get in touch with your family and let them know you're safe?'

'How do you know about my family? Have they been here?' Bill asked, panic-stricken.

'No dear, we read it in the paper,' said Dot.

'Did your wife do that to you?' said Larsen.

Bill thought for a moment. If Ruth hadn't bought him the car, he wouldn't have had the accident. After all, he wouldn't have tried the back road in the old Volvo. He nodded his head.

'Don't worry, love; you'll be safe here with us. We can take care of you till you work out what you want to do. We've helped men and women in your situation before.'

'Thanks, I just need time to think. I'm all confused.'

'Those are nasty scars, how did you get them?' asked Beryl.

'I was in a car crash.'

'Were you a passenger?' Dot asked.

'No – I was driving – I had been drinking – the police are going to arrest me and put me in jail. I was banned for three years and given a suspended jail sentence – someone died in the accident.'

'How can we best help you?' said Beryl.

'I don't know. I am so confused. I just want to get away. Sometimes I wished I had died in the accident.'

'Your feelings are quite natural,' said Larsen. 'After my wife died I went to pieces. I blamed myself. I turned to drink and lost three months of my life in an alcoholic haze. I couldn't look after my daughter and ended up giving her to her grandparents to bring up. I'd lost everything, including my own self-respect.'

'What did you do?' said Bill.

'It was buying the *Leviathan* and going back to sea that changed my life.'

'What's the *Leviathan*?' said Beryl.

'My yacht – it's been lying in the harbour for the last five years. That's why I'm here; I have an opportunity to go chartering again.'

'Fine for some,' said Bill. 'I'm stuck here with the police looking for me everywhere.'

'What about children? Do you have any?' Larsen queried.

'None of my own; my wife has three daughters from her first marriage. They like the country club life and have lots of friends. All I am is a househusband, cheap labour; spend my days mopping up after them. All I hear is, Bill is dinner ready, Bill where's my coat, Bill I'm hungry. Honestly I've had enough; I'm ready for a change.'

'I know that feeling well,' said Larsen.

Bill stood up. 'I'm tired and my head hurts – why won't the pain go away?'

'Did your doctor prescribe anything for your headaches?' asked Beryl.

'He prescribed lots of pills: little white ones, long green plastic beans and some yellow ones that taste disgusting. I don't take them anymore.'

'Edward, would you mind helping Dot take the tea things through to the kitchen? I'll tidy up in here,' said Beryl.

Bill looked puzzled but said, 'yes, of course.'

As soon as Bill was out of earshot Beryl asked, 'How was your trip to London, Captain?'

'Fine, I've given notice to my landlord, packed up my clothes, what little I have and I'm ready to go to sea again. At least, I will when I get the *Leviathan* overhauled.'

'What about crew?'

Larsen smiled, 'I've managed to get in touch with the guys who sailed with me before. All except the cook, he's got married and his wife is expecting. The others will be here in a few days.'

'Captain, I was just wondering.'

'If I would offer the job to Edward, is that what you were going to say?'

'You took the words right out of my mouth.'

'I'd need to interview him first, I'm particular when it comes to crew.'

'I'll call him, if that's all right?' said Beryl.

'Why not?'

Beryl went through into the kitchen and returned with Bill and Dot.

'Edward, before you go off to bed, the Captain would like to ask you a couple of questions.'

'OK.'

'Can you cook?'

'You ask that because I am a househusband?'

'Let me try another. Are you clean?'

'I bathe every day.'

Larsen shook his head. 'Let me see your arms, roll up your sleeves.'

Bill rolled his shirt sleeves up above the elbows and stretched out his arms.

'Good. You can roll them down again.'

'What was that in aid of?'

'I don't want any junkies on my yacht.'

'Oh, I see, I think.'

'You said you are wanted by the police?'

'I told you someone died in the car accident; it wasn't my fault. I had only had a couple of drinks and, yes, the police are after me,' he said.

'And you want to get away from it. Have you ever been to sea?'

'Three years in the Navy, I think. Why?'

'You *think* you did?'

'The accident earlier—I hit my head and my memory is a bit hazy about some things.'

'What branch were you in?'

'I was a chef.'

'So you know how to cook?'

'A bit, I was only in for three years.'

'I am looking for someone to live aboard and work as cook on my yacht,' said Larsen. 'Do you think you could cope with that?'

'I could live aboard and get paid for my work?'

'Yes, are you interested?'

'What about money? How much would I get paid?'

'As your duties will involve provisioning as well as cooking, your pay will be 800 per week; we pay in US dollars or Euros as they are both readily convertible in most places in the world.'

'Really? When do I start?'

'Consider yourself on the payroll. And you want to be called Edward?'

'Yes.'

'Edward what?'

'Just Edward for now.'

'Look, there will be eleven of us on board for up to a year, I don't like evasiveness. Edward isn't what people call you, is it?'

He sighed and slowly shook his head. 'According to the driving licence and cards in my wallet my real name is Edward, but I seem to be called Bill.'

'Do you have a passport with you? You can't leave the UK shore without a passport.'

Bill shook his head, his countenance fell.

'Don't worry, I know someone who may be able to sort out a passport for you,' said Larsen. 'So, Edward, what's going to be your full name?'

'Edward Cook, how's that?'

'As a name, it'll do. I'll call my friend and see what we can sort out. He will want to know details such as age and have a recent photo. Right now, I am off to bed. I'll see you in the morning.'

'Wait – what do I call you?'

'Captain Larsen will do. Goodnight cook, Cook.'

The door of opportunity had opened, and Bill felt himself being drawn through into a new world.

14
First day

'Good morning, Captain.'

'Good morning, Edward. Eaten breakfast?'

'No, I've just come down. Mind if I join you?'

'Be my guest.'

'This is exciting,' said Bill, 'I've been awake since five trying to think of what I'll be doing on my first day.'

'Ah. Today won't be a workday per se, more of a getting acquainted day.'

'Not sure what you mean?' Bill said, forking the yolk of his egg.

'I've got to go to the yard where the *Leviathan* is currently moored and secure its release. Then I need to find another yard suitable for her overhaul and get her transferred.'

'What will I be doing?'

'Here,' he said, passing Bill a folder, 'hold on to this. It contains my correspondence with the yard. Look severe and say nothing, I'll do all the talking.'

Intrigued, Bill followed Larsen out the door and into a waiting taxi.

'Where to?' said a familiar voice.

'Same place as yesterday, Terry.'

'Going sailing today?'

'No, were just going to sort out some issues about my boat.'

'What kind of boat do you have?'

'Sailboat, I used her for charter work in the Caribbean.'

'Nice work for some. Now me, I get seasick on the Sandbanks ferry. Not my wife though, she loves sailing. Maybe you can take her out for the day; she'd love that, how much for a day trip?'

'We were charging $8,000 a day in the Caribbean, one week minimum.'

'Crikey! What's it called, the *Queen Mary*?'

Larsen didn't have time to answer; they had arrived at the yard. He paid the fare and as they got out, he handed Terry half of a fifty-pound note, and said, 'Like to earn the other half?'

Terry grinned, 'I've got nothing to lose, it's my lunch break.'

'Good, we'll be back before dessert,'

'Listen, before we go in, do you have problems with this yard? If so I can recommend a better one.'

'Go on.'

'You could try Baron's. I used to work for them; they're on the other side of the harbour.'

'Why did you leave?'

'Worked there for years, till they got quiet, kids needed feeding, mortgage needed paying.'

'You're the second person that has recommended Baron's. Thanks.'

The yard offices, containing Grindley's office, consisted of a single-story corrugated steel shed with windows covered with strong steel mesh. There was under-cover parking space for two cars at the far end.

'I would like to see the yard manager, please,' Larsen said to the receptionist.

'He's out in the yard, like to leave a message?'

'Yes, tell him Captain Larsen's here with his solicitor to take his yacht away.'

Bill tried not to show his surprise at the news of his promotion.

'And the name of your boat is?'

'*Leviathan*, shall I spell that for you?'

At the mention of the yacht's name the look of indifference on her face changed to worry and she picked up her mobile.

'Mr Grindley, sorry to interrupt you,' she said, then winced and held the phone away from her ear. When the tirade eased, she continued, 'The owner of the *Leviathan* is here with his solicitor. They're here to remove it from the yard. Yes, I will tell him that, yes – yes – yes – certainly,' she hung up and, with a flushed look said, 'Mr Grindley says you must wait here for them to come over.'

Them, thought Larson as the image of a bunch of drunken deckhands with marlinspikes came to mind.

Grindley and gang must have entered through another door because three minutes later the intercom sounded with a rude buzz and Grindley's nasally voice said, 'send Mr Larsen in.'

Not even a please, observed Larsen. As he entered Grindley's office he bumped his head on the top of the doorframe. Being six foot two had its problems.

Grindley was sitting, head bowed, looking at some papers on his desk. He was not alone; another figure silhouetted by the glare of the sun through a side window was seated across from him. The lawyer, thought Larsen, at least there was no gang with marlinspikes.

Still not looking up, Grindley gestured to the other empty chair. 'Sit down, Mr Larsen.'

Larsen picked up a spare chair and placed it to his left and motioned for Bill to sit. Finally, when the tension had built to Grindley's satisfaction, he looked up at Larsen, smiled, and indicating his companion said, this is Mr Marley; he represents the company when it comes to legal issues.'

Before Larsen could speak, Grindley looked back down again at the spreadsheet and continued, 'You have been a considerable inconvenience to us, Mr Larsen. We have been very lenient with you these last five years. Many a time we could have rented the slip to more than one yacht owner and subsequently this has cost us a great deal. In view of this sorry history we've decided to force a sale of your boat to recover our losses. It is estimated that the sale should generate sufficient funds to cover the yard's expenses and leave a small balance for you. In fact our solicitor, Mr Marley,' he said looking up and licking his lower lip, 'is in final negotiations with a buyer. All we need is your signature on this release and we will take the problem off your hands.'

Marley turned to look at Larsen and grinned. Larsen doubted there was a buyer for the *Leviathan*. Even if she were to be sold, the difference between what he owed, and her value was considerable.

Larsen caught Bill's eye and smiled. Then, filling his lungs with air, he leaned forward till his face was inches from Grindley's. 'You and Marley are nothing more than maggots in the apple of life.'

Before Grindley could say a word, Larsen leaned back and reaching into his briefcase threw a bundle of £50 notes on the desk. Grindley was speechless. His hand, thin fingered, talon-like, quivered as it hovered over the bundle. Then, like a starving cat grabbing a dying rat, he pulled the bundle to him and started to count. As he did so he pressed the intercom, 'Millie, bring in the *Leviathan* account.'

Moments later Millie entered with a folder and carefully laid it on the desk. Her jaw dropped when she saw the money.

'£53,450 pounds exactly; make sure to count it carefully,' said Larsen, 'and I want a written receipt. Give it to my solicitor.' He nodded to Bill. 'Also, I'm making arrangements for Baron's to tow the *Leviathan* to their yard for a refit.'

'But Captain Larsen, we have ample facilities here at our yard,' said Grindley, spreading his arms in a pleading gesture.

'Oh, it's *Captain* Larsen now. Baron's surveyor says there are thousands of pounds of damage to the yacht. Did you know that there are four feet of water in the bilges? And – against my explicit instructions — there are hippies living in there, smoking pot! You're lucky I have gone against my solicitor's advice and am not suing you for damages.'

◆

'You enjoyed that! Do I get a raise?' asked Bill.

Larsen looked at him, shook his head, and chuckled, 'You'll do.'

As they got in the taxi, Larsen said, 'Terry, take us to Baron's.'

They stopped in a carpark outside a yacht chandlery. There was a small mini market on one side and a café on the other.

'This is Baron's?' asked Larsen.

'The office is inside on the left beside the sales counter. You go straight through the chandlery to get to the boatyard,' explained Terry.

Through the window at the back of the chandlery they could see the boat yard. Baron's looked as though it had seen better days. Just a few boats were hauled out and being worked on.

'Good morning, can I help?' asked the receptionist.

'Yes, I need to have some work done on my boat and your yard was recommended.'

'Oh, who recommended us?'

'Two people: the bartender at the Admiral Aubrey, and my taxi driver, Terry.'

The receptionist smiled and said, 'He's my Dad.'

'I thought there was a resemblance,' said Bill.

'Can you tell me what you want done?'

'It's quite a lot,' Larsen said, passing over his handwritten list.

'Ah,' she said, reading it, 'You'll definitely have to talk to Mr Baron about this. She pressed the intercom and said, 'Mr Baron, you have a customer.'

'Send him in and ask him if he wants coffee, I could do with a cup.'

CEO Robert Baron it said on the door. Larsen pointed the name tag to Bill and smiled, someone had felt-tipped out the letter *T*.

Baron turned away from staring through the window, put out his hand to Larsen and said, 'Robert Baron.'

'Captain Larsen, and this is Edward, my purser.'

'How can we be of assistance, Captain?'

'I need some work done on my boat before I go transatlantic,' he said, passing the list to Baron.

'This is quite a lot of work. How big is your boat?'

'One hundred and five feet.'

'It's not the *Leviathan*, is it?'

'Do you know it?'

'Certainly, we know the *Leviathan*. Is she still wallowing in the mud at Grindley's?'

Larsen nodded and said, 'still in Grindley's mud bath. Could you bring her over for me? I'm short of a crew at the moment.'

'Dave's my yard manager; he oversees all the work done here,' said Baron, pressing the page button on the tannoy, 'Dave, can you come to the office, please?'

There was a knock on the door and the receptionist came in with the three coffees.

'Bring a cup for Dave as well would you please, Sandra? He should be joining us in a minute.'

Five minutes later Dave knocked and came into the office.

'Dave, this is Captain Larsen and Edward, his purser. He's the captain of the *Leviathan*. He wants us to overhaul her before he goes transatlantic.'

'Hallelujah, there is a God!' said Dave. 'We've watched the *Leviathan* deteriorate for years – so sad, such a wonderful boat.'

Baron smiled and said, 'Don't worry Captain; we'll get her shipshape in no time for you.'

'And at a price no doubt,' said Larsen.

'There is that of course,' said Baron.

'Listen,' said Larsen, 'I don't have unlimited funds for the overhaul but I really want to see *Leviathan* back under full sail. Like she used to do; her rail down, defying storms, throwing green seas over her shoulder like they were but mere ripples on a windless day by the seaside.'

'We will need to survey her first before we can give you an estimate for the repairs. I presume she's still over at Grindley's?' said Dave.

Larsen nodded.

'Let me check the tides,' said Baron picking up a tide calendar from his desk. 'How much does she draw, Captain?'

'Seven foot six, with a clean bottom.'

'Next high tide today is not till eleven-thirty this evening, it's a 2.2 should be no problem – except the men will have gone home by then.'

'I'll help,' said Sandra, putting down Dave's coffee, 'and I am sure Dad would want to join in.'

'That makes six, perfect,' said Baron.

'Er, after last night I was hoping to turn in early,' said Bill.

'Fine,' said Larsen.

'Let's meet back here at six o'clock,' said Baron. 'The sun will have set but with the work lights on *Little Toot*, we shouldn't have a problem seeing what we're doing.'

'*Little Toot?*'

'It's the yard's runabout. Terry's, Sandra called it that when she was a little girl, and the name sort of stuck.

At six-fifteen they climbed onto *Little Toot* and set out to retrieve the *Leviathan*. No one challenged them as they came alongside *Leviathan*. They, tied her to the work boat, untied from the pontoon, and slowly manoeuvred out into deeper water. Although they were only moving at three knots Larsen felt the old magic come back as they motored down the channel past the bridges and into Poole harbour. With Baron's steady hand, they tied up at Barons just before midnight.

Larsen stood on the holding dock under the floodlights and looked at his lady.

'Well,' said Baron, 'she's here.'

'I'm going to stay on board tonight,' said Larsen, 'no telling what state the hull is in, can't have it sink at the dock.'

'I'll get a pump,' said Dave, 'if the boat does spring a leak you should be able to keep it afloat till you can call for help.'

'What time can we haul in the morning?' asked Larsen.

'There'll be plenty of water by eight,' said Baron. 'We'll warp the boat round and get it into the cradle by nine, bottom cleaned, and in the boat shed by noon.'

◆

As they sat in the café next morning eating breakfast, Baron asked, 'When would you like the work to be done by?'

'You have five weeks. I am late for the Atlantic and I don't want to run into any early hurricanes.'

'Ah, that might be a problem,' said Baron.

'Suppose I pay up front in cash, will that help?' Larsen picked up his briefcase, placed it on the table, and opened the top.

The tide of stress went out of Baron's face. 'It's not so much the cash, though that's very welcome, it's going to be how much work needs doing to the boat in the limited time we've got,' he said, suddenly looking five years younger. 'Dave should have completed the survey by lunchtime, and I'll have an estimate for you by the end of the day.'

'Great,' said Larsen.

'I'll get Sandra to call around and see who's available to work. As you probably realise, this is the quiet time in the year for boatyards and I only have a skeleton crew on hand, but I'm sure we'll manage.'

♦

Bill had a job – but he'd tossed and turned most of the night, finally falling into a troubled sleep as the church clock struck four. He'd been wrestling with the dual problems of immediate cash and how he would cope with cooking three meals a day for eleven people.

15
Doubts

'Morning, Beryl, said Bill as he walked into the kitchen.

'Morning – it's almost lunchtime,' responded Beryl, with a grin.

Bill looked at the kitchen clock, 'It's only eleven-thirty, still morning in my book.'

'You've missed breakfast,' said Beryl chuckling. 'Would you like a sandwich to tide you over till lunch?'

'Yes, please. I'll put the kettle on.'

'Edward, I was wondering,' said Beryl as she made Bill's sandwich, 'are you sure you should be moving on to this yacht with a man you have only just met?'

'Oh, I won't be the only person on board. Including me, there will be a crew of five plus six passengers.'

'How big is this yacht?'

'I have no idea. He is going to take me to see it today. Oh, he's also going to see if he can get me a new passport.'

'Be careful. How do you know you can trust him?' said Dot, shaking her head.

'You've met him, does he seem dangerous to you?'

'No. He seems a decent sort of chap.'

'Beryl I do need some advice, though. I know you haven't been charging me the full rate for my room, but even so the money I have isn't going to last me very long and although I will be paid by the Captain, I don't know when.'

'How long will what you have last?'

'I estimate a few weeks at the most.'

'I see. Your bank cards may be no good now.'

'Why not? There must be plenty of money in the accounts.'

'Were they joint accounts?'

'Yes, why?'

'There are some facts of life you need to know about, dear. When someone in your circumstances goes missing, the first thing that their nearest and dearest do is to block access to all the joint bank accounts. It's standard police advice. Just like if someone steals your wallet.'

'Oh dear, it's worse than I thought, then. What am I going to do? It could be months before I get paid.'

Beryl concentrated on the soup she was stirring then said, 'Why don't you talk to the Captain? Maybe he'll give you an advance on your wages.'

'I don't know, feels like begging.'

'If that's the worst you have to do in this life you've got off easy.'

'Thanks for the advice, Beryl. Be back in a moment, going for my jacket.'

When he came back, he found Larsen standing in the reception area talking to Smith; he beckoned Bill to wait while he continued with his conversation.

'How are the repairs going, Captain?'

'Barons hauled the *Leviathan* out on the railway this morning. I will see the surveyor's report later today. Repairs will probably be quite extensive.'

'Just give me the bare bones, Captain,' interrupted Smith. 'You will be able to sail in five weeks, right?'

'As long as there are no surprises, yes.'

'That's what I like to hear. Now, I would like to set up a meeting with you and our guests in the next few days. When would be convenient for you? How's Friday next week?'

'You want me to ask what time?'

'I knew we would get along. Shall we say ten o'clock?'

'In the morning? I'll probably be busy on the boat.'

'No, Captain, ten in the evening. Beryl says the restaurant will be empty by then. How are you doing with crew? I have some very suitable sailors I can get for you.'

'I have made contact with three of the crew who used to work for me; they will be joining me next week sometime and I've hired a new cook.'

'Good, I look forward to meeting them. Goodbye.'

'Mr Smith?' said Beryl as the doors swung closed behind Smith.

'Oh, hello Beryl Yes, that was Mr Smith.'

'He does have a way about him, doesn't he?' she said, laughing. 'Will you want dinner this evening? Dot's making her special lasagne.'

'Look forward to that.'

'OK, I'll make sure she keeps some for you. What about lunch?'

'I'll need to freshen up first, slept in my clothes on a bunk last night.'

'Shall I meet you in the restaurant?' suggested Bill.

'Good idea, see you in a few minutes.'

As they sat down for lunch, Larsen asked, 'Ready to go to work?'

'Yes.'

'Look, I think I will just call you Edward. You'll find most of the crew and the team will call each other by their first names as well.'

'Except you?'

'Except me, I will always be Captain.'

'That's fine. Have you had a chance to talk with your friend about a passport for me?'

'I just talked to him. He wants me to send him a passport size photo of you. We can get that done on the way to the yacht.'

'Isn't it illegal to forge a passport?'

'You could have your name changed by deed poll if we had time, but we don't so all we are doing is saving time. That's the way I look at it.'

'I suppose, it makes sense when you put it that way.'

♦

'Where to?' asked Terry, as they got into the taxi.

'Do you know where this photo studio is?' Larsen said, passing over the note with the studio address on it.

'Yes, it's at the rear of the precinct shops. We'll have to go down Hill Street and in the back way.'

From the outside the studio looked like it had seen better days. The sign above the door, faded and only partially readable said: *Jones the Photographers 24hr service.*

Larsen had to give the door a good push to open it. Inside was dark with faded yellowing strip lights and smelled of cats. The floor showed signs of the many footsteps that had trodden it over the years. Yellowed family portraits lined one wall. Shelving lined the opposite wall behind the counter with tired and misshapen empty camera boxes sitting on them.

The photographer appeared out of the gloom at the rear of the studio.

'My friend needs a passport photo,' said Larsen, 'and you were recommended.'

'By who?'

'You mean by whom,' said Bill, suddenly embarrassed by his outburst.

'I don't know anybody by that name, do you want the photo or not?'

'Lead on Macduff,' said Larsen, 'we're obviously wasting your precious time.'

It didn't take the photographer long and as they were about to leave, he said, 'are you coming to collect or do I need to send it somewhere?'

'Ah, Mr Smith recommended you and unfortunately I don't have his address.'

'I'll call him when it's ready. Now, I'll need a name, signature, fingerprints and date of birth. Here on this paper, make sure it's clear, we don't want any problems. I expect Mr Smith will get in touch with you directly. And my name is not Macduff, good day,' he said scurrying back into the depths of his studio.

'All sorted?' asked Terry, as they got back in the taxi.

'Yep, take us to Baron's please, Terry.'

Bill was surprised and slightly disappointed when they pulled up in a car park in front of the yacht chandlery. A high galvanised chain-link fence extended from the side of the café along the edge of the car park. It turned sharply to the left at the end of the car park and terminated on a high brick wall. Behind it he could see the masts of sailboats, none of which could be more than thirty feet high.

'Is this the marina where your yacht is berthed?' he asked.

Larsen sensed Bill's uneasiness, 'Yes, it's at this marina; there's a boat repair facility behind the chandlery.'

'Oh, I was beginning to wonder.'

'Come on then, ye of little faith, follow me.' he said, laughing heartily while swinging wide the door to the chandlery.

They went in, past the sales counter, racks of turnbuckles, shackles and anchors, and on to the rear of the store with its shelves of paint and varnish. Through large glass doors Bill could see boats of various sizes propped up on the concrete yard. Some had their masts removed while one was being water-blasted to remove the accumulation of weeds and barnacles from its bottom.

They went through the doors with Bill now wondering where this yacht that would sleep eleven people and cross the oceans in comfort could be.

They had to step to the side to avoid the large travelling crane that had just deposited a small power boat onto the yard. A crew of hands were putting the last of the props under the boat to shore it up. As they walked between the parked boats, he couldn't see any boat over forty feet in length. He was totally confused when Larsen walked through a small door into a large steel building and said, 'Here we are, here's your new home.'

All sorts of bizarre ideas started to flow through Bill's mind.

Larsen smiled and put out his hand. 'Trust me, it's really in here.'

He nervously stepped out of the warm early morning sunshine and into the cool gloom of the building. It took his eyes a few minutes to acclimatise to the dim light of the boat shed.

The sound of pneumatic sanders filled the air; the atmosphere was a rich aroma of wood shavings, tar, and linseed oil. Directly in front of him was a large rusty steel cradle on train wheels. Scaffolding extended in both directions. Workmen's legs, in white overalls, dangled from the scaffolding boards. He looked up at the cradle and realised there was a very large yacht sitting inside.

'This – this is your yacht? How big is it?'

'*Leviathan* is one hundred and five-foot-long, seventy-eight on the water. Would you like to see inside her?'

'I thought you said it was a sailboat? It doesn't have any masts,' he commented as they carefully made their way to the end of the shed and daylight.

'They were removed for maintenance. They're on the spar benches on the other side of the shed,' said Larsen.

The yard workers had hung a string of work lights from stern to stem illuminating the shed in a tired yellow glow. A series of ladders attached to the scaffolding provided access up to the deck.

'You first,' said Larsen.

The only time in his life Bill had climbed scaffolding was when the roofers had done work on the house and, at a dare from the twins, he'd gone to the top trembling with fear.

He stood on the side deck and looked forward. It took him a few moments to get his balance. Owing to the fact the yacht was not in the water, the up-sloping deck now sloped down. He leaned down and wrote his new name in the dust on top of the coach roof.

'Ready to go to work?' asked Larsen.

'I suppose so,' he answered, wondering who he was supposed to be cooking for.

'Follow me,' Larsen said, descending the companionway into the main saloon.

Bill followed Larsen below, dodging another string of suspended work lights. As he stepped onto the companionway steps, Larsen said, 'Watch your head on the hatch combing.' Bill was about to ask what the hatch combing was, when his head came into contact with it. They both said *ouch* simultaneously; he winced; Larsen grinned.

In the dim light to his left Bill could just make out the shape of the main saloon table. Turning to the right he asked, 'is this the kitchen?'

'On a boat it's called a galley.'

'Oh, off course it is.'

'Since you will be cooking for eleven on this trip, you will have my cabin,' said Larsen. 'It's here.' He opened a well-varnished door on the left at the bottom of the companionway steps.

'Where will you sleep?' Bill asked sheepishly.

Larsen grinned and said 'I'll sleep on the bunk in the chart room. It will be fine as I'll be doing most of the navigating on this trip. I'll explain general terminology to you later when I have time, the rest you'll have to pick up as you go, though I expect it will come back to you as your memory returns. This is your cabin.'

Bill opened the door and stepped in. It was difficult to make out the interior due to the poor light.

A door on the left opened into a private toilet with a shower. 'A head,' corrected Larsen. To the right of the entrance door was a small bookshelf stuffed full of books and opposite the door was his bunk. Bill was pleased to see it was a wide bunk with storage underneath. Immediately on his left he saw a small writing desk with mirror above and a chair tucked neatly underneath.

'Suitable?' asked Larsen.

'When can I move in?'

'Hold on a minute, you'll have to wait a couple of days. There is no DC power on the yacht; the engine and batteries are being serviced. Although I suppose we could get the shore power connected—in fact that would be a good idea as you will need power on while you are cleaning. I'm afraid there's no water; you'll need to bring it on board by bucket for now.'

'I don't mind,' he said, with a feeling of excitement growing inside him.

They went back into the main saloon. There was dust everywhere, but not even the smeared condiments could take away from what was the splendour of a magnificent yacht.

'Sorry to do this to you on your first day at work, but someone has to clean it. I doubt if there's anything on board suitable for cleaning, so you'll need to go to the market. I've opened temporary credit accounts both there and at the chandlery. Anything you need just charge it to the *Leviathan* account; I'll settle the bill before we leave. Oh, the same goes at the café, we will eat there till *Leviathan* is back in commission, any questions?'

Bill shook his head.

Larsen continued, 'I have to go see Dave first, then into town so I won't be around most of today. Tell you what, why don't you come with me to the office, and I'll see if I can find someone to show you around the yard?'

♦

'Morning Bob, Dave,' nodded Larsen, 'I've brought Edward along so he can get to know his way around *Leviathan* and get started making her ship-shape inside.'

'Morning, Edward,' said Dave, 'you certainly have your work cut out; I have seen what those bast—vandals did to the interior. Has the captain shown you where things are yet?'

'Er, no, we've just arrived.'

Baron pressed the intercom, 'Sandra, is the coffee ready?'

'I am just on my way in.'

'Captain. Coffee for you and Edward?'

'Yes, please. Edward?'

Bill shook his head. 'No thanks.'

'Sandra, make that three coffees, please.'

Seconds later the door opened, and Sandra entered with three steaming mugs.

Baron picked up his cup, 'Sandra, could you take Edward around the yard and show him where things are? He will probably need to get cleaning stuff from the market, so it would be a good idea to introduce him to Mrs Phillip. Also, while you are doing the rounds, introduce him to Pete in the chandlery and Betty in the café.'

'Sure. Ready, Edward?'

'Yes, let's go.'

'First let's see if Pete's in the store, then Mrs Phillip in the market and finally a cup of tea in the café, you'll like Betty.'

They left the office, walked through the chandlery and round to the market.

'Pete this is Edward, he's one of the crew on the *Leviathan*.'

'Pleased to meet you, Edward,' he said, shaking Bill's hand. 'What do you do on the yacht?'

'I am the cook.'

'That sounds like a lot of work. If you need any propane we have plenty of cylinders out at the back, you won't need to go into town for it.'

'Thank you, I'll remember that when the time comes,' he said, although he hadn't a clue what he was talking about.

Next on the tour was Mrs Phillip.

'Pleased to meet you, Edward. Your captain came in yesterday and said someone would be coming by. We have lots of fresh vegetables, dried goods and some tinned when you need them.'

'Thank you, Mrs Phillip. It will be a while before I need the food. I have to clean the interior first; the previous tenants have left quite a mess.'

'Not to worry, we have what you need I'm sure. Cleaning goods are on aisle five.'

'Thanks, I'll stop by later when I've made up a list of what I need.'

'Fine, we're open seven days a week and late on Friday and weekends. Goodbye Sandra, Oh Winston called, said he'll be a little late.'

'Who's Winston?' asked Bill as they walked past the chandlery to the café.

'He's Mrs Phillip's oldest son; we are getting married in September.'

The sign on the cafe door advertised *breakfast served all day*.

'Betty, this is Edward, he's the cook on the *Leviathan*.'

'Sandra – what can I get you?'

'I'll get this, Sandra. Can we have two cups of tea, please Betty?'

'Where would you like to sit?'

'I seem to live in front of windows these days. Why change a habit? That one over there looks fine.'

As they sat down, Bill asked, 'So what does Winston do?'

'He's a research chemist; he works for a pharmaceutical company just outside London.'

Bill nodded. 'That sounds important. And where are you going on your honeymoon?'

'We're going to Jamaica to meet some of his family, then on a cruise.'

'Sounds fantastic. Wish I could go somewhere exotic.' Then he remembered he would be. In a few weeks he'd be off across the Atlantic to the Amazon. He smiled inside.

Their conversation was interrupted by the arrival of Dave. 'Thought I'd find you both here,' he said sitting down at their table, holding a well-used plastic coffee cup. He noticed Bill looking at it and explained, 'refills are free at Betty's. I buy a fresh cup of coffee every January and spend the rest of the year refilling it. Just one of the perks of the job.'

'Mr Baron said you're the yard manager?'

'Call him Bob, we're all on first name terms here,' said Dave.

'Then who calls him Robber Baron?' asked Bill.

'Ah, you saw the name tag on the door to his office. He did that himself; it's his sense of humour. So, you're the cook on the *Leviathan*. Not going to be very busy for a while, are you?'

'I have the whole interior to clean first.'

'Ah yes, what a mess.'

'It's quite dark inside the yacht,' said Bill, 'Captain Larsen said he would ask you about some shore power.' He was using the words that Larsen had used without understanding their meaning.

'No problem, the engineers' just finished servicing the batteries and engine.'

'What about water? The captain said I would have to carry buckets on board for cleaning.'

'We'll rig up a ship-to-shore connection. The galley seacock has not been refitted yet so I'll get one of the lads to connect a temporary drain. Anything else?'

'Not that I can think of at the moment.'

'Tell you what, as soon as you've finished your tea I'll walk you back to the yacht and show you where things are.'

'Wonderful.'

'Edward, I have to get back,' said Sandra, as she got up to go, 'the phones get real busy at this time of the day, so see you around.'

'Have you met Pete yet?' asked Dave as he and Bill walked through the chandlery on their way to the *Leviathan*.

'Yes, Sandra introduced me earlier. We also went round and said hello to Mrs Phillip.'

'Good, in that case let me show you where the toilets and the laundry are. The laundry is only for the yard staff, but we make exceptions sometimes. It works on tokens; you can get them from Pete.'

They left the laundry block, walked across the yard, and went into the boat shed. The smell had changed to that of fresh paint.

'There are about a dozen shipwrights working in here on the yacht at the moment,' said Dave. 'The masts have been removed and are lying on the spar benches. Would you like to see them?'

They walked to the end of the shed, ducked under the stem of the *Leviathan* and picked their way around a large pile of anchor chain.

'That's the main anchor chain; it's just going off to be re-galvanised.'

'I'm sorry? You need to explain that.'

'Old chains get rusty and sometimes need re-galvanising to extend their life. Before we launch *Leviathan,* the chain will be hoisted up on to the deck and stored below.'

Bill bent down and grabbed the end of the chain to lift it and found out just how heavy it was.

'Don't worry,' said Dave, 'the *Leviathan* has a very good powered windlass, should only take a few minutes to haul the chain on board.'

As they walked back down the shed, he explained. 'The mizzen mast is close to sixty foot in length and the main mast is about a hundred – you'll get a good view from up top.'

'That's not for me,' said Bill, 'I like to keep my feet on the ground.'

Dave introduced Bill to the workers as they passed on their way to the stern.

'This is Edward; he's the cook on the *Leviathan*. He will be working inside, cleaning.'

The deck was a hive of activity. A crew of painters were sanding and filling the paintwork on the top of the coach-roof. This time Bill watched his head as he climbed down the companionway.

When he got below he found Dave talking to a young man dressed in blue overalls.

'Edward, this is Steve, the engineer who's been working on the engine and batteries. He's just turned on the internal power for you. The main circuit board is in the chart room, but you won't have to worry about that, while at sea it will be the engineers' job to look after the electrics. The cabin lights have small switches on the side, see,' he said, demonstrating. 'Most everything onboard runs on the batteries except the mains outlets and they are 110 volts. Just think of the yacht as a large caravan. If there's anything heavy or awkward that you want to move just ask any of the guys in the shed, I've told them to help you if needed. To use the water just turn on the tap, same as in a house, except at sea the water comes out of a tank.'

A very large caravan, Bill thought. 'No, nothing comes to mind at the moment. Thanks, I'll shout if I need help.'

'Good, then if you are ready to get to work, Captain Larsen and I are off to deliver the sails to a loft in Wareham, shouldn't be long.'

After Dave left, Bill stood and looked around the interior of the *Leviathan*. This was to be his home. What a mess! He looked up through the octagonal skylight at the yellow work lights and wondered what it would be like staring up at the stars at sea.

On his left, directly behind him was a fireplace with a large video screen over the mantelpiece. Immediately to his left was an 'L' shaped cushioned settee, with a space with bar stools that backed onto the galley. Behind the galley was the chart room.

The galley, he saw now he had turned on the lights, was surrounded by a wide varnished teak countertop. Opposite the galley was his cabin. Directly on his right was the main saloon dining table, also in varnished teak with four dining chairs hooked to the cabin floor, *sole,* Larsen had corrected him, and a long heavily cushioned bench seat against the port hull.

He turned and walked downhill into the guest cabin area. On his left, there was a small double cabin with two single bunks and an ensuite shower and toilet. It was the same with the cabin on the right, except the lower bunk was a double. Forward of these was the main guest cabin. It had a full double bunk. The bathroom had, in addition to a shower, its own varnished wooden bathtub.

Glad I'm only the cook, he thought, I wouldn't want to keep this lot clean, I wonder whose job that will be? Another puzzling question, where did the crew sleep, surely not on the settees?

No good standing here, he thought, time to get to work. He climbed the companionway and was about to walk aft to the ladders when he realised that he hadn't looked all the way up front yet.

He stepped off of the companionway and turned left around the coach roof, to walk forward. If it hadn't been for the lifelines, he would have been quite uncomfortable walking forward along the narrow side deck this high off the ground. Just past where the main mast would be, he saw another hatch. He slid it open and looked down into the dark. He felt around inside and found a light switch. Turning it on, he saw a large cabin with one double bunk and a large single. He climbed down the steps and into the cabin, it had its own toilet, *head* he corrected himself and forwards of that there were two more single bunks.

So, this is where the crew sleeps, he said to himself. Bit cramped but very functional.

16
DCI Ross

'Mum, that car with the two men is still parked outside the house,' said Hannah.

'Probably fishermen waiting for the weather to change,' Ruth replied.

'Maybe they are spies,' suggested Rachael.

'Don't talk nonsense,' said Abigail. 'Breakfast is ready, come and eat it while it's still hot.' Then, looking out the window to the rear car park, she added, 'That policeman is back.'

'I'll go see what he wants; you girls finish your breakfast.'

Ruth opened the door as DCI Ross was about to press the doorbell.

'Sorry to disturb you, ma-am. I wonder if we might clarify a couple of items in your statement?'

'Any news about my husband?' asked Ruth as Ross stepped into the hall accompanied by a plain clothes police officer and a uniformed woman PC.

'Sorry, ma-am, nothing new at the moment, except this,' he said, removing a small backpack from an evidence bag. 'Is this your husband's, ma-am?'

Ruth looked in the backpack, pulled out Bill's jacket, phone, and the letter from the court. 'Yes, it's the one I bought for him last Christmas. Battery's flat on the phone, as usual, and the letter from the court, unopened. Where did you find it?'

'It was handed into security in the mall. No wallet though. It might be a good idea to call the bank and find out if any money has been withdrawn from your account.'

'Yes I'll – I'll do that.'

'Don't give up hope, Mrs Drysdale.

'This is Detective Sergeant Wood and PC Johnston,' he indicated by a wave of his hand. 'PC Johnston will sit with your children while we talk; the front room should be fine.'

Ruth led the way while PC Johnston went into the kitchen.

Ross nodded to Wood, 'You say you all went out to dinner the evening prior to your husband's disappearance?'

'Yes, that's correct; we went to the Harbour View restaurant.'

'And you arrived home a little before midnight?'

'Yes.'

'Good food was it, ma-am? Our tenth anniversary is coming up in a couple of weeks and I would like to take my wife somewhere special.'

'The food was excellent; I am sure you and your wife would have a lovely time.'

'Mrs Drysdale,' interrupted Ross, 'did your husband enjoy his dinner?'

'Yes, I think he did – yes I am sure he did.'

'Do they have a good wine list, ma-am?' asked Wood. 'My wife went to one of those wine-tasting events last year when we were in France and considers herself a bit of an expert now; wouldn't want her to be disappointed.'

'The wine was excellent; your wife will not be disappointed.'

'Red or white, ma-am?' queried Wood.

'What?'

'Your husband, ma-am, did he have red or white wine with his dinner?'

'He had a beer before dinner then we had white wine with the dinner and ended the meal with cognac and cheese and biscuits.'

'Did you finish the wine, ma-am? I prefer beer, you get more for your money,' said Wood, writing in his notebook.

'Yes, we probably did.'

'Did you drive home?' asked Ross.

'No, we'd booked a taxi. Look, what has this got to do with my husband's disappearance?'

'Was he recently involved in a car accident?'

'Yes, I've already told you that. He ran into the back of a car on the M3.'

'What about the one on the country club road?' asked Ross.

How the hell do they know about that, Ruth wondered? 'I – er, he swerved to avoid a black panther and ran into a tree.'

'Black leopard ma-am, there's no such animal as a panther,' said Wood, 'one of those misconceptions of life, least so my daughter said. It was in her homework a couple of weeks ago.'

Ruth shook her head in dismay, turned and walked over to the bay window and stared out over the sea. She stared for a moment at the smoke rising above the horizon from the funnel of the cross-channel ferry.

'Was your husband a happy person, ma-am?'

Ruth turned and stared at Wood for a moment. 'Just what are you implying, sergeant?'

'Nothing, ma-am. Sometimes when people are under stress they do strange things.'

'Did you have an argument when you returned from dinner?' asked Ross.

'About what?'

'You tell me. For instance, did his drinking cause you concern?'

Ruth thought for a moment; she suddenly realised where the interrogation was headed. 'Yes.'

'Did you say anything to him about it when you returned home?'

'Yes.'

'Did you argue?'

'No, er, well – we may have said things that we shouldn't have.'

'Did you go out again that night?'

'No, of course not.' As she said it, she remembered going out for the milk and cereal, then realised she'd just told Ross they'd been drinking at dinner.

Ross looked at her, shook his head and said, 'You're on CCTV at the grocery store buying milk and cereal at ten past eleven. We are looking for your husband Mrs Drysdale, not trying to catch you driving under the influence. Was he with you?'

'No. He was at home in bed.'

'Did you go anywhere else while you were out for cereal, ma-am?'

'I drove out to the chain ferry; I needed fresh air and time to think.'

'And your husband was at home in bed?'

'I've already told you he was in bed, what are you driving at inspector?'

'Just wondering if when you got home, you put the girls to bed, then instead of going out on your own, you took your husband for a drive, to talk things over. Maybe you wanted to explain to him how important your work was and the upcoming general election. You went to the ferry and you both got out for the fresh air. There was an argument and he walked off. Maybe, having had too much to drink, he slipped and fell in the water. You weren't able to rescue him and decided it might be for the best if he was out of your life.'

'Inspector that's an obscene suggestion, besides, how did his backpack end up in the mall?'

'We only have your word that it's his.'

'Inspector, you have a cesspool for a mind.'

'Just doing my job Mrs Drysdale, just doing my job. So you just returned home and went to bed?'

'Yes.'

'Was he asleep?'

'I don't know. I made up a bed on the settee.'

'Did anyone see you at the ferry?' asked Ross.

Ruth shrugged her shoulders. 'It was tied up; don't know if anyone saw me, I wasn't looking for anyone.'

'You say you went down to the beach with the children in the morning. Was your husband awake or sleeping?'

'He was fast asleep; I didn't want to wake him, so I wrote a note and left it on the kitchen counter.'

'Did your children see their father before you all went out, ma-am?'

'Their stepfather, no, I told them he was not feeling well but would probably join us later.'

'So, the last time the children saw their stepfather was at dinner the previous evening?'

'Yes.'

'Thank you, Mrs Drysdale,' said Ross, rising to leave. He turned as they were about to go out the door and asked, 'Do you have a recent photograph of your husband, Mrs Drysdale? We would like to circulate it and also we would like to make a statement to the press.'

Ruth shuffled off down the corridor and returned with a recent photo of Bill and handed it to Ross.

'Those two men in the car out the front,' asked Ruth, 'are they your men?'

'Not directly. They're special branch, as are the two at the rear of the house. They are there to keep a watch on your house; you are a very important lady, Mrs Drysdale. I understand the work you do is much appreciated in certain government circles.'

'I can take care of myself; I don't need a bodyguard.'

'Mrs Drysdale, until we can ascertain what has happened to Mr Drysdale, we can't afford to take any chances. How long will you be staying in Canford Cliffs?'

'I suppose till we hear something definite, or at least the end of the week, then the girls need to get back to school.'

'Understandable. Mrs Drysdale, please let us know if you decide to return home. Good day.'

17
Provisioning

As Bill descended the companionway, laden with cleaning stuff, a voice said, 'Careful, the cabin sole is up.'

He stopped and bent his head forward to look inside the cabin. One of the shipwrights was shoulder-deep in the bilges with a section of the cabin sole lifted.

'It's OK, just watch where you step,' he said.

'What are you doing?' Bill asked, stepping into the galley.

'Replacing a worn-out hose; can't have it springing a leak at sea.'

'Will it take you long? I need to get to work.'

'About half an hour. Cup of tea would be nice.'

'I'm sure I can manage that. Milk and sugar?'

'Milk, two sugars, please.'

By the time tea had been drunk and the cabin sole replaced Bill had cleaned the refrigerator and was head and shoulders into the freezer.

♦

'It took me almost an hour just to clean the refrigerator,' Bill said to Larsen on his return. 'I still have to go through the boat and get all the crumbs and mouse droppings out of the drawers. Thankfully, I haven't seen any signs of cockroaches. Is there a vacuum cleaner?'

'Yes, there is a small canister vacuum somewhere – lives in one of the lockers under the drinks cabinet, I think. Now Edward,' he continued, '*Leviathan* is due to go back in the water sometime next week. We need to start thinking about provisioning for the voyage. Will you work out a provisioning list for me? I don't expect you to have done a shopping list this large or complex before, so can you have a think about it and we will discuss it later?'

'Oh, OK, I'll put something together for you.'

'Good. I have to go out again and won't be back before it's time to stop for the day. Why don't I tell Terry to pick you up at five-thirty and I will see you in the hotel for dinner about seven, OK?'

'Sounds great, I'm famished. I've been so busy I forgot to stop for lunch.'

'Don't do that at sea, you must eat to keep up your strength.'

'See you at dinner then,' Bill said, as Larsen climbed up the companionway.

Bill poured a cup of coffee, went to his cabin and up on to his bunk to think. It was two worlds, he mused. In the cabin was peace and tranquillity while across the boat was the galley, his nemesis. Bill looked at his reflection in the mirror and wondered how was he to go about making a provisioning list. In fact, what was a provisioning list? He shook his head at his foolishness. He needed to think; he needed more than a cup of coffee.

It was then that he noticed the books on the shelf. They didn't appear to be in any rational order: not by alphabet, subject, size or author. He threw himself into sorting them.

While waiting for Terry he leafed through a couple of the cruising books. One especially stuck out. It was just what he was looking for, *How to Keep Your Crew Fed, Fit and Happy*. Opening the book at the index he looked at the chapter headings and saw to his joy one called 'Provisioning for going offshore'. He glanced at his watch, picked up the book and headed for the car park. Terry was already waiting for him.

'Good day at work?' asked Beryl, as Bill walked past the reception desk on his way to the restaurant.

'Yes thanks.'

'The captain is waiting for you.'

'How was your day?' asked Larsen.

'Fine, once I got started. Did you know that ketchup and mustard are equally hard to clean when they have dried out? Thanks to Mrs Philip's recommendation I was able to get it all off. The kitchen – sorry, galley, has had an initial clean. Tomorrow I'll go through all the cupboards and wash them down with bleach. There were some rotting vegetables under the sink that have left a bit of a stink. Dave was telling me it is vitally important to keep cupboards clean of food scraps otherwise they can attract cockroaches.'

'You certainly have been busy. Dave's right: cockroaches can be a big problem, especially when you get into the tropics. I remember being told by a deckhand that one night, because it was too hot below, he was sleeping on deck and woke to find the little blighters nibbling the dead skin on the soles of his feet.'

Over dinner Larsen recounted some of his more colourful experiences as a charter captain in the Caribbean.

'Was dinner all right, Captain?' asked Beryl, as she cleared the dishes from their table. 'Can I get you anything else?'

'The dinner was lovely Beryl, thank you. If I didn't already have a cook I would be asking you.'

'Not me you wouldn't,' laughed Beryl, 'I like both my feet on dry land,'

'It's been a long day,' said Bill, 'I think I will go to bed early. I hope you don't mind, Captain, but I've borrowed a rather interesting book from the *Leviathan* and I would like to get started on it.'

'No problem, read them all, I have, several times,' he said, getting up from the table. 'See you at breakfast.'

'Good night, Captain.'

'Would you like a nightcap, Edward?' asked Beryl.

'I'd love a cup of cocoa, please.'

'Come through to the kitchen when you're ready,' said Beryl, as she moved off to clear the other tables in the restaurant.

Bill went up to his room with a steaming mug of cocoa and, after showering, climbed into bed and started to read *How to Keep Your Crew Fit Fed and Happy*. He managed half of the introduction before he was sound asleep.

18
Mr Smith

By nine-thirty Bill had finished cleaning the accumulation of dust and debris in the cabins and moved on to the crew quarters. Larsen had gone to London to collect the charts for the voyage, so Bill went to lunch at Betty's on his own.

'When does the *Leviathan* go back in the water?' asked Betty, as she made Bill's sandwich.

'Sometime next week, strangely, I don't know if I get time off at the weekend.'

'I'm sure you will. He can't work you seven days a week – can he?'

'It doesn't matter if I do have to work; I have nothing else to do anyway, may as well keep busy.'

'Do you want to help me in the café?'

'I'd love to, but I'll need to ask the captain first.'

'You won't have to work that hard. We do mostly breakfasts and burgers at the weekends.'

'That's OK, I won't mind. Anything to keep my mind occupied.'

'Here's your sandwich. Do you want a drink?'

'No thanks; I've got the kettle on in the galley.'

Bill returned to the main saloon and his book. When he turned to the section on keeping watch, he found out to his pleasure that the cook on a large vessel wasn't expected to stand any watches. The downside was he would have a long day, starting early preparing the breakfast, then lunch, and finally dinner. On top of all of this he would be expected to keep the boat tidy and do the laundry. Then he realised he hadn't seen a washing machine anywhere on board. He'd need to ask the Captain about that.

His lunch was interrupted by the sound of footsteps on the scaffolding steps. Whoever it was stopped on the companionway and said, 'Edward Cook?'

'Down below, in the main saloon.' Bill felt pleased with himself. He was coming to grips with nautical terms.

The legs belonging to the voice descended into the main saloon. It was Smith.

'Edward Cook?'

'That's me.'

'Sorry to disturb you; I have your passport.'

'Oh, I had forgotten all about that.'

Smith opened his briefcase and took out a large manila envelope and removed Bill's new passport. 'It looks a little used. Don't worry, we do that deliberately.' He reached back into the envelope and pulled out some more papers. 'This is your driving licence; you do drive, don't you?'

Bill nodded.

'Here are two credit cards in your name; each has a positive credit of five hundred pounds. PIN numbers attached to the backs. The cost comes out of the captain's cruising budget. This is your national insurance number, and here is your NHS medical card. This is a paid invoice from the gas company, and finally a letter from your solicitor stating your divorce is final and he is sorry that you did not get the custody of your children.'

Tears came into Bill's eyes as he felt the irony of losing yet another family, albeit an imaginary one.

'Do you have a mobile phone?'

Bill shook his head.

'You can have this one,' Smith said, passing Bill a slim orange phone. 'It's a pay-as-you-go one. It should have credit already on it. You'll find the number written on the tape on the back.'

Their conversation was interrupted by the arrival of Larsen.

'Ah Captain, just delivering the documents to your cook, how's the refit going?'

'Fine, we are ahead of schedule.'

'Would you gentlemen like coffee?' asked Bill.

'Please,' said Larsen.

Smith shook his head.

Larsen turned to Smith and continued with his report while Bill busied himself in the galley.

'The sails are at the sail loft; the engine only required a good service, which will be complete as soon as we are back in the water. The masts are being repainted as we speak. The bottom paint is going on tomorrow then all the through hulls with the seacocks can be fitted. The prop shaft and propeller have just come back from the machine shop. So it looks like we will be back in the water Monday or Tuesday.'

'What about the masts? When will they go back up?'

'The masts will be stepped the day after we go back in. It's too big a job to do the same day. All of the standing rigging is new, so has to be cut to length and the ends re-terminated.'

'Are you planning to stay here at this yard till you depart?'

'No, we will go over to the harbour. The water is too shallow here and I don't want the bottom paint to get damaged at low tide.'

'Good to hear your progress, Captain,' said Smith, standing. 'I will be away for a few days so I will see you next week at the Admiral Aubrey.'

'Your coffee, Captain,' said Bill.

'Well, I see you have your passport,' said Larsen, 'and credit cards and a mobile phone. I'll take the number – it could come in handy. Is this the number on the back?' He turned it over in his hand.

'Yes, that's what your Mr Smith said.'

'*My* Mister Smith?' laughed Larsen. 'You've got it the wrong way round, he doesn't belong to us; we belong to him.'

'Oh, never looked at it that way.'

'What have you got going this afternoon?'

'All the bedding has been washed and aired. I plan to spend the rest of the day ironing the sheets, re-hanging the curtains and finish by stuffing the mattresses into their covers.'

'Good, I'm going to see Bob, then check on the progress of the painting of the masts.'

Just as Larsen was about to leave, Bill said, 'Can I ask a question?'

'Certainly.'

'Do I have to work the weekends as well as through the week?'

'No, not while in dry dock.'

'I was talking to Betty and she said she could do with some help in the café this weekend. I thought it would be a good opportunity for me to cook for a lot of people at once.'

'Marvellous idea. Go right ahead. Just tell Terry what time you want collecting in the morning.'

Bill went to bed early. He wanted to be fresh for the next day's work. By the time he had read the chapter on provisioning three times he understood better what was involved. Glad I won't be getting up at four in the morning, he thought.

The captain wasn't at breakfast, but Dot handed Bill a message to say that he'd gone to the boat early. When Bill arrived, he was greeted by both Larsen and a strange smell emanating from the side door of the boat shed.

'They are applying the bottom paint,' he said, seeing Bill's expression. 'It's a mix of epoxy resin and copper powder. It works the same as covering the bottom with sheets of copper but is much cheaper and more suited to a hull shape like the *Leviathan*. It will be a while before we can get on board.'

'Why do you have to work so fast?' asked Bill.

'In this temperature, when mixed, the epoxy will be too hard to apply after forty-five minutes. That is why there are two crews working non-stop.'

'Do they get a break during the day?'

'Not today they won't,' said Dave, smiling. 'I've arranged with Betty to provide lunch. She might want a hand to prepare it, if you've got time?'

'Certainly,' said Bill, 'as I can't get onto the boat, I've got plenty of time.

When Bill returned, Larsen and Dave were deep in conversation at the end of the shed.

'Tomorrow,' said Dave, 'the lads will paint the topsides and the boot stripe, then we will install the zincs, seacocks, shaft and propeller and put the *Leviathan* back in the water Monday.'

Bill saw a grin grow on Larsen's face.

♦

On Saturday morning Bill was up ready and waiting for a non-existent Terry. As he stepped out into the street Terry arrived, tyres screeching.

'Sorry I'm late, have you had to wait long?'

'No, just got here myself, you look rushed,' Bill said, fastening his seat-belt.

'Poole FC is playing away at Alresford today and a couple of supporters had car trouble and almost missed their coach, so it was Terry to the rescue.'

At the mention of Alresford, Bill shivered; it was the last place he wanted to be.

Betty was already in the kitchen when Bill arrived.

'Good morning Edward, had your breakfast yet?'

'No, thought I would eat here, if that's all right?'

'Fine, I have some bacon under the grill already—would you like a full breakfast?'

'Sounds great, how can I help?'

'You'll find the cutlery in the trays and the mugs are hanging from the hooks. Would you like some toast? You can have brown or white?'

'Brown will be fine.'

'Would you see if the papers have arrived, please? The boy usually puts them in the box at the side of the front door.'

Bill picked up the pile of newspapers. Glancing at one of the headlines he saw that another MP had been caught handing out favours to one of his friends.

'Where do the papers go, Betty?'

'They go on the small table beside the condiments. Wait a moment though, before you do that, take this pen and write, 'Not to be taken out of the café' across the top of each.'

Putting the pen down, Bill glanced through the local paper. He almost dropped it when he turned to page seven. There, smiling out at him was a picture of himself. The article that went with the picture read:

> *Concern is growing for missing father-of-three, Bill Drysdale, resident of Alresford. He was last seen on Saturday evening with his family. Anyone having information regarding his whereabouts should contact the police.*

♦

'Busy day?' asked Larsen as Bill joined him at the dinner table.

'I never realised how many shades of yellow, egg yolks can have,' he said, looking at the menu.

'I just eat them. How are you getting on with the provisioning list?'

'I talked to Mrs Phillip; she's going to introduce me to her sales rep on Tuesday. I should have a shopping list ready by the end of the week, except for a couple of items I'm having trouble with.'

'Such as?'

'Canned and dried food are not too difficult to organise, it's the fresh food that can be problematic. Can you give me an idea how long each stage of the voyage will be?'

'You certainly have been doing your homework. I plan to head for Falmouth first; it will act as a shakedown cruise, hopefully we won't need to make any adjustments to the boat. Depending on the weather we will sail a westerly course till we are well clear of Lands End, then run south west down to Madeira. This will keep us away from the Spanish coast, a potentially dangerous lee shore, and its busy coastal shipping. It is a long run, depending on weather could take between seven and twelve days. From Madera to the Cape Verde islands, say six to ten days. Although, if we run into contrary weather; it could take longer.

'When we reach the Cape Verdes we will head roughly west along the trade wind route for Barbados and then before we get to Barbados we'll head south west for Brazil and the Amazon River. I haven't worked out the exact route for that leg, but if we allow twelve days for the passage it should suffice. Does that help?'

'It's a start. I will spend some time on the list tomorrow.'

'Ah tomorrow, Dave says the *Leviathan* is ready to go back in the water. Originally, we were planning on launching first thing Monday, but it seems that *Leviathan's* arrival has raised the profile of the yard and there is another large yacht due in for a haul out on Wednesday. Dave would like to get the holding dock cleared as soon as possible. So we've agreed to put *Leviathan* back in the water early tomorrow morning. She will sit in the cradle till high tide, which will be at five-thirty then floated over to the holding dock.'

'Why does she need to sit in the cradle all day? Surely if she is back in the water early in the morning we could move her then?'

'Two reasons: first we will let *Leviathan* sit in the cradle as the tide rises, then if there are any major problems it is a simple job of hauling her back out of the water.'

'And second?'

'Low tide, not enough water.'

'Oh, I see. Do you envisage any problems?'

'Not really, the yard has done a superb job of the refit. I would like you to be on board tomorrow morning before the launch and spend the day watching for leaks. Dave and I and a couple of the yard's fitters will be there checking the rigging, so you will be our eyes and ears on board during the day. We'll now be stepping the masts on Monday. Tuesday the engine fitter will be back to complete the service.'

'Well, I must get to bed then, I have a busy day tomorrow,' he said, his eyes glistening with excitement. 'Oh, I must see Beryl about the Bill for my room first.'

Larsen shook his head and said, 'That's my responsibility. As you are part of my crew your board and lodging expenses comes under my running costs. Do I understand you want to move aboard full time?'

'Isn't that what you meant?'

'No, not really, but you could if you wanted to. The yacht will be fully functional by then and I suppose it would be good for security if someone is on board. Before you go though, there are some formalities that need to be taken care of. I need you to sign your crew contract.'

'Crew contract, what's that?'

'Any time a yacht goes overseas the captain becomes legally responsible for the welfare of all the crew. The contract states what the responsibilities are of both the captain and the crew.'

Bill looked down at the contract that Larsen had placed in front of him.

'It says my job title is Purser/Cook, I don't understand?'

'As purser you will be responsible for the administration of the yacht's finances, as regards to provisioning and purchase of spare parts if they are needed and deal with many of the port officials when purchasing and taking on board stores. You will also need to visit the port captain's office daily when we are in port for any mail that may have been forwarded to the yacht. If you read through you will see the complete list of your responsibilities.'

Bill looked at the contract, skimming through the short document. 'Can I take this away and read it first?'

'Sure. We won't be leaving for a couple of days yet; take your time.'

Bill stood up from the table and went through to the bar to see Beryl. On the way he almost walked into the doorframe and decided to read his contract later.

'Hello Bill, how was your day?'

'Beryl, I never want to see another egg in my life.'

'That bad?'

'No, not really, just a busy day. We are launching *Leviathan* tomorrow instead of Monday. The Captain wants me to spend the day on board watching for leaks. I will be moving on board tomorrow and he said he will pay for my room as I am one of the crew.'

'We'll miss you when you've gone.'

'I'll miss you both as well, although I should be back to this side of the harbour on Wednesday. Captain Larsen has made arrangements with the harbour master to berth the *Leviathan* at the dock outside. I was wondering, Beryl, you wouldn't happen to have a spare suitcase I can borrow for a couple of days, would you?'

'I am sure we can find something. We always have spares; you'd be surprised what people leave behind, I'll dig one out this evening and leave it at reception for you.'

19
Launch day

Dave and Bob were waiting for them at the end of the boat shed. They exchanged pleasantries and watched the yard workers remove the scaffolding from the rear of the boat shed exposing the stern of *Leviathan* and its freshly applied name in gold leaf.

One of the yard workers came over from the boat shed. 'We're ready to launch, Dave.'

'Right, we'll stop her just above the keel. Before we launch though, I think we should get the anchor chain back on board, it will save us hassle if we do it now.'

As Bill walked towards the *Leviathan* the morning silence was broken by the deafening roar of an ancient diesel engine. Bill watched with fascination as the cables attached to the cradle became taut and, very slowly, the *Leviathan* was eased out of the boat shed and down the rails to the water.

'Look at all this dust and debris,' he said, as Larsen climbed on board and handed him his suitcase.

'You can sweep up the big bits and wash off the dust with a hose when we get into the bay. There is a deck wash standpipe beside the windlass. It is plumbed to a pump on the engine.'

'Good. Do you think anyone wants coffee while we wait?'

'Good idea, bacon butty would be even better.'

'I could make you one in a couple of minutes; except we have no gas. Pete mentioned that if I wanted any he could sort it for me.'

'I'll go ashore and talk to Dave, back later.'

Larsen came aboard in the middle of the afternoon and checked the bilges. 'Dry as a bone, that's what I like to see.'

'Can I replace the cabin sole now?' asked Bill.

'Yes, looks like *Leviathan* will be fine; I'll turn on the bilge alarm before I go, just in case.'

'Are you all done with the masts?'

'As ready as we can be. Dave wants to do the main mast first thing in the morning before the wind gets up.'

They were interrupted by a knock on the hull. 'Captain, we're ready to move.'

'Ok Dave, be right with you,' said Larsen.

It only took a few minutes to warp the *Leviathan* out of the cradle and over to the holding dock.

'Are you sure you'll be all right on your own?'

'Yes, I'll be fine. I'm actually looking forward to the peace and quiet.'

'OK then, in the meantime you have my phone number if you need me. I'll stop by before sunset, just to make sure all is well. Dave has given me the key to the side gate of the yard, also a second key for you should you need to go out. He asks that if you do go out to make sure you lock it after you.'

On the spur of the moment Bill offered, 'Would you like me to make dinner for you? It will only be a seafood salad with French bread.'

'Sounds fine, how about seven-thirty?'

'Your wish is my command,' said Bill, smiling.

As soon as he was alone Bill made a cup of coffee and, taking his notebook and copy of *How to Keep Your Crew Fed, Fit and Happy*, went up to the cockpit and sat down at the table to plan Tuesday's shopping trip.

♦

Larsen arrived promptly at seven-thirty.

'Hmm,' he said, looking around, 'the *Leviathan* is looking more like she should. You have been busy.' He passed Bill a chilled bottle of *Shloer* carbonated grape juice.

'Dinner's ready.'

'Great, but before we eat, I'd like to check the bilges, should only take a few minutes.'

'Cheers,' said Bill, holding up his glass.

'Cheers,' said Larsen in return. 'You staying warm enough?'

'Yes. The weather has been so mild for February.'

'Newspaper says it's close to a record. Did you see the sunset this evening?'

'Yes, it was magnificent.'

'We should see a lot more of these before we are back in Poole again. In fact, with the clear sky this evening we should be able to see Vega.'

'Vega, what's that?'

'Vega is one of the stars in what's called the summer triangle. The other two stars are called Deneb and Altair.'

'Do you know the names of lots of stars?'

'Just the main stars to do with navigation. Although these days with GPS navigation; it's not really necessary to know them all.'

'At least your satnav system won't take you down any narrow country lanes. We used to get huge trucks trying to get down the lane outside our house – how long do you think the voyage will last?'

'All going well, we should be back about this time next year. That is if you decide to stay for the whole trip.'

'Why wouldn't I stay for the whole trip?'

'Some people are not suited to life at sea: the first storm and they go to pieces. While for others life at sea is second nature. Most get sick for the first few days, while others never get over it.'

'What about you, do you ever get seasick?'

'It has happened; but being the Captain I just have to endure. I'm usually fine after a couple of days. Then, no matter how rough the motion of the sea, it doesn't bother me. How about you, have you ever been seasick?'

'A few times, when I used to sail with my father, but the worst was when I was in the Navy. We were out on patrol in the north Atlantic and a message came through that there was Russian nuclear sub in the area. We spent the next ten days criss-crossing the ocean, all in a force ten gale. I expect I will be fine on the *Leviathan* though.'

'Glad to hear that,' Larsen said, refilling his glass. 'How are you doing with the provisioning?'

'I was working on it before you came, I could go over it with you now if you want?'

'No time like the present,' he said, gesturing with his hands.

Bill returned from below with his list and a bottle of wine. He noticed Larsen looking at the bottle and said, 'Are you driving?'

'No, Terry drove me over.'

'Oh, I just wondered, we've been drinking grape juice all evening.'

Larsen shook his head slowly and said, 'I don't drink any more, not since – ah, never mind, another time.'

Bill smiled and thought, we all have our secrets. He picked up the bottle of juice and asked as he poured Larsen's drink, 'Do you have any hobbies?

Larsen shook his head and said, 'Not anymore, used to do a bit of horse-riding, western mostly.'

'Really?' said Bill, smiling at the memory of his attempt to decide what type of captain, Larsen was. 'I could imagine you dressed in crimson. Calling the hounds, yoicks and tally ho, that sort of thing.'

Larsen shook his head and laughed. 'I only rode when I lived in the States. Samantha's parents owned a stable in Los Altos, in the West Bay.'

'I rode when I was a teenager. I had my own horse, Rifleman, beautiful horse, 14.2 hands, all muscle, and fire. Won three firsts and many seconds in the junior cross-country events.'

'Any hobbies now?'

Bill shook his head. 'Tell me about Stephanie.'

'She's nineteen, studying at Stanford for a degree in law. She's going to apply to work for the FBI when she graduates.'

'Are you married?'

Larsen smiled. 'No.'

'Dating?'

'Not for several years.'

'Can I ask why not?'

Larsen sighed and took in a deep breath, 'This all happened a few years ago – when I was still drinking heavily. One night I staggered home drunk and found my girlfriend in bed with another man. I lost it, threatened to beat them both within an inch of their lives. He got out of bed, grabbed an empty beer bottle from the nightstand, and went to lunge at me. The bottle hit the metal headboard and broke as she stepped in between us.'

'Did she die?'

'No, thank God. The broken edges of the bottle just slashed her arm. She needed hospital treatment but made a full recovery.'

'What did the police say?'

'Nothing,' he said, shaking his head, 'it was all put down as domestic argument; they didn't give a damn.'

Bill picked up his glass, paused; then put it back down.

'I've not been able to trust myself with a relationship since,' Larsen said. 'I can't see anyone putting up with me and my lifestyle.'

'More juice?'

'No thanks, I'm fine, but you go ahead if you want some.'

Bill shook his head and said, 'None for me either. I'm ready for some coffee. Need a clear head tomorrow, how about you?'

'Clear head or coffee?' Larsen said laughing and then adding, 'Black coffee for me, please.'

Looking at the provisioning list as they sipped their coffees, Larsen said, 'How did you arrive at these figures? I'm impressed.'

'I used the book I found in my – your cabin and went by the number on board and the government requirements of five a day for fruit and vegetables.'

'Looks really thorough, have you worked out any menus yet?'

'Yes. I have about two weeks' worth here,' he said, passing them over. 'I'm assuming from the reading I've been doing that the run south across the Bay of Biscay can be really rough. I will be making two stews to cover the first couple of days, one a beef and the other chicken. I'll keep them in large Thermos flasks; after that, depending on the weather, I will cook as we go.'

'Have you thought about the trip to Falmouth? The south coast between here and Falmouth can get quite rough.'

'What about a hearty vegetable soup for the first night at sea? I can bake a couple of large loaves of bread to go with it. Then, depending on the sea and weather, I will cook something appropriate.'

'That sounds eminently suitable.'

'I need to find somewhere to get the freshest fruit, vegetables, eggs, and meat. I thought I would ask Mrs Phillip tomorrow.'

'I know a place, at least somewhere you can find a supplier. It's a country hotel called *The Fallen Angel*; Mr Smith took me there for a meal. The waitress said they only serve fresh produce from a nearby organic farm. You could call them and get the phone number of the farm that supplies them.'

'Thanks; that should save me some time.'

'Tomorrow I will issue you with your cash float so you can start buying in what you need. You'll need to get an accounts book when in town so you can keep a record of your expenditures.'

Bill nodded and wondered what other surprises the captain had in store for him.

'Will we be fishing as we go?' Bill asked. 'The book says fresh fish can be a good addition to the daily diet.'

'Fishing from a fast-moving yacht is a hit and miss affair. I normally encourage it, sometimes we get a surprise.'

The conversation was interrupted by the sound of a car horn.

'That will be Terry, I asked him to collect me at eleven,' said Larsen. 'I didn't realise it was that late.'

Larsen stood and said, 'Thanks for the lovely dinner; I look forward to many more.'

Bill stood, smiled, and thought; so do I.

After Larsen left Bill took the dishes down below, washed them, and then returned to the cockpit with a fresh cup of coffee and a thick woollen blanket. He stretched out on the cushions, covered himself, and stared up at the night sky looking for the Captain's Vega while sipping his coffee – complete with its Scottish ingredient.

20
Elijah

Bill woke, startled by the sound of footsteps on the side deck. He looked towards the sound and was confronted by the sight of total stranger looming over him, his hands in his jacket pockets.

'Morning sleepyhead, been out here all night?' he asked, in a deep American drawl.

'What time is it?' Bill said, sitting up and stretching. 'And who are you?'

'Seven-thirty, and the name is Elijah Gates. I'm the boson on the *Leviathan*. You must be Edward? Captain Larsen said you had moved on board.'

'Oh, I hadn't expected anyone for a few days yet.'

'Captain called, I had nothing on, work I mean, so I was glad to accept the offer of going back to sea.'

'You're an American?'

'Yeah, born in Greenwood in the state of Mississippi but raised by my uncle and aunt in Cambridge, England.'

'You've' still got an accent.'

'Although I grew up in England, I never lost my love for the States. When I reached eighteen, I volunteered for the military service, spent twelve years in the US Marines.'

'What happened to your parents?'

He looked down at his feet and said, 'They died when I was young.'

'How sad, it must have been awful for you.'

'I learned to live with it.'

'Have you sailed much with the captain?'

'About seven years full time, till five years ago. We sailed mostly in the Caribbean. I joined the *Leviathan* after my time in the US Marines.'

Before Bill could enquire further, Elijah said, 'How about you? How long have you been sailing?'

'I used to sail a bit with my father and I did a stint in the Royal Navy.'

'You'll do fine; the Captain's a very good judge of anyone's abilities and character. He's a fair man to sail under.'

'I am coming to that conclusion. What's brought you down here this early? Are you planning on moving on board?'

'No, I'm staying at the Admiral Aubrey till the end of the week; then we will all be moving on board.'

'All?'

'Stephen Foster, and John Grey.'

'Who are they?'

'Stephen is the ship's engineer; he looks after all things technical. John is a shipwright, part-time paramedic and, like all of us, does his stint as a deckhand.'

'It appears the captain has all eventualities covered.'

'That's why I like sailing with him, and since you asked I'm here to supervise the stepping of the masts. The main mast is being stepped in a few minutes, want to watch?'

Bill looked over at the boatyard. A tall, gangly crane was being driven slowly towards the yacht; the masts were already sitting on wheeled dollies at the edge of the dock beside the recently serviced life raft.

'I'll be right back, I need to change,' Bill said, as Larsen walked out of the chandlery. He was back on deck fifteen minutes later with a re-heated cup of coffee in time to watch the main mast lifted up in the air and lowered down into the *Leviathan* with the mizzen following shortly after.

The stepping of the masts didn't take long and by the time Bill had made them all lunch, both masts were secured and the life raft lashed down and secured in its cradle.

'Edward,' said Larsen, 'Elijah and I are going to call the loft to see if the sails are ready for collecting, should be back in fifteen minutes.'

'OK.'

Bill watched them leave, then look at the riggers, noticing they seemed to be concerned about something. They kept gesturing to the top of the mast. Bill's curiosity got the better of him and he walked up the deck to see what the fuss was about.

'Anything wrong?' he asked.

The taller of the two riggers, holding a hank of rope replied, 'we have a bit of a difficulty. This halyard is supposed to be hanging from the mast instead of in my hand.'

'Does that mean one of you needs to go up the mast?'

'That's the problem – neither of us is quite suited to going up the mast,' he said, patting his waist. 'Young Trevor would go up, but since we were supposed to be stepping the masts tomorrow he has gone off diving today.'

'Where are you going to find someone at this time of day?'

The two riggers looked at each other, then at Bill, and smiled.

'Oh, no you don't! I am not going up there. I'm a cook, not a monkey.'

'Oh, come on, Edward,' said the large rigger, ripples of laughter shaking his ample body, 'you'll be up and down again in no time.'

Bill didn't know why he said yes, but after he was glad he did. Once they had strapped him into the climbing harness and sat him in the bosun's chair they hauled him up on the main halyard. It was then a simple job to thread the errant halyard through the block and drop the end down to the deck.

'Ready to come down?' they shouted up at him.

'Not quite, give me a couple of minutes,' he shouted back.

Secured in his climbing harness and seated in the bosun's chair, he turned his head to admire the view. From his vantage point, looking to the left of the mast he could see all the way to the chain ferry and Brownsea Island. To the right of the mast he could just make out the Admiral Aubrey and Poole quay, their intended berth till they were ready to go to sea.

'I'm ready to come down now,' he shouted.

'Too late, we're off home, see you later.' They laughed loudly, ignoring his pleas.

Bill watched as Larsen and Elijah exited the chandlery and walked across the yard to the *Leviathan*.

'Captain Larsen,' he shouted, 'they won't let me down! I need to pee.'

'Do you hear something?' said Larsen, pretending to survey the horizon.

Bill watched them shrug their shoulders and pretend to look over the side. Finally, Larsen looked up and said, 'I think you can let him down now.'

'Thanks a lot,' Bill said, as he stepped out of the safety harness. 'I enjoyed that, *thanks* – did you know you can see Poole Bay from up there?'

♦

Two hours later Larsen thanked the riggers and waved them goodbye, *Leviathan* was finally ready.

'Edward, could you join me below for a minute, please?'

'Sure, be right there.'

When he got below, Larsen was seated at the saloon table with the same briefcase Bill had seen Smith give Larsen.

'I have your cash float for the provisions. I suggest you keep it locked in the safe in your cabin and take out what you need as it is required.'

Larsen opened the briefcase and took out a large bundle of Euros, GB pounds and US dollars.

Bill had never seen such a large bundle of cash at one time before and it showed on his face.

'Impressive, isn't it? You'll need a cash book to keep track of it and I want an accounting of your expenditures before we leave each port.'

'I'll lock it away immediately. Oh, I don't know the combination,' he said, still awestruck by the amount of cash.

'It's up there,' Larsen said, pointing to the ship's registration number carved in the main cabin beam. 'It's the middle six digits.'

Bill smiled and picked up the folder with the cash and went into his cabin to lock it away in the safe.

'We should all be seeing Poole Bay next week, the sails will be ready for Elijah and I to collect on Friday morning,' said Larsen as Bill exited his cabin.

'When are the other two crew members arriving? Are they staying at the Admiral Aubrey as well?'

'Stephen should be here tomorrow to oversee the engine servicing and John will join us later this week. We'll all probably stay in the hotel till Sunday, said Larsen, looking at his watch. 'We're done for the day so I think it's time to head for the hotel. Care to join us for dinner, Edward? You have your gate key and you can get a taxi back to *Leviathan* after.'

'Thanks, yes, sounds great.'

Being Monday night, it was open mic in the bar and after dinner they all went through and found a table close to the lone microphone. The same bearded performer did the announcing, played a couple of songs and just before the break said, 'Ladies and gentlemen this evening is very special, directly after the break we will be opening with some blues music.'

After the scramble for beer and glasses of wine at the break, the announcer called for silence. 'Ladies and gentlemen, please give a warm welcome to our special guest—all the way from Cambridge – Mister Elijah Gates!'

Bill turned to Elijah, astonished. Elijah grinned at Bill, ambled over to the microphone, and lifted one of the guitars from its stand. He perched on the stool in front of the microphone, smiled at the audience and said, 'I'd like to start with a song called *'I believe I'll lose my mind'*. Then we'll just see where we go from there.'

Thirty-five minutes of finger-picking blues later, with sweat dripping off his brow, Elijah said, 'Ladies and gentlemen, you've been a wonderful audience and I'd like to finish with a very special song written by the great Rev Garry Davis, *'Sometime I Wish'*

As Bill watched Elijah, their eyes met. Bill got a lump in his throat and realised Elijah was singing especially for him. Bill involuntarily wiped a tear from his cheek as he listened to the lyrics.

Elijah stood to the audiences' rapturous applause, thanked them, and after playing two encores returned to the table.

'Elijah, that was incredible,' said Bill. 'I have never been so moved in all my life.'

'Thanks, Edward, the atmosphere's perfect, not like some I have played in,' he smirked. 'I could do with a drink.'

'My round,' said Larsen, 'Beer all round?'

'Could I have a large red wine?' asked Bill.

Larsen bought him a small red wine.

'Elijah, would you see Edward back to the boat? He doesn't look too steady on his feet,' Larsen said. 'Terry will bring you back.'

'Sure thing Captain, see you in the morning.'

Elijah intercepted Bill as he returned to the table, 'Captain said for me to see you home, Edward. Terry is waiting outside.'

'My wine, I didn't finish it – just a minute.' Bill tottered over to the table and swigged down the remaining wine, put his arm over Elijah's shoulder and said, 'Ready, take me home sailor.'

21

Launch day

Bill woke at six-thirty, his head throbbing in time to the sound of someone snoring in the stateroom.

He dressed and quietly opened his cabin door. Elijah, covered by a blanket, was sleeping soundly on the starboard settee; the snoring was coming from the port settee. *Who's that*, he wondered, must be a friend of Elijah's. Bill walked quietly into the galley and put the kettle on. Elijah woke as Bill poured the boiling water into the cafetiér.

'Ah, that smells great.'

'Good morning, sailor. Want some breakfast?'

'Yes please,' he said, sitting up and yawning. 'What's there to eat?'

'How does eggy bread and bacon, with fresh ground coffee sound?'

'What's eggy bread?'

'Bread dipped in beaten egg then fried,'

'Ah, you mean French toast,' he laughed.

'Yes, of course that's what I meant.'

'Lovely,' he said, 'I'll just put my bedding away.'

'Who's that?' Bill said, pointing to the snoring form on the port settee.

Elijah grinned and answered, 'That's Stephen; he showed up at the hotel just as we were leaving last night, don't you remember?'

'All I remember is your guitar playing and a glass or two of wine.'

'Stephen, wake up, it's morning! Want some breakfast?' boomed Elijah, throwing a cushion at the prostrate form.

Stephen snorted loudly, opened his eyes, sat up and briefly looked around the cabin. Then, as the question of food penetrated his consciousness, he said, 'whatever's cooking I'll eat; I'm famished.'

'I'm cooking eggy bread and bacon.' said Bill.

'That'll do nicely; any chance of a cup of tea?'

'Yep, do you want milk?'

'Please, and two sugars.'

After breakfast Bill left Stephen and Elijah to their business and went into his cabin to collect the provisioning list.

◆

'Good morning Bill,' said Mrs Phillip as Bill put his shopping bag on the counter. 'This is Mr Patel, the gentleman I told you about.'

'Good morning,' he said shaking, Bill's hand. 'I understand from talking to Mrs Phillip that you would like to purchase some provisions for an upcoming voyage?'

'Yes, I have a list already made out,' he said handing it to him.

'Oh my goodness, this is quite a list! I'll need some time to go through it. I notice that it's mainly dried and canned goods, will you need any fresh fruit, vegetables or meat? We can also supply frozen food.'

'I was going to call a local restaurant to find out where they buy their produce from,' said Bill.

'Which one is that?'

'The Fallen Angel, do you know it?'

'Do I know it? They are one of my best customers. I tell you what, give me a couple of minutes to get my other catalogues and I'll meet you in the café.'

'Instead of the café, how about we meet on board the *Leviathan*? I have all my notes there. Also, can you supply alcohol?'

'Oh most certainly, everything you require. See you in a few minutes then, er, where is the *Leviathan*?'

'Go through the chandlery and you'll find her tied up at the holding dock. You can't miss her; she takes up the whole dock.'

As he approached the *Leviathan*, Bill could hear the engine running. Climbing on board he saw the dock lines were taut and a brace of mallards were nibbling at the mud and weeds stirred up from the propeller wash. Going below he found Elijah and Stephen seated at the saloon table having coffee with the engineer.

'I'll need the table in a few minute, will it be clear for me to use?' he asked.

'Yes, I'm done for now,' said the engineer, 'the engine needs to run for another hour and that will be its service complete. In the meantime, I'm off to look at another yacht, be back in about an hour.'

Bill heard the engineer's footsteps depart to be replaced by a different set. 'Come aboard, Mr Patel,' he said, through the open port.

As he opened his catalogues, Bill said, 'The kettles' just boiled, I'm having coffee, would you like a cup?'

'Could I have a tea please, no milk or sugar.'

Bill poured himself another coffee and two and a half hours later with a full shopping list established, delivery day set for Thursday at Poole Quay and a cash deposit paid, Bill said goodbye to Mr Patel.

Next, he made for the car park, and Terry's taxi. He needed some personal items and the stationery that he would require as the ship's purser.

'Thanks, Terry. Can you pick me up in forty minutes?' he said as he got out.

'Sure, thing Edward, I have two other trips to make, I'll see you back here at quarter to five.'

Running late as usual, Bill was about to step out of the stationer's when he saw two uniformed police officers walking towards the front door. He was trapped; they had found him.

Turning and pretending to look at a rack of pens and pencils he tried to work out what to do. Out of the corner of his eye he could see the police standing patiently outside the shop, inside, the staff were preparing to lock up for the day. In desperation Bill mingled with a group of schoolchildren making their way to the front and the door. Bill walked out of the shop trying to look like part of the group.

The ruse didn't work. The younger of the policemen walked right up to him and said, 'Excuse me sir; I wonder if you could help us? We're looking for this man – have you by any chance seen anyone fitting his description?' He handed Bill a photo.

Bill was stunned; it was a photo of himself. It had been taken last year at the club when Ruth had hosted the twins' birthday party. Bill recovered his composure and said, 'No, sorry, I haven't seen him. I'm new here.'

'Thanks, sir.'

His hands continued to tremble as he watched them walk over to another shopper.

On returning to the *Leviathan*, still shaken by the event, Bill was met by the sound of voices emanating from the crew's quarters. Curious, he walked forward and looked down the hatch to see two pairs of legs hanging off the bunks, one each side of the cabin, and one mop of dark hair standing in between.

'I recognise the legs but who is the hair?' he said.

The hair turned to look at him, 'John Grey at your service, you must be Edward.'

'Nice to meet you, John, are you moving on board?'

'Yes, the captain said we may as well move on board since we are all here, he'll join us tomorrow. Apparently, the hotel needs the rooms for guests.'

'In that case I'd better get started with dinner, any requests?'

'How about southern fried chicken and grits?' said Elijah.

'That's a trip into town. I think I have most of the makings for sweet and sour chicken with rice; that do?' He hadn't a clue what grits were and a trip to town was the last thing he wanted right now.

Three smiling faces told him yes.

'I'll call you when it's ready.'

A quick trip to Mrs Phillip produced the remaining items for the dinner plus extra bacon, eggs and bread for breakfast.

Bill was pleased with his first attempt at feeding the crew; even if the sweet and sour sauce came from a jar and the rice was boil-in-the-bag. Plenty of time to learn as he went along, he thought to himself.

'Stephen, John, I know of some of Elijah's past – how about you two?' he said, pouring coffees.

Stephen and John looked at each other and shrugged their shoulders, John spoke first.

'I left school and home at eighteen and joined the Royal Navy. I spent twelve years in various places around the world. I trained initially in weapons engineering. When the last ship I was on went in for a complete refit, I volunteered for duty as a medical orderly at Hasler during its final years as a military hospital. Not many jobs require training in heavy weapons in Civy Street. When I was discharged from the Navy I applied for a job as a paramedic with a local ambulance service. Then while on holiday in the Caribbean I met up with Captain Larsen and rest they say is history.'

'Married?' Bill asked.

'Divorced, one daughter, I never could settle down. My ex's now happily remarried to a solicitor.'

'What about your daughter, do you get to see her very often?'

'Not very often, they live in France near Nice.'

'Oh, that's sad, Stephen, what about you?'

'My family are quite wealthy, and I grew up needing nothing, sort of spoilt you might say. I went to university to study civil engineering. The family expected me to join the family firm. During my gap year I went out to Mozambique as a volunteer. While there I helped build a school for some orphaned children. It was quite an eye-opener for me, having never seen such poverty before. When I returned, I had lost all my ambition to complete university. After much wrangling with the family I gave up my studies and as a compromise to my father I applied for a commission in the Royal Marines where I trained as an engineer. Like John I served twelve years before leaving the service. I never could settle down either. I met the Captain while I was on holiday in the Caribbean.'

'The three musketeers,' said Bill, laughing.

'I suppose that makes you D'Artagnon,' said Stephen, laughing.

Bill shook his head, 'Can't be, I don't know how to use a sword.'

'What about you then, Edward?' asked John. 'What brought you here?'

'I would rather not talk about my past if you don't mind. Now, are you guys going ashore this evening?'

'Not tonight, it's an early night for us,' said Elijah. 'We're moving the *Leviathan* over to Poole Quay tomorrow and there is a lot to do before we can untie.'

'Ok, as soon as I have tidied up from dinner, I am going to turn in early as well; I've got work to do to get ready for the delivery of the provisions on Thursday. Stephen, will you turn the freezer on for me, I need to get it chilled down for the frozen food delivery.'

'Sure thing.'

Bill set his alarm clock for six am then climbed into his bunk, with a glass of his Scottish nightcap. He wasn't sure what time the crew would be awake but thought that six should be early enough.

The engine burst into life at five am, waking Bill from a deep sleep. Dressing in a hurry he went on deck.

The *Leviathan's* decks were awash with light from the spreader lights. 'What's happening, why are we up so early?' he asked Stephen who was busy coiling down one of the dock lines.

'If we're not in mid-channel by low water we'll miss the advantage of a rising tide.'

Bill looked at Larsen at the wheel; he was engrossed in rotating the *Leviathan* slowly about a spring line. Great sulphurous-smelling watery clouds of grey silt emanated from the stern of the yacht as Larsen alternated between forward and reverse while the engine idled. Bill watched, fascinated, no one said a word. Imperceptibly the bow of the *Leviathan* swung round till it was facing out to Poole Bay.

When Larsen was satisfied with the yacht's position he nodded to Stephen, who undid the fixed end of the spring line and pulled it in, then went below to turn off the spreader lights. They were now in total darkness except for the channel markers and the distant lights from Poole Quay and the town behind.

Larsen pushed the throttle lever gently forward and slowly the *Leviathan* moved under its own power for the first time in several years. Bill saw a smile grow on Larsen's face.

Larsen kept the speed down to three knots while they navigated within the outline of the narrow channel and the moored yachts. At the main shipping channel, he turned the *Leviathan* to starboard and headed up the channel to the port of Poole. Just before they reached the bascule bridge Larsen turned the *Leviathan* about and motored down, against the incoming tide to their berth alongside the quay. The previous week he had negotiated a temporary berth alongside the main quay, directly in front of the Admiral Aubrey.

Bill was pleased to see Dot and Beryl standing on the quayside waving as though he had just returned from an around the world voyage.

'Edward, welcome back,' said Beryl as Bill stepped off the gangway and on to the quayside. 'How are you, have you settled in all right, would you like breakfast?'

'Yes, and if it's ready, I have to dash into town when the shops open, but I'll have more time this afternoon for coffee if you are free.'

'Look forward to that; see you later then.'

♦

'What's for dinner tonight, Edward?' said John, as they sat down at the saloon table.

'Lasagne, garlic bread and salad,' Bill replied.

'Smells great,' said Larsen. Then addressing the assembled group, he continued, 'Friday evening I will be meeting the guests. All being well they should be moving on board next Wednesday. As you know we are one crew member short and I am hoping that one of them would be suitable to work as a deckhand during the voyage.'

'What about me?' asked Bill.

'Thanks Edward, but you will have your hands full with cooking. I'll see who's fit from the team when I meet them Friday evening. Now, who's doing what tomorrow? Stephen, you first.'

'I've arranged for a fuel delivery tomorrow morning at five am. I managed to get it delivered for less than the local price and it will be fresh fuel. Should be fuelled before traffic gets busy on the quay, or the harbour master kicks up a fuss.'

'Good, any time we save money is fine by me. See Edward for the cash and make sure you get a receipt. John, what you up to?'

'I contacted a local doctors' clinic this morning and one of the doctors is going to write a prescription for the drugs we will require for the medical kit. While I'm at the clinic I will also set up appointments with the practice nurse for our inoculation jabs.'

'Sounds like you have both got your hands on the tiller. You can get what cash you need from Edward; just make sure you get receipts. Elijah?'

'As I know where all the storage space is, I'm going to help Edward with storing the provisions when they arrive.'

'That's good, it looks like we will be ready to depart next week then, two weeks early; Mr Smith will be pleased.

'Know anything about our guests?' queried John.

'All I know at present is there are six of them.'

22

Dr Kaufmann

Friday morning Larsen and Elijah collected the sails from the loft in Wareham and set to re-hanging and covering them. It was just as well the day was wind free as Larsen wanted all the sails run up the masts to inspect them.

As a thank-you for the very large order, Mr Patel gave Bill a case of his favourite Scottish ingredient, which was now secreted under Bill's bunk.

Bill had their dinner ready for seven-thirty and at nine, while he cleaned up, Larsen and the crew headed for the Admiral Aubrey.

'Let me go in first,' said Larsen. 'You wait a few minutes then come in and sit at separate tables, away from me. I won't introduce you to our guests this evening as I would like to know how they act when I am not around, and if they are really who they say they are.'

Larsen entered by the side door and saw Smith sitting at a side table talking to a lanky, grey-haired man in his late forties.

'Captain Larsen, let me introduce you to Doctor Kaufmann; he's the leader of the team you are taking to the Amazon.'

Kaufmann stood and extended his hand to Larsen.

Larsen reached out and clasped Kaufmann's limp and sweaty palm.

'Captain Larsen, Mr Smith has been singing your praises. Glad we could finally meet. Sit with us for a minute before we go through.'

'Thank you,' said Larsen, sitting down facing Kaufmann.

'Can I get you a drink, Captain?' asked Smith.

'I'll just have a coffee.'

'Doctor Kaufmann, can I refresh your drink?'

'Ja, same again, double whiskey,' Kaufmann said, downing the dregs in his glass and passing it to Smith.

'Captain Larsen,' said Kaufmann, 'where's your crew?'

'They're busy this evening, there's lots to do before we go to sea.'

Larsen's musing was interrupted by Smith returning with the drinks.

Larsen sipped his coffee and watched as Kaufmann took a deep gulp of his whiskey.

'Captain,' asked Kaufmann, 'how big is your boat? I don't want to share a cabin. My team is just working-class muscle, they can share, not me.'

'Not to worry Doctor, we've reserved the master stateroom for you, you won't have to share.'

'Quite right Captain, I'm the one in charge on this expedition, I shouldn't have to share with anyone.'

'Shall we go through to the restaurant?' said Smith 'I believe the team will have finished their dinner.'

There were five of them seated around a large table in the corner of the dining room. Larsen noticed the five empty and two half-empty wine bottles in the middle.

Three of the team had whiskey glasses in front of them and were busy arguing about football. The fourth was singing softly to himself and the fifth was drinking coffee.

They stopped talking and looked up as Kaufmann stopped at the table.

'Guys, this is Captain Larsen of the *Leviathan*; he and his crew will be taking us to the Amazon.'

'Good evening, gentlemen,' said Larsen.

The three whiskey glasses stared, the singer tried to focus and the coffee cup, Larsen noticed, was thoughtfully assessing him.

'Captain, let me introduce you to my team,' said Kaufmann.

He started with whiskey glass one and went clockwise around the table, 'This is Andrew Davis, Simon Jones, Hugo Martinez, Tony Edwards and Marcel Galan.'

'Good evening,' said Larsen, 'on behalf of the crew and myself I would have welcomed you aboard tomorrow, but as we have just come out of a refit we are not quite ready to have you board yet.

Some house rules while on board: smoking is only permitted on the lee deck, downwind if you don't understand the terminology. Alcohol will only be served at mealtimes or while at anchor, and no drugs, your bags will be searched when you come aboard.

'The weather for the trip should be tolerable – we are not expecting to encounter any hurricanes. Before we depart, I will need to collect all your passports and health certificates if you have them.'

Larsen shook his head and scratched his ear as he looked at four sets of bored faces staring back at him.

'I believe Mr Smith has arranged for you to stay here at the hotel till Wednesday. Providing there are no setbacks, we should be leaving for the Amazon early on Thursday morning.

'I do have one small request. We are one crew member short and I was wondering if any of you had any sailing experience and would like to volunteer as a deckhand? There isn't any pay involved, just the excitement of night watches, being called out of your bunk in the middle of the night and getting wet.'

Four pairs of alcohol-sodden eyes stared at the tablecloth while coffee cup thought for a minute then said, 'Captain, I have experience. I was in the Spanish Navy.'

'Thank you, Mr Galan. We are going out for a shakedown sail tomorrow morning at seven am; if you were on board by six for breakfast, it would give you time to meet the crew.'

'Thank you, Captain. I will see you on board at six.'

Larsen turned to Smith and Kaufmann. 'If you gentlemen will excuse me I have a yacht to get ready. Good evening.'

As he walked through the bar he nodded to Stephen to follow him outside.

Stephen joined him a few minutes later, 'all well with our guests?'

'I have invited one of them, a Spaniard, to work as an extra hand for the crossing; he'll join us in the morning. Keep a special eye on him for me this evening will you? You can't miss him, he's the sober one with the pony tail.'

Larsen and Bill sat at the table playing cards waiting for the crew to return. The clock struck eight bells as the sound of footsteps was heard on the deck.

'Would you all join me for a minute before you turn in?' requested Larsen, 'I'd like to hear your assessment of our guests.'

'If you gentlemen will excuse me,' said Bill turning off the galley lights, 'I'm off to bed, see you at breakfast.'

'Night Edward,' said Larsen as his door closed.

'We did as you said,' said Stephen, 'we kept our identities out of the conversations. Galan appears to be whom, and what he says he is. According to his story, he spent twelve years in the Spanish Navy. When he left he found he couldn't find a proper job. He tried several, even worked as a hairdresser, then, when the opportunity to work in the Amazon came up he jumped at it.'

'Did he say what his job was on the team?' asked Larsen.

'Not really. Apparently he speaks some Portuguese.'

'That could be very useful, and the rest?'

'Your Mr Smith left a few minutes after you and the rest kept to themselves all evening,' said John.'

'All except Martinez,' said Elijah, 'they call him Marty. Kaufmann calls him Hugo, not sure if there's more to their relationship. All I know is he's a real sleazeball, almost got glassed by a Scotsman wearing a kilt. When he wasn't on the prowl, he told racist jokes in front of Elijah, laughing as he did, saying it was all a bit of harmless fun. Kaufmann drank all evening with the rest and told bawdy stories, mostly about soiled underwear.'

'What a shower of shites,' said Larsen, shaking his head. 'Time to turn in, we have an early start in the morning, and we don't want to look bad in front of our new crew member by being late for breakfast, do we?'

23
Marcell

'There will be six for breakfast this morning, Edward,' said Larsen. 'One of the expedition team has agreed to join us for the crossing. I have invited him along for the weekend to find out if he is suitable as an additional crew member.'

'Not a problem, I've made plenty.'

'Good.'

Just then there was a knock on the deck.

'Hello, the *Leviathan*, permission to come aboard?'

'That, if I'm not mistaken, is the sixth member of our crew – he's early,' said Larsen looking at his watch, 'I like that.' He climbed partway up the companionway ladder and called, 'Come aboard, breakfast is about to be served.'

Bill picked up the kettle from the stove and poured boiling water into the cafetiér. Hearing new feet on the companionway ladder, he looked up and almost fainted.

'Edward, are you all right?' asked Larsen. 'You look like you've seen a ghost.'

'Yes – I'm fine, just stood up too fast, really – I'm fine.'

'Edward, this is Marcel Galan; he'll be joining us for the weekend. Marcel, this is Edward, our cook.'

'*Buenos Días Señor,*' he said, bowing his head slightly.

Bill nodded his head in reply, then abruptly turned and made himself busy in the galley wondering what Marcel was doing here. The last time Bill had seen him was with Marcie in his arms and them disappearing out the door of the club dining room.

Yesterday at the stationers, being confronted by the police had been shocking enough, but now, what was he to do? He couldn't hide from Marcel; they would be stuck together on board for the next year. At least Marcel hadn't said anything, maybe he had forgotten him? After all, he had had his hair shortened and restyled. He desperately needed time to think.

Bill was spared for the moment when the rest of the crew descended the companionway steps.

'Gentlemen, I'd like to introduce you to Marcel Galan,' said Larsen. 'He'll be joining us for the weekend. Is breakfast ready, Edward?'

'Coming right up,' he said, having recovered a certain modicum of composure.

After serving breakfast he retired to his cabin to think and consult with his Scottish friend. When he heard the crew climb the companionway he came out and busied himself clearing the table and galley in preparation for going to sea.

Once, when he had been sailing with his father, the whole contents of the galley lockers had relocated from the starboard side to port as a result of him not locking the doors properly; he was not about to let history repeat itself.

Ten minutes later the engine burst into life and the now familiar smell of diesel exhaust drifted into the galley displacing the lingering smell of breakfast. It took him a moment to regain his balance as the *Leviathan* eased forward under the surge of propeller.

Bill looked out of the port and watched as the scenery changed from luxury yachts tied up across the channel to the expanse of Poole Harbour.

Content that the galley and main saloon were secure and ready to go to sea, he poured himself another mug of coffee and added some of his Scottish ingredient. He went up on deck and walked back to the cockpit.

'That's a large ship ahead of us,' he said to Larsen.

'It's the *MV Barfleur*, a car ferry, twenty thousand tons and drawing about twenty feet loaded, headed for Cherbourg. They run a daily service for cars and foot passengers. They will have a crew of about ninety for a passenger list of twelve hundred, that's almost one crew for every twelve passengers, we'll have one for one.'

'Bit large to be operating in such a small harbour and the ferry crossing doesn't look wide enough for it.'

'Oh the channel's wide enough. The only issue they have is at low tide, the ship's deep draught can cause problems if it catches the chains from the ferry.'

'How do you know all that?'

'It's a captain's job to be aware of all that is going on around him – and I mean all,' he said, looking directly at Bill.

Bill turned and stepped out of the cockpit and made his way over to the stern rail. After Larsen's remonstration he found his coffee had lost its taste.

They followed the ferry down the channel, past the chain ferry and out into Poole Bay.

Bill reached into his jacket pocket for a hanky and found he still had his wallet there from his last trip into town. He took it out just as Larsen pushed the throttle full forward. He lost his balance and grabbed for the rail, dropping his wallet over the side.

The wallet didn't sink; instead, it swirled in the propeller wash for a moment disgorging all of its contents, including the only photos he had of the Ruth and the girls.

He stared at the three faces till they shot away, bobbing in the wake of the *Leviathan*. He almost called the captain but then thought it was better this way. They were the last tie to his past; it would be all new from here.

Dark clouds of exhaust came from the funnel of the ferry as it turned to starboard and headed out into the open channel. Larsen turned the *Leviathan* to port and into the open bay.

They motored for a further ten minutes before Larsen backed off the throttle to an idle and turned the *Leviathan* into the wind.

'Elijah,' said Larsen, 'I think we'll try the drifter, we'll set the main out on the port side and as long as it doesn't block the wind, set the mizzen on the starboard side.'

In what seemed seconds to Bill, the crew had all the sails up and tied off, and Larsen turned the *Leviathan* downwind. Bill watched Larsen's face relax as the yacht accelerated under the power of the wind in her sails. He reached down, turned off the engine, and set the shaft brake. The steady throb of the engine was replaced by the rhythmic thump of waves, as they were tossed aside by *Leviathan's* bow, and the gurgling of the sea, running along the hull.

With all the sails trimmed, Larsen set a course due east towards The Isle of Wight, while Bill went below to make sandwiches for lunch.

It took him longer than he expected as he had to frequently go up on top for fresh air. Lunch finally made, Bill returned to the cockpit and curled up, trying to get his stomach to settle. It didn't take long as the direction of travel towards The Isle of Wight, being downwind, allowed for a fairly stable passage.

'Tired?' asked Larsen, noticing the lack of colour in his face.

'Sorry, was I nodding off?' Bill replied yawning.

'I find lying on the bowsprit platform very relaxing when running downwind, just make sure you are wearing your lifeline harness, don't want you to fall overboard. There should be some cushions in one of the forward lockers, ask Elijah.'

Lying on the bowsprit platform was indeed serenely peaceful. With the huge drifter sail towering over him, it was like being at the foot of a multi-coloured cliff. The drifter, acting like a megaphone, caught the murmur of voices of those sitting in the cockpit and carried them downwind to him, lulling him to sleep.

He was awakened by a splash from a wave and headed below to the galley, wondering, how he would ever cope in rough seas. Making the sandwiches while sailing a few miles offshore had been bad enough; what would it be like in mid-Atlantic in rough weather?

Three hours later, a mile from the red and white tower of The Needles lighthouse, Larsen put the *Leviathan* about and headed back across Poole Bay.

'Edward,' said Larsen as the *Leviathan* settled on her new course, 'I plan to anchor for the night off Studland and, owing to the nice weather, I think a barbeque would be a fitting end to such a glorious day.'

'Oh, I thought we were going back to the quay tonight.'

'No, we'll anchor out tonight, then tomorrow we will sail a triangular course getting us back into Poole sometime early Monday morning.'

'I'll go dig out some steaks from the freezer. How long before we reach our anchorage?'

'With this wind, we should be at anchor just before sunset.'

'Good; the steaks should have defrosted by that time. If not, a few seconds in the microwave will bring them up to room temperature.'

They anchored west of the Old Harry rocks just below the Studland headland. He was still nervous of being around Marcel; several times during the day he saw Marcel staring at him with a puzzled look on his face.

That evening, as he cleaned up in the galley, Larsen called them all together.

'Right gentlemen, as of now we are on cruising routine. Marcel, sorry to do this to you, you have First Watch. Should be easy; just check our bearings regularly to make sure we don't drift off our anchorage during the night. Elijah, you will take Middle, John you have Morning and Stephen you'll be on the Forenoon Watch. As you'll all remember from when you sailed with me before I expect you to be on watch at least ten minutes before you are scheduled.

'Meal times are: eight for breakfast, twelve noon for lunch and eighteen hundred hours for dinner. If you are on watch during meal times, arrange with Edward to have something brought up to you if you don't want to wait till you are off watch.

'First thing in the morning we will do a practice launch of the dinghy and, since it is in the water, a couple of you may as well go ashore and see if you can find me a newspaper. Launching the dinghy will be good practice for later in the voyage. John, would you call the coastguard on sixteen after you come off watch in the morning and let them know not to get their knickers in a twist? Tell them we will be practising man overboard drills in the bay for an hour or so. After that we will head to the Isle of Wight again. Then out into the channel and through the night getting back into Poole Harbour, tying up at the quay early Monday morning, any questions?'

'Yes,' interrupted Bill from the galley, 'where do I fit in?'

'Sorry Edward, I assumed you already established your own routine. As I said earlier, you are excused from watches. If you have the meals ready for the times I just stated that should suffice. You will get requests for teas, coffees, and sandwiches from time to time from the crew and guests. You will need to have hot drink makings available for the night watches when you are not in the galley.'

'Thanks, I thought that would be the case, I just wanted to be sure.'

After breakfast Bill went up on deck and watched them launch the dinghy. Stephen and Marcel returned about an hour later with copies of the *Guardian, Telegraph,* and the *Daily Echo.*

'Right gentlemen, as they say in the movies, hands to your stations,' said Larsen, laughing.

Bill had slept well the previous night, the sound of waves rippling down the side of the hull and his exhaustion had soothed him into an untroubled sleep.

Today he was pleasantly surprised to find it easier to work in the galley.

'You're getting your sea legs,' remarked Stephen in passing. 'It's the main reason for having a shakedown sail, it gets most of the vomiting out of the way before the guests join us.'

Feeling excited, Bill went to his cabin with his morning coffee and this time, the Scottish ingredient stayed under his bunk. He glanced at the broadsheets and then picked up the *Daily Echo.*

On page two he read:

> *A wallet found floating in Poole Harbour is thought to be that of missing man, Bill Drysdale. Dorset police confirmed that a fisherman had picked up a wallet and that no further statements will be issued till its ownership has been established.*

Bill felt sad for a moment then put the paper down and got on with working out the menu for the next twenty-four hours. For lunch, he made sandwiches of sliced beef that he had barbequed the previous evening. Dinner would be Shepherd's Pie, providing he could learn to work the stove while it was swinging in the gimbles, from side to side.

♦

After dinner he poured a coffee and went and sat at the saloon table with John and Stephen.

'You look bushed, Edward,' said John.

'Is it that noticeable?'

'It's the fresh air and the constant motion of the boat. You'll get used to it, best way in the world to lose weight and get fit,' said Stephen.

He finished his coffee then, remembering about the hot drinks for the night watch, boiled the kettle, and filled a large thermos with hot water before turning in for the night.

He woke with a start when the *Leviathan* changed course at one-thirty am, then remembered Larsen said they would be sailing out to the main shipping channel before turning and heading back to Poole. He slept fitfully for the next two hours, finally falling back to sleep.

His alarm went off at six. He got dressed and went up on deck. Although Stephen had relieved John, they were both in the cockpit talking in hushed voices.

'Morning men, either of you hungry or want anything to drink? I won't be starting breakfast till about seven thirty.'

He made them bacon butties to go with their tea then returned to the galley to prepare breakfast.

'Good morning, Edward,' said Larsen as he came out of his cabin.

'Morning Captain, sleep well?'

'Yes, thank you. It's good to be back at sea again. Breakfast smells great.'

They ate in the cockpit as the *Leviathan* motored up the channel to the quayside.

As soon as they were tied up, John went off to see Terry about hiring a minibus for Tuesday's trip to the clinic. Larsen went off to the Customs and Excise Office to collect the clearance papers, while Elijah, Marcel, and Stephen went into town to do some shopping.

Larsen returned an hour later, fuming. 'Edward, do you have all those receipts for the stores?'

'Yes, they are in my cabin.'

'And guest passports? They should be on the bottom drawer of the chart table.'

'Yes.'

'I've just been to Customs and Excise. These,' he said, holding up a fistful of forms, 'will need to be filled in before we can leave. Some officious little bastard can't tell the difference between a charter yacht and the *Queen Mary*. He said if I don't fill them in, he'll not issue our clearance papers. I'd like to tie him to the bowsprit in a North Atlantic gale!'

Bill struggled to keep back a grin and hurried off to get the relevant receipts and passports. He returned to find Larsen, after his tirade, back to his normal polite self.

It was a struggle to work through the forms and, as his handwriting was neater, Larsen chose to let Bill fill in the paperwork.

'It's good that we haven't loaded any bonded stores, and don't carry any firearms' said Larsen, when they finished.

'Why is that?'

'It just keeps things simple, for instance firearms are not allowed into the UK without a special licence and like bonded stores, such as alcohol, they need to be stored and sealed in a secure locker by Customs and Excise till the vessel is out of UK territorial waters.'

'We don't carry any guns, do we?' he asked.

'No, of course not, that's against the law,' Larsen said, smiling smugly.

'Captain, I was wondering if we could have a bon voyage party? We could invite all the people who have helped get the *Leviathan* ready.'

'Sounds interesting, I'll think about it and let you know when I return.'

Forms completed; Larsen stepped onto the quayside just as John stepped out of Terry's taxi.

'Need to go somewhere, Captain?' asked Terry.

'Yes, can you take me to Customs House, please?'

◆

That afternoon Bill invited Beryl and Dot to afternoon tea on the *Leviathan*.

'How are you settling in, dear?' asked Beryl, as they got to the bottom of the companionway ladder.

'Fine. Would you like to see my cabin? It's just there on the left.'

Dot and Beryl entered through the open door.

'This is all yours?' said Beryl from inside. 'It's certainly cosy.'

'The shower and toilet are included; it's normally the captain's cabin,' Bill answered from the galley while putting the kettle on.

'Where does he sleep?' asked Dot.

'In the chart room, it's behind the galley on the right at the foot of the ladder. It's not very large, mostly the chart table and a bunk that runs behind and under the cockpit. Bit too cosy for me, but he doesn't seem to mind. Says he is close to what is going on, like a pilot on a plane. Kettle's boiled, or would you like to see around the yacht first?'

'It can wait,' said Beryl,' let's see the cabins first.'

Bill led them forward past the saloon table and showed them the guest cabins.

'What luxury,' said Dot, 'you're a very lucky man.'

'And all cabins have hot and cold running water,' added Bill.

'Where do the crew sleep?' asked Beryl as they returned to the main saloon.

'They have their own quarters beyond the main cabins. You go up on deck and climb down some steep steps to get there.'

As Bill made the tea, Dot said, 'How do the crew treat you, the only non-sailor on board?'

'Absolutely fine, it's like having a bunch of big brothers. They tease a bit, but that's all.'

'You'll need to watch the guests; they could be trouble if you're not careful.' advised Beryl.

'Why, what's wrong with them?'

Beryl looked around and, in a conspiratorial tone, said, 'One word – alcohol. They drink like fish and the foreign one, the one they call Marty, never let yourself be alone with him. I've seen his sort before, all joking and smiles on the surface, but inside a boiling cauldron of deceit and viciousness.'

'Thanks for the warning, Beryl. I'm sure I can take care of myself but, just in case, I'll keep out of his way. Thankfully the captain has the liquor locker key and only permits alcohol at mealtimes.'

'None the less, be careful,' said Beryl.

'I made a Victoria sponge cake this morning,' said Bill, 'would you care for a slice with your tea?'

'Yes please,' said Dot, 'just a thin slice.'

'Beryl?'

'Yes, please Edward, but I'll have a slightly larger slice than Dot, Victoria sponge cake is one of my weaknesses. No guessing on the others.'

Bill cut three slices and put them onto plates he had on a tray. As he lifted the tray it hit one of the brass poles on the end of the galley counter and deposited the tray, plates and cake all over the floor.

'Damn, damn, damn!' he shouted, stamping his feet on the cabin sole.

'Edward, come and sit down for a moment,' said Beryl, 'Dot can take care of the mess. You look all in.'

'I am – there's been so much to prepare for the voyage. I've been working every day from breakfast till late into the night.'

'You must sleep like a log, being that tired,' said Beryl.

'I probably would if it weren't for the nightmares. I thought I was done with them, but they're back.'

'Right, that settles the matter; you're taking the evening off and spending it with us.'

Bill started to protest but Beryl wasn't having any of it.

'When the captain returns, I will simply tell him you need time off like anyone else. In the meantime, let's have that cup of tea. Dot, pass the teapot, and will you cut some more of that lovely cake?'

They'd had two cups of tea before Larsen returned. When he saw the determination in Beryl's face; and the exhaustion in Bill's, he thought better of arguing and acquiesced to Beryl's request.

'We'll take good care of him, Captain, don't you worry,' said Dot as they stepped down onto the quay.

They entered the Admiral Aubrey by the private entrance and went through the kitchen to Dot and Beryl's apartment.

'Dot,' said Beryl,' will you go and see if Michelle is in? If she is, ask her if she would like to go out to dinner with us this evening. I'll call Terry and see if he is free to drive us. In the meantime, Bill, you can have your old room for the night – you know where the key is. Why don't you go freshen up and we'll see you in a few minutes?'

Bill looked at Beryl, cocked his head, shrugged his shoulders, and smiled.

'Ah, what to wear,' said Beryl, 'I don't suppose you go out to dinner very often?'

Bill shook his head.

'Don't worry,' said Beryl, 'Cinderella will go to the ball. Right, let's see what we have in Aladdin's cave.'

Bill looked at her, 'Aladdin's cave?'

'As I said to you a couple of days ago, it's amazing what some of our guests leave behind. I'm sure there will be something suitable that you could wear for the evening.

♦

It was one-thirty when they returned, Michelle said goodnight and went straight to bed as she had to get up early.

'Fancy a nightcap before you turn in, Edward?' said Beryl.

'Aren't you two tired?'

'We're used to these hours. Just because the bar closes for the evening, doesn't mean the work stops. Dot and I are quite often up till gone midnight.'

'Oh, I never thought of that. In that case, what's on offer?'

'How about an Irish coffee?'

'Sounds fine to me.'

'Just go through to the bar with Dot, I think the fire should still be burning.'

Dot pulled the curtains shut and placed a couple of logs on the still smouldering fire.

'Your coffee, Edward,' said Beryl, putting the tray with three steaming cups on the small table by the fire. Dot handed Bill his cup of milky coffee. Bill sniffed the steam rising from the froth and detected the heady smell of his Scottish ingredient.'

Taking a sip he said, 'Thanks Beryl, this is just what I needed.'

'Enjoy yourself this evening, Edward?' asked Dot.

'Yes thanks. It's been ages since I enjoyed myself so much. Dinner was great and the dancing afterwards was just what I needed. Bit noisy though, my ears are still ringing. I feel like I have been taken apart and put back together.'

'That's what I like to hear,' laughed Beryl.

Just then the fire burst into life with large orange flames curling round the dry oak logs and wisps of smoke drifting up the chimney.

'You can't beat a real fire,' said Beryl.

'We have one on the *Leviathan*,' said Bill.

'You won't need one on the Amazon,' said Dot.

'If I go,' said Bill.

'Having second thoughts?' said Beryl.

'No, I don't think so. I'm just confused.'

'What's really on your mind?' said Beryl.

'I thought I knew – now the dreams have come back.'

'They're just dreams, dear,' said Beryl.

'But they're so real, Beryl – I'm scared – I feel something terrible is going to happen to me – it's like a premonition. I need to go away before the police catch up with me. There was an article in the weekend *Echo* about me. The police were asking the public to watch out for me.'

'I'm sure they are just worried about you,' said Dot.

'No – you don't understand – they want to lock me up.'

'Why would they do that? It was just an accident,' said Beryl.

'I've killed before.'

The room went silent; even the fire stopped crackling.

'Edward, I think you should take a deep breath and explain what you mean,' said Beryl.

♦

'My name is really Edward William Drysdale; most of my friends call me Bill, including my wife's children. But you'd already know that from the newspapers, I've seen you hide them when I came into the room.'

'Is it something to do with the recent accident?' asked Beryl.

'Yes, but not directly, it's more to do with something that happened when I was young.'

'You poor dear,' said Dot.

Bill shook his head and said, 'It's not what you are thinking.' He paused for a moment then went on, 'I am also responsible for the death of my little brother.'

Dot looked at Beryl.

'I think you need to explain that,' said Beryl.

'It was an accident.'

'And now, the recent car accidents?'

'Yes.'

'And you blame yourself for all of these accidents.'

'Yes. What am I to do? I feel so guilty.'

'Well, I need more coffee,' said Beryl 'Would you like one?'

'Please.'

Beryl got up and went over to the bar and poured another coffee for Bill.

'Your coffee, now, take your time, we're listening.'

'This happened many years ago when the family was on holiday in Scotland. It was early September and we were in the middle of an Indian summer. I was seven and my brother George was five. One evening, it was too hot to sleep and no one wanted to go to bed, I decided to go for a walk with George. It was still light and very warm, mother said not to go near the river – but I thought it wouldn't matter if we just paddled at the edge and got our feet wet – we splashed about in the shallows and then crossed to the other side on some large stones. I crossed back first and as I reached the far edge, I turned to watch George. Halfway across – he – he slipped on one of the wet stones and fell into the water – hitting his head on a rock. The water just – just carried him off down the stream. His body was never found.'

'What about your parents?'

'Mother cried herself to sleep for years and my father was heartbroken.'

'So, you're an only child? No brothers or sisters?'

Bill nodded.

'After the memorial service they never spoke about it again. They just locked the door in their minds to the room with all the memories and threw away the key, shutting me out.'

'Did you ever try to talk to them about your feelings?' asked Beryl.

'Once, but mother burst into tears and took to her bed for a week. Dad just clammed up; he couldn't discuss it, and spent the week fussing over mother.'

'How sad for you,' said Dot. 'Must have been difficult growing up in such a house.'

'It wasn't always bad. I learned not to bring up the subject and as soon as I was able, I left home and joined the Navy.'

'What about your wife? And you must have friends who'd listen,' said Beryl.

'She'd just tell me to buck up and get on with things, and my friends – as you call them – well, it would just cause embarrassment if I talked to them.'

'What happened to your parents?' asked Beryl.

'Nothing. They grew old with their ghosts, and I got busy with life, the Navy, university, and marriage. My parents still live quite close and I see them almost every week. My father runs a very successful electronics' firm.'

'Have you ever talked to the girls about this?'

'No, never. How could I? They're my wife's children, I only adopted them.'

'So, you have been keeping this secret all these years?'

'Yes.'

'Like Joseph Marley, you carry too many chains; it is not good for you,' said Beryl

'Joseph Marley? I don't understand.'

Beryl shook her head and said, 'He is a character in a book by Dickens.'

'Oh, of course, *A Christmas Carol*.'

'Right Edward, you said, *if you go*. Are you having doubts about the voyage?' said Beryl.

'A couple of days ago, when we were passing the ferry, I put my hand into my pocket to get my wallet and it fell over the side. The only photos I had of the girls floated there staring at me. I felt terrible, yet at the same time I knew it was too late to change my mind and this was fate's way of making me say goodbye.'

'It's never too late to change your mind, dear,' said Dot.

'I suppose, but I can't face going home. They will never forgive me, they will hate me, and the police will arrest me.'

'Edward, I'm sure they will forgive you. And your accident, surely that's all it was – an accident?' asked Beryl.

'Why would they forgive me? I'm a terrible person. I killed my brother and the image of that motorist who died on the M3 as he was hit by the truck, haunts me day and night. I'm running away. I'm not worthy of being forgiven, I may as well keep on running. I can't go back. It's not like I broke a chair that a lick of glue will fix, or a lost credit card that a call to the bank will sort out. How do I bring my dead brother back to life, bring that motorist back to life or go home and live as though nothing has changed? No, it's hopeless. I have made a real mess of things. I may as well continue as I started and go sailing. Maybe I'll find a new life at sea, or if I am lucky just drown, that would sort all the problems.'

'Edward, you can't spend your life running away from yourself. One day, sooner than later, you will have to decide whether to keep on running or stop and face the music.' said Beryl.

'Well as far as I am concerned, they can wait. Beryl, I've made up my mind. I'm not going back. This evening, talking with you and Dot has shown me my whole life has been about pleasing everyone else and not having any time for myself. It's time I had my own life.'

24
No going back

Bill stared out the window through the driving rain at the *Leviathan* tied up at the quayside. The decision had been made; there was no going back.

Mid-morning, he was included when Larsen's crew and Kaufmann's team piled into the minibus to head for the clinic. Martinez squeezed in beside him, rubbing Bill's thigh, pretending to feel for his seat belt. But before he could say anything, Elijah turned and said, 'Edward, there's a spare seat up front with the Captain.'

Grateful to have escaped his encounter with Martinez, Bill excused himself and stood up.

Martinez stood to let Bill out and, grinning at him with tobacco-stained teeth, his breath smelling of vomit, said. 'Nice meeting you, Eddy boy, Hugo will brush your hair for you, any time. Then he turned to Elijah, 'That's one I owe you – boy.'

Bill saw the muscles on Elijah's neck tighten then relax as he answered, 'OK, I'll put it on the slate. You can pay me any time you like – janky.'

Bill looked in the driver's mirror as Kaufmann shouted, 'Sit down, Hugo. The driver won't go till we are all seated.'

Bill saw Martinez make a two-fingered gesture to Elijah's back before sitting down.

♦

Bill rose early next morning to make sure all the cabins were ready and now, as he sat at his desk listening to the rain drum on the coach roof he wondered if it would be this wet on the Amazon.

'Good morning, Doctor,' said Larsen to Kaufmann as he and his team came aboard.

'Good morning, Captain. I have made everyone wear proper footwear, just as you requested.'

'Thank you, Doctor. The purser will show you to your cabins; he's waiting below.'

Bill led them forward to their cabins. 'Doctor Kaufmann, I've put you in the main stateroom. Mr Davis and Mr Jones, you are in the starboard side cabin. Mr Edwards and Mr Martinez you are in the port side.'

Martinez pushed past Edwards and grabbed the lower double bunk for himself.

By mid-afternoon the rain had eased to a light drizzle, allowing the crew to finalise their preparations for departure the next morning.

During the day Kaufmann and his team migrated back to the bar at the Admiral Aubrey.

Late afternoon, Betty, Bob, Pete, and John stopped by with a gift followed by Dot and Beryl bearing a cake. Terry, with Sandra and her beau, followed by Mrs Philip, also arrived late afternoon, and before he realised what was happening, Bill found the day descending into a bon-voyage party.

Next morning Bill woke with a raging headache and realised that the crew at least had to be fed before they untied. He doubted any of Kaufmann's people would be up before midday, especially after the quantity of alcohol they had consumed.

Dot and Beryl waved them off from the quay just before seven o'clock and to their surprise the boatyard crew had piled into *Little Toot*, and met them mid-harbour to wave and cheer them on their way.

This time they were ahead of the ferry and passed out into Poole Bay on their own.

25

A lost wallet

'Mum,' said Abigail, 'he's back again.'

'Who's back again?' asked Ruth applying her mascara.

'That policeman, the one who was here last time,' said Abigail.

'I'll get it, you finish your breakfast.'

'Good morning ma-am,' said Ross as Ruth opened the door, 'sorry to disturb you. I wonder if I might have a word – are you all right?'

'Yes, just a bit stressed, haven't been sleeping well, think I've got a tummy bug. Have you any news about my husband?'

'Sorry ma-am, it's still early days yet but we do have this,' Ross said, holding up a large clear evidence bag. 'Is this your husband's wallet?'

Ruth took the plastic envelope and stared at it. It definitely looked like Bill's wallet.

'Can I take it out?'

'Yes, ma-am.'

Hands trembling, Ruth opened the bag, extracted the wallet, and looked inside. There were no photos or credit cards. It was Bill's though. On the inside, in a pocket on the right, was a business card from Bill's councillor. She'd put it in there hoping Bill would remember to use it when the urge to drink got a hold of him. There was no doubt in her mind the wallet was Bill's.

The look on her face was all Ross needed, 'It was handed in to the police station yesterday by a fisherman,' said Ross.

'Inspector,' said Ruth, 'we'll be returning home tomorrow, there's nothing more for us here.'

26
Shake down

As they cleared the entrance to Poole Harbour, Bill went back to the stern with a pair of binoculars. He scanned the beach looking at the early risers along the promenade and then gazed up to the houses on Canford Cliff. The binoculars settled on a balcony on the first floor of one of the flats.

As three sad faces stared back at him, he involuntarily stepped back, lost his balance, and tripped over the stern-locker hatch.

Stephen heard the crash.

'Elijah, it's Edward, I think he's walked into the mizzen boom,' he shouted over the sound of the engine.

Elijah clambered over to the prostrate form.

'Edward, what happened, you all right?'

'I'm fine; just lost my balance, tripped on the hatch.'

'Elijah, take him below and have John take a look at him,' said Larsen, 'he should be in the chart room.'

Elijah helped Bill down the companionway steps and eased him onto the settee.

'What happened, Edward?' said John.

'Nothing, honestly, I'm fine. I slipped on the wet deck and fell. Really, I'm fine.'

A few minutes and a cup of sweet tea later he had sufficiently recovered to return to the galley.

'If you are all right Edward, I am going back on deck,' said Larsen.

As they were still under the lee of Durlston Head the motion was quite gentle, allowing Bill time to think. *Those little angels, what have I done?*

His thoughts were interrupted by Kaufmann dressed in his pyjamas, staggering into the main saloon. 'Is that coffee I smell? I take mine with milk and two sugars, I'll have it in my cabin while I dress.' Then as an afterthought he said, 'Is it always this rough at sea?'

'Oh no,' said Bill, 'we're not out in the channel yet, the waves get much higher out there.'

Kaufmann's face went two shades lighter. 'Forget the coffee,' he said, heading back to his cabin.

As the engine note dropped to a murmur, Bill took advantage of the lull in the boat's motion and carried Marcel's breakfast up to the cockpit.

'You all right?' he asked.

'I'm fine, just lost my footing. Eat your breakfast while it's hot.'

'Thanks.'

Bill sat down in the lee of the dodger and watched as the sails were raised. A few minutes later with the sails set and trimmed and engine off, *Leviathan* healed under the press of the wind and headed out into the channel.

Larsen returned from inspecting the sails and stepped into the cockpit. 'Hold this course for now, Marcel.'

Bill looked at Larsen; he was at one with his ship.

'I doubt your compatriots will be joining us this morning, Marcel,' said Bill.

'I'm not surprised; they drink like fish and none of them have been to sea on anything other than a cross channel ferry.'

'Kaufmann came out of his cabin for a coffee,' said Bill, 'he felt the motion of the boat and headed back to bed.'

'As expected,' said Larsen. 'Have you known them long, Marcel?'

'No, only met them a few weeks ago.'

'How did you meet?'

'I was in between jobs. A chap I met in a pub told me about the expedition and said they were looking for someone who spoke Portuguese and had small boat handling experience. He gave me Kaufmann's mobile number. I called, agreed to meet up with him and here I am.'

'Are they paying you well?'

'They're taking care of my expenses plus some cash up front and I get a cash bonus when we return.'

'I didn't realise that UNESCO trips were profit related?'

'They're not, Kaufmann is working on a private venture. It's a project to help the local natives export their handmade crafts and he's also working on a European distribution network for them.'

'Busy man, and quite a philanthropist, our Doctor Kaufmann,' said Larsen thoughtfully.

'Captain,' said Bill, 'your breakfast is ready.'

'Thanks.'

Bill followed Larsen down the companionway steps, Larsen to the chart room, and Bill to the galley. Larsen came back out a couple of minutes later and stopped at the galley counter to watch a developing spectacle.

Martinez, unshaved and hair dishevelled, had come out of his cabin, and was standing beside Davis.

'Move Davis, that's my seat.'

'I was here first.'

Martinez grabbed Davis's ear and gave it a twist.

'*Yeow!*' said Davis as he got up from his chair and moved to the lone seat on the settee.

'What's for breakfast, *Eddy boy*?' said Martinez, leering at Bill, 'and why is the boat moving? It's doing my head in.'

'Feeling queasy, are you?' asked Elijah.

'What's it to you – boy?'

Bill and Larsen watched, wondering what was going to happen next, Elijah turned to Bill and said, 'Edward, do you have any more fried eggs? Those last ones were really nice, especially the ones with the runny yolks. And while you're frying, how about some more sausages, and beans?'

Bill caught on to what Elijah was up to, smiled, and said, 'How about some more black pudding and fried bread to go with it? I need to soak up the leftover oil in the frying pan.'

'Yeah, bring it on – *Eddy boy,*' he said with a huge grin on his face.

Martinez, his face like Kaufmann's earlier, had turned two shades lighter. He stood with his hand over his mouth and staggered off to his cabin. Davis smiled and moved back to his original seat, then got up, excused himself and returned to his cabin.

Larsen shook his head slowly and smiled.

They didn't see Kaufmann or his team again till they dropped anchor in Falmouth.

◆

'Well men, eighteen-thirty on Friday evening in Falmouth Harbour. Considering how the weather's been we have made good time with this leg,' said Larsen. 'John, Elijah, when you've finished your coffee would you launch the dinghy?'

'Sure thing, Captain.'

Larsen turned to Marcel. 'What are your plans for this evening?'

'Kaufmann wants me to go ashore with his team; I suppose being part of their team I should go with them, and you?'

'I was going to take the crew ashore for dinner and be back on board by eleven.

'Luxury,' said Marcel shaking his head, 'I will have to put up with them getting blind drunk, filling their bellies with kebabs then throwing it all up as soon as they get in the dinghy, that's their idea of a good night out.'

They were interrupted by Kaufmann, 'What time will we be leaving in the morning, Captain?'

'We set sail at nine.'

'My men and I are going ashore this evening; they need some time on land that's not constantly moving.'

'The liberty boat will be coming back at twelve; those of your team who are not on board by then will have to swim,' said Larsen.

'Captain, may I remind you that I am in charge of this expedition and I will say when we return.'

'And may I remind you that I am in charge of the voyage and the yacht. Liberty boat at twelve and we leave at nine am sharp.'

'Another thing,' whined Kaufmann, 'why is the boat so unstable? It was bouncing all over the place.'

'That's life on a small yacht on the open sea,' said Larsen. 'This leg of the voyage was the easy part, tomorrow we head out into the Atlantic and then you'll really see waves.'

'I've seen them forty feet high,' said Elijah. 'Liberty boat is ready, Captain.'

'Thanks, Elijah.'

'Twelve sharp, Doctor Kaufmann.'

Stephen rowed Kaufmann and his team ashore then returned for the crew.

'Since you have the task of feeding us three meals a day every day Edward, I thought it only right you choose where we go for dinner tonight,' said Larsen.

'Anywhere I choose?'

'Anywhere your heart desires.'

'How about we just go ashore and ask at the taxi rank? They'll know where the best food is.'

♦

'Stephen,' said Larsen when they got on board after the evening ashore, 'will you go back and wait for our guests? Then when you return join me in the main salon. 'Edward, will you make me a hot chocolate, please? I want to catch the shipping forecast; I want to find out when this storm will blow through and what is waiting for us when we head out in to the open sea tomorrow.'

He waited for Kaufmann's bedraggled revellers to turn in before he started.

'I've checked the weather report for the area south and west of the English Channel and I am afraid it is not good. There is a force five north westerly storm due and I want to avoid being driven into the Bay of Biscay, where it is expected to be force seven. It's my intention to beat out to the west before heading south-west for Madeira. It will be uncomfortable for us for a couple of days and probably worse for our guests. But it will be much kinder when we head south-west as we will be running before the wind and weather. By the time we get south of Biscay we will pick up the southern branch of the North Atlantic current and hopefully better weather, any questions?'

'Yes what about our guests?' queried John. 'It's too late to give them something for sea sickness; I suppose it would be a waste of time anyway.'

Marcel added, 'After this evening's shenanigans in the pub I expect we won't have to worry about them, I doubt we will see them for days.'

'Stephen, John, first thing in the morning before we sail, I want you to go through their cabins and set up the lee cloths on their bunks. I don't want them being bounced onto the cabin sole and breaking bones and I don't care if they protest. Edward, you have something to add?'

'I have made two hearty stews for us, they will be in the Thermoses in the galley, the red one on the left is beef and the green one on the right is chicken. Bread is in the bread box on the counter, I made it fresh this morning so it should keep well for the first few days. I have some slices of cold meats, cheese, tomatoes, and lettuce in the fridge if anyone wants a sandwich. Fruit is in its usual place in the hanging net. Hot water for drinks is in the third Thermos beside the stove, I will keep it topped up for you.'

'I'm hungry already,' said John.

'Right,' said Larsen, 'I'll stand watch till one, who's on Middle?'

'I am,' said Elijah.

Early Saturday, with the anchor up and lashed down on the deck, the *Leviathan* headed out of Falmouth Bay, on into the English Channel and the biggest adventure of Bill's life.

27
Alarm at sea

'How are you coping, Edward?' asked Larsen, helping himself to a large mug of beef stew.

'Fine, until we hit those really big waves. The noise of them crashing on deck is frightening; it feels like we have hit a wall and it's just fallen on top of us. Other than that, I'm getting quite used to it, unlike our guests who I've not seen since Falmouth.'

'Hmm, we'll be changing course soon. You'll find the motion of the boat will ease quite considerably. I expect you will have a full table for breakfast in the morning.'

Larsen hadn't reckoned on the softness of Kaufmann's team and even by the next day, none of them were up and about.

'Captain, I'm worried about our guests,' said Bill, as he served him his lunch. 'I've hardly seen any of them. Davis and Jones came into the galley earlier and had some soup, then went back to their cabin, that's all.'

'I'll have John check on them, make sure they are not getting too dehydrated.'

♦

It was early afternoon the next day before any of the guests rose.

'Good afternoon, Doctor Kaufmann,' said Bill. 'How are you feeling?'

'I'd feel a damn sight better if the boat would stop moving.'

'Oh, you'll get used to it. Hungry?'

'Ja, what have you got?'

'Fresh fruit, cheese, sliced ham and warmed bread rolls with coffee.'

'I'll just have coffee, cheese and a roll,' he said, sitting down at the table beside Stephen and Elijah.

'Do you want milk and sugar in your coffee?'

'Two sugars, no milk.'

'I'm making stew and dumplings for dinner tonight; maybe by then your team will feel well enough to eat.'

'I hope so. It will do them good to get up and eat something.' Then turning to Stephen, he said, 'When do we get to Madeira? I need to stand on something that is not moving all the time.'

'Day after tomorrow, as long as the wind stays as it is. We won't be staying long. Just long enough to top up the water and fuel.'

'But my men, they will need time ashore. All this motion is not good for them, it is making them sick.'

Stephen's reply was cut off by the shrill ring of an alarm bell.

'What's that?' asked Bill.

Larsen came hurtling down the companionway ladder as Stephen dashed ahead of him into the chart room.

'It's the bilge alarm!' shouted Stephen. 'We must be taking on water.'

Larsen turned and got down on his hands and knees at the foot of the companionway ladder. He pulled on one of the brass rings on the cabin sole, lifted the floor hatch and shone his torch down into the gloom of the bilge.

'I can see running water and there is some oil as well; it's coming from the stern,' said Larsen.

'I'll check the engine room,' said Stephen heading for the chart room and access to the engine. Larsen followed, they reappeared fifteen minutes later.

'Well, are we sinking Captain?' said Kaufmann, fear of drowning apparently overcoming his seasickness.

'No, Doctor, we are not sinking. The seal on the rudder shaft is leaking more than it should. Unfortunately, due to all the steering cables and the motion of the rudder quadrant we are unable to stop the leak while underway. We will make repairs when we reach Madeira. It will mean an extra day there. It also adds a day to our arrival time at the Amazon.'

'That's not a problem. Sinking in the Atlantic, now that *is* a problem.'

'What will happen to the water in the bilge, Stephen? asked Bill. 'And will we have to listen to the bell all the way to Madeira?'

'No. I'll reset the alarm and the bilge pump will keep up with the leak, it has a float switch. Every time the water gets to a certain level the pump starts pumping the water over the side. See, nothing to worry about.'

'Good. In that case I'll get on with dinner.'

Next morning, Bill had a full complement of guests and crew at breakfast. He felt he finally was doing what he signed on for.

◆

Two days later, as he was cleaning the last of the breakfast dishes, he heard a commotion above. Curious, he went up on deck to find everyone staring off to the port side.

'What's got everyone's attention, Stephen?'

'They are watching an airliner landing on Porto Santo,' he replied, pointing.

'Wow, it looks like it's going to crash into the mountain.'

'No, it'll be fine. The airport is up on the hill, the runway runs diagonally across almost the whole island. It's quite an exciting landing if you have never been there before.'

'I suppose you have?'

'Two years ago. The beaches on the eastern shores are magnificent.'

'Someday I'll be that lucky. How long till we reach Madeira?'

'We should be tied up by twelve this morning; we're headed for the harbour at Funchal.'

'That will please Herr Doctor,' Bill said, smiling. 'How long will the repairs take?'

'Shouldn't be more than a couple of hours. It's the oil leak that I am concerned about. It could only come from the engine.'

'That does sound bad, any ideas?'

'Loose sump plug, or maybe a loose hose clamp or oil filter. Either way I am afraid it will be down to you to clean out the oil from the bilge when the repairs are complete.'

'Why me? I'm the cook, not an engineer.'

'Don't take it personally. It's simply the fact that you are the right size for getting down deep in the bilges, we're all too large for that.'

Bill grinned. 'That's a bit of a back-handed compliment, thanks,' he said, and headed back below to finish clearing up.

As the morning wore on there was a noticeable air of excitement growing on board. At eleven he heard activity on deck in preparation for arriving in port, so he poked his head out of the hatch to watch.

'What's that large building that looks like a bridge on the beach?' he asked.

'That's the airport,' said Stephen. 'The structure on stilts is the extension to the runway.'

'That's weird; I've never seen anything like that before. You been here as well?'

'Yep, I worked as a mechanic, repairing English cars in a garage in town.'

Just then Marcel excused himself, pushed past and went below to call the harbour master on the radio.

They tied up at the jetty between a couple of fishing boats, and Stephen went to work.

'Ah, Captain Larsen, how long will we be here?' asked Kaufmann.

'I expect the repairs to take a couple of hours, then we need to take on water, and I think we will take advantage of the market and get fresh provisions. So we stay one night and leave tomorrow morning about nine.'

'Ja, that's what I thought. In that case we will go ashore and take in the sights; we will be back for dinner at six.'

None of the crew was sorry to see Kaufmann and his team go ashore. It gave Stephen uninterrupted time to resolve the oil leak.

'What was it?' queried Bill, as Stephen came out of the chart room.

'Nothing more than the oil filter not being screwed on tight enough.'

Bill climbed down into the bilges with a bucket, detergent and rags to clean up the spilled engine oil.

Next it was up forward to tidy the crew quarters. By the time he had completed cleaning them it was time to return to the galley to prepare lunch.

After lunch he headed for the guest cabins. Kaufmann's was simple; he just had to make the bed. As he fluffed up the pillow, his hand came into contact with a small velvet pouch. Curiosity got the better of him and he loosened the drawstrings, shaking out the contents. They weren't what he expected; lying on the pillow was a large pile of chunks of rough glass.

'Uncut diamonds,' said a voice behind him.

Bill looked round guiltily to see Marcel staring at his find. 'Probably using them to fund his expedition; I'd just put them back and forget you saw them,' he said, winking. 'It'll be our secret – for now, anyway.'

Davis and Jones had evidently tried to do some tidying themselves, whereas Martinez and Edwards' cabin smelled of sweat and vomit.

Bill opened the hatch and pulled the bedding back to air, then went into the toilet. Evidently, they had been unsuccessful in depositing the contents of their stomachs into the head and had vomited all over the back of the toilet.

Taking a deep breath, he pulled on his rubber gloves and got down on his hands and knees to scrub the vomit off the back of the toilet. His hair kept flapping in his face, and it wasn't long before he realised his hair had as much muck in it as the rag he was using to clean up with. As tears ran down his face, he wondered why he was doing this. At home he had a warm bed to sleep in, regular meals, a nice car, and a kitchen that didn't try to turn on its end every time he started to cook. Even Mrs Parker went home at night.

'Oh, Eddie baby, what a sight for a weary sailor,' said a voice behind him.

He jumped in surprise and turned his head to see Martinez standing in the cabin doorway fondling his crotch while staring at Bill's backside.

Before he could say anything, Elijah said from behind Martinez, 'You said you were getting a clean shirt, do it and get out.'

'OK sailor boy, just thinking what any red-blooded sailor would think. No harm in that, is there, boy?'

Bill watched in awe as Elijah barged his way into the cabin, grabbed Martinez by the throat and pushed him up against the bulkhead, so that his toes barely touched the cabin sole.

'Listen you weasel. Not now, but one day – you and me – we're going to have a quiet talk, somewhere we won't be interrupted, and I will stuff that stupid grin so far down your throat, that when you sneeze you'll bite your ass. Do you understand me – janky?' he dropped Martinez onto the floor.

Bill watched as Martinez's face turned from the white of fear to the red of anger then to a shade of demonic grey, as he said, 'Any time you want – boy.'

'Collect your shirt and get your ass out of here – now,' said Elijah.

Bill tried not to smirk as he watched Martinez take a clean shirt from the locker, drop the sweaty one on the floor then leave.

'That's the second time you have come between me and Martinez. Thanks.'

'No problem. Any time he becomes a nuisance, just let me know and I will gladly take care of the little rat. Oh, by the way, the captain says we are going to leave after breakfast in the morning. He thought you might like to go ashore to the market with Marcel. It's got the reputation of being one of the best markets in Madeira.

'Yeah – that sounds wonderful – thanks.'

Now what was he to do? So far Marcel had kept to himself and hadn't shown any sign of recognising him. Maybe he had been waiting for a time when they were alone together? But perhaps it didn't matter; they were no longer in England. What could he do?

Kaufmann, followed by his entourage, showed up at the yacht just in time for dinner.

'What's for dinner? I'm famished,' he said, sitting down at the saloon table.

'Where is Mr Martinez, Doctor?' said Larsen.

'Ah, he has met a pretty Señorita in town and he sends his apologies to the cook,' said Kaufmann, turning to Bill and grinning.

'He's not planning to jump ship, is he?' said Larsen.

'Nein, nein, not at all, 'said Kaufmann, 'don't worry, Captain, he'll be back in plenty of time.'

'He'd better. I have his passport.'

Kaufmann and team went ashore again directly after dinner and didn't show up till ten after two in the morning.

'Now where is Mr Martinez, Doctor?' asked John.

'Deep in the arms of love, Mr Grey. Don't worry, he'll show up when he is good and ready.'

The blue lights of the police car brought John up on deck at three-thirty.

'Where is your Captain?' asked the uniformed policeman.

'I'll get him for you, please wait.'

Larsen was a light sleeper and was up by the time John got to the bottom of the companionway steps.

'Is that the police, John?'

'Yes.'

'Did they say what they wanted, or should we guess?'

'Probably Martinez, he still hasn't returned.'

Larsen stepped off the *Leviathan* down on to the dock.

'Captain Larsen of the yacht *Leviathan*,' he said, extending his hand to the policeman.

'Capitan Diego of the Santa Cruz Police, at your service, sir,' the policeman replied, shaking Larsen's hand.

'What can I do for you, Captain Diego?'

'You can come to the police station and remove your crew, please.'

'Ah, that will be Mr Martinez, we've been wondering where he had got to. If you can just give me a minute?'

He turned to John. 'Go wake Doctor Kaufmann, and tell him to bring his wallet, there's bound to be a fine to pay, and I don't see why I should get stuck with it.'

Marcel came on watch at four, just in time to welcome Larsen and Kaufmann and the bruised Martinez back on board.

'What happened to him?' asked Marcel.

'Got involved in a drunken brawl with one of the door staff,' said John. 'Kaufmann's now much lighter in his wallet.'

Bill was awake and in the galley before the sun was up

'You do a double watch?' Bill asked as Marcel came down the companionway steps.

'Yeah, John needed his sleep more than me.'

'What would you like for breakfast?'

'I'll take whatever you are making. Still going fishing this morning?'

It took him a moment to understand what he meant. 'Er, yes, just as soon as I have finished with breakfast. Is the market far away?'

'No, we can walk to it, but I think we'll take a taxi, need to be early for the best choice of produce.'

'Where is the market?' Bill asked Marcel as the taxi sped along the sea front.

'It's near the old city of Funchal. It's inside and has two floors. It's not only a fish market; they also sell exotic flours, vegetables and all sorts of fruit.'

♦

They were back on board just before nine. The engine was running, oil leak fixed and the sail covers off; the *Leviathan* was ready to resume her voyage.

As they headed back out to sea, Bill went below to prepare the guests' breakfasts.

'Good morning, Edward.'

Bill looked up from the counter where he was slicing salami for lunch.

'Good morning, Mr Edwards. How are you today?'

'Jim—all my friends call me Jim. I'm fine and a bit hungry, for the first time at sea. What time is it?' he said, looking round for a clock.

'Ten to eleven, there's a clock over the fireplace. What would you like to eat?'

'Any chance of an omelette with some grilled bacon and a cup of tea to go with it?'

'Sure. Be ready in a couple of minutes.'

It wasn't long until the smell of grilling bacon enticed the other guests out of their cabins.

'What's that island over there, John?' asked Davis.

John glanced at the compass, 'that's La Palma.'

'Aren't we stopping there?' asked Kaufmann. 'It has wonderful scenery and terrific restaurants.'

'No, the Captain says we head straight for the Cape Verdes islands,' said John, smiling at Kaufmann's discomfort.

'I'm going to talk to the captain about this. I'm in charge of this expedition and I will decide where we stop.'

Kaufmann stepped into the chart room. 'Captain, the chap on the wheel says we are not stopping at La Palma. Why not?'

'Firstly, because I say so, and, secondly, we have entered the hurricane season and I don't want to be caught out crossing the Atlantic. I have just checked the long-range weather report and it shows clear for the next few days at least. I plan to stop at Mindelo on the Cape Verdes long enough to take on water and top up the diesel tanks, then it is full sail across the Atlantic, and the Amazon.'

'Oh, OK, that does make sense now you explain the circumstances. Thanks.'

Kaufmann turned to leave, then stopped, turned and said, 'Captain, I have been thinking. I am worried about my team, they spend all their time lying about or sleeping. It can't be good for their health or morale. Would it be possible for them to help out on deck and help your crew on the helm during the day watches? If they only did two hour stretches it shouldn't tax them too much. In fact, it'll do them good to get out in the fresh sea air and should we run in to any bad weather your crew will have been rested that bit more and be able to deal with whatever the Atlantic throws at us.'

'I don't see why not. Let me work something out.'

'Good. Do you want a coffee? I'm getting one for myself.'

'Yes, please, black no sugar.'

Kaufmann was back in ten minutes.

'Thanks for the coffee. How does this schedule look to you?' said Larsen, handing a sheet of paper to Kaufmann.

Larsen had worked out the schedule making sure that Elijah and Martinez didn't share a watch.

'Looks fine to me, I'll pass it round.'

They put in to Mindelo at five-thirty and were back at sea heading west before any of Kaufmann's team was out of their bunks.

'Isn't that the Cape Verdes over there John?' said Jones, coming on deck to take his spell at the wheel.

'Yes, that's one of the islands.'

'Why didn't we stop?'

'We did – at five-thirty this morning.'

'Oh well, there'll be plenty of shore time for us when we get to the Amazon.'

'Here,' said John, 'hold this course,' he said pointing to the compass, 'I'm going below for a minute.'

He was back in ten with a thick sandwich and a cup of steaming vegetable soup.

'Doesn't this boat have an autopilot?' asked Jones.

'Yes, but the captain says while we have a big enough crew we steer by hand, it keeps us busy and attentive while on deck. The *Leviathan* sails herself mostly, so it's not a great chore to steer. I prefer it.'

'Could I see how the autopilot works?'

'Sure, let's wait till the change of watch then I'll take you below to the chart room and you can see how to set it.'

'Thanks, I look forward to that.'

◆

By lunchtime on the third day life on board had settled to a benign regime of eating, sleeping, and watch keeping. Earlier in the day, Larsen had the drifter set wing and wing with the main to catch the steady trade wind, now carrying them westward at an average 200 miles a day.

Chores complete Bill climbed out of the cabin and went forward and lay down on the sail bag on the bow platform. The gentle breeze combined with the slow rolling gait of the *Leviathan* soon had him dreaming.

He was high in the mountains watching a river flow between boulders capped with snow. A shepherd started talking in a German accent to his dog; Bill struggled to make sense of what was being said and realised he had been dreaming and it was in fact Kaufmann. The sound of Kaufmann's voice had been carried on the wind to the drifter sail that towered over Bill.

Bill raised his head and glanced back at the cockpit. It definitely was Kaufmann's voice, and he was talking to Martinez. Bill raised his head some more and saw that they were alone in the cockpit.

'Did you talk with your friend before we left?' Martinez asked.

'Yes, he assured me that everything was still on schedule. He'll meet us at the dock.'

'How will he know when to expect us?'

'He said not to worry. Mauro works in the dockside cafe; he'll let our friend know when we arrive.'

'Can we trust him?'

'What choice do we have?'

'When will we know that our terms have been agreed to?'

'We'll know by the time we get to the anchorage.'

'What about the crew?' queried Martinez.

'I'll leave them to you, that's more your speciality than mine,' said Kaufmann.'

'Galan, do we still trust him?'

'Good question Hugo. Have you noticed when we go ashore, he sometimes disappears then manages to join us just as we are ready to go back on board?'

'Yeah, I followed him when I went to meet up with the barmaid from the Casa Del Sol, but lost him in the back alleyways. Got the impression he knew I was following him. Then as I was heading back from saying good night to Margarita, I saw him coming out of the port Captain's office. He said he was checking up on his sick mother back home.'

'Wonder if he really has a sick mother?' said Kaufmann.

'He did check out, didn't he?'

'Of course, he did, at least that's what I was told by Smith. Do you think I'd just let anyone join this venture? But just in case Hugo, keep a close eye on him, he might just be expendable.'

'Huh, how do we know we can trust Smith?'

'He's all right. He's pretty much put this deal together for us. Don't forget, it was he who found this boat for us.'

'All the same, maybe we should keep Galan on a short lead.'

'Good idea Hugo.'

'The big black one has invited Stephen to go with him to see his family in the US,' said Martinez. 'That'll just leave the Captain, Grey and the cook. When the time comes, I'll take care of them.'

'And the cook?' said Kaufmann.

His reply was lost in the sound of the *Leviathan* plunging into a wave.

What were they planning? Bill wondered. He waited till he saw Stephen come on watch to relieve Martinez and Kaufmann, and then headed below to the chart room to talk with Larsen.

'What do you think he meant, Captain?'

'Good question, Edward. Where's Marcel?'

'I saw him head forward to his bunk.'

'Perfect, let's not say anything to Marcel. Not sure which side of the fence he's on. This will just be between our crew. Can you get Elijah and John and meet me and Stephen in the cockpit?'

'What will I say if Kaufmann asks what's going on?'

'Tell him we're getting ready for our arrival in Brazil.'

'That'll work, back in a minute.'

Stephen made the pretence of steering, while keeping a lookout for any signs of Kaufmann's team.

When the crew had assembled in a huddle behind the spray dodger, Larsen had Bill repeat the conversation he'd heard between Kaufmann and Martinez.

'What'd you think Captain?' asked John.

'If I was a betting man, I'd say the good doctor has plans to take command of the *Leviathan*.'

'But why?' said Stephen. 'He's already dictating where and when we go.'

'I think we're fine for just now, Stephen. He still needs us to get him to his destination. It's the return journey that bothers me. That's probably why he wanted his team to get some experience with handling the *Leviathan*?'

'But they've no experience of handling a boat this size in heavy weather,' added John.

'That's Kaufmann for you. Edward anything else, find anything unusual when cleaning their cabins?'

Bill shook his head then remembered the uncut diamonds under Kaufmann's pillow and Marcel's advice to say nothing about it.

'Uncut diamonds you say, what the hell does he need them for,' said Larsen.

'Marcel said it was to fund Kaufmann's private venture,' replied Bill.

'Were their many diamonds?' asked John.

'Just a small handful.'

'I suppose,' said Larsen, 'if the diamonds quality was of low grade it could make sense.'

'This just confuses the issue,' said John. 'Do we trust Galan or not?'

'I think,' said Larsen, 'we too will keep Señor Galan on a short lead.'

28
Coffee and chat

Enough was enough. Ruth dialed the local CID office and asked for DCI Greyson.

'Harry, its Ruth, any chance you need a coffee? I could do with a chat.'

'Give me thirty minutes and I'll meet you at that new café on Broad Street. There's someone I want you to meet, that is if they're available.'

Ruth drove into town wondering who this person was. She parked in the on-street area and walked across the road to the café. Ten minutes and a cup of coffee later, Harry arrived with a tall dark-haired woman. Ruth stood and waved at them.

'Thanks for coming, Harry.'

'Anything for a friend. Ruth, this is Sergeant Reynolds, she's the division police liaison officer.'

'I'm sorry to hear of your husband's disappearance, Mrs Drysdale,' she said, sitting down.

Teas and coffee delivered, Reynolds continued, 'Mrs Drysdale, what you have been experiencing is quite common in cases such as yours. Every year in the UK anywhere up to 200,000 plus, missing people reports are filed; thankfully the majority of these cases are cleared up quite quickly. But unfortunately, there are a small number that are never cleared up.

Some runaways stay in the same area that they formerly lived in, never travelling further than a few miles from their departed home. Some say it helps them to know their way around, and which shops to go in to without giving away their identities. They are more familiar with places where they can sleep securely and possibly find casual cash in hand work.'

'Where does my husband's case fit in?' asked Ruth.

'It's difficult to say at this point – time is the best weapon we have in our arsenal.'

'I just don't know what to think,' said Ruth, staring into her cup. 'I expect him to come through the door at any moment. Every time the phone rings I wonder if that's him, whether he's been in an accident and lost his memory, or worse.'

'You have three daughters, Mrs Drysdale?'

'Yes. Abigail, the eldest, she's thirteen, and twins Hannah and Rachael, they're eleven.'

'How are they doing at school?'

'Abigail is doing fine – but the twins, according to their teachers, are struggling. I have a meeting at the school next week.'

Reynolds nodded and said, 'That's quite common. The younger ones find it harder to understand, sometimes they may blame themselves.'

Ruth smiled and shook her head. 'It's not only the girls who blame themselves. I wrack my brain trying to think of what I did wrong.'

'Can't sleep, or have trouble getting to sleep?'

'Most nights – tried drinking myself to sleep one night, failed miserably and woke with a raging hangover, couldn't keep food down for three days after.'

'How about church? Some people find solace in prayer and the support they get.'

Ruth shook her head again. 'I grew up in a church-going family but when I went off to university life just got in the way.'

'The Pinocchio syndrome,' said Reynolds.

'What's that?' asked Harry.

'Not an official medical definition. It describes what happens to a young man, or woman, when they leave home for the first time. The siren-call of the bright lights of the city, with its entrapments, and diversions, that can lead them astray.'

'Oh that,' said Harry, chuckling at an old memory, 'I lived there for a couple of years, knew every street and bar.'

Trying to bring the conversation back to the subject on hand, Reynolds asked, 'What about family finances?'

'There are no problems there. I'm a QC, and my husband's father is managing director of Multi Layer Ltd, they design and build miniaturized electronic components. I'm also a director. We do a lot of work for the MOD; keeps three thousand people in gainful employment.'

'How about appeals in the newspapers, local radio or television?' she asked Harry. 'Have those been tried?'

'Local and national papers, yes; we haven't tried local radio or television yet.'

Reynolds nodded. 'Right, here's what I propose. We'll get you interviewed on local radio and then I'll see if we can get you on the next edition of *Crimewatch* – but, of course Mrs Drysdale, when people disappear they don't always want to be found.'

29
Brazil

'Is that the coast of Brazil?' asked Bill, as he handed Larsen a coffee.

'Indeed it is. We're heading for the mouth of the river.' Larsen replied. We'll motor in slowly; I don't want to come this far and run into a sandbank in sight of land.'

The sound of the engine starting brought Kaufmann up on deck.

'What's happening, Captain? Are we in trouble?'

'We have arrived, Doctor. Those lights are the lights of Macapa; we should be at the dock just before breakfast.'

'Good. As soon as we've tied up, I'm going ashore. I need to make arrangements.'

'Doctor, no one goes ashore till customs and immigration procedures have been completed.'

'Of course, Captain, please excuse me; it's the excitement of being so close to the work. All the months of preparation are about to pay off.'

'You're excused, Doctor,' said Larsen, wondering what Kaufmann meant by the term, *pay off.* 'John, will you hoist the Q flag? Let's hope the Brazilians know what it means. Edward, I think early breakfast is in order.'

They were met by a high-powered police launch. A uniformed officer gestured to them to follow and tie up behind a large river ferry. At the dock they were boarded by a team of stern-faced Federal Police Officers. Bill watched them through his cabin porthole and noted their smart uniforms, the handcuffs, and serious looking side-arms on their belts.

On boarding, the senior officer approached Larsen, 'Captain Carrasco, I'm the senior officer here. Welcome to Brazil. May I see your ship's papers and the passports of all on board?'

'Shall we go below?'

'Lead on.'

'Bill, would you make us coffee, please?' said Larsen as they sat down at the table. Larsen opened a thick folder and passed the contents to Captain Carrasco.

'Your papers all seem to be in order Captain. May I give you some advice?'

'Certainly,' said Larsen.

'I am sure you are aware that drug trafficking in Brazil is not tolerated.'

'Certainly, it is the same in my country and I don't condone it in any way.'

'I'm sure you don't, Captain. Unfortunately, some Europeans come here thinking they can just do as they wish in our beautiful country and it is my duty to assuage them of those ideas.'

Larsen was relieved at the professionalism shown by the Brazilian immigration authorities, although he was bothered by the police captain's directness in discussing drug trafficking.

Kaufmann's introductory papers from UNESCO added an air of authority to proceedings and after many cups of coffee and much handshaking they were cleared to travel into the interior.

'Doctor Kaufmann, now we have arrived, my crew and yacht are at your disposal. Let me know when you are ready to proceed, will you?'

Kaufmann raised an eyebrow at Larson's sudden acquiescence, then took the initiative and said, 'Well thank you, Captain, finally you have come to your senses. I will go ashore this afternoon to make contact with my local people; I'll take Mr Martinez with me. The remainder of my team are free to come and go as they see fit. I will let you know when we are ready to proceed up the river. Good day.' Sniffing the air, he turned and went off to his cabin.

'What are the orders for the day, Captain?' asked John, as the crew assembled round the saloon table after Kaufmann's team had gone ashore.

'First, we'll set the awning. Then, John, would you go with Edward to do his shopping? There are bound to be markets where you can find fresh produce. Also, you might like to check out the pharmacies and see what they have. You never know what health problems we may run into on the river and at least you'll know what remedies are generally available. Stephen, you and I will go and see what we can do about getting diesel for the trip up the river. Elijah, I am afraid it falls to you to stay on board and keep watch.'

'That's not a problem. Gives me time to wash down the sails and get them under cover. This tropical sunshine will be hard on them.'

'Right, gentlemen, if there are no further questions, we have our duties for the day,' Larsen said, standing. 'We may not be at sea, but life on board goes on. While we are ashore, you must carry your passport. All citizens are required to carry ID. As we will be living in their country for the next eight months or so, we should get used to doing things their way. One other thing – Elijah, I don't trust Kaufmann or his team, especially Martinez. He's trouble, watch your step with him. I think he has it in for you.'

'I'm way ahead of you on that score, Captain, just waiting for a suitable moment.'

'Elijah, that's not what I mean, just keep clear of him, I don't want you to get hurt.'

'I can take care of myself, Captain; my time in the US Marines taught me that, I promise you. I won't start anything.'

'It's not the starting that bothers me, Elijah.'

John and Bill stepped off the gangway and headed along the promenade while Larsen and Stephen went off to find the harbour master and fuel.

When John and Bill returned, they were greeted with the sight of yellow plastic fuel containers festooning the side decks of the *Leviathan*.

'Looks like we were both successful,' said Bill to Stephen, as he and John passed up their bags of fresh produce.

Later in the afternoon Kaufmann and his team, minus Martinez, returned to the *Leviathan* for dinner.

'Well, Doctor, were you successful in meeting your contacts?' asked Larsen.

'Ja, we sail for Manaus first thing in the morning. Then we will meet up with our guides and proceed up the Rio Negro to our anchorage.'

'We probably won't be doing much sailing, Doctor. The river may be wide but I think motoring will be the order of the day. Will Mr Martinez be joining us?'

'Ja, he is visiting with friends. Don't worry, Captain, he'll be with us in plenty of time.'

'OK, we still set off at nine am,' said Larsen.

Just after dinner, when Bill was in the galley cleaning up, the conversation in the main saloon turned to the crossing the line ceremony.

'How many of you have done the crossing the line ceremony?' queried Larsen.

All of his crew put up their hands, Davis and Galan did likewise while Jones, Edwards, and Kaufmann looked blank.

'What about you, Edward?' said Larsen.

'I don't know what it means,' he replied.

'It is a ceremony to celebrate the first time a sailor crosses the Equator,' said Larsen.

'What's involved?' he said nervously, squeezing a dish cloth and not really wanting to find out.

'It's simple really; you just get dressed up in your party clothes and get wet.'

'I don't know,' he replied.

'On cruise ships they use a small swimming pool to represent Neptune's court.'

'Relax Edward, it's only a bit of fun,' said Stephen.

'Captain, we can't afford the delay,' said Kaufmann. 'We must get up the river.'

'Of course, doctor, we'll set sail at nine tomorrow morning, if that suits you?'

'Ja that will do nicely.'

Next morning at eight, just as Bill was cleaning the skylight, a car drove up and Martinez disgorged himself. He stood straight, saluted the driver, and then staggered over to the *Leviathan*.

'Glad to see that you have decided to join us, Mr Martinez,' said Stephen.

'At your service, sir. Wouldn't want to miss the trip up the river, hope you have plenty of paddles?'

Stephen just shook his head at Martinez's attempt at humour.

'I suggest you come on board, Mr Martinez; we are about to depart.'

The movement of the boat, combined with the smell of exhaust, was too much for Martinez. He headed straight for the rail and vomited over the side, much to the amusement of those assembled on the quayside.

'Mr Martinez, if you have finished, I think you should go below, some of us have work to do,' said Larsen, annoyed at being interrupted in a conversation with Kaufmann.

Martinez wiped his mouth with the back of his hand, grinned at Larsen and Kaufmann and staggered off below.

♦

Bill was slicing salami for sandwiches when the engine note died to an idle, bringing Martinez out of his cabin.

'What's up, we there yet?' Then, shaking his head and grimacing, he said, 'Got any coffee, Eddie baby?'

'My name is Edward, Mr Martinez and to answer your question, yes, I've just made some. I presume you would like it strong and black?'

Martinez thought for a moment, then sat down with a wide grin on his face said, 'Yes, Eddie baby, I like it strong.'

Bill put down the knife and poured Martinez a large black coffee, put it on the counter, and then returned to slicing the salami.

'Over here, Eddie baby, bring it over here.'

'Mr Martinez, I am the cook, not your servant. If you want your coffee, come and get it yourself – if you're able.'

Instead of getting up, Martinez sat there mesmerised watching Bill slice the salami. Bill watched him stare for a few minutes then Martinez grimaced and grabbed his crotch. He shook his head, got up from the table, collected his coffee, and went up on deck.

'What are those buildings on stilts at the edge of the river, Stephen?' said Bill, delivering his lunch.

'Not sure, maybe small warehouses. Doctor Kaufmann, what do you think?'

'Ja, they're probably small warehouses to store farmers' produce prior to collection for market.'

'Looks more like houses to me,' said John. 'Most river people are poor and don't own much. What you see is all they have.'

'Look at the river – what's happening?' asked Bill.

'It's the confluence of the Amazon and the Negro,' said Larsen, 'the Amazon river water contains large quantities of silt, while the Negro river is clear and contains decaying plant chemicals – making its colour blackish.'

'Reminds me of something I drink at parties,' said Stephen.

◆

They arrived in Manaus six days after setting out from Macapa. Kaufmann arrived on deck as they tied up at the main jetty next to a Policia Federal patrol boat; Larsen noticed that he looked a little nervous.

'Something bothering you, Doctor?'

'Nein, nein, it's all these blasted flies, they're everywhere. Can't we tie up somewhere else?' he said, swatting the air. 'I'll be happier when we are away from here. Tomorrow, Captain, I will meet with the guides who will be taking us up the river.'

'Guides, Doctor? How many will there be?'

'Just one for this part of the river. When we get to our anchorage we will be joined by the rest. They have proper river boats that can navigate through the tributaries and get us to the places where a yacht the size of yours could never get to.'

Next morning turned into evening before Kaufmann's guide showed up. He arrived in a narrow river launch and tied up alongside the *Leviathan*.

'Captain, this is Paulo Gusmao. He will be guiding us to our anchorage in the river Negro.'

'Señor Gusmao, pleased to meet you.' said Larsen, extending his hand.

'Unfortunately, Captain, he only speaks Portuguese. I'll get Mr Galan to translate for us.'

'Certainly, Doctor. I will also need to be able to communicate with the guide as we go up the river tomorrow.'

'Mr Galan, this is Señor Gusmao, he will be our guide to the anchorage. Unfortunately, he doesn't speak English so you will have to act as our translator.

'*Boa tarde senhor, como está?*'

'*Muito bem, senhor.*'

'Tell him,' said Larsen, 'we're leaving at eight tomorrow morning.'

'He says, he'll be here at ten to eight.'

'Good. Would you thank him for me?'

'I'm sure you will agree that it was too late this evening to set out? That's why I suggested eight tomorrow morning,' said Kaufmann, after the guide had left.

'Eight is fine, Doctor. Now, if you will excuse me, I have charts to look over. Don't want to come this far and run into trouble, do we?'

'No, we certainly don't want to run into trouble,' replied Kaufmann.

'Edward,' said Larsen,' we'll be leaving at eight in the morning. Since we will be motoring, let's have breakfast at seven.'

'*O café da manhã será, às sete horas,*' said Bill.

'I never realised you spoke Portuguese,' said Larsen.

'You never asked. I learned to speak Portuguese while working in Portugal during my summer breaks from university.'

'That's very interesting. But let's not tell the Doctor, shall we? He already has a lot on his mind.'

'OK.'

30

Up the Amazon

'I never expected to see a bridge that big on the Amazon River,' said Stephen. 'Marcel, can you ask the guide about it?'

'He says it connects the city of Manaus with Iranduba. It is the only bridge on the Amazon River. He says it's not technically on the Amazon, as it only crosses the Negro, which is what we are motoring on now.'

'Just can't get over how people can live right on top of the river, I'd always worry about getting swept away in the night,' said Bill to John while they sat on the coach-roof in the shade of the awning.

'I doubt it happens very often. The river is wide and has many alternative routes to the sea. I once read that it can rise twenty metres. Normally it floods inland through the forests. That's why the houses are built on stilts.'

'Just the same, the idea of waking up to piranhas in my bed would make me have nightmares!'

'Marcel, ask our guide how long it will be before we reach our anchorage,' said Larsen.

Translating back into English, Marcel said, 'Five days, then we should be close, he says.'

'Bit vague for a river guide; ask him to explain.'

'He says that the river is quite high and he doesn't want us to run into submerged trees or old buildings. He is not used to piloting large sailboats with deep keels in these conditions.'

'Now he tells us,' said Larsen, shaking his head. 'Stephen, I think a bow watch is in order, I want someone on the bow all the time we are underway.'

♦

Late in the afternoon of the fifth day they set bow and stern anchors in a small cove just off a short sandy beach. Larsen had them run out long spring lines to trees on the riverbank.

'What are those discs on the dock lines for, Stephen?' queried Bill.

'They stop rats and other rodents from walking up the dock lines and getting on board.'

'First piranha, now rats! What next?' he asked.

Martinez,' said Stephen looking over Bill's shoulder. 'What's he doing?'

'I'll bet it's no good,' said Elijah.

Martinez was standing on the end of the short jetty which jutted out from the beach, talking very animatedly with the river guide.

'Is there a problem, Mr Martinez?' shouted Elijah.

Martinez stopped talking and looked at Elijah for a moment, then shouted back, 'Nothing for you to be worried about – boy.'

'Ignore him,' said Bill, 'he's just trying to rile you.'

Elijah took a deep breath. 'Well, he sure is succeeding. I swear to you, Edward, one day he'll get his comeuppance and I hope it's me that delivers it.'

'Stephen, why can't we just tie up to the jetty?' asked Bill

'Not enough water. Remember Poole, when we re-launched the *Leviathan*? Also we'll get a better breeze and less insects out here.'

'How do we get ashore?'

'I'll set up the dinghy on an outhaul.'

'What's an outhaul?'

'It's a loop of line run through a block on the dock at one end and the other block tied to a cleat on deck. The dinghy is tied to the loop. When you want to go ashore, you get in the dinghy and pull yourself hand over hand to the dock. If someone on the boat then needs the dinghy they just pull it back, see, simple.'

Early next morning a sleek river launch with three men aboard arrived and tied up against the fenders alongside the *Leviathan*.

'That must be the Doctor's guides,' said Larsen, putting down his coffee cup. 'Doctor, you have visitors,' he said, knocking on Kaufmann's cabin door. 'Doctor, do you hear? I think it's your guides, are you awake?'

'Ja, ja, Captain Larsen, I'll be right there.'

Kaufmann came out of his cabin and opened Martinez's door as he passed. 'Hugo, your services are required in the main cabin – now. And put some clothes on.'

Stephen showed the three strangers down into the main saloon as Martinez staggered out of his cabin, zipping up the fly on his shorts. Edward busied himself in the galley while Larsen and the crew went up on deck to set the side awnings.

'Doctor would your visitors like coffee?' asked Bill.

'Ja, I'm sure they would, and I will have my breakfast now.'

'Me too, Eddie baby,' said Martinez.

'Hugo, where are your manners? Ask our visitors if they would like something to eat,' said Kaufmann.

They all shook their heads to the food but nodded yes to the coffee.

'Captain, we will be leaving shortly and be gone for a couple of weeks. Since one of the guides speaks English quite well, we won't need the services of Mr Galan. I thought he could stay with your crew and be useful,' said Kaufmann.

Edward looked at Marcel as Kaufmann made this pronouncement and saw his face momentarily freeze as though he was trying to understand what he had just heard. Then, just as quickly, it relaxed and he said feigning hurt, 'Ah Doctor, I was looking forward to seeing the interior of this fantastic jungle. Now I'll end up being nothing more than a deck-hand.'

'Don't worry, Mister Galan, I'm sure the captain will find something for you to do.'

'Thank you, Doctor, I can always use an extra hand. A boat this large can be a bit of a Forth Bridge.'

'Forth Bridge? I don't understand, Captain.'

'The Forth Bridge in Scotland – as soon as the painters have got to the end it is time to start painting all over again.'

'Ja, ja, now I understand, some of your humour, very good, Captain. Now if you'll excuse us, we have some work to do ourselves.'

Larsen nodded to his crew to follow him up on deck.

After Kaufmann and his team had left in the river launch for their two-week trip, Larsen asked Bill what had been said between Kaufmann and the guides.

'They talked mostly about the whereabouts of various tribes and when a certain tribe would be available to deliver, sounded to be a lot of double talk.'

'What do you mean?'

'Well, what was said in Portuguese was not always what was translated into English. I think the doctor was trying to lay a false trail with his answers in English. Oh, also they said something about Señor Galan; I was boiling the kettle and only heard part of what was said. Something about him not being suitable, and him not being who he said he was. Didn't make any sense to me as the kettle whistle drowned out the rest of the conversation. Also, I think the doctor understands some Portuguese.

'Captain don't you think it odd that a team of ecologists would set out on an expedition with so little scientific equipment? All they appear to have is Kaufmann's laptop, which he's left behind, and a mixed collection of tablets and smart phones, which probably won't work here on the river.'

'Just what I thought; he's up to something. I doubt if he is in any way interested in rainfall on the river. Good work, Edward.'

'Thanks, Captain.'

'What have you got planned for today?'

'John found an Indian who speaks some English. He's invited us to visit his village. Be a good opportunity to see if we can acquire fresh fruit and vegetables. Not so sure about the meat, though. I think we'll stick to fish.'

♦

The next two weeks went fast, and it was a bit of a disappointment when the sound of twin outboard motors announced the return of Kaufmann with its attendant disruption.

'Successful trip, Doctor?' asked Larsen.

'Ja, very successful, Captain.'

'How long will you be on board for?'

'Just long enough to get fresh clothes and a good night's sleep, then we'll be off again. The Amazon is a very big river captain, full of all kinds of interesting sights to see and people to meet.'

31
At anchor

During their time at anchor Bill had made friends with some of the families in the local village and had arranged to have the *Leviathan* supplied with fresh produce, and much to Bill's delight, he'd become an unofficial uncle to the children of the Diaz family.

'Just what does he need us for?' asked Larsen as Kaufmann set off again on one of his trips. 'He is gone for three weeks at a time, returns for a couple of days then he's gone again. I tell you, Elijah, he is up to no good. I have trouble believing him when he says he keeps all the data on his laptop. Just glad I don't have to justify his expenses.'

'Talking of expenses,' said Elijah, 'since you have things under control here and it is so quiet, I thought now would be a good time to fly to the States and visit with my family. It's been six years since I have seen my grandparents. Stephen says he'd like to go with me; he's never been to the South.'

'Sounds fine,' said Larsen, 'I've got John, Marcel, and Edward to keep an eye on things while you're gone. How will you get to Manaus?'

'I'll get one of the local fishermen to take us down river.'

'Bit unusual, but I suppose it will work,' said Larsen. 'When do you plan on leaving?'

'Tomorrow, if we can get a lift.'

'OK, let Edward know and he'll advance you some of your pay. Let him know how much you need, there should be plenty of US dollars in the safe.'

Next morning, just as the sun was rising, there was a cautious knock on the side of the hull.

'Elijah, Stephen, I believe that's your taxi,' said Bill.

'I'll help with your bags,' said John.

Bill, Larsen, John, and Marcel stood on the deck and watched Elijah and Stephen as the small craft disappeared round the bend on the river.

Two days later, they required the services of the fisherman again. Larsen had woken with a stabbing pain in his right side.

'What do you think, John?' said Bill.

'With his symptoms: severe pain in the right side, vomiting, foul-smelling breath, elevated temperature – and the help of my medical dictionary, I would say it's a case of appendicitis. There's very little I can do for him on the boat. I am not trained to do surgery; all I can do for him is to give him painkillers and antibiotics.'

'Will that do?'

'No, he needs hospital treatment urgently, and probably surgery.'

'Right, I'll go see if I can round up a friendly fisherman,' said Marcel.

He returned five minutes later. 'The captain is very fortunate; Elijah must have paid handsomely for his ride down the river. They're out there now arguing whose boat is faster.'

Bill and Marcel watched John and Larsen go round the same bend in the river that Elijah and Stephen had taken two days before.

Bill found it strange being on the boat without Larsen. He'd been with him every day for months and now he had only Marcel to keep him company.

Bill went down the ladder and got busy in the galley. Feeling a presence on the other side of the counter, he turned. Marcel stood looking at him.

Bill asked, 'what would you like to eat for lunch?'

'How about elephant?'

'I'm sorry, we are completely out of elephant,' he said, wondering what Marcel was up to.

'Are you sure, there is one in the cabin right now.'

'Oh dear,' Bill thought, Marcel's gone mad and I am alone with him till Kaufmann returns.

'You're missing what I am getting at, Mr Bill Drysdale. I've been puzzling for months where I know you from, then it clicked when you pushed your hair back and I saw your scars.'

'Oh dear, and I thought I was doing so well. I suppose it doesn't matter now anyway. The Captain knows everything, including my phony identity; in fact, he helped me get my passport.'

'Relax Edward; I have no intention of telling anyone your real identity.'

'Good. What's a hairdresser doing on a charter yacht on the Amazon river?'

'Remember when we met in the hair salon, I told you I used to be in the Spanish Navy? I missed the sea and when this opportunity came up I said *why not*, that's all.'

'How is your mother, she was sick wasn't she? At least that's what you told Marcie.'

'Ah, Marcie.'

'Yes, Marcie. You do remember her, don't you? You gave everyone at the dance the impression that you two were an item. I suppose you've left her in the lurch wondering what's happened to you.'

'We have something in common then, don't we?'

Bill shrugged his shoulders and said, 'I suppose we do. Will you ever go back to her?'

'How about you? will you ever go back to your family?'

'No, too much water has passed under the bridge. Besides, I couldn't if I wanted to – they'd never take me back, I was just in their way.'

'Pity, your family seemed to be such nice people.'

'If you say so. So, Señor Galan, since we are destined to sail the seas together, tell me, what can the ship's cook make you for lunch?'

'How about a salad? I'm not really hungry.'

'Fine. Salad for two coming right up.'

'Going into the village this afternoon?' asked Marcel.

'Yes. I said I would sit with Mrs Diaz boys. She has a doctor's appointment this afternoon and won't be back before sunset.'

'Couldn't one of the other mothers have looked after the boys?'

'I suppose they could. But since I've become sort of one of the family, she asked me if I would sit. The boys call me their uncle Ed.'

'You shouldn't get too attached. The day will come when we say goodbye to all of this.'

A tear formed in Bill's eyes. 'I realise that. But till that day comes I'm going to continue to be Uncle Ed to my – my boys.'

'Are you all right?'

'Yes. I'm fine, just some old memories floating to the surface.'

'We all have our share of them.'

'What's yours?'

Marcel shook his head and said, 'someday – maybe. But in the mean time you've got your boys waiting for their Uncle Ed.'

'What have you got planned?'

'Some of the village fishermen have asked if they can fish off the *Leviathan*. Apparently we are floating directly over the best fishing hole in miles.'

As the days passed, they settled into a relaxed routine, Bill doing the cooking, cleaning, and visiting the village, while Marcel tended to the dock lines and did maintenance as needed while swapping stories with the village fishermen.

Late one afternoon, a week after John and Larsen had headed off down the river, Kaufmann returned to the *Leviathan* alone.

'Doctor, where's your team?' asked Bill.

'I could ask you the same question, what has happened to your shipmates?'

'Elijah and Stephen have gone to the US to visit Elijah's family. Should be back in a couple of weeks, and the Captain and John have gone to the hospital. Captain Larsen has suspected appendicitis.'

'Oh dear,' said Kaufmann, a smile growing on his face. 'I hope he gets well soon. I'm almost done with my work and am eager to return to England.'

'Where's your team, Doctor?' asked Marcel.

'Oh them, they are staying overnight at one of the villages. There's going to be a big all-day celebration tomorrow in our honour. I was coming back to the boat to invite everyone. It's only up the river a couple of miles. It'd be a new experience for you both, much livelier than the local villages you usually visit.'

'We couldn't go and not leave someone on the boat,' said Bill.

'No problem, I'll stay on board with a couple of my guides during the day. You've seen how competent they are with their own boats. I assure you; no harm will come to the *Leviathan*. You can stay in the village for the afternoon celebrations then return and I'll join my men for the evening. You won't be gone any longer than your usual trips into the local village.'

'What do you think, Marcel?' asked Bill.

'I suppose it won't harm us or the boat to be gone for a few hours. She's been tied up here all summer without incident and you say you will stay on board the entire time, Doctor?'

'Most certainly, Mr Galan, I will busy myself stowing all my samples.'

'What do you mean by samples, Doctor?' asked Bill.

'Why, all the native goods that I am taking back with me. Surely Captain Larsen told you I was setting up a European import business to sell the craft work of the river Indians?'

'The *Leviathan* is not a cargo boat, Doctor; it has limited space to store goods. Where do you propose to put them?' said Bill, remembering the trouble he had storing all the provisions he had purchased from Mr Patel.

'Oh, that's not going to be a problem – I had a look under my bunk, there's plenty of space there.'

'You have thought of everything, Doctor,' said Marcel.

'Of course, I have. My backers wouldn't put me in charge of this type of expedition if I wasn't capable.'

'How do you propose we get to this village, Doctor?' Marcel asked.

'No problem, I'll have Mr Martinez take you in the *Leviathan's* dinghy. He's due back this evening. I'm sure he won't mind returning to the village. I understand he has become quite friendly with one of the natives. When you've had an enjoyable afternoon with our river friends, he will bring you back.'

'I'm not sure. The *Leviathan* has never been without a crew member since we left and I wouldn't want to have something happen while we are gone,' said Bill.

'What could go wrong? As I've already said, my native friends are extremely competent at looking after boats on the river. And there will be at least five of us on board at all times. I can assure you nothing will go wrong with my plan, it's perfect.'

Later that evening, Bill lay in his bunk and tried to figure out why Kaufmann was so eager to get them off of the *Leviathan*. Nothing made any sense to him. One minute he treated them like his servants then all of a sudden was worried about their personal welfare and didn't want them to miss a party. Bill resolved to discuss it with Marcel in the morning.'

32
Prisoners

When he arose next morning, Bill found Martinez and Marcel in the main saloon waiting for him.

'Ready to go to the ball, Eddie baby?' said Martinez.

'No, I haven't had my coffee yet. And Mr Martinez, for the last time, I am not Eddie, or your baby, or any other thing. Do you understand?'

'Sure thing – Eddie baby.'

'Let it go, Martinez. Can't you see he hasn't had his coffee yet?' said Marcel.

'Yeah, *Edward*, drink your coffee then we can go to the *party*. Your *pumpkin* is waiting alongside.'

'If you gentlemen will back off, I'll go get my backpack. Mr Martinez, I suppose there will be food at this party?'

'Plenty, don't you worry about food, Brazilians know how to party.'

Marcel wrapped his camera in a spare tee-shirt and packed it in a small rucksack along with a couple of water bottles.

'Here, you'll need these, the sun is hot on the river,' Marcel said, handing Bill a wide-brimmed straw hat and sunglasses.

It took two hours to reach the small jetty and the trail leading into the jungle.

'Are we going in there?' said Bill, looking at the trail.

'Sure, we are. Worried about spiders and creepy crawlies, *Eddie baby*?' said Martinez.

'No, just wondered.'

'Just keep close and follow me, I'll get you there.'

Bill had imagined they would have to hack their way through the jungle with machetes but was relieved to see a well-worn track leading away from the river.

After they'd been walking for about twenty minutes, Martinez stopped and looked around.

'What's the matter?' asked Bill.

'I think someone is following us.'

'Is that unusual? Lots of people must walk on this track. It looks well-trodden,' said Marcel.

'We have been walking quite slowly and I would have expected whoever is following to have caught up with us by now. You two hide in there,' said Martinez pointing to an opening in the undergrowth. 'I'll walk back and take a look. It's probably just a wild animal, nothing to worry about, back in a moment.'

Bill looked at Marcel. Marcel gestured his finger to his lip and gave a slight shake of his head. 'Certainly Mr Martinez, I am sure you're correct. Probably just a wild animal foraging for food,' said Marcel. 'We'll just wait in here,' he said as Martinez crept slowly back down the track.

'Marcel, what's going on? Are we in danger?' asked Bill.

'Possibly. Let's wait here and see what happens. I don't trust him one bit.'

Martinez had gone about thirty yards when a shot rang out. He fell to the ground, groaning loudly.

'Is he hit?' said Bill.

'Not sure, wait here.'

'Not likely, I'm coming with you. I'm not staying here on my own.'

They got within twenty feet of Martinez when he pushed himself up on one elbow. 'Run, get away, they're illegal loggers, they will kill you if they catch you.'

'Sorry, can't leave you to die here in the jungle,' said Marcel.

They got another three paces when a fusillade of shots rang out and bullets ricocheted off the ground at Bill and Marcel's feet. Bill looked at Martinez; he appeared to have breathed his last.

'Quick,' said Marcel, 'we've got to get out of here.'

'Is he dead?'

'Can't tell, you heard the gunshots.'

They forced their way through the undergrowth till they came to a small clearing. Bill was the first to emerge. Marcel jumped in front of him and pushed Bill back into the undergrowth as one of the loggers fired his rifle.

Marcel collapsed face down on the ground. Bill didn't know what to do. A few seconds was all he had before two of the Indians burst into the undergrowth and grabbed him. Bill tried to fight them off but one of the Indians hit him hard on the head with the butt of his rifle.

◆

Bill came to in a hut with strangers standing over them. One bent down and picked up Marcel's rucksack. He rummaged through it, shook out the camera from the tee-shirt, and laughed at his prize. He threw the rucksack to the floor and they left, locking the door behind them.

Bill lay there for a few moments waiting for his head to clear and his eyes to be accustomed to the gloom. History was repeating itself; he was back in a prison cell. Not a freezing, damp, vaulted brick one like Zhukovski's, but a round hut made from cut-down trees, with no light or window, or even a battered bucket to pee in, a cell none the less. With what light there was he looked at the tear in his shirt and realised he had been shot in the arm.

He prodded gently and realised it was just a flesh wound. It would hurt for a while but shouldn't cause him any problems. It would leave a scar though – another one for the gallery.

Bill rolled over and looked at the bullet hole on Marcel's shirt. It looked bad. A large patch of wet blood darkened the shirt.

'How do you feel?'

'The bullet missed – my lung, I think,' he said, wincing and slowly exhaling. 'Thankfully it went through the strap buckle on my rucksack first.'

'How do you know it missed your lung?'

'There's no blood in my mouth – is there?'

Bill looked in Marcel's open mouth and shook his head.

'Good – I'll require surgery sooner than later – if we live long enough.'

'You really think they will kill us?'

'I'm sure of it. If they are illegal loggers – or worse, they won't want any witnesses to their presence.'

Bill crawled over to the door and found it firmly locked from the outside. He then worked his way around the inside of the hut; about three feet from the left side of the door he found a gap in the poles that made up the walls.

'What did you mean, *or worse*? What can be worse than illegally cutting down the rain forest, they're the lungs of the world?'

'It's nothing to do with the forest. These people aren't loggers. Do you see any chainsaws, trucks to haul logs, or even bonfires burning? I think logging is just a front for something more sinister. See or hear anything?'

'Not much. It appears that this hut, like the rest, is built on stilts. There's a campfire burning about twenty feet to the left. There's a bunch of Indians sitting round talking and laughing.'

'Do you recognise any of them?'

'No, why would I?'

'Just a hunch. Though I do wish I could hear what is being said,' said Marcel.

Bill turned his head, so his ear was to the gap in the wall.

'It doesn't make sense. One of them says something about them keeping us for ten days, and then we're to be lost in the jungle. They speak a different dialect here in the jungle, not sure if I heard correctly.'

'I didn't realise you spoke Portuguese.'

'The captain said to keep it a secret between us.'

'Wise man. Now, how are we going to get out of here? I'm afraid I am not much help with this bullet in my chest.'

'How about I hide behind the door and hit the guard on the head when he enters, then we jump down and run off into the forest? No – that only works in movies. I – I'm sorry, Marcel, my mind isn't working properly. Does it hurt much? And don't say, *only when I laugh*.'

'Relax Edward, I promise I won't laugh – though I could do with some of that stuff that John gave the Captain. I think the bullet has lodged between two of my ribs – and is tearing at the muscle tissue, oh shit – I think it's started bleeding again.'

Bill bent down and examined Marcel's shirt. 'This will sting a bit,' he said, carefully pulling Marcel's shirt away from the wound. 'No, you're all right, you're sweating, and it's tricking down your side. Need to keep the wound clean, can't let it get infected.'

As Bill dabbed away the dried blood with a clean corner of Marcel's shirt he noticed a small round grey object. 'I've found the bullet,' he said excitedly,' shall I try and get it out?'

'With what?'

Bill undid a button on one of the pockets of his shorts and pulled out a pair of tweezers. 'How about these, I use them to pull the bones from fish before cooking them.'

'You carry them with you?'

'Just a habit, they're small and easily lost.'

Bill reached into the other pocket and pulled out a small hip flask, Marcel look at him, puzzled.

'You can't trust the water around here,' Bill said smiling.

Marcel shook his head. 'You're – so resourceful.'

Bill pulled the discarded tee-shirt out of the rucksack and tore off a piece to make a cleaning rag. The rest he tore into strips.

'Lay still, I don't have much light.'

Bill went to pour some of the contents of the flask on to the rag but changed his mind and took a large swig. 'I needed that,' he said before pouring a liberal amount on to the wound and the tweezers.

It took a couple of tries to grab the small bullet but eventually he managed to remove it. He looked at it, then over to Marcel, who was sweating profusely.

'Sorry, did it hurt much?'

'Only when I laughed,' he said, grimacing.

'Sorry, first time at surgery, I'm doing brain surgery next week and needed the practice.'

'Anything left in that flask?'

'Sorry, I was being selfish. Here, let me help you.'

Bill poured a good slug into Marcel's mouth, making him cough. 'Careful, you'll start the wound bleeding again.'

'Thanks, I needed that,' he said, mimicking Bill.

'That's what I like to hear. Dead men don't laugh. Right, let's get you bandaged. I'll need you to sit up, if you can.'

Marcel rolled over on to his good side and using his forearm pushed himself up into a sitting position against the wall.

Bill finished surgery by binding a whiskey-soaked pad of tee-shirt to the wound. 'There, that should keep it clean till we get you to a doctor. Want another swig?'

He nodded yes; Bill handed him the flask.

'Hope he doesn't speak German,' said Marcel, wiping his mouth with the back of his hand.

'Oh, I've completely forgotten about Doctor Kaufmann. I wonder if he is out looking for us and Martinez,' Bill said, staring through gaps in the walls of the hut.

When Marcel didn't reply he went over to check if Marcel was all right. There was nothing to worry about, he had drifted off to sleep and was snoring softly.

Later that evening they were brought a meal of fish and rice with a plastic bottle of water to share.

'Why are we here?' asked Bill.

The Indian who had brought their food ignored him and left, locking the door behind him.

'At least we won't starve,' said Marcel. 'They must have a reason for keeping us alive; that at least gives us some hope.'

'What is this – stuff?'

'Don't ask, just eat it.'

'What did you mean by *hope*?'

'As long as we are locked up in here and not tied to a stake, we have a chance of escaping.'

'Good, I like that kind of news. Can we leave now?'

'Not yet, the taxi's not here.'

'Drat, and I thought we were off home.'

The shadows lengthened till the only light in the hut was from the campfire. As everyone drifted off to their huts for the night, Bill and Marcel were let out one at a time under escort to go to the toilet before they were locked up again for the night.

By the second day Bill decided it was time to do something constructive about their situation. Marcel was getting feverish; his temperature had risen, and he was floating in an out of consciousness.

Early in the evening of the second day, after they had been fed, Bill found a couple of broken and loose floorboards at the rear of the hut.

It appeared that something heavy had been dropped on the floor at some time and had cracked both the boards. An idea started to form in his head; he rummaged through a pile of discarded boxes and old nets in the shadows of the hut and found a bent fishing spear. Trying not to make more noise than was necessary he pushed the tip into the gap between the floorboards and pried them up. Breathing hard with excitement he found there was enough of a gap in the floor to lower himself to the ground.

'What are you doing?' Marcel asked, during a lucid moment.

'Sorry, I thought you were sleeping. I'm just doing a bit of reconnoitring. Don't worry; I'll be back in a minute.'

'Edward, be careful, this is not a game. These people will kill you given half a chance.'

Bill dropped down to the ground and found there was enough room to walk, while crouching, under the hut. He stopped at the front of the hut and hid in the shadows of the crude wooden steps.

The Indians were all seated round the campfire laughing and joking. Occasionally one of them would stand up, point at the hut, make a rude gesture, and laugh. Bill felt he knew who the butt of the joke was and didn't like the thought one bit, maybe it was time to get his hair cut. Only too well did he understand what was to be their fate; piranha food.

Bravado overcame him and he crept out from under the hut and made his way in the lengthening shadows around the camp to get closer to the fire. He took refuge behind a beaded curtain in a small lean-to that appeared to be used for the preparation of meals.

He was stunned. Sitting on the far side of the blazing fire, not fifteen feet from him, was Kaufmann.

His first reaction was to run out and say, 'Here we are,' but Marcel's caution made him push deeper into the shadows. He realised

Kaufmann did in fact only speak a little Portuguese and was talking through one of the river guides to the group. He appeared content, though quite drunk, swapping bawdy jokes with the others round the fire.

Bill wondered if it was safe to come out. After all, drunk though he might be, he was still the same arrogant Kaufmann he had come to know during the voyage.

Bill made his mind up. Marcel needed medical help and it was quite possible that Kaufmann didn't realise they were prisoners. He stepped out from behind the curtain into the shadows of the lean-to in time to see three figures emerge from the jungle on the far side of the clearing. The air of joviality round the campfire descended into a hushed silence.

Kaufmann turned to see what had attracted the attention of those seated opposite him. Bill climbed back into the darkness of the curtain.

Two of the newcomers were Indians, the third looked Hispanic. Kaufmann stood and shook hands with the Hispanic visitor. It appeared from their conversation that they hadn't met before.

Bill moved out from behind the curtain to get a better view and hear the conversation as another bottle was opened and passed around.

Kaufmann said, 'Well, Señor Plata, tell me, have you been successful in your quest?'

Plata roared with laughter and replied, 'Ah yes, Doctor, much success, but many problems yet to be sorted and there is the small matter of an angry husband, a local politico.' Taking a swig from the bottle, he went on, 'You know what, Doctor; married men shouldn't neglect their wives.'

'Ja, indeed I do,' he said. 'Shall we go somewhere we are not overheard and you can tell me what has happened? Maybe I can be of assistance.'

'Certainly Doctor. No need to burden our friends with information that would lay heavy on their minds.'

They got up and walked directly towards the lean-to where Bill was hiding. In a panic he stepped back into the darkness, unable to escape as Kaufmann and Plata approached.

'Well, Señor Plata, tell the good doctor what ails you,' said Kaufmann.

'I concluded my business a few days ago, but unfortunately there is still the issue of the local politician. So here I am on the run.'

'Bad luck, Señor, but I suppose to make an omelette one must break many eggs.'

'Yes, yes, that's it. Can I tell you something, Doctor? I believe we are men who think alike; I am sure we will get along well.'

'So it wasn't an angry husband, my friend?' said Kaufmann.

'Well, not really, it was a business deal that went spectacularly good for me, much profit for my cause. My competitor, on the other hand will probably go bankrupt and be extremely upset when he realises what has happened. As for my men, they can slip into the forest and never be troubled. Me, I have a restaurant, a wife and many children to look after. I must make great haste and get back home.'

'You're a drug runner?' asked Kaufmann, looking worried.

'Certainly not, I never touch the stuff,' said Plata.

'Then it's gold. I'll bet you've discovered a treasure trove of some ancient Inca king?' laughed Kaufmann.

Bill watched as Plata's face became very serious.

'Doctor, it is good that we are friends and we talk where no one hears us. Let us keep this conversation to ourselves; otherwise this information could be very unhealthy for you. Do you understand?'

'Ja, ja, it was just a bit of German humour, that's all. I'll forget what I said.'

'Good, I am glad to hear that. Now, as you have partially guessed, during my travels I do sometimes come across gold in the form of coins, jewellery and artefacts as well as other items of value. For a fee, to cover my expenses, I pass them on to those who have the ability to appreciate what I find. Doctor, what I do must remain a secret, many lives depend on it.'

'I assure you Señor Plata, my lips are sealed.'

'Good, now you understand my reticence in using commercial transport.'

'What will you do?'

'I will get one of the Indians to take me down river to Manaus. I hope to get a berth there on one of the freighters that ply the coastal routes and have them drop me off at a suitable place.'

'Where would the suitable place be?'

'Playa San Carlos, it's on the northern coast of Venezuela, just past Caracas.'

'Suppose I said I could get you there – for a suitable fee?'

'You've a ship?'

'It's not exactly mine. I have chartered a fine ocean yacht and since my work is almost complete, I plan to sail in the next couple of days. It should be a simple job to sail up the coast and drop you off before we head across the Atlantic.'

'And what would this journey cost me? I don't have a lot of cash, although I hear it is sometimes acceptable to work one's passage.'

'Can you cook?'

'Yes, as a matter of fact I can.' Plata said laughing at a private joke. 'Why would you ask that?'

'We seem to have lost our cook. In fact the whole crew is missing, one-way or another.'

'What happened to them?'

'Two went off to the USA, two to the hospital, and the other two went missing in the jungle. My team have looked for them, but unfortunately we must presume them dead.'

'So sad, and you have claimed salvage on the boat and now you require a crew to sail it for you?'

'Yes and no; I made provision for crew on the way over the Atlantic. I have a standby crew all ready and waiting.

'I like the way you think, Doctor. Suppose I were to pay you in silver?'

Kaufmann's jaw dropped. 'Ja, ja, that would be most suitable.'

Kaufmann you greedy rat, thought Bill.

Plata shook his head. 'Don't get too excited, Doctor, it's only a few pieces of eight.'

'Pirate treasure!' exclaimed Kaufmann.

'I doubt it, Doctor, probably just leftovers from when the Spanish were here; it was quite a common currency. In fact, in the fifteenth century it could be found as far away as Ireland.'

Bill thought Plata's reply was lost on Kaufmann; his mind wandering in a dream of untold riches, the graveyard for many a weak mind.

'When can I board?' asked Plata.

'Join us tomorrow. We can return together.'

'I need to collect something first. Can you wait two days? I can join you then?'

'Ja, two days' time it is. Any of these Indians can take you down the river to the boat; they know where it's anchored.'

'Will you go back this evening, Doctor?'

'No, I don't like being on the river after sunset. Besides, the evening's entertainment hasn't started yet; I'll go back in the morning with my crew. They'll be joining us later this evening. They are currently busy. In the meantime, shall we re-join the party?'

Bill waited till they were seated by the fire before he came out of hiding and made his way back to the hut and Marcel.

Bill found the opening in the floor and saw that Marcel had been enlarging it.

'Where have you been? I was starting to worry you weren't coming back.'

'We don't have time for that. Marcel, we have to get back to the *Leviathan*, the doctor plans to sail off and leave us behind.'

'Slow down. Catch your breath and tell me what you have found out?'

Bill told Marcel about the conversation between Kaufmann and Plata.

'Are you sure the doctor called the other person Plata?'

'Yes, of course I'm sure, I was as close to them as you are to me. Why does that matter? Are you all right? You're sweating heavily.'

'Just a bit of a fever, I'll be all right, but quick, you're right, we've got no time to lose.'

'Just a bit of a fever? Marcel, you are dripping with sweat.'

'It'll have to wait. Here, help me loosen this board.'

Working feverishly, they managed to get a third floorboard loose. Bill watched as Marcel pushed his way through head-first and onto the ground.

'Are you sure you can manage this?'

'What choice do we have? I'm sorry, but you'll have to help me walk. My legs are a bit weak.'

Without drawing attention to themselves, they managed to work their way around the camp and back to the track to the river. Having to make their way through the bush at the side of the path made the trip more difficult, but it was just as well for as they got close to the river, they could hear raised voices coming their way. They crouched down behind a large bush as Davis and Jones went past.

'I wonder where Edwards and Martinez are?' said Bill.

'Probably stayed on the boat,' said Marcel.

'Stay here in the bush. I'll go see if there are any more surprises waiting for us,' said Bill.

'Be careful,' said Marcel. 'I need to rest anyway.'

Crouching down, Bill made his way through the undergrowth and arrived at the river's edge in time to see Martinez and Edwards arguing about something. Bill crept closer till he could make out what was being said.

'That's all you get. Take it or leave it, it's your choice,' said Martinez.

Bill wasn't able to hear Edwards' reply, but the hand gesture left nothing to the imagination.

What happened next stunned Bill. Martinez took a knife from his pocket and threatened Edwards who, in return, pulled a machete from his belt and took a swing at Martinez. As the heavy blade swung harmlessly past Martinez's head, he struck home and buried the knife in Edwards' side. Edwards gave a grunt and fell sideways to the ground and lay still. Martinez bent down, put his foot on Edwards' chest and pulled the knife from the dead body, wiping the blade clean on Edwards' shirt. Bill watched in horror as Martinez rolled the body into the river, laughed, and returned the rude gesture to the disappearing body.

This was too much to think about. What was important was that they got back to the *Leviathan*. Marcel's wound needed treating and Kaufmann's plan had to be thwarted. Getting to the *Leviathan* would solve both these problems.

Bill made his way back to Marcel and whispered to him what he had just witnessed. It was just as well that they were still off the track and in the undergrowth as Martinez passed ten feet from them.

'I wonder where's he off to?' said Bill.

'The Indians' camp,' said Marcel. 'Come on, get me to the dinghy and back to the *Leviathan* before I pass out.'

Bill was glad it was such a short distance. Marcel was becoming delirious again and had started to sing quietly in Spanish.

Bill untied the dinghy from the small jetty and using the oars to steer, let the current take them down river. Thankfully the sun hadn't set completely, and he was able to make out the silhouette of the *Leviathan*.

All the way down the river he wondered how he would deal with any Indians left on board. He was both relieved and angered to find the boat empty. Now it was just the task of getting Marcel on board. With Marcel's help Bill managed to get him below and on to the settee.

'This may hurt,' he said dribbling hydrogen peroxide on to Marcel's wound. Next, he dabbed it dry then dressed it. Bill covered Marcel with a blanket and watched him drift off to sleep.

In the shower Bill discovered how bad his own wound was. There was an ugly red weal on his arm, about four inches long, which had now started to weep.

Marcel was still sleeping, and when Bill checked his temperature, he sighed with relief to see it had dropped a degree. Marcel was on the mend, but what to do next? At least he would have the night to think things through.

Bill made a large mug of hot chocolate, grabbed a blanket from his cabin and made himself comfortable on the settee opposite Marcel. Within minutes, he was fast asleep.

33
Dr Drysdale

Bill woke to the smell of fresh coffee. Opening his eyes, he was surprised to see John in the galley.

'Hungry?' John asked.

'I could do with a cup of coffee. When did you get back? Where's the captain?'

'One cup of coffee coming right up, early this morning and the captain's fine, he's asleep in the chart room. I'll wake him in a minute.'

Bill sat up and looked across to the settee. 'Where's Marcel?'

'Relax, he's having a shower. I checked his wound and re-bandaged it; nice piece of surgery you did. Want to take over being doctor?'

'Definitely not. I've had enough surgery to last a lifetime.'

'Marcel said you were shot as well. How are you?'

'The arm is fine. I've had worse sunburn.'

'Let's have a look; you can't be too careful.'

While John was dressing Bill's arm, Larsen came out of the chart room.

'Morning, Captain,' said Bill.

'Morning Edward, boy, that looks nasty. Does it hurt much?'

He thought of saying, *only when I laugh*, but just said, 'I've had worse sunburn.'

Larsen said, 'Are you up to making us breakfast, Edward?'

'*Oui, mon capitaine.*'

'What's got into him?' Larsen said to Marcel as Bill wandered off to the galley.

'I think he's happy you're back. He's really had a hard time these last few days. You'll find out just how bad when he updates you.'

'Oh, good, I'm looking forward to that – I think.'

Bill made them scrambled eggs and joined them at the table.

'I'll go first,' said Larsen. 'Thanks to John, I made it to hospital in time to have my appendix removed, excellent care from the staff and as you can see I've made a complete recovery and am now ready to get back to sea. John?'

'Well as the captain has just said we got to the hospital in time for surgery – any longer and no captain. While the captain was in the theatre I called Elijah's family and left a message for Elijah to call me. It was late the next day when he did. I brought him up to date on the captain's health and told him all was well. Elijah said they were going to head back in a couple of days but as it would take at least five days to get to Manaus he said they would call us on the sat phone to see if we had left for Macapa before coming up the river. If we had, they would fly to Macapa and meet us there.'

'Edward, your turn,' said Larsen.

He told his story, starting from the moment that Larsen and John left, up till he woke to find John in the galley.

'Marcel, do you have anything to add?' asked Larsen.

'No, I think Edward covered everything; remember I was delirious for most of the time, so my memories are rather confused.'

'What about this chap Plata? I wonder who he is?' mused Larsen.

'If he is who I think he is, then he is a bit of a folk hero,' said Marcel. 'Several years ago, when I was still in the Spanish Navy, I got posted to our Embassy in Caracas. Part of my job was to keep my ear to the ground, read the papers and send reports on what was happening in the country back to our Foreign Office. The name of Plata appeared quite often in the underground papers. He was seen as a bit of a Robin Hood figure, altruistic to the extreme, supports local charities. He has a reputation of being a treasure hunter. He owns a restaurant in the city of Playa San Carlos, the poorer you were the cheaper the bill at the end of the meal.'

'What about drugs?' said Larsen.

'No, the one thing he would never touch was drugs; that's one reason he was so loved by the people.'

'Sounds like quite a character, I look forward to meeting him – I think,' said Larsen.

'A trip to Venezuela was not on the itinerary, was it, Captain?' said John.

'No, but Kaufmann will probably argue that the charter is time-specific not location-specific. So, a visit to Venezuela could be, by his definition, part of the itinerary, especially if he thinks there's a profit to be made.'

'What about hurricanes? Going into the Caribbean will put us in line for any late ones that pass,' said John.

'I'll check the weather projections in a minute. Of course this is all based on Kaufmann being ready to leave and this chap Plata still requiring a passage to Venezuela,' said Larsen.

'What about Edwards?' asked Bill.

'Hmm, good question. I am not sure what the law is on this situation. What you saw Edward, could have been an act of self-defence. If it happened on board or while at sea, I could deal with it, but since it happened ashore in another country I believe it is out of my hands.'

'The way I see things,' said Marcel, 'I think we should keep what we know to ourselves and wait and see what Kaufmann has to say when he comes back on board.'

'Fine by me,' said Larsen. 'Right, shall we get ready for our visitors and more importantly, get ready to leave the jungle and go back to the sea, where we belong?'

Kaufman arrived by river launch mid-afternoon and was obviously shocked to see Bill in the galley.

'What are you doing here?' he blustered.

'Preparing the evening meal, where else should I be?' said Bill, cocking his head and shrugging his shoulders.

'I thought – I mean, you have been absent for several days. We have searched everywhere for you, and Mr Galan, is he here?'

'Mr Galan is fine. He is resting in his bunk. He was shot in the chest by the same Indians that shot Mr Martinez. They imprisoned us in a hut for two days. We managed to escape last night while they were enjoying themselves and make our way back to the boat. I doubt if we could ever find their camp again.'

'Could you identify any of them?' asked a worried-looking Kaufmann.

'No, we were unconscious when they took us into the jungle, and it was dark last night when we escaped. It was luck that we managed to find the river and the dinghy and make our way back to the boat.'

'How terrible it must have been for you both,' said Kaufmann, visibly relieved. 'We've been gravely worried.'

'We?' said Bill.

'Ah,' said Kaufmann, 'Mr Martinez was very lucky, he pretended to be dead and when the Indians went off to find you, he managed to escape.'

'Good afternoon, Doctor,' said Larsen coming out of the chart room. 'Who are the "we", you refer to, Doctor?'

'The chiefs of the local tribes, Captain, they were very helpful in the search.'

'Pity you were unsuccessful in your search for my crew, Doctor. Where are your men now? Still out searching?'

'Ah – yes, we are also looking for one of our own men, Captain. Mr Edwards is missing. Apparently, he and Mr Martinez were coming down the river in the dark; the launch hit a submerged log causing it to tip poor Mr Edwards overboard. I fear he is gone. Our Indian friends say he has probably been eaten by the piranha.'

'Sharp teeth, those piranha. Strip a man to the bone in minutes,' said Larsen. 'I'll enter the details in the log.'

Bill shivered at the thought and continued with the preparation of the evening meal.

'Will they be back before sunset, Doctor?' said Larsen.

'Ja, the Indians say it is futile to search any longer and a waste of time in the dark. I fear Mr Edwards will be staying when we leave.'

'And when will that be, Doctor?'

'Er – I think I should be ready tomorrow; yes, that should be enough time.'

'Enough time for what, Doctor?'

'Oh, for instance, my team will need time to get ready for the trip and you know how good at sea they are. I will need time to get all my records stored away and, er, Captain, something I need to discuss with you. While we were working in the jungle I met an explorer from Venezuela and I thought since we would be going up the coast on the way home it would be a simple matter to make a slight detour and drop him off at his home port.'

'And where would his home port be, Doctor?'

'I can't give you an exact latitude and longitude, but it's called Playa San Carlos, just along the coast from Caracas.'

'Doctor, are you aware of what time of the year it is?'

'Ja, of course I am, it's early spring here and in England summer has just passed.'

'That's not what I am referring too. It obviously has passed your mind that we are still in hurricane season. If we make this little detour for your friend, it will take us straight into the path of any hurricane that decides to come roaring by.'

'Then, Captain, you'll just have to steer a course and avoid any that come our way. And may I remind you once again, that you, your crew, and this boat are at my disposal? I'm paying for this charter and you'll go where I say. Señor Plata will be joining us tomorrow morning and we leave the moment he is on board. Is that understood?'

'*Jawohl, mein Herr.*'

'There's no need for sarcasm, Captain, just follow my orders and keep us out of storms.'

Kaufmann sniffed the air as though a nasty smell had just pervaded the atmosphere and walked off to his cabin.

'I'd love to tie him to. '

'To the bowsprit in a North Atlantic gale,' interrupted Bill. 'Don't let him rile you, Captain; he's just a self-opinionated prat.'

'You're right, he is a prat. I'll be in the chart room if needed.'

Kaufmann's team, minus Edwards, arrived just before dinner. Martinez was the last on board.

'Mr Martinez,' said Bill, 'we thought you had been killed.'

'I was just lucky. I figured you two had been captured so I returned to the boat to get help. We've been looking for you both for days but we've been unsuccessful.'

You lying pig, thought Bill.

'Never mind, we are both fine,' Bill replied. 'Dinner will be early this evening; the doctor informs us we will be leaving early tomorrow and I have a lot to get ready before we depart.'

'Whatever you say, Eddie baby.'

'Mr Martinez, I am not now, nor ever will be, your Eddie baby. Now piss off, I've got work to do.'

'*Oh*, listen to him.'

'Hugo, leave him alone, he has a lot to do and I want my dinner,' said Kaufmann.

Martinez shrugged and went off to his cabin. As he passed, Kaufmann said, 'Hugo, since Mr Edwards is no longer with us, I have arranged for a friend of mine to share your cabin with you; it will only be for a few days.'

'Where we taking him to?' asked Martinez.

'Just along the coast from Caracas, isn't that right, Captain?' said Kaufmann.

'Yes, that's correct, should take us about ten to fifteen days, depending on the winds and weather. And supposing we don't encounter any hurricanes.' replied Larsen.

♦

Plata joined them mid-morning, complete with enough baggage to make the average tourist wilt.

'Been on a safari, Señor Plata?' asked Larsen.

'One has to be prepared for all eventualities, Captain, especially when one travels alone.'

'So it seems. If you follow Edward, he will show you to your cabin.'

34
John Plata

'Good to have you back,' said Larsen, helping Stephen and Elijah on board with their cases. 'Sorry to have cut your trip short, Elijah.'

'Not a problem, I'll catch up with them this winter; that is if we don't have any charters scheduled.'

'Nothing planned. I was thinking of wintering in Poole and taking the *Leviathan* back to Bob's yard to prepare for next season's charters.'

'Have you two had dinner?' asked Bill.

'Sort of,' said Stephen, 'we ate at the airport while we waited for the taxi. Could do with a coffee if there's some; where's Kaufmann's team?'

'They went ashore. Kaufmann's in the main saloon writing his report,' replied Larsen as he followed Bill below.

'How long till dinner, Edward?' asked Kaufmann.

'Ready for six,'

'Excellent, should have completed writing my report by then.'

'Must be quite a report, doctor,' said Larsen, 'You've been at it since we left the anchorage.'

'Must get it right, captain, there's a lot to tell. Besides I'm sure you've noticed how good a sailor I am, can you see me sitting and typing my report while the boat is bouncing all over the place?'

'No doctor I can't, and of course, you must be able to justify your expenses?'

'Yes, there is that. And then there is the matter of poor Mr Edwards. I suppose his family will need to be told, I seem to remember him saying something about children.'

'Ah yes, the matter of Mr Edwards disappearance, I've mentioned his demise in the ships log.'

'Thank you, Captain,'

'Who's going to read your report, doctor?' asked Bill.

Kaufmann smiled and said, 'in all probability very few will. Most will read the introduction then flip through the pages to the conclusion.'

'Then why spend so much time writing it?' asked Larsen.

'You said it yourself, Captain. Need to justify the expenses. Now, if you'll excuse me, I need to get ready for going out to sea.'

'Elijah – coffee?' asked Bill.

'Coffee's fine, but why are we going into the Caribbean, we're still in hurricane season?'

Larsen came out of the chart room with a copy of the *Atlantic Pilot*. 'Our friend here, the doctor, has brought a friend with him and we are to drop him off in Venezuela before we head home. He's bunking down in Martinez's cabin.'

'Where's Edwards?' asked Elijah.

'Good question,' said Larsen. 'According to the doctor, while Edwards and Martinez were coming down the river, they apparently hit a submerged log. Edwards fell overboard, never to be seen again.

'Piranhas probably had him for dinner,' said Elijah, as Larsen whispered what had really happened. 'So, who is our mystery guest?'

'Señor Plata, according to the doctor, is a Venezuelan explorer who needs to get home. Apparently, he is afraid of flying, hence the boat ride. First thing in the morning, Elijah and Stephen, the awning needs to come down. Edward, can you and Marcel go ashore and get what provisions you need for the voyage? I don't plan on stopping before we get to Bermuda and John, will you arrange for the necessary fuel and water?'

'We're not stopping in Venezuela?' said Stephen.

'No, we have no papers or reason to stop there. Señor Plata will be met by friends who will ferry him ashore.'

'Bit clandestine, isn't it?' asked John.

'Needs must, we don't have time to get involved in domestic politics. Remember, he's not listed on the passenger or crew manifest. It would cause too many questions if we docked,' said Larsen, as Martinez, Davis, and Jones clambered down the companionway ladder.

'You're back! I thought.'

'I very much doubt it. You thought you would just sail off and leave us behind Mr Martinez, is that it?' interrupted Elijah. 'Sorry to spoil your party, but we live here.'

Elijah grinned at Martinez then climbed the companionway steps and went forward to his cabin.

Martinez thumped the galley counter with his fist and headed for his cabin.

'It's nice to see her ready to go to sea again,' said Bill to Marcel, 'especially after these last few months tied up in the jungle.'

'Yes, and it is good to be heading home at last, albeit via a slight detour.'

◆

The faint aroma of diesel exhaust drifted in through the open port. It has begun thought Bill. We're on our way home.

The *Leviathan* headed out into the Atlantic and northwards to the channel between Tobago and Trinidad.

All through the summer on the Amazon, Bill had wondered what he would feel when this moment arrived. Now it was here he felt nothing: no panic, no fear, just emptiness. For a moment he thought of jumping ship, saying to Larsen he wanted to stay and make a new life for himself here in Brazil, but he had no visa and very little money to start again. Bermuda, on the other hand, had loads of hotels and restaurants where he could get a job. He would settle down to a new life and then of course he had several months of back pay coming his way, that would help. So, he did have money and *could* start a new life for himself. He finally had a future to look forward to.

Within minutes of leaving the river mouth, Kaufmann and his team took to their bunks.

'They're not very good sailors, are they, Captain?' said Plata, coming on deck on the third evening at sea.

'No, they certainly aren't, but that's their problem and of course it keeps them out from under my feet. Edward, on the other hand, has the most work keeping them fed. I told him to let them fend for themselves, but he seems to have some hidden motive. I just let him get on with it.'

They were interrupted by Stephen coming into the cockpit.

'Evening, Stephen. How's the weather report for the Caribbean?'

'Still clear, no hurricanes forecast. There is a report on the NOAA website about a tropical depression off of the African coast, though.'

'Let's hope it stays there. Where's Edward, Stephen? I could do with a cup.'

'I'll ask him to make you a fresh one. He's still up, says he has a lot to do, not sure what he's on about.'

'Señor Plata, would you like coffee?' enquired Larsen.

'Could I have hot chocolate?' said John, from the wheel.

'I'll have coffee,' said Plata, 'and, Captain, my friends call me John. Señor makes me sound like some Spanish nobleman, which I can assure you I am not.'

'Two Johns on a boat at sea – sounds like the start of a joke,' said Stephen, laughing.

'And tell me, John, what exactly are you then?' asked Larsen.

'Good question, Captain. To the world I am just a poor Venezuelan businessman trying to make my way through life without creating too many waves. I share the ownership of a small restaurant with my wife and do a bit of travelling.'

'Your coffee, gentlemen,' said Bill, placing two mugs of coffee on the table before passing John his hot chocolate.

'Is it true you have a sliding scale of charges for meals in your restaurant?'

'Ah, my reputation travels. Yes, it is true.'

'Isn't that bad for business? Don't the wealthy stay away?'

'No, Captain, they brag about how much they were charged. It's pure snobbery. I love it, and so do my children.'

'Your children? Do you mean the ones in the orphanage?'

'You've been doing your homework, Captain. Yes, I support an orphanage for those left behind by drugs and AIDS.'

'I heard it from Marcel.'

'Ah, the good Señor Galan, we have talked a little since I boarded. I think we understand each other.'

'Tell me how you got involved in the orphanage.'

'When I was nineteen, my younger brother died from a drug overdose. My father went after the dealer and beat him to death. The gang took revenge and burnt our house down, with my parents and little sister tied up inside. I vowed revenge. Not by violence but by rescuing as many children from the web of drugs as I could.'

'And how do you manage that, you being on your own?' asked Larsen.

'I'll tell you a story, Captain. Due to the destructive power of the drug trade, I have made many friends in many countries.'

'Isn't that dangerous for them?'

'Ask my friend Alejandro. He lost two sons. He has nothing else to lose and Brigit, she lost a daughter, and of course Father Morales, he is constantly fighting a private war to keep his pupils from being sucked into the sordid world of drugs and prostitution. These are just examples, Captain, I could tell you about hundreds of cases just like them.'

'Isn't what you are trying to do futile?'

'Captain, a wise man once said, all that is necessary for evil to triumph is for one good man to do nothing. Just think Captain, one man, not ten, not an army, just one man standing up to evil. That's what I do; to do anything else would be anathema to me.'

'John, all I can say is the world needs more like you.'

'Thank you, Captain.'

'So, what have you been up to that you have to avail yourself of our transportation?'

'I was in the interior on business and had the opportunity to take advantage of a spectacular business deal. I was able to pull it off, but unfortunately my competition will not be happy when they find out what has happened.'

'Well, you can't win them all,' said Larsen.

'Maybe, maybe not,' said Plata. 'Captain, the real reason I can't fly home from Brazil is that aeroplanes sometimes crash.'

'Are you saying that they would kill a whole aeroplane load of passengers to just get you?'

'Si, that is the way they work.'

'And I thought I had a difficult life with the Kaufmann.'

'Ah yes, the good doctor. Captain, he is bad news; watch your back with him. He is what I think you English say as slippery as an eel.'

'Well put. But I can assure you, John, we have his measure.'

♦

'*Sea of sunshine and adventures, full of stories about pirates and pieces of eigh*t, *say the holiday brochures.*' said John, in his best Robert Newton accent.

'Not if you have to get up at five in the morning to prepare breakfast for you lot it's not,' said Bill.

'We'll be in the Caribbean later today and then you'll see how nice it is. We'll be running with the currents and the trade winds, perfect weather to run downwind.'

Bill was in the galley cleaning up after dinner when he felt the motion of the boat change. So much for running downwind, it was more like the beat out into the English Channel when they'd left Falmouth at the start of the voyage.

'It's going to be a long night, Edward,' said Larsen, as he headed for the chart room. 'Better get the kettle on.'

'What's up? Why's the motion so rough? John said we'd be running downwind with the trades.'

'There's a storm developing out in the Atlantic. I'm just going to check how it's doing,' said Stephen coming out of the chart room. 'That depression we were watching, it's turned into a fully-fledged hurricane. It's on the move at about fourteen knots; looks like it will track between St Lucia and Jamaica about noon tomorrow.'

'What's its name?' queried Bill.

'Werner.'

Larsen burst out laughing, shook his head and said, 'Typical, typical, that's Kaufmann's first name.'

'Sounds like, *wiener*,' laughed Stephen.

Bill shook his head and went back to filling the Thermoses with soup.

'Do they say what course it's expected to follow?' asked Larsen.

'The latest projection is for it to travel somewhere north of Barbados then curve in a north-westerly direction.'

'How soon till we get to Plata's drop-off area?'

'About ten this evening, if the wind stays as it is.'

'If Werner is still out in the Atlantic, we should have time to get to the drop-off before things get really bad,' said Larsen. 'Let's keep a continuous watch on it. Don't want to get caught with our pants down. I suggest you all get as much sleep as you can before we reach Caracas, because you're not going to get much when we turn and head east.'

'Elijah, where are we?' said Kaufmann. 'Can't we go ashore soon? This constant motion is not good for me. I can't think.'

'Just off the coast of Venezuela, Doctor. That glow in the distance is Caracas. We'll be dropping Señor Plata off soon, then Bermuda's the next stop. Should be there the middle of next week.'

'Next week? I can't possibly wait that long; I'm going to be sick. This is too much.' Kaufmann pushed past Larsen as he came on deck.

'Anything to report, Elijah?' asked Larsen.

'The sea feels different and the wind is now coming at us from ahead.'

'Right, I think we need to get prepared for some rough weather, set the auto pilot and follow me below; we need to be prepared for the worst.

Edward, we need coffee, and Stephen, can you get John and Marcel here?' said Larsen.

'First thing, Stephen,' said Larsen when everyone was seated at the saloon table. 'What's the latest on the weather system?'

'Bad news I'm afraid: it's now a category five hurricane with winds of up to one hundred and twenty miles an hour and still moving west at an average of fourteen knots.'

'Just what I was afraid might happen. Let's look at the chart and see what options we have,' said Larsen.

The main saloon table was cleared, and the chart of the Caribbean Sea laid out on it.

'Right everyone, this is where we are,' said Larsen, marking the chart with a soft pencil, 'and this is where we will be dropping Señor Plata.

This timeline,' he said, drawing a curved line across the chart, 'is where the hurricane is expected to track. We can't go into any of the harbours around here. Señor Plata's presence would create too many unanswerable questions and I certainly don't fancy having the *Leviathan* impounded. As far as I can see our only option is to come about and head east till the worst of the hurricane has passed us by.' He drew another line on the chart. 'Then we'll head north towards—well, let's just see where we end up.'

'Out into the Atlantic?' said John.

'Let's hope not; we'll end up backtracking too much if we do. Initially, the wind will come at us off of the port quarter as we track east. It will still be on our port quarter as we round to the north, then as the hurricane moves further away the wind will come round to our starboard quarter and eventually the trades should return.'

'Storm sails?' asked Elijah.

'Not at the beginning,' replied Larsen, 'we'll start with a full reef in the main and inner staysail, but I imagine we'll end up with bare poles and towing warps to control the speed, at least till the sea moderates. None of you, as far as I know, have ever experienced what we are going to face during the next twenty-four to forty-eight hours. It will be extremely noisy, and violent movement will be the norm. Parts of the *Leviathan* that have never leaked will drip with water, every surface will be either damp or wet, so make sure you have one hand for yourself and one for the boat.'

'What about Kaufmann and his team?' asked Bill.

'Let sleeping dogs lie. They'll know soon enough when it gets rough,' said Larsen. 'They're better off in their cabins, out from under our feet anyway.'

'Watch keeping, Captain?' said Stephen.

'I want two of you on watch at all times, one steering and one watching. I don't mind how you share your time at the helm. The relief pair can sleep, if that's possible, down below here in the main saloon. I don't want you to be forward in your own cabins, I want that hatch completely watertight. John, make sure the bilge pumps are ready and open the cockpit storm drains. As we'll probably be running down the wave fronts, the worst thing I envisage will be we get knocked sideways and broach, that could lead to us being rolled and dismasted. Or of course, as an alternative, we could surf down a wave and get pitch-poled at the bottom. I'm not trying to scare anyone, just want you all to be prepared for the worst.

'I'll make sure the cable cutters are ready,' said Elijah, 'just in case we have to cut any damaged rigging loose.'

'Stephen, Marcel, rig the lifeline jackstays and get the warps out of the locker,' said Larsen.

'I'll set them up on the stern and while we're at it we'll rig the running backstays, 'said Stephen. 'When we go to bare poles they'll come in handy for steadying the masts.'

'One very important point,' said Larsen, 'would all of you please remember to keep the main hatch closed – unless of course you are going in or out. It's surprising just how much water can get below if it's left open. We'll be running down some pretty big waves and, should one of them break over the transom, it won't only be the cockpit that fills with water. Edward, the galley is your responsibility. It looks ready; do you have any of that soup left?'

'Yes, I've still got chicken and beef in the freezer; I'll heat them up and put them in the Thermoses. I made some fresh bread this morning, so feeding you all shouldn't be a problem.'

'Good, just make sure you put everything away when you are done – hopefully we won't have to deal with flying sinks.'

Bill looked at Larsen.

'Don't ask; if you don't know, it won't scare you,' he said.

Bill thought for a moment then returned to extracting the frozen soups from the freezer.

'No-one will go on deck,' continued Larsen, 'without foul weather gear or their lifejackets and harnesses. In fact, keep them on at all times; you will sleep, eat, and pee in them till we are through the storm. If you go on deck make sure you are clipped to the life line jackstay before you exit the cabin. It's unlikely you will be able to get any sleep but if you need to nod off for a few minutes make sure you are securely wedged into a corner or tied to something substantial. Right, you all know what to do, let's get busy; I'm going on deck to check if we can see Señor Plata's transport.'

It was a coal-black night; the city lights of Caracas reflected off the low scudding clouds that now obscured the stars and moon. The sea looked black and deserted except for the white wave crests reflecting in the glare of the cabin lights, a good night for a bad storm, thought Larsen.

The bustle and noise of the engine starting brought Plata and Kaufmann on deck.

'Is all this for me, Captain?' asked Plata.

'No, John, there is a hurricane on its way and we need to prepare for some rough weather. We will be at your rendezvous point in about half an hour.'

'A hurricane, you say. I hope you are a good seaman, Captain, and your vessel is strong. The last time we had a hurricane through here it caused devastation.'

'I am sure we will be fine. Just got to make sure we're ready. Talking about being ready, are you?'

'Yes, I'll just bring up my bags.'

'Why can't we just go into harbour till it's passed?' whined Kaufmann. 'Then we could drop Señor Plata off at the jetty.'

'We don't have visas or paperwork to enter Venezuela,' said Larsen.

Plata reappeared with his bags, assisted by Bill and Marcel.

'Can't see your transport yet, John. Are you sure this is where you agreed to meet?' asked Larsen.

'Don't worry, Captain. My friends are well used to rendezvousing at sea in the dark. You'll know when they are here.'

A few minutes later the growl of twin v12 engines, minus navigation lights, announced the arrival of Plata's ride. It rounded on to the lee side and made way alongside in time with the *Leviathan*.

'See, I told you they would be here, Captain,' said Plata, throwing his bags over before following on board. With a cheery wave they were gone, chased by their own rooster tail.

'But – but my money,' moaned Kaufmann, his protestations lost in the growl of the rapidly disappearing fast-boat.

'Relax, Doctor. It's gone to a good cause.'

'What do you mean?'

'Señor Plata promised he will give the money to charity.'

Kaufmann stood for a few minutes staring into the night, then, realising he was out on deck wearing only a shirt and shorts, turned green and headed for the leeward rail. Larsen grabbed his shirt in time to prevent him from falling overboard.

'Steady on, Doctor, maybe you should go below. There's some very nasty weather coming this way.'

Wiping the vomit from his face with his sleeve, Kaufmann nodded. 'Yes, you're right, I need to go and lie down. All this stress is making me ill.'

'Captain, there's something we need to show you—in the chart room,' said Stephen.

'Lead the way, I'm right behind you.'

♦

'Well, what's got you excited, John?' Larsen queried.

'I got quite good at looking at the radar screen when I was in the Navy, so as we were drifting, waiting for Plata's ride to shore, I thought I would use our radar and see if I could spot them.'

'And did you?'

'No, at least not till they were almost alongside. It's this blip over here, right on the edge of the screen, that caught my attention,' he said, pointing to a bright green dot.

'Probably just a fisherman.'

'That's what I thought at first, then just before Plata's ride showed up the blip changed course, appeared to accelerate and headed for our position.'

'Coincidence?' suggested Larsen.

'Not likely, as Plata's go-fast came alongside the blip slowed and matched our speed and direction. Then when the go-fast took off, the blip turned and accelerated after it.'

'More likely one of Plata's so-called friends, trying to grab him before he gets to shore.'

'I don't think so; it gave up the chase after a few minutes, probably not able to match the go-fast's speed,' said John, 'then it changed course and is now shadowing us.'

Larsen left the chart room, climbed halfway up the companionway steps and shouted to Elijah on the helm, 'Elijah, count to thirty then fall off the wind, ten, no make that fifteen, degrees. Stay on that course for three minutes, then come back on to the original course.'

'Fifteen degrees to port in thirty seconds, Captain,' repeated Elijah.

'Right, John, let's see what our shadow does with this,' said Larsen.

Four pairs of eyes watched the second hand on the chronometer count the remaining seconds. The motion of the *Leviathan* eased as it fell off the wind for three minutes before returning to the original course.

'Well, there's no doubting it, we are being followed. But who would be out here playing silly games with a hurricane bearing down on us?' pondered Larsen.

'Plata's enemies; they couldn't catch him so now they are after us?' suggested Stephen.

'No gentlemen, I think we are looking at a Venezuelan coastguard cutter. They are out on patrol and saw Plata's go-fast rendezvous with us. Since they couldn't catch him, they are probably wondering what we are up to. John, show Edward how to watch the screen; it would be a good idea keep an eye on it. I want to know if it decides to close on us. In the meantime, I want everyone on deck. We have more important business at hand. We've got a hurricane on the way.'

Bill had now been at sea long enough that the effects of the boat slamming into the waves, the noise of the wind in the rigging and green sea falling on the deck no longer bothered him. But this was different; Larsen had brought the *Leviathan* round on to a new course, due east. One minute he felt like he was going up in an elevator then *Leviathan* would tip forward and accelerate down the wave. The sound of the wave-tops rushing past the hull as the boat settled waiting for the next wave made him nervous. Marcel and Stephen, seated in the port side settee, chuckled at his discomfort.

'You two can wait for your drinks,' he said, pouring hot water into the insulated travel mugs for the night watch.

Timing the motion of the boat, he carefully climbed the companionway steps. He hooked his fingers through the handles on the mugs with one hand and the handrail with the other. He'd managed two steps across the bridge deck when six hundred gallons of cold sea charged into him. Without dropping the cups, and still standing upright, he slid across the bridge deck and into one the guard rail stanchions. If it hadn't been for his personal lifeline and harness he would have disappeared between the guard rails into the boiling maelstrom of the sea.

Elijah got to him first. 'Are you all right, Edward?'

'I think so. My right arm is sore; I hit it on the stanchion. At least, thanks to the lids, I didn't spill your drinks.'

'That doesn't matter. You're more important than any hot drink. Here let me carry the cups. You hold on to me and we'll get you to the safety of the cockpit.'

'That's quite a trick, Edward. When did you learn that one?' asked John.

'Not so funny – I think I have done something to my arm. It hurts quite badly.'

'John, I'll take the helm with Elijah,' said Larsen. 'You take Edward below and look at his arm. We can't afford for him to be injured.'

Bill held on to John with his good arm and they went below. Much to his relief after examining it, John said, 'It's just bruised, it'll be fine in a couple of days. In the meantime, no more showing off, OK?'

Bill nodded, then, zipping up his coat, followed John back on deck, and climbed into the cockpit as the first squall of the evening hit.

'How's Shadow?' shouted Larsen.

'He's disappeared. I checked before I brought up the drinks,' Bill shouted back. The thought of being chased across the sea on a wild night reminded him of the Lapland forests. He shivered and wondered if Thornton had had the same feeling of excitement.

'Shall we stream the warps, Captain?' asked Elijah.

'Not yet, this squall will soon pass, and I'd like to see how well the *Leviathan* takes to running downwind in these winds. As long as we have steerage and don't start surfing too fast, we should be all right. As far as I remember, she's never been through a storm like we will see during the next forty-eight hours and I am curious to see just how well she does.'

'Will it be anything like when we set out from Falmouth?' said Bill, looking a little worried.

'No, nothing like that, 'said Stephen. 'It'll be much worse!'

Bill punched his arm and said, 'Cold soup for you tonight, my friend,' then laughed and headed below. Just a few more days and they would be tied up in Bermuda; this would be all over. He could start his new life, sleep in a proper bed, and even go out for a meal in a restaurant without first having to cook the meal.

Kaufmann and his merry men were another matter. All night he could hear them groaning. The smell of vomit pervaded the atmosphere down below. Bill was looking forward to being able to open all the hatches and clear the air. Unfortunately, the cleaning-up fell to him and he definitely wasn't looking forward to that.

In the early hours of the morning he heard someone praying. Typical, he thought, like calling the insurance company for coverage after the accident. Bill spent the night and most of the next day ferrying cups of hot soup and warm bread or hot chocolate to those on the helm, while trying to avoid the sporadic squalls.

Every time the motion eased, Larsen would turn the *Leviathan* away from the east and slowly, degree by degree, bring her round until about three in the morning on the second day they were sailing almost due north.

'How are we doing, Captain?' asked Bill.

'Looking at the compass and the condition of the seas, I'm pretty sure we've crossed behind the hurricane and it is well to the north-west of us now. We'll keep heading north for a while. When the seas have settled we'll head for—well, we'll just head for somewhere; I'll check our position and decide where then.'

Although they were now out of the storm's way, the winds and heavy seas kept up all through the night and into the next day.

♦

'Morning, Edward,' said Stephen.

'Good morning, men,' he replied to Stephen and Marcel. 'I was wondering if you wanted to wait for breakfast or would you like it here at the helm?'

'If you could do one of your special breakfast rolls, I'll eat it here,' said Marcel.

'Me, too,' said Stephen.

'Fine, do you want the egg with a soft yolk?'

'Any way it comes, thanks.'

Bill was halfway down the companionway hatch and had just unclipped his lifeline when he heard the noise; it was like an express train, he said later. He managed to grab onto the hatch coaming and waited. A rogue wave had just broken over the stern. He turned in time to see Stephen and Marcel sitting waist-deep in Caribbean Sea. The lifeline stanchions behind them were sticking up out of the foam, and a wall of water was boiling down the side decks towards the open hatch. The coach roof split the wave and Bill watched as gallons of frothing water spilled over the bulwarks and back into the sea as *Leviathan's* stern lifted on the passing wave.

He gave a sigh of relief, but as he was about to resume his descent into the boat he froze. Eighty-five tonnes of *Leviathan* violently pitched forward and accelerated down the surface of the wave. Ahead was a sheer wall of green sea, towering over the *Leviathan*. Bill watched transfixed as the bowsprit ploughed into the wall and kept going till green water covered the whole of the foredeck and washed over the top of the coach roof. He realised in horror that a third of the *Leviathan* was now under water.

Before *Leviathan* could rise out of the hole, the top of the wall of water collapsed on the deck and roared angrily along the coach roof. Hundreds of gallons of cold sea water, and Bill, poured down the companionway. He ended up trapped under the saloon table, lying on the cabin sole splashing in eighteen inches of sea water, with books, cushions, soggy vegetables, and magazines floating around him. John and Marcel were on the floor in a heap at the far end of the saloon.

Larsen shot out of the chart room. 'Is everyone all right? Edward, what about you?' he said, helping him to his feet.

'Yes, I'm fine. Are we sinking?'

'No, I don't think so.'

'What happened? I mean, where did the wave come from?'

'It is one of those situations where two waves arrive in one place at the same time and we were there to meet them. It's just one of the pleasures of ocean sailing during a hurricane. John, get the pumps running. Marcel, on deck, let's find out what and where the damage is.'

In spite of the amount of water that had landed on the deck and poured down the companionway hatch, little damage had been done. All the cushions were wet, water had splashed up on the bulkheads, pages from well-read novels floated like lilies in a pond, yet the galley, and chart room suffered no ill effects. The guest cabins fared better due to the cabin doors all being shut. The bilges were full of sea water, but once the main engine had been started the pump cleared them quickly.

'That must have been the largest wave I have ever seen,' said Stephen, as they sat in the cockpit munching on their belated breakfast rolls at eleven in the morning.

'I've had enough to last a lifetime,' said Bill.

'What's the damage below, Edward?' asked Larsen.

'Mostly wet cushions, a few books that will never be read again. The water drained into the bilges quickly. Some got into the lower lockers but that doesn't matter, I mostly keep pots and pans down there. My cabin door was shut so little water got in there, thank goodness.'

'Pity it didn't get into the guest cabins – have you smelled the pong coming from them?' said Elijah.

'Thanks for reminding me,' said Bill, 'I'm the one who will be cleaning them when I can get in. I can't believe that no-one came out of their cabins. They could have drowned and not known about it till they met their maker.'

It just was past midnight when the wind eased and the wave pattern steadied enough for the reefs to be shaken out of the main, mizzen, and staysails. A semblance of normality had finally returned to the *Leviathan*.

'Where we headed, Captain?' said John, munching on a huge cheeseburger.

'St Kitts, and Cockleshell Bay.'

'Sounds fine to me,' said Marcel, 'I could do with going ashore in the dinghy and lying on the beach for the day.'

Bill resigned himself to staying on board and went back to cleaning up the mess left behind from the wave, all the time dreading what he would find in the guest cabins.

♦

'Who's on watch after you, Stephen?' asked Bill, handing Stephen his mug of hot chocolate.

'Ah, tastes great, thanks,' he said, taking a careful sip. 'It's the Captain. You know how he likes to be on deck when we enter a new anchorage.'

'How long before we reach it?'

'Just before sunrise, if the wind stays fair; I reckon about another five hours. The moon will still be up, so we should have plenty of visibility.'

'In that case I'm going to turn in; the crew will want breakfast early.'

'Night, Edward pleasant dreams,' said Stephen as Bill descended the companionway steps.

'If only,' he said.

Without turning on the light, Bill entered his moonlit cabin. He shut the door behind him and reached over his bunk to open the porthole. A strange smell permeated the air, like cat pee.

Before he could do or say anything, Martinez had grabbed Bill from behind by his hair, pulled him close and mashed his knife-laden hand over Bill's mouth, splitting his lip.

Fear, the taste of his own blood and the smell of sweat and tobacco emanating from Martinez's hands made Bill retch. He saw his last bottle of whiskey lying on his bunk, half-empty. The rat had drunk most of it. Bill had planned to celebrate his first night on dry land in Bermuda by drinking it dry; now it was almost gone.

'Now, Eddie baby, not a squeak out of you; you and me, we've got something to sort out. Why don't we have a little drink together, and have a chat like good friends.'

'That's my whiskey you've drunk, arsehole.'

'I'll drink to that,' said Martinez, still holding Bill close from behind, the stubble of his unshaved face snagging in Bill's long hair, Martinez placed the tip of the knife against Bill's cheek.

'You see the knife? good, then you'll be nice to Hugo.'

Bill recoiled in fear as he recognised Martinez's knife – the one he used to kill Edwards.

Slowly, with deliberation, Martinez placed the knife on the bunk, the point towards Bill with the sharp edge of the blade glinting in the moonlight.

Like a volcano erupting, years of pent up anger and frustration boiled over and Bill lunged for the knife.

'No you don't,' said Martinez making a grab for, but missing, Bill's wrist.

Bill managed to struggle free from Martinez and swung round, elbowing Martinez in the face. In the ensuing struggle the knife slashed Bill's face.

'You'll pay for that Eddie baby. Now give me the knife. Slowly now, we don't want an accident, do we?'

'Fuck off; the only way you'll get this knife is in the belly, just where you stuck Edwards.'

Martinez froze. 'You're going to be very sorry you said that Eddie baby. Cause now I'm going to have to stick you too, and such a pity, I had all sorts of plans for us.'

Bill backed off till he was against the toilet door. 'Stay back, I mean it, I'll stick you.'

'No you won't, you wouldn't want to hurt your Hugo now would you. Why don't you give me the knife and we'll have a little drink together, talk things over friendly like.'

'And Edwards, will we talk like you did with him?'

'No, I don't think so. He had it in for me and I was simply defending myself.'

'That's not what I saw.'

'So you say. Now give me the knife and we'll talk this over, like friends do.'

'You're no friend of mine.'

In a flash Martinez grabbed Bill's wrist and wrested the knife from his hand. In the struggle Martinez tripped over the chair leg and crashed to the floor.

'Edward are you all right?' came Larsen's voice, from the other side of the door.

'Not a word or I'll cut you like a piece of salami,' whispered Martinez as he got to his feet.

'I'm fine, bad dream,' he blurted out.

'Bastard,' Martinez snarled, 'we'll finish this later,' he said stuffing his knife into the waistband of his trousers.

Larsen opened the door and saw Bill leaning on the toilet door and Martinez leaning against the bunk.

'What's going on, and what are you doing in here Mr Martinez?'

'I couldn't sleep. I was heading for my cabin when I saw Eddie coming down the stairs, and thought. What an opportue time to complement him on the fine food he's been making for us these last months, especially since we'll be back in England soon.'

'Is that so, Edward?' asked Larsen.

'Yes, it's just like Mr Martinez says.'

Larsen shook his head and said, 'bring me a coffee when you come up on deck, will you?'

'I'll be right there,' he said shakily.

As fast as he could, Bill got out of his cabin and went into the galley. As he poured Larsen's coffee, he caught sight of the shadow of Martinez heading forward to his cabin.

'Coffee, Captain,' he said, offering the cup to Larsen.

'Thought you were turning in?' said Stephen.

Bill shuddered at the recent memory and replied, 'Too hot below, I – I thought I'd sit up here till it cools down – that's all, maybe sit up and watch for the sunrise.'

'OK, if you're sure.'

'I'm sure.'

'Should be a magnificent sunrise,' said Larsen, 'low humidity and no clouds all the way to the horizon. What have you done to your face?'

'I cut it on one of the toggles when I opened the porthole.'

'You need to have John look at it. I don't want you getting an infection.'

'It's OK really, only a scratch.'

'You cold?'

'A little,' he said, shivering.

'Why don't you put a coat on? We still have several hours before sunup.'

'Honestly, I'm fine, I was too hot below; the cool air is just what I need. I'll get a coat if I get too cold.'

The last thing he needed right now was to go below and be confronted by Martinez.

The ship's clock struck two am and Stephen stood up from the wheel, 'That's me done for the night; I'm going to turn in for some shut eye before we reach our anchorage.'

'Night, Stephen,' said Larsen.

'Night, Captain, Edward,' he said, as he headed forward to the crew's quarters.

'I think I will go below to put on something warm,' said Bill. 'Stephen, could you have a quick look at my cabin light switch? It didn't work earlier.'

'Sure.'

Bill nervously followed Stephen down the companionway ladder. Stephen stepped in to Bill's cabin and turned on the light. 'It seems to work fine now.'

'Oh, it must have been stuck.'

Satisfied that Martinez hadn't returned, Bill thanked Stephen, shut and locked the door behind him then turned and vomited into the toilet. Breathing heavily, he wiped his mouth with a tissue before pulling off his clothes and climbing into the shower. He almost scrubbed himself raw trying to wash away the memory of the assault.

After pulling on jeans and a clean shirt, he grabbed his jacket from its peg on the door. he looked at the cut on his face in the mirror; another war scar. It had stopped bleeding but did look like it might need stitches. He applied a couple of steri strips and put a couple in his jacket pocket in case the cut started bleeding again. With the recent attack still fresh in his memory he returned to the cockpit.

'That looks more sensible; you'll be much warmer in those clothes.'

'Yes – thanks, you're right, I feel much better.'

Bill sat down in the shelter of the dodger, shivered, yawned, and curled up in the shadows.

He woke from the fog of sleep, stretched and sighed as the memory of the previous evening filtered into his consciousness.

'Breakfast, Edward?' said Larsen.

'Oh, yes please,' Bill replied, and then realised Larsen was telling him it was time for him to go make it.

As he stood to go below, Bill saw lights in the distance. 'Where are we?' he asked.

'Those are the lights of St Kitts. We'll be there in about an hour,' said Larsen.

◆

Bill heard the sound of the anchor hitting the water as he set out the plates for the crew's breakfast.

'Gentlemen,' said Larsen at the table, 'after the last few days of atrocious weather I think we deserve a day ashore, before we go Transatlantic.'

'Does that include our guests?' asked Elijah.

'Everyone,' replied Larsen.

'I'd like to stay on board,' interjected Bill.

'Why? We could all do with a day on the beach,' said Larsen.

'I've got too much to do, and besides what if something happened while we were all ashore?'

Larsen saw the look on Bill's face and said, 'as you wish. You're right; it will be good to have someone on board just in case.' Turning to Elijah, he said, 'How did the inspection go?'

'Stephen and I went over the rigging, checked the spars and the sails. It looks like we have got through the storm unscathed.'

'I've checked the engine room and the bilges are clear,' said John.

'Edward, how about your areas?' said Larsen.

'That's one of the reasons I need to be here while you are all ashore. There is a lot to clean up before we go to sea again. I had Marcel give me a hand to check the provisions and as far as we could see, there's been no loss there, just wet cushions, some loose vegetables, and rugs.'

♦

Bill stood at the rail and watched as the crew and Kaufmann's team went ashore in the dinghies. He would have enjoyed a day sunbathing on the beach but needed time to think about how to deal with the menace of Martinez.

Bill settled himself on the side deck, peeling the vegetables and watching the activities on the beach through binoculars. Tidying the interior could wait. He noticed that Larsen had organised a game of volley-ball between some of the crew and the guests.

Within half an hour of them landing, a mist started to form. It drifted in from the open sea and made it difficult to see what was happening on the beach. A cold chill settled around his shoulders. Bill shivered and, picking up the binoculars stared at the beach; someone was missing. Still holding the knife he stood up to get a better view.

The mist was getting thicker. He could hear the voices on the beach, but it was now becoming difficult to make out who was who. Try as he might, he couldn't see Martinez anywhere.

He had definitely gone ashore, Bill reassured himself; he had watched Martinez through the binoculars all the way there and seen him get out of the dinghy. Both dinghies were still pulled up on the beach. Then Bill saw someone outside the surf line, swimming purposefully towards the yacht. Bill watched, horrified, as every powerful stroke brought the swimmer closer. It could only be Martinez.

Martinez arrived amidships and trod water while catching his breath and looking for the best way to get on board. He tried to reach up and grab the toe-rail but failed and slid back into the water.

'Come on, Eddie baby, help your Hugo on board. We've unfinished business.'

He tried again to reach the toe-rail but once again failed. Then like a seal looking for salmon, he breast-stroked round the stern to the starboard side of the yacht. He saw what he needed; the tail end of the spare dinghy anchor rode hanging over the side.

'Not long now, Eddie baby,' he said, before grabbing the rope.

Martinez started to pull himself up but only managed to get out of the water to his waist before the rope slipped and he fell back. 'Son of a bitch, hold the rope!'

Like a rabbit in a car's headlights, unable to prevent the inevitable moment, Bill stood frozen to the spot and watched.

Martinez tried again to pull himself out of the water; once more the rope slipped and he plunged back. 'Tie the rope off, shit face!' he screamed.

The more Martinez swore at Bill the more frightened Bill became.

Martinez stopped pulling on the rope, tied the tail end around his waist and leaned back on the rope to rest, staring at his quarry.

Bill was petrified with fear, realizing the inevitable was about to happen.

Rested, Martinez once again started to pull himself hand over hand out of the water, 'third time lucky, Eddie baby.'

As Martinez was about to grab the toe-rail, the rope slipped again. This time the chain that was attached to it rattled noisily over the side scraping Martinez's face and making it bleed.

'You'll pay for that – arsehole.' He spat out the words while wiping blood from his face with the back of his hand.

Bill watched in horror as the anchor fluke caught on one of the lifeline stanchions.

Martinez reached up to the chain. Their eyes locked.

Bile rose in Bill's throat, little beads of sweat formed on his brow; he tried to call for help but all that came from his mouth was a squeak.

As Martinez's hand grabbed the toe-rail, Bill dropped his knife and grabbed at the anchor to try and release it from the stanchion, but it was stuck fast. In frustration, he picked up his knife and stabbed at Martinez's hand, missing it by a whisker as the tip stuck in the toe-rail.

'This is fun,' Martinez said, laughing.

Bill tried to release the knife, but in his struggle, he pushed the knife handle down.

Like a miniature guillotine, the knife hinged on its trapped point, and neatly severed Martinez's fingers and thumb. As the severed fingers fell on the deck, the knife came free and Martinez, screaming in agony, fell back in the water. Fuelled by demonic anger and oblivious to the pain and blood spurting from his severed finger stumps, he grabbed the chain and once again tried to pull himself out of the water.

Before his weight was fully on the chain, Bill bent down and freed the anchor. Their eyes met and for the first time Bill saw the look of fear in Martinez's eyes; he understood what was about to happen. Triumphantly and with deliberate slowness Bill threw the anchor over the side.

For a moment nothing happened, and then they both turned towards the anchor as it descended through the crystal-clear water to the bottom.

Just before the anchor hit the bottom, it pulled Martinez under till just his head was out of the water.

Bill watched Martinez frantically tugging at the rope while kicking with his feet, until he was lost in a cloud of blood and froth. Bill crouched down and holding tight to the nearest stanchion, hung over the side, wondering – was it finally over?

Without warning, Martinez's blood-soaked hand shot up out of the water and grabbed Bill's hair, threatening to pull him down into a watery grave.

Still holding his knife Bill tried to cut his hair to rid himself of the monster whose face was now out of the water, staring at him with a death grin. With a last frantic swipe, he tried to cut Martinez loose. The knife missed its intended target, pierced Martinez's left eyeball and embedded itself in his brain.

As life left him, Martinez let go and sank back into the water, still reaching up to Bill, the stubs of the fingers of his right hand just below the surface. Mesmerised, Bill watched as Martinez floated, tethered by the anchor, just below the surface. It didn't take long for the fish to start nibbling at the blood-soaked stubs of his fingers and the remains of his eyeball.

In a state of post-adrenalin shock, Bill was petrified that even now Martinez could return to life and resume his assault on him. Bill stared at Martinez's fingerless hand, still reaching up in a death grasp, and couldn't help feeling a pang of sorrow for him. Bending down, Bill picked up Martinez's fingers from the deck and one at a time dropped them over the side, saying, 'this little piggy went to market, this little piggy stayed at home, this little piggy had roast beef but this little piggy had none. And this little piggy,' he said, looking at Martinez's thumb, 'went wee, wee, wee, all the way home.'

35

Fight on the quarterdeck

'Captain, where's Martinez?' asked Elijah.

Larsen looked around and shrugged his shoulders. 'Don't know, he was here a minute ago.'

They looked out to where the *Leviathan* was anchored, barely discernible in the mist.

'Quick, get John, and tell Stephen and Marcel where we are going. I'll bet the rat has swum back to the boat,' said Larsen.

They pushed the dinghy out into the sea and started rowing.

'I don't like this one bit,' said Larsen. 'Last night, I found Martinez in Edward's cabin. He said they'd just been talking. Martinez had the gall to say he was complementing Edward on his cooking.'

'What did Edward say?' asked Elijah.

'He confirmed Martinez's statement. But what neither of them realised was I saw a half-drunk bottle of whiskey lying on Edward's bunk.'

'It's no secret about Edward's drinking,' said John. 'Smell it on his breath frequently, still he's a damn good cook.'

'That's not the issue I'm worried about,' said Larsen. 'Did you see that cut on Edward's face this morning? He said he cut it on the porthole toggle last night.'

'Thought it looked too clean, more like a knife slash,' said John.

'The reason I went into his cabin,' said Larsen, 'was I thought I heard them fighting, now I'm certain Martinez cut Edward's face with a knife, and now he's gone back to the boat to confront Edward.'

'If he has laid a finger on Edward, I swear Captain, you'll have to.

'Relax, Elijah, nothing will have happened,' he said, wishing he could believe his words.

Tying the dinghy to one of the stanchions they climbed on board.

'Edward, is Martinez here?' said Larsen.

Bill sat, arms folded, not answering, just staring off into the distance.

'Edward, what's the matter? What's happened, are you all right?'

Hickory dickory dock
the anchor went plop
the slimy rat got quite a shock
and never came up again.

'What's the matter with him? If that rat has touched him, I swear I'll tear him to pieces and feed him to the fish,' said Elijah.

'Martinez's feeding fishes, fishes like Martinez.' Bill laughed, and then started shaking uncontrollably.

'He's not below decks,' said John.

Larsen grabbed Bill by the shoulders and said, 'Pull yourself together Edward. What's happened, where's Martinez?'

Elijah looked down at the bloodstains on the toe-rail then at the cloud of fish formed directly below him. The last time he had seen something like this was when he dropped his dinner over the side when at anchor in Kingston. Inspiration caught his imagination and grabbing the boathook that was lying on the coach roof, he prodded at the fish.

'I've found him. He is feeding the fish, John, have a look. He really is feeding the fish.'

'What is it?' said Larsen.

'We've found Martinez; he's anchored to the bottom.'

'Well, I'll be,' said Larsen, leaning over the rail. 'I've never seen him look so peaceful,'

'Is that a knife sticking out of his face?' said John.

'Never mind his face, John, let's get him on board before he attracts a passing shark,' said Larsen.

He pushed a loop of rope round the body of Martinez and using a halyard they pulled it to the surface and on to the deck.

'John,' said Larsen, 'take Edward to the cockpit and Elijah, bring a sheet or something, we'll need to cover the body.'

'What shall we do with all his jewellery?' asked Elijah. 'He must have thousands tied up in those rings and the necklace.'

'You mean his trophies? I say we bury them with him,' said Larsen.

'I know,' said Elijah, 'why not give them to Edward? Sort of compensation for what he's been through.'

'Do you really think he would accept them after what has happened?' said Larsen.

'Not sure, I'll hold on to them for now. Who knows what he'll feel like later?'

'How is he?' asked Larsen, as John joined them on the side deck.

'He's in shock; I've made him a cup of strong sweet tea. You can probably ask him what happened in a few minutes. If he was responsible for Martinez's condition, I don't know what thoughts must be going round in his mind.'

They stood and talked for a few minutes before they joined Bill in the cockpit. They waited patiently while he sipped his tea till he was ready to talk.

Starting from the previous night's encounter in his cabin he told them everything that took place.

'I should have seen the signs, it's my fault,' said Larsen.

'It's nobody's fault captain, it's just the way life treats me. Just another dead body for me to remember; I'm worried this is becoming a habit.'

'Elijah, will you take Edward below? John and I will take care of Mr Martinez.'

'Ahoy, sailing ship *Leviathan*, this is the US coastguard cutter USS *Alviso*. Stand by to be boarded.'

'What the hell – who is that?' exclaimed Larsen, staring into the mist.

'It's Shadow. There they are, just breaking through the mist over to the left,' said Bill, as Elijah led him below.

They watched as the cutter USS *Alviso* slowed, dropped its anchor, and reversed. Within minutes a small patrol boat, fully loaded with armed and helmeted sailors, was lowered from the stern. It came alongside and one of the sailors climbed on board the *Leviathan*.

'Acting Captain, Lieutenant-Commander JR Crow asks, where is your Captain? And says you are to prepare to be boarded.'

Larsen smiled at the young sailor, pulled his shoulders back, placed his fists on his waist and looking him straight in the eye, said quietly, 'I'm the Captain. Tell your acting Captain, Lieutenant-Commander JR Crow, that I am attending to some ship's business. I'll be available to talk with him in half an hour. In the meantime, get out of my way, unless you are willing to help.'

'Yes sir, I mean no sir. I'm to secure the vessel until further orders and to ascertain who the Captain is.'

'I have already told you, I'm the Captain. Now excuse me,' Larsen looked at the name badge on the sailor's life vest, 'Petty Officer Janski, I have an urgent matter to attend to. John, here's the sheet.'

'Thanks, Captain. Shall I cover him up?'

'Yes, and since young Petty Officer Janski is doing nothing while he waits for his acting Captain to arrive, get him to help you.'

'Certainly, this way, sailor,' said John, as he led the way to the starboard side deck.

'Holly shit man – is that his knife sticking out of his eye? Who did that?'

'That's what we are trying to find out,' replied Larsen.

'I'll need to inform my command and control about this.'

'Whatever, go ahead. In the meantime, get out of the way,' said John. Bending down he grabbed the knife with his right hand, placed his foot on Martinez's mouth and pulled the knife out of the eye socket. He finished by wiping the blade on Martinez's shirt. It was all Janski could take; he turned and vomited over the side.

Within minutes a second boat arrived, this time bringing Lieutenant-Commander JR Crow. As he boarded, he said,' Captain, you, and your crew are under arrest. You will be taken to the *Alviso* for questioning.' He turned to the sailors in the first boat and shouted, 'You men, get out of there and secure this vessel. *Now*, do you hear?'

A garble of, *Yes, sir's*, came from the boat as the sailors scrambled to board the *Leviathan*.

'Janski, where's this body?' shouted Crow.

'Here, sir, under this sheet.'

Crow bent down and pulled back the sheet. 'Nasty piece of work, missing fingers as well I see.' He stood up. 'Captain, who did this, who is the perpetrator?'

'That's what I was investigating when your men interrupted us.'

'Never mind that now; we'll soon get to the bottom of it when you are on the *Alviso*. Janski, get them on the RHI and back to the *Alviso* – now.'

'I don't think so,' said Larsen.

'You don't have a choice, Captain, I'm ordering you. Get in the RHI.'

'For a start, you do not have the authority to order me anywhere. I outrank you. Captain is still senior to the rank of Lieutenant-Commander. Secondly, you are on a British vessel. You, my friend, are trespassing.'

Larsen was not sure of his ground, he needed time to think and he hoped by stalling he would at least have time to get the loud-mouthed Crow on the defensive.

'All right, you can leave one of your crew onboard. The rest come to the *Alviso*.'

'John,' said Larsen, 'Take care of things while we're gone, we'll be back shortly.'

Crow interrupted, 'That, Captain, will be for our Captain Delaware to decide. You have more crew below?'

'Yes, the purser and the boson,' answered Larsen.

'Get them up here, Captain. I think there is more going on than you're telling me and I mean to get to the bottom of it.'

John went to the companionway and called,' Edward, Elijah. Captain says can you come up on deck?'

Bill climbed the steps first and stood on the deck beside the coaming; Elijah followed close behind.'

'What do we have here?' asked Crow as he walked over and stood towering over Bill.

Larsen saw the muscles on Elijah's arms flex and his hands ball into fists; he imperceptibly shook his head. Elijah relaxed.

'My, you're a pretty one,' said Crow running his fingers through Bill's hair, 'you a friend of Dorothy's?'

'I'm nobody's friend – *creep*,' said Bill not understanding Crow's jibe.

'Feisty young filly! And my, what a specimen we have here.' Crow said, looking at Elijah. 'You two an item? Do tricks and things, entertain the guests?'

Elijah moved slightly in front of Bill and stared straight into Crow's eyes.

'Cat got your tongue, *boy*? I'm talking to you – you hear me?' Crow said and spat on Elijah's foot.

Larsen went to move. One of the sailors stuck his M14 into Larsen's back; the boarding party crowded round, watching the developing spectacle.

'I'm talking to you, *boy*,' Crow continued. 'You know you shouldn't be associating yourself with white folks, even if they are a friend of Dorothy.'

The boarding party laughed at Crow's jibe, eager to see where this was going.

Larsen looked at Elijah and once again shook his head slowly from side to side; Elijah stood still and silent.

Crow pulled his revolver from its holster and pointed it at Elijah's left knee. 'Tell you what, *boy*, you and me, on the flight deck of the *Alviso*. One on one – then we'll find out who the real man is. When I've finished with you, you'll wish you had shown me more respect, boy. You see, me and my family, we're used to dealing with your type. My grandpa used to hang your sort in the trees down by the bayou, once they did three in one night. They had to cut them down early and throw them in the river—didn't want the bodies to put off the tourists.'

Larsen saw Elijah was at breaking point and knew it was just what Crow wanted: an excuse to shoot.

Bill grabbed Elijah's arm and pleaded, 'Elijah, please, he's just trying to get you annoyed. Don't listen to him, please.'

Larsen clenched his fists and, raising his arm, swung to the right as hard as he could. His clenched fist struck one of the sailors full on the side of the face, sending him sprawling into the sea, his M14 spattering bullets harmlessly into the air. The sailor directly to the left hit Larsen hard on the back of the neck with his rifle butt, Larsen collapsed on the deck.

'Well, what do we have here?' said Crow, looking down at Larsen. 'You shouldn't meddle with the men of the *Alviso*, Captain. Get up, or do you want my men to help you? Janski, I told you to get them all in the RHI and back to the *Alviso*, now.'

'Not so fast,' said John.

'What now?' Crow turned, looked at John and said, 'Be careful with that knife, boy, no need for anyone to get hurt. I was just joshing with your man, bit of southern humour, that's all. Let the sailor go and we can get on with the business at hand.'

While the sailor was being helped out of the water, Larsen picked up the dropped M14 and, pointing it at Crow's back, said, 'John, put down the knife please; the blade could be contaminated with AIDS, you know what a scumbag Martinez was.'

John withdrew the knife from the throat of the sailor and put it on the coach roof.

Crow turned back to say something to Larsen then saw the M14 barrel pointing directly at him. 'Captain, for pity's sake, let's not start a war over such a trivial matter; put the gun down, please.'

'You, sir, are a disgrace to your uniform and your country. I'll put down the gun after you apologise to Colonel Gates.'

'Colonel Gates? But I thought.'

'I doubt it,' interrupted Larsen.

'Say you're sorry, Mister Crow,' said Bill.

'We're waiting,' said Larsen.

'All right, I'm sorry. Now, would you and your people please get in the RHI? Your man can stay on board while you are gone. Also, Captain, bring the crew's passports with you.'

'Elijah,' whispered Bill, 'what's an RHI?'

'It stands for rigid hull inflatable.'

'Why can't they just speak regular English, like us? It's no wonder the Americans are so misunderstood around the world.'

'Edward, Elijah,' said Larsen, 'let's go. Hopefully their Captain is a reasonable man.'

'Captain Larsen, if it is of help we can take the deceased to the *Alviso*. We have facilities to deal with it there,' said Crow.

Larsen thought for a moment, shook his head and said,' He's been my responsibility so far. No point in changing things now. We'll give him a burial at sea after we are under way.'

'I knew Elijah was in the US Marines. Didn't realise he was a Colonel,' said Bill to Larsen as they crossed to the *Alviso*.

'He doesn't talk about it. He had a rough time in Iraq. I just said that to rub Crow's nose in the dirt. Colonel outranks Lieutenant-Commander, and Crow knows that.'

The trip from the *Leviathan* to the *Alviso* took a few minutes. Larsen was pleased to see that the mist was now completely obliterating the beach. There was no need to complicate matters by mentioning Kaufmann and his three – no, now his two team members. He had only brought the five passports with him and had deliberately omitted to bring the logbook.

Larsen, Bill and Elijah were escorted up the gangway and taken to what Larsen assumed was a holding room. He handed in their passports, had their fingerprints taken as well as having their irises photographed, shades of 1984, he thought.

From there they were taken to a detention room with two doors and no portholes. There was one long table with four chairs behind. Seated at the table were the Captain of the *Alviso* and a civilian, flanked by two Marines. Larsen looked at the civilian, he was wearing dark glasses: either CIA or homeland security.

The captain looked every bit a captain, white hair tucked neatly in his cap and enough gold braid to float a bank.

'You're the Captain of the *Leviathan*, Mr Larsen?' said Captain Delaware.

'It's Captain Larsen. I have my Master's Ticket, and I am the owner of the *Leviathan*. We're returning to England from a trip to the Amazon.'

'And you, sir, what's your position on the yacht?' Delaware asked Bill.

One of the Marines sniggered.

'Something funny, sailor?' asked Delaware.

'No sir, just trying not to sneeze – *sir*.'

'Good. Next time, sailor, excuse yourself first.'

'Yes, *sir*.'

'Go on, sir,' said Delaware.

'I'm the purser.'

'And you, sir?' he said to Elijah.

'Main duties are boson and deck hand, sir.'

'You're an American?' he said when he heard Elijah's accent.

'Yes, sir, born in the States and raised in the UK by my uncle and aunt, my parents died when I was five.'

'And you have dual citizenship?'

'Yes, sir.'

'Sort of convenient, isn't it?' the civilian commented.

'It's never convenient when you lose family,' replied Elijah.

'That's not what I meant. Citizenship without responsibility, that's what I'm talking about. Lots of young men your age fought and gave their lives for their country while you were lazing about in jolly old England.'

Elijah inhaled slowly. Chest expanding, shoulders rising, he looked at the civilian. 'It's Colonel Elijah Gates, retired, you are talking to. I served twelve years in the Marines and commanded some of those fine men you are talking about. What have you done for your country, besides pushing a pen?'

'My apologies, sir, I had no idea you were in the service. I am sure you're aware how difficult a job we have of protecting our citizens. Sometimes the enemy is very clever – look at 9/11; we must always be on guard.'

Trying to extricate himself from his embarrassment the civilian turned to Larsen and said, 'That's a lot of very beautiful yacht for one man to own, Captain. Did you win the lottery?

'Mister whoever you are, no one speaks to me while hiding behind dark glasses.'

The civilian reached up and removed his glasses to reveal two small beady eyes, set close together either side of a narrow bony nose. 'Agent Harrison, homeland security, my job is to keep our borders safe and free from filth and scum, like the dead fish on your deck, Captain.'

'Thank you, Mr Harrison, and to answer your question, I pensioned out of the Merchant Navy and bought her with my savings.'

'Unusual route to England Captain, do all English sailing boats go into the Caribbean to get to England?' asked Delaware.

'I thought it would be interesting to look at some of the sailing grounds for future charters. Captain Delaware, you must know yourself from sailing in that area, what the pilots say about the Venezuelan waters. I just wanted to find out first-hand.'

'Who were you rendezvousing with, Captain?' said Harrison.

'I'm sorry; I don't understand your question.'

'Two nights ago, just off the coast of Caracas, you stopped and put someone over the side on to a fast-boat. Who was that, Captain?'

'I didn't stop and put anyone over the side.'

'Captain, we followed you. We saw you turn on your radar, slow down and rendezvous with a fast-boat. Then when you saw us on your radar you changed course to see if we were following you. When you saw we were, you tried to shake us off by sailing into the path of the approaching hurricane, a very risky manoeuvre for a ticketed Captain.'

'Captain Delaware, we are on our way home to England. Our cruise had ended a month early and I thought a slight detour into the Caribbean was not out of order. I checked for hurricanes before I changed course and found that there were none forecast. We got as far as Aruba before I found out there was one on the way. The slowing down and subsequent changing of course you saw was nothing more than us getting ready for the bad weather.'

'Why didn't you put into port and wait for the storm to pass?' said Harrison. 'After all, it was only a short journey to a secure harbour.'

'Agent Harrison, I assume that you are not a sailor, or you would understand the actions I took. First, for us to go into port would have meant probable destruction. Why do you think your naval standing orders say for your ships to put to sea in hurricane weather? Secondly, we couldn't outrun it, so the only choice left was to sail south east under its path and let it pass behind.'

'What about the fast-boat that you rendezvoused with?' asked Harrison, 'were you asking for directions?'

Larsen shook his head. 'We were too busy getting ready for a hurricane to pay attention to any fool who would be out in that weather.'

'You have not filed a sail plan saying you would be anchoring at the island.'

They were interrupted by an aide bringing a document folder to Harrison. He read the contents then turned to Delaware and whispered while pointing to something.

'Captain, what's your business in these waters?'

'We stopped to check over the boat. Hurricanes do terrible things to boats at sea. As far as I am concerned international naval law permits any burdened vessel to go into any port or anchorage when threatened by or suffering from the effects of bad weather.'

'Captain Larsen, what was the dead body doing lying on your deck?' asked Harrison.

Crunch time thought Larsen. 'Captain Delaware, can I have a word with you – in private?'

Delaware turned to Harrison and had a whispered conversation. Harrison got up and left.

'Sergeant at arms, escort Colonel Gates to the wardroom. He's my guest.'

As soon as Elijah had left, Delaware said, 'Right, Captain Larsen, I am eager to hear what you have to say. Shall we go through to my cabin, we'll be more comfortable there.'

Delaware reached for a crutch from the back of his chair and stood up. 'I broke my ankle last night while we were chasing you across the Caribbean. You're quite a sailor Captain, I would never have had the balls to do what you did.'

That's why Crow was going on about being acting Captain, thought Larsen.

'Can I offer you and your boson a Drink, Captain?' asked Delaware when they got to his cabin.

'I'll have black coffee, please,' said Bill,

'I'll have the same, 'said Larsen.

'Make that three,' said Delaware to his steward.

Coffee in hand, Larsen told Delaware everything, except he left out any mention of Plata and Kaufmann. He let Delaware assume that Edwards and Martinez were crew members of the *Leviathan*.

Bill gave his account of what had happened with Martinez the previous night at sea and the subsequent incident that morning.

'Captain, to lose one is unfortunate, to lose two is careless,' said Delaware.

'Oscar Wilde,' said Larsen.

'Yes, he was a very interesting character, got in a lot of trouble if I remember correctly. I tend to read a lot while at sea, Captain; television has no appeal for me.'

'Me neither, Captain Delaware,' said Larsen.

They were interrupted by Delaware's steward entering the cabin.

'Excuse me, sir,'

'Well, what is it, man?'

'Doctor Perkins' apologies sir, he says that Lieutenant-Commander Crow is getting ready to fight Colonel Gates, on the flight deck, sir.'

'What I would give to be rid of this tiresome imbecile,' said Delaware.

'Four knights with swords?' said Larsen.

'Very good, Captain, but I'm afraid there aren't any on board just now, so I'm stuck with Crow for the present. Tell the doctor we're on our way,' he said to the steward.

'Yes, sir.'

'I didn't think fighting was allowed on board naval ships,' said Larsen.

'It's not; this will be put down as a grudge match. In the Navy we are allowed to work out our differences in a boxing ring; it's seen as more dignified and supposed to be easier to control the outcome.'

'Padded gloves and a referee, I see what you mean.'

'He'll near kill your man, Captain; Crow's a vicious, sadistic bastard.'

'Why don't you get him transferred to another ship?'

'Not so easy; his father is a rear admiral, sits on the Committee on Appropriations; all but writes my pay cheque. Between you and me and these four walls, Crow is an embarrassment at home to the family. He drinks heavily, gets in fights, chases any female in a skirt, married or single. So daddy got him a job on the *Alviso*, sort of keeping him out of harm's way. No, I'm afraid I'm stuck with him for now, or until your four knights show up.'

'How about a very fit black knight?' said Bill.

'What, your Colonel Gates? I'm sorry, son,' said Delaware, shaking his head. 'Crow will chew him up and spit him out; I've seen him do it many times before.'

'I doubt it, Captain, Elijah can take care of himself.'

'You reckon he's that good son? Oh, if only that were so. If only I could dream of it for a moment, just savour the thought, Crow gone for good.'

They were disturbed by the steward returning.

'It looks bad, sir, Lieutenant-Commander Crow has most of the ship's company back there, got them all stirred up and they are baying for blood, sir.'

'Right then, shall we go and put an end to this madness I'm still the Captain, regardless of what Mr Crow thinks.'

◆

They left Delaware's cabin and made their way along the companionway, up two flights of steps and emerged onto an open gun deck one level above the flight deck.

The scene below reminded Bill of his school days. Someone would pick a fight with a fellow pupil; word would get around and by the end of the school day most of the school would be assembled to watch the two protagonists punch out their differences.

He watched as Crow, stripped to a pair of gold-coloured satin boxing trunks, strutted around flexing his ample muscular torso.

Elijah, seated on a stool, attired in a pair of standard issue white boxing trunks, stared at the deck in front of him.

'Shall we go down?' said Larsen.

'No, Captain Larsen, if I went down it would be tantamount to my approval of this spectacle. Grudge matches are, as I said, permitted, but I fear this will be more than that. Also, I imagine Brubaker will be keeping a book on the fight, and that is definitely against Naval Standing Orders.'

'I understand,' said Larsen.

'Mind if I go down and wave the flag?' said Bill.

'No, not at all, give my regards to your man, and son, tell him from me to give Crow a good thumping.'

'Will do, Captain,' said Bill, laughing.

A few minutes later Larsen waved to Bill and indicated that he was on his way down.

'Captain, I'm worried he's going to kill Elijah. You have to stop the fight,' said Bill.

'Now hold on a minute, Edward, no-one is going to get killed. Captain Delaware assures me this will be just a grudge fight, with boxing gloves, so no one is going to get hurt.

'Well, if you're sure,' he said.

'Yes, I'm quite sure,' said Larsen. He turned to Elijah. 'How are you?'

'Eager to get on with the fight, Captain, really looking forward to making him eat his words.'

'Elijah, why on earth are you going through with this? Crow is Delaware's problem, not yours.'

'Just fancy knocking him down a peg or two. Besides, he insulted Edward, can't let him get away with that.'

'That's no reason to get into a fight,' said Bill. 'Honestly, it didn't bother me; I've been called worse.'

'Captain, Edward, people like Crow only know one thing, and that's being confronted and dealt with in the manner they understand. With Crow that's the fist – you saw him point his gun at me. He really was looking for an excuse to use it.'

'But Elijah,' said Larsen,' he's a good foot taller than you and you can't help but notice he is substantially bigger.'

'Captain, all I can say is, remember Drake and the Armada.'

'You think you can out-box him, then?'

'Sure thing,' said Elijah, 'done it before to better fighters than Crow.'

They were interrupted by the arrival of Brubaker and the announcer.

'You guys want to put some money on your man? I'll give you three to one.'

'What's that mean?' asked Bill.

'It means,' said Brubaker, 'that if your man wins, and it's not very likely, I'll pay you three dollars for every dollar you bet.'

'Make it five and you got a deal,' said Elijah.

'Cash up front, man, can't collect from a corpse,' said Brubaker, laughing and shaking his head from side to side.

'Cash up front it is, then,' said Bill, reaching into his pocket and taking out three crumpled fifty-dollar bills. 'They've been there since we left Brazil, keep forgetting to put them back in the safe. Don't worry,' he said to Elijah and Larsen, 'it's my money, I was going to buy one of those handmade blankets in the market before we left Macapa – just didn't find one I liked.'

Elijah shook his head slowly and shrugged his shoulders; he knew what Bill really meant.

Brubaker took Bill's fifties and wrapped them round a roll of money as big as a tin of beans. 'How about you, Captain?' he said to Larsen. 'The lad has faith in his man, what about you?'

'Take an IOU?'

'Sure thing, you don't leave the *Alviso* till you pay up, though, how much?'

Larsen looked at Elijah; he shrugged his shoulders and smiled back.

'All right,' said Larsen, 'how about five hundred dollars?'

'Fine by me,' said Brubaker, laughing, 'this is going to be the easiest money I've ever made.' He turned to Elijah. 'What about you, son, got faith in yourself?'

Elijah just shook his head and continued to stare at the deck.

'That's telling,' said Brubaker, as he walked off.

'Mister Gates,' said the announcer, 'I could do with some background info. Have you boxed before?'

'I did a bit when I was in the service. Not a lot,' said Elijah.

'Any knockouts?'

'I've had a few.'

'Any professional bouts?'

'I only boxed while in the service.'

'Oh good, keeps things simple.'

When the announcer had left, Larsen said to Elijah, 'Captain Delaware was saying Crow's a bit of a problem, real troublemaker, wished he could be shot of him.'

Elijah's answer was interrupted by the arrival of Delaware's steward. 'Excuse me, Captain Larsen, Captain Delaware asks, would both of you join him on the gun deck?'

'Captain,' said Elijah, 'tell Captain Delaware I might just have a solution to his problem with Crow.'

Bill followed Larsen up on to the gun deck.

'Captain Larsen,' said Delaware, 'how's your man?'

'If I was Lieutenant Commander Crow, I'd be filling in my transfer request right now.'

'Oh, Captain, you give me hope to believe. Now, does your man have a second?'

'He has our purser, Edward.'

Delaware looked at Bill and shook his head. 'Nope, that won't do, Crow is such a slime ball he'll get up to all sorts of trickery to beat our – I mean, your man. Here's the deal: I've asked Jack Broughton, our chief engineer, to be your man's second, if that's all right with you?'

'That's fine by me,' said Bill.

'Good, he has a great deal of experience in the ring, and he knows all Crow's tricks.'

'Where is he?' said Larsen.

'Down there, at the back of the crowd beside the Marines, and Captain, I think it would be better if we remained up here. Your purser can go down, though. If any questions are asked in future we can say we were in my cabin discussing navigation issues and weren't aware of the fight.'

'Whatever, Captain Delaware, if it helps you get rid of Crow, I'll go along with your subterfuge.'

Delaware raised his hand and signalled Broughton as Bill returned to the ringside, then pointed to Elijah. Broughton nodded and made his way through the crowd to where Elijah was sitting.

'Elijah Gates, I presume?'

Elijah looked up.

'Jack Broughton. Captain Delaware thought you could do with a second.' He looked at Bill. 'Where's your Captain, son?'

'He's with Captain Delaware, up on the gun deck,' Bill said, looking up and nodding to them.

Elijah looked up and smiled at Larsen, then turned to Edward and said to Broughton, 'This is Edward; he's my second.'

'Pleased to meet you, Edward. Now, down to the business at hand, Elijah, do you know anything about your protagonist?'

'He's got a big mouth, should be easy to hit.'

'Hmm, that's a start, let me fill you in on our Mr Crow. To begin with, I've seen him fight many times and it wasn't pretty. He's reputed to be the biggest and strongest man in the fleet. Regularly bench presses five hundred pounds for the hell of it, and he's a scrapper, not a boxer, with a very powerful right hand.'

'What about his science and stamina?'

'Well, as I said, he's not a pretty fighter. Has always gone the distance and never been knocked down.'

'Hmm, it's going to be an interesting challenge. I think I'll just wing it for the first couple of rounds, should be able to figure out his weaknesses by then.'

'If you're still in one piece. 'I tell you, he's one tough cookie, why do you think he chose to wear training gloves? He can do more damage with those.'

'Elijah,' said Bill, 'it's still not too late to back out; I don't want to see you get hurt.'

'Edward, relax. The only one who is going to get hurt is Lieutenant-Commander Crow; that I promise you.'

Further conversation was curtailed by the announcer. 'Ladies and Gentlemen, this fight is supervised by PHS Lieutenant-Commander Perkins and sanctioned by the United States Coast Guard Standing Orders which promotes the wellbeing of enlisted men through sporting activities. This will be a fight of ten rounds of three minutes each, with a knockout or submission terminating the fight immediately and, should it be necessary, the referee's decision is final.'

He paused for effect. 'And now – introducing, in the red corner, all the way from England in – the sail-boat over there,' he sniggered, and then recovered his composure, 'somewhere in the mist.'

The crowd turned to where the announcer was pointing and made gestures of staring of into the distance while laughing out loud.

He continued, 'Wearing white trunks, with a record of a few fights, unknown knockouts, at five foot eleven inches and weighing two hundred and fifteen pounds. Give him a warm *Alviso* welcome: Mr Elijah Gates.'

An unenthusiastic cheer, some raspberries, and a few catcalls rang out.

The announcer continued, 'And now, in the blue corner, from the USS *Alviso* and wearing the gold trunks, with a record of thirty two and O, twenty nine knockouts, with twenty-two in four rounds or less and seventeen in the first round, at six foot four inches and weighing two hundred and forty pounds, let's hear it for our very own, Lieutenant-Commander Crow.'

The crowd erupted in a rapturous cacophony of cheers, whistles and cries of encouragement for their champion.

As the noise died down, the referee called the protagonists to the centre of the ring for his pre-fight instructions and inspection of their gloves. Satisfied that they were ready, the referee signalled for seconds out and the start of the fight.

As the referee stepped back, the bell sounded for round one. Crow hit Elijah hard on the face with a left jab, sending him sprawling into the ropes. The crowd roared their approval. Elijah bounced back and managed to avoid Crow's right hook to the face and hit Crow's undefended jaw with a short right-handed jab. Crow countered with a wild left-handed hook, which whistled safely over Elijah's head. Crow stumbled and grappled Elijah round the neck jabbing at his face and ribs before the referee stepped in. As the referee withdrew his hand, Crow swung at Elijah, who managed to duck under the powerful punch and right-jabbed Crow in the ribcage. Crow grunted and started to back-pedal to gain time and recover his wind. The bell sounded for the end of round one.

'What do you think, Elijah?' said Broughton. 'Can you get the measure of him?'

'Already have; he's no boxer. More of a back-alley scrapper, very untidy, but quite predictable.'

'Seconds away, round two,' cried the announcer, enthusiastically ringing the bell.

With his gloves up, Elijah was ready for Crow. He didn't have long to wait. Crow assumed his reticence to be that of fear and launched straight in, arms milling like a threshing wheel. Elijah stepped back and hit the passing Crow hard with a right-jab in the ribcage again. Crow yelled in rage and turned, kicking Elijah behind the right knee. Elijah fell to one knee, but before he could stand up, Crow hit him hard on the side of the face with a right hook, sending him sprawling onto the deck. The referee stepped in and started the mandatory eight-count. Elijah was on his feet by four and stood there listening to the referee count the final four. At the count of seven, Crow sent a vicious right jab over the referee's shoulder and hit Elijah square in the face. Elijah fell to the deck a second time. The crowd were jumping up and down in a frenzy of excitement, encouraging their man to *finish the Limey*. The bell rang for the end of the round.

Bill sponged blood, snot and sweat from Elijah's face while Broughton asked, 'Elijah, do you want to call it off?'

'Are you kidding? I'm enjoying this.'

'Elijah, how can you say that?' said Bill. 'He's killing you, you won't last another battering like the last round. Please, I implore you, give up before it's too late, I can't take any more.'

Elijah smiled at Bill, patted his arm, and said,' Honestly, I'm fine. You'll see.'

'Seconds away, round three,' cried the announcer.

Elijah started the third round by dancing backwards, managing to avoid Crow's wild punching while continuing to work on his ribcage.

Crow stepped forward and stood on Elijah's left foot, smiling and hitting him with a left-right combination to the face before the referee told him to get off Elijah's foot.

While swearing at the referee and continuing to stand on Elijah's foot, Crow lunged forward and head-butted Elijah hard on the face. Crow stepped back and watched Elijah crumple to the deck, blood pouring from a split left eyebrow. Crow raised his arms in the air and bellowed loudly. 'Who's the greatest and why am I so good at it?'

The crowd screamed their admiration.

Bill was at breaking point and picked up Elijah's wet sponge from the bucket and threw it at Crow, hitting him on the back of the neck.

'What simple minded moron wants to dice with death?' Crow bellowed. 'Come on, who did it, own up and I'll kick your ass from here to Yokohama!'

'I'm not going to Yokohama,' yelled Bill.

'Well, if it's not the feisty little Dorothy from the sailboat. After I've finished with your boyfriend, I'll sort you out, good and proper.'

Whistles and catcalls emanated from the crowd.

The referee had stopped counting and the ringing of the bell for the end of round three gave Elijah time to get back to his corner.

The referee went over to Crow to remonstrate with him about his conduct. During this elongated time-out Brubaker reappeared.

'You should have given up when you had the chance, man. Give up now before it's too late and you can still walk away from here.'

Elijah raised his head, stared at Brubaker, and said, 'in the words of a great man, *I've not yet begun to fight*, Mister Brubaker. It's you who should have given up before the fight started.'

'Bullshit man, you're all in, one more round and they'll be carrying you off on a stretcher.'

'Want to bet on it?'

'With what, your boy had the only cash amongst you. You're for the chop – why would I take an IOU from you?'

'I've got something better than money. Edward, reach into my right-hand jacket pocket.'

Bill reached down to Elijah's coat and took out Martinez's gold.

'Will this do?' Elijah said.

Brubaker stared at the assortment of medallions and rings before answering, 'Must be a couple of grand here in gold, and these diamonds and rubies must be worth five grand at least. Sorry, son, that's too rich for me.'

'What you got there, Brubaker?' yelled Crow.

'The sailor wants to bet his jewellery against you winning.'

Murmurs of, 'pirate treasure,' and 'Spanish gold,' rippled through the crowd.

'What's its value?'

'Seven or eight grand,' answered Brubaker.

A collective sigh went up from the crowd.

'What odds did you give him?' shouted Crow.

'Five to one,' said Brubaker.

Crow thought for a moment. A hush descended on the crowd as they waited for their hero to make a decision.

'I'll cover it, take the bet.'

The crowd roared their approval.

'OK, you're on,' said Brubaker, pocketing the gold. 'This is like taking candy from a baby. I feel sorry for you, son – you're a born loser. Give up while you can. You don't belong here.'

Brubaker went back to the crowd who were eager to see the treasure. The bell rang for round four. Elijah got to his feet and staggered slowly towards the middle of the ring. Crow, sensing victory was within his grasp, launched a pile-driver of a right cross at Elijah's eyelid. Elijah ducked and rammed home a left jab to Crow's ribs. Crow grunted and bent to the side in pain.

'That's winged him,' said Broughton to Bill.

'What do you mean? Is that good?'

'Watch Crow, see, he is keeping his right elbow low and to his side; it means he is hurt bad, maybe a broken rib in there. He's protecting his ribs; he won't be able to use his right arm to punch as readily as he wants.'

'Go on, Elijah, hit him again! Show him what you can do,' shouted Bill.

Momentarily distracted, Elijah turned to smile at Bill. Crow saw his opportunity and made good use of it by landing a hard left jab to Elijah's forehead sending him sprawling onto the deck.'

'Oh shit, what have I done now?' said Bill, the colour draining from his face.

Elijah was back on his feet by the time the referee got to nine. Once again Crow launched a punch at Elijah's forehead, aiming for the cut just above his left eye. Elijah fended the punch with his left hand and launched a well-directed cross at Crow's nose. It landed centrally, splitting it from top to bottom. Blood poured down Crow's face and, if it weren't for the bell, the fight would have been over.

Fortunately for Crow his seconds managed to staunch the flow of blood and get him ready for the next round.

'Seconds away, round five,' called the timekeeper.

Elijah stood and stretched, like a bear coming out of hibernation, rolled his shoulders and raised his fists.

'This is where it gets interesting,' said Broughton to Bill.

'I don't understand.'

'See how Crow's standing, both feet flat on the ground, and his shoulders, they're dropped. Also, look at his body, straight and vertical, like a tall tree waiting to be felled by the woodsman's axe. Now look at Elijah, see how he's standing. He's on the balls of his feet, head over his front left foot and his right leg straight out behind him. His left fist in front of the right, and both tight against his chest under his chin. His body swaying like a snake getting ready to strike its prey. He's ready to attack or defend as needed. This is where science counts and brawn looses.'

Sensing something was different but not being able to identify it made Crow wary about charging in. Elijah advanced a few paces and Crow stepped back to stay out of punching range. Each time Elijah stepped forwards Crow stepped back till he had his back against the ropes.

The referee reached for the top rope and gave it a tug. Crow involuntarily stepped forward and drove at Elijah's face with a left jab. Elijah blocked it with his left and threw a right hook to Crow's right elbow.

Crow arched forward in pain; Elijah followed hard with a right uppercut. Crow staggered back and fell onto the ropes, where he stopped. He stood there panting, left arm round the top rope for support, trying to catch his breath.

The referee started to count, 'One – two – three.' The crowd were silent, what was happening to their champion? Cries of 'Come on, sir, you can do it,' and 'Give him hell,' and 'Knock his head off' echoed around the ring.

'Four – five – six,' intoned the referee. At 'seven' Crow let go of the top rope and shuffled forward, his face contorted with pain and anger. Elijah smiled, which made Crow even angrier, an anger which overrode the pain in his ribs.

He strode forward and bellowed, 'Now you, you insignificant piece of shit, you're going to feel the full weight of my fury! You'll wish you never decided to cross swords with me.'

The crowd loved it and shouted their approval. This was their champion of old, full of anger and about to perform violence on his opponent.

Elijah dropped his hands to his side and turning his hands out, opened his palms in a gesture of, 'Come on then, do your worst.'

The bell sounded for the end of the round. Crow raised his fist in a gesture of anger then returned to his corner.

'Elijah,' said Broughton as he sat down,' you need to wind this up. Crow is going to get a second wind and you'll have to do all this work again.'

'I'm way ahead of you, I'm sure he has a couple of broken ribs, and that's just a start.'

Bill watched Crow and his seconds. One of them took an aerosol spray and applied it to Crow's right-side ribcage.

'Seconds away, round six.'

'Jack?' said Bill, watching Crow shuffle after Elijah as he danced backwards round the ring, 'I thought Crow was guarding his right ribs with his elbow, so why is he trying to hit Elijah with his right fist?'

'Probably used an analgesic painkiller spray; football players use it all the time. It temporarily takes the pain away and lets the players keep going,' said Broughton.

'Isn't that cheating?'

'Not if your name is Crow.'

'Cheat!' shouted Bill.

Crow made a rude gesture at Bill, and then resumed his pursuit of his opponent.

Elijah stood and waited for Crow to attack. He only had moments to prepare. Crow lunged with his left. Elijah ducked and was hit by a vicious right uppercut to the face. Elijah replied with a right jab to Crow's ribs; Crow grunted in pain and fell on the ropes before staggering back to his corner.

'Elijah, you're bleeding,' Bill shouted, in a panic.

Elijah reached up with his glove to his eyebrow, and then looked at his glove. The blood was not from the eyebrow. He carefully felt the left side of his face. The salt from sweat on his glove told him where the cut was. He had a gash about three inches long on his left cheek. He looked over to Crow's corner. Crow was smiling.

The referee stepped in front of Elijah, looked at the cut and called Broughton into the ring. Crow's corner started yelling that Crow had won, Elijah had thrown in the towel; the fight was over.

The referee raised his hands and shouted to the timekeeper that there had been a foul. The cut was not caused by the boxing glove.

Crow left his corner and started shouting at the referee.

'Lieutenant-Commander Crow,' said the referee,' you know better than I what caused the cut. Now get back to your corner. Any more of that and I'll declare the visitor the winner.'

Crow went silent and returned to his corner.

'Elijah,' said Broughton, 'that's a bad cut. He must have had something concealed in his glove.'

'That's why he slid back along the ropes to his corner, he had to get rid of what he was holding,' said Elijah. 'Can you stop the bleeding before the bell?'

'You're not going on, Elijah,' said Bill. 'How much more punishment do you have to take? I can't bear it. I have enough pain to bear as it is; this beating from Crow is too much.'

While Broughton worked on his cut, Elijah said,' Edward, listen to me, it's really all right. Although it doesn't look like it, I am winning.'

'Winning!' he exclaimed. 'One more of those and you'll bleed to death.'

The bell went for the start of round seven. Elijah and Crow stood. The referee called them both to the middle and made them touch gloves.

'That's the last bell you'll hear,' said Crow.

Elijah replied, 'Ask not for whom the bell tolls, for it tolls for thee, my friend.'

'Piss off!' Crow took a swing at Elijah's face, hoping to restart the bleeding. Elijah ducked the punch and jabbed at Crow's ribs again. The analgesic spray was wearing off. Crow winced and dropped his guard.

Elijah hit Crow in the face with a left jab, then a second and a third, and followed with a right cross.

Crow was now incapable of avoiding the barrage. Elijah repeated the move, following Crow as he staggered backwards around the ring, then made a third onslaught and a fourth. As well as the swollen and bloodied nose, Crow now had one eye starting to close up and was having difficulty seeing Elijah's punches coming.

Elijah hit him again with a left. The crowd yelled, 'Left,' and each time Elijah hit Crow with a barrage of blows, the crowd followed with, 'Left, left, left right, left.' Crow could only stagger backwards with each blow in time to the crowd.

Elijah noticed the small flecks of blood on Crow's lips and smiled. It was time to end this contest. With a well-timed left jab he broke Crow's nose, which started bleeding again. He followed swiftly with a right hook and broke his jaw then, to complete the blitz, drove his fist hard into Crow's ribs. Crow collapsed onto the deck.

All went quiet, the only sound on the flight deck came from the referee: 'Eight – nine – ten – out.'

♦

'Well, Captain Larsen, Colonel Gates, son,' said Delaware, 'it certainly has been an interesting day. Are you sure you can't stay for dinner?'

'I'm sorry,' said Larsen, 'but that hurricane of a few nights ago will be making its way north-east soon and I don't want to get caught by its remnants in the Atlantic, maybe another time.'

'Pity, I wanted to show my appreciation for what you did for us. Thanks to your ministrations, Colonel Gates, Mr Crow has nothing to crow about now.'

'How is the creep?' said Bill. 'In pain, I hope, especially after what he did to Elijah.'

'I've just come from the sickbay and until he gets his jaw wired up and the broken ribs sorted, he will continue to be in serious discomfort.'

'Good. I hope he suffers for a long time,' said Bill.

Delaware turned to Larsen and said, 'As soon as we get you back to your yacht, Captain, we are headed for San Juan. Crow will be taken ashore there for medical treatment.'

'What will happen to him?' said Larsen, 'I mean after he's recovered from his injuries?'

'That's the beauty of the whole situation. When I visited him in the sickbay Crow was full of excuses about what happened to him.'

'You mean,' said Bill, 'he didn't realise you knew what had really happened?'

'Apparently so,' said Delaware, 'Crow said he was attacked and was only defending himself, typical of the man, always trying to shift the blame on to someone else.'

'What did you say to that?' said Larsen.

'I told him I had made enquiries, and apparently there were no witnesses. I told him I got the impression that everyone involved was trying to protect him.'

'What was his reply?' said Ruth.

'He actually asked me what he should do.'

'What did you advise?' said Larsen.

'I suggested that it would be better for his career if he volunteered to be transferred to shore duty.'

'How did he take it?'

'He shook his head and said he couldn't, his reputation would be ruined.'

'Just what you'd expect from such a slime-ball,' said Bill.

Delaware continued, 'I said I would put in my report that he had suffered his injuries in the line of duty.'

'And?' said Larsen.

'He jumped at the offer. The ink's still wet on his transfer request.'

'So he gets away with it. Where's the justice in that?' demanded Bill.

'Ah, but he's not getting away with it. My steward informs me that there are already several videos of the fight on YouTube. Apparently some of the sailors who have crossed swords with Crow are getting their own back.'

'Poetic justice,' said Bill, laughing.

'What about Brubaker?' asked Elijah.

'Can't wait to get off the *Alviso*, his little gambling spree has broken his and Crow's bank. There are a lot of very unhappy sailors who put money on Crow – he did pay up, didn't he?'

'Every penny,' said Bill, 'we even got the jewellery back, although I'm sure I won't be wearing it.'

'Glad to hear that,' said Delaware. 'Colonel Gates, how are you? I see our medical staff has taken care of your injuries.'

'Yes, thank you, sir. The cut to my face is only superficial. I heal quickly so I should be right as rain in a couple of days.'

'One more thing, Captain, are you sure we can't help with your former crew member?'

'No thanks. Better if we take care of his funeral. We'll do it tomorrow, on our way to Bermuda.'

'OK, Janski will take you back to your yacht. In the meantime I've got a little celebrating to do. You're not the only ones who had a bet on Colonel Gates.'

Delaware shook hands with them, turned, and walked off whistling quietly to himself while doing a Charlie Chaplin walk.

36

Burial at sea

Within minutes of Janski's farewell, the RHI was back on board and the *Alviso* was on her way to San Juan.

'John,' said Larsen, 'call Stephen and ask him to get everyone back to the *Leviathan*. It's time we were out of here and on our way home. And don't say anything to Kaufmann about Martinez, or the coast guard. I'll do that when he's back on board.'

'Sure thing Captain. Oh, by the way, I've prepared Martinez for his departure.'

'What did you do?'

'Stitched up the sheet and put some weights by the feet. I've left the head exposed, in case identification was necessary.'

'I doubt it will be necessary. In fact, it would be a good idea to not let on to the doctor what actually took place—I'll just say he had an accident while swimming back to the boat.'

'Sure thing,' said John.

'Is that what I think it is?' said Bill.

'Yes, you're looking at a very dead Mr Martinez,' replied John. 'Elijah, what happened to you?'

'I had to educate the Lieutenant-Commander about his manners,' said Elijah. 'I believe he has learned his lesson well.'

The shore party arrived, full of good humour, and climbed on board.

'Doctor Kaufmann, can I have a word, please?' said Larsen.

'Ja, what is it?'

'It's about Mr Martinez. I'm sorry to say he had an accident while swimming back to the boat.'

'Oh dear, is he hurt bad? Where is he, in his cabin?'

'No, Doctor, I'm afraid he's dead.'

'Oh no, that can't be! What will I do now? I needed him for my project; he was so strong and resourceful.'

'You still have two team members left,' said Larsen, pointing to Davis and Jones.

'*Dummkopfs*, both of them, they're nothing more than hired hands.' Kaufmann's voice rose. 'Mr Martinez, he had brains. I know he didn't always show it, but behind the façade was a very competent worker – and a good friend.' He stared off into the distance for a moment, then said, 'Excuse me, Captain. I have some serious thinking to do.'

'What was all the noise about?' said Davis as Kaufmann pushed past, 'sounded like you were having a party.'

'That was the US Coast Guard ship *Alviso*,' said John, 'apparently they have been following us for the last couple of days.

'What was that about the coast guard?' Kaufmann said, the blood draining from his face.

'They saw us drop off Señor Plata and wanted to know what we were up to,' said Larsen.

'What did you say?'

'I said we hadn't dropped anyone off, what they saw was us getting ready for bad weather.'

'Did they believe you?' asked Kaufmann anxiously.

'Why shouldn't they? We've done nothing wrong,' said Bill.

'Is there a problem, Doctor?' said Larsen.

'Nein, nein, Captain, all is well,' said Kaufmann. 'Just like you I need to be aware of what is going on around me.'

'What's got into him?' said Bill to John, after Kaufmann had gone below.

'Who knows?'

'And why do we need to wrap up Martinez? Can't we just throw the bum overboard?'

'It's tradition, Edward,' said Stephen, laughing. 'Traditionally the unfortunate sailor would be wrapped in old sailcloth with the last turns of the needle being passed through the nose and weights tied around his ankles to make the body sink.'

'That's gruesome! Why would you stick the needle in the nose?'

'To make sure they're dead.'

'Oh – sounds logical enough,' said Bill. 'Have you done that to Martinez?'

'No, not yet, I was waiting to find out if Kaufmann needed to identify the body. Captain says it's not necessary.'

'Here, let me,' he said, bending down and grabbing the needle, 'can't leave it to chance, got to make sure.'

Stephen and John watched as Bill pulled the flaps of sheet tightly over Martinez's face and started to sew up the sheet while singing softly to himself,

*'In through the front door
out through the back
over the roof and pull out the slack.'*

'Not bad for a first timer,' said John, as Bill completed the sewing.

'It's quite tough pushing the needle through the nose,' he said, 'but quite enjoyable knowing he's not coming back from where he's going. When's he going over the side?'

'Captain wants to do it early tomorrow morning once we've cleared the island and are in deep water,' said John.

'Right then, I'm off to get dinner ready,' said Bill.

'Make it quick, Edward, we'll be setting sail in about an hour,' said Stephen.

Bill put one of the polythene bags containing soup in the microwave, set it to defrost, and got busy buttering bread.

Something had changed; he felt different but couldn't quite put his finger on it. Martinez was gone, well at least he would be first thing in the morning, but that wasn't it.

He'd fallen into Poole Harbour, temporarily lost his memory, become employed to work as a cook on a luxury yacht, been sold off for who knows what to some jungle Indians, survived a hurricane, almost been knifed, killed his attacker in self-defence, been arrested by the US Coast Guard, and finally been a second at a grudge fight.

Then he realised what it was. The moment had arisen when he saw Elijah beat Crow in the fight. It had also been him fighting in the ring with his demons and he had won. He was now truly free to do what he wanted.

Getting off the *Leviathan* in Bermuda and starting a new life was the answer. No more cooking in a moving galley, cleaning up vomit, sharing living quarters with a bunch of men. Though most of the time it had been fun, he now knew what he wanted. No more running away. He would settle down to a quiet life. He would miss the men, though, Elijah especially; he'd really grown fond of him.

He'd get a small apartment overlooking the sea, and a nine to five job. Not six to midnight if the weather was bad. He would get a small dog and go for walks when he got home and, best of all, no more dreary English winters with the cold and rain.

He poured the soup into mugs as the engine note died away. He felt the now familiar movement as the *Leviathan* heeled under the press of the evening wind.

'Lovely to be under sail again,' he said to John as he delivered his soup. 'Where are we?'

'We're just past the west coast of the island. Be back in the Atlantic in about an hour. The weather's set fair and should be a pleasant sail all the way to Bermuda.'

'What was that?' said a worried-looking Kaufmann, who had just come on deck.

'I said the weather should be fair for our run to Bermuda.'

'Captain Larsen never said anything about going to Bermuda. I have important business to attend to as soon as we get back. I don't have time to waste sightseeing in Bermuda.'

'You'll have to take it up with the Captain. I just follow orders,' said John, smiling to Bill over Kaufmann's discomfort.

'What do you think that was all about?' Bill asked as Kaufmann strutted off.

'Your guess is as good as mine. The man is a complete mystery to me.'

'I'll go see what I can find out.'

Bill stepped down the companionway and into the galley, setting about washing dishes whilst listening to Kaufmann arguing with Larsen.

'But, Captain, I have reports to hand in. Decisions have to be made based on my work. I can't hang around in a tourist port while your men have a jolly ashore.'

'Doctor Kaufmann, if you'll just listen to me instead of getting all excited. I will tell you why we are going to Bermuda. We need fuel for the generators, and I presume you still enjoy having a shower?'

'Ja, what's that got to do with stopping in Bermuda?'

'That's the only place this side of the Atlantic where fuel and water are available. The alternative would be going west to Florida then retracing our steps, and besides Bermuda is on our way across the Atlantic. Even if we could catch rainwater from the sails we would still need to stop for diesel. If it's any consolation to you, we will only be there long enough to take on fuel and water.'

'That's better,' said Kaufmann, visibly relaxing. 'How long will that take?'

'Depends how busy the fuel dock is; we may have to anchor out till space is available. One to two days, I imagine.'

'More than that, Captain, I will need to get ashore and call my people. They'll be wondering where I have got to.'

'Call from here,' said Larsen,' we have a sat phone you can use.'

'Ja, I know that, but all the same, Captain, I would feel better using a landline. My work has generated some very sensitive information and I can't have it leaked till after it has been reviewed by my peers.'

'Whatever, Doctor, whatever,' replied Larsen, pushing his hair back with his hand.

As he climbed the companionway steps, he stopped and said,' Edward, I could do with a haircut and possibly so could some of the men. Should have plenty of time when we get to Bermuda.'

'Er, sure, no problem,' Bill replied. But this *could* be a problem, he wasn't planning to hang around and cut hair. As soon as they were tied up he wanted to get ashore and check out the accommodation and work scene. He would have enough money to keep him going for a while but that wouldn't last forever, so the thought of spending time giving haircuts caused him some alarm.

Bill watched Kaufmann go forward to his cabin and shut the door behind him; he wondered what the sensitive information was. How could rainfall measurements be sensitive, unless he had found a way of using the information for commercial use?

While they were anchored in the river Bill had met some of the jungle Indians who were growing fresh produce and selling it commercially through the local Brazilian markets. According to what he had been told, it was a fast-growing industry and the climate enabled a round-the-year crop. Maybe Kaufmann was working on setting up his own business, importing what they grew to Europe? If that was so, although it didn't make sense, what were the packages that he had stowed under his bunk? Definitely couldn't be vegetables.

Then the truth dawned on him: Kaufmann was feathering his own nest at the expense of UNESCO. Bill figured that there probably wasn't any rainfall data. Kaufmann was nothing more than a cheap fraudster; he was letting them fund his business dealings.

♦

Larsen had the sheets eased for the funeral and let the *Leviathan* fall off the wind. The boat wallowed in the swell while everyone was assembled on the lee side deck.

Martinez's body, still wrapped in the sheet, was placed on a makeshift stretcher and turned so the feet were pointing over the side. Stephen and Elijah stood each side at the head, holding on to the stretcher.

John and Marcel, with Bill in between, stood behind Elijah. Davis and Jones, still smarting from Kaufmann's remarks, stood a few paces forward holding on to the lifelines. Kaufmann stood beside Larsen, facing the body.

Satisfied that all was ready, Larsen said in his most solemn voice, 'Let us pray. We brought nothing into this world, and it is certain we can carry nothing out. The Lord gave, and the Lord hath taken away; blessed be the Name of the Lord. For as much as it hath pleased Almighty God to take unto himself the soul of Mr Hugo Martinez, here departed, we therefore commit his body to the deep in the sure and certain hope of the Resurrection to eternal life, through our Lord Jesus Christ.'

Stephen and Elijah raised the head of the stretcher till Martinez's body slid into the sea.

Bill looked at Kaufmann; he was crying.

The sound of a few shuffled feet and a muted chorus of 'Amen' broke the silence.

The normal sea-going pattern soon re-established itself. Kaufmann and team went to their cabins, while Bill returned to the galley and the others to their duties.

37
Bermuda

'What were all those numbers you were reciting?' Bill asked when Larsen came out of the chart room.

'Part of the clearance procedure for docking in Bermuda. Harbour Master wants to know all about our radios and beacons,' said Larsen. 'We have been instructed to tie up at the holding dock and wait to be cleared.'

It didn't take long to clear immigration and Larsen was pleased to find there was a place on the fuel dock where they could tie up for the night. Fuelling would be first thing in the morning.

Bill realised that by the time they had tied up and had their evening meal it would be too late to go ashore. As soon as he had the galley cleared he made a cup of coffee, went into his cabin, and shut the door behind him. So close, he thought, as he sat on his bunk and stared out of the porthole at the lights of St George. His thoughts were interrupted by a knock at the door.

'Yes, who is it?' he said.

'It's Captain Larsen; can I have a word, Edward?'

'Yes, sure, come on in.'

'Edward, I've been meaning to have a talk with you,' he said, standing in the doorway.

'About what?' Bill said, his voice betraying his nervousness.

'Look, we've been together for several months. We've experienced more events than most people will in a lifetime, especially you. Surely we know each other well enough that you can confide in me? What's bothering you?'

Bill hesitated for a few moments, then said, 'I have been meaning to talk to you, but wasn't sure how to bring it up. I'd like to leave the *Leviathan* in Bermuda and start a new life for myself, if that's all right with you. The voyage is almost over; you'll be back in England in a few days so I didn't think I would be missed. Bermuda is British, so I won't need a visa. Between the winnings from Elijah's fight with Crow, the money I have saved, and the rest of my pay, it should keep me going till I find work.'

'Bermuda is not quite British and although you have some money set aside, it's not that simple to live there,' said Larson. 'As a visitor you can stay only three weeks and if, as a crew member you wanted to disembark here in Bermuda, you should have informed immigration authorities at least several months ago.'

'Then it's hopeless,' Bill said, tears starting to form in the corners of his eyes.

'Look,' said Larsen, 'I plan to sail at five tomorrow afternoon. Why not go ashore first thing in the morning and have a good look around? Go to real estate agents, the ones that do rentals, and find out what it costs to rent an apartment. Have a look at the situations vacant section in a local newspaper, see what jobs are available. Come back to me and we will discuss this again. Then if you still want to give it a try, I'll talk to the immigration people; they seem to be quite pleasant.'

Bill's eyes dried and a big smile came over his face. 'Thank you, Captain.'

'Good night, Edward.'

The look on his face next afternoon told Larsen everything.

'You were right, only millionaires and criminals could afford the prices I was quoted. I just don't know how anyone can afford to work and live here. I guess you're stuck with me for the rest of the voyage.'

'Good, I wasn't looking forward to anyone else's cooking, I've tried that before, and I think I actually lost weight. Welcome back.'

'Thanks for being so understanding,' Bill said, visibly relaxing. 'Right, soup and sandwiches for the night watch, I've got to get busy, excuse me.'

38

In the Doldrums

Three days out of Bermuda, Bill woke to the *Leviathan* rolling from side to side, the familiar sound of the sea rushing along the sides absent. He dressed and went on deck.

'Why have we stopped, Stephen?'

'Can't you tell?' he said stretching out his arms, palms up. 'There's no wind.'

'But there's always wind. Where's it gone? There was plenty last night when I turned in.'

'The wind blows where it may; it's beholden to no-one.'

By the third day Bill had had enough of lying out on deck.

'I'm bored, and claustrophobic,' he said to Elijah. 'The sea looks so flat, makes me think I could go for a walk on it.'

'I wouldn't try it. It is 4,500 metres deep,' said Elijah. 'You could try getting in the dinghy and letting out the line. Some sailors do this; they say it gives them a feeling of true isolation.'

'Sounds like an idea, I think I'll try it.' He grabbed some cushions and a hat while the dinghy was being put over the side.

'Before you go off, I need to change the painter; the one on the dinghy is only two metres. You'll need a much longer one to get the real effect,' said Stephen. 'Elijah, pass me that spare line, the one on the coach roof.'

Bill climbed down into the dinghy and pushed off from the side of the *Leviathan*. The dinghy slowly drifted till he was floating 100 feet away.

He lay back on the cushions, placed his hat so the brim shaded his eyes, and stared at the horizon. He looked in an arc from south to north; there wasn't a cloud in sight, nor any ripples on the surface of the ocean. The *Leviathan*, still and listless, looked like a toy sitting in a pond on a summer day. He pulled the brim of his hat further over his face, closed his eyes, and thought of Bermuda and what might have been.

'Hello, Edward.'

Startled, he sat up and looked for the source of the voice.

'Over here.'

He was sure he had heard a voice, but there was no sign of anyone, not even the tell-tale ripple of a swimmer from the *Leviathan*.

'Not over there, over here.'

Bill turned, looked over the transom of the dinghy, and was surprised to see a young man floating head and shoulders out of the water.

'Who are you? Where did you come from?' Bill sat up and looked around for signs of another vessel. 'You're not from the *Leviathan*, Where's your boat?'

'I don't live on a boat Edward; I live here.'

'Where?'

'Here, in the sea. This is my home.'

'You mean to say you just float around?'

'Sometimes, depends on the weather. When it's calm and sunny I like to float on the surface.'

'And when it's not nice?'

'Down below, with my friends.'

'There are more of you?'

'Of course, I've lots of friends.'

'But you can't just live in the sea, you'd drown.'

He smiled and wrinkled his nose at Bill. 'You don't recognise me, do you?'

'Of course, I don't recognise you; I've never seen you before in my life.'

'But you have, don't you remember? It was a long time ago. We were on holiday, it was midsummer. A very hot evening, we went for a walk.'

Bill looked at him; there was something about his eyes. 'George! But you're dead, you drowned – I killed you – I saw you washed down the river – we never found you.'

'I know, that was a sad day. It was quite a shock. But all the same, you didn't kill me.'

He reached up, pulled himself partially out of the water, rested his arms on the gunnel, and stared into Bill's face.

'How are you, big brother? You look troubled, what's bothering you?'

'I've killed again – twice.'

'Look, you didn't kill me. I lost my footing and fell and hit my head. You had nothing to do with my death. It was an accident; accidents happen. That's why they're called accidents.'

'That's what Ruth said.'

'She's smart; you should listen to her.'

'It's too late for that.'

'It's never too late to forgive, or to be forgiven.'

'You dying made it too late; Mr Ambrose dying in the car crash made it too late, and Thornton, it was too late for him the moment he got in my car; running away from my family made it too late; killing Martinez made it too late. Don't tell me it's never too late.'

'As I've already said, my death was an accident; I don't blame you for that.'

'But four people have died because of me?'

'Alcoholism is an illness. Would it, say, be your fault if you became ill from flu, or you caught malaria while on the Amazon?'

'No, it happens to lots of people.'

'My point exactly.'

'But you don't catch alcoholism.'

'That's true, but nonetheless it is still an illness.'

'And running away from my family, what illness is that?'

'You were scared, emotionally exhausted, and you simply took the easy way out. Stress does terrible things to your reasoning.'

'I suppose it was stress that killed Martinez?'

'No, you definitely *did* kill him, but that was self-defence and nobody would blame you for what you did.'

'Still, I feel guilty all the time. I suppose that's why I drink; I drink to forget.'

'And does it work?'

'No.'

George slid off the gunnel and back into the water. 'Well, give it up. I've got to go now.'

'No wait; there are still lots to talk about! You can't leave me now,' Bill cried, leaning over the edge of the dinghy.

◆

'Elijah,' said Stephen, 'what's Edward up to? He looks like he's talking to someone.'

'You're right,' said Elijah, holding the binoculars to his eyes.

'Better keep an eye on him,' said Larsen, as he stepped into the cockpit, 'too much sun can cause sunstroke.'

'Too long in the sun already,' said Stephen. 'Should we pull the dinghy back?'

They watched in disbelief as Bill slid over the side of the dinghy and under the water.

'Now what's he up to?'

'Nothing good,' said Elijah, as he kicked off his deck shoes and dived over the stern rail.

'He hasn't surfaced,' said Stephen, as they watched Elijah swim towards the bubbles on the surface.

'Get John, Stephen, I think his services will be needed.'

Elijah arrived at the spot where Bill went under and, after filling his lungs with as much air as they would hold, upturned and dived after Bill. He swam down the trail of diminishing bubbles until he could just make out his form in the cerulean blue of the ocean. Bill had stopped swimming and hung there, suspended in the water, looking like a rag doll someone had discarded. Elijah reached down and, cupping Bill's chin with one hand, struck out for the surface.

As they reached the surface Elijah wrapped his free left arm round the dinghy painter and yelled, 'Stephen, pull us back, he's not breathing.'

Desperate for signs of life, Elijah looked at Bill's face. Unable to detect any breathing Elijah pulled Bill's face to his, pinched his nose with his left hand, tilted Bill's head back, and as he floated on his back, commenced mouth-to-mouth resuscitation. It was a difficult manoeuvre. As Stephen pulled on the rope it tried to pull Elijah's hand away from Bill's nose.

As they came alongside the *Leviathan* Stephen and John jumped down into the dinghy and, with as much care as they could, passed Bill up to Larsen and Marcel who laid Bill on the coach roof. Within seconds John was back on board and by Bill's side.

'How is he?' asked Larsen.

'Not good, very weak pulse, but at least he's not dead.' He turned Bill's head to the side and waited for a moment; a trickle of sea water dribbled from his nose and mouth, then he coughed and vomited. John waited for the spasms to cease then checked Bill's vital signs again. He shook his head, smiled, and said, 'Poseidon will rise to live another day.'

'Stephen,' said Larsen, 'get Bill a blanket, can't have him go into shock. John, what do you recommend?'

'Bed rest and fluids, water that is. Bill should be fine in a couple of days.'

Stephen returned with a blanket.

'Here, let me do this,' said Elijah, taking it from him. He bent over, unfolded the blanket, and covered Bill's shivering, prostrate body.

'I'll check his bunk,' said John. 'Could you carry Bill below?'

'Well?' said Larsen as John came out of Bill's cabin.

'He's awake, just. I've told him he needs to rest, get his strength back.'

'Can I see him?'

'Sure, but keep it short, he does need to rest.'

♦

Larsen knocked and went in. Bill was lying on his side facing the cabin door. His eyes were staring at something a million miles away.

'How are you?'

Bill looked up at Larsen and replied, 'I should have drowned. You should have let me go.'

Larsen shook his head. 'Too much sun, that's all that's wrong. You'll be fine after a couple of days' rest. Stephen says there won't be much wind so you may as well lay back and sleep. The boys can make the meals while you rest, it'll do them good.'

'And what about me, when do I get to feel good? All I feel is guilt.'

Larsen looked at Bill and, trying to sound as patient as he could, said, *'forgive yourself.'*

'I don't deserve to be forgiven. Not after what I've done.'

Larsen shook his head, breathing out through clenched teeth. Reaching over to the shelf he grabbed a book, spilling several others onto the floor, and threw it onto the bunk. 'Here, read this. It'll tell you all about forgiveness.'

He left the cabin, shutting the door behind him.

Bill sat up, picked up the book, and looked at it.

'How to have a great day, and a fantastic future it read down the spine, just what he didn't want to read, another self-help book. He'd read enough of those to last three lifetimes.

A call of nature got him out of his bunk. On the way back he picked up the books that had fallen out of the bookshelf and returned them to their places, all except the last one.

It was Larsen's Bible, zipped tight in a leather case. He shook his head and went to put it alongside the others when he noticed that the zipper wasn't done up all the way round and a piece of blue paper was sticking out. Curiosity got the better of him and, unzipping the cover, he opened the Bible at the blue paper.

It was a letter, or rather several letters, bound together by a dried-out rubber band. He looked at the front of the pack; the first letter was addressed to *Captain Larsen, MV Sargasso, c/o Madison Lines, Bilbao, Panama.* A large stamp *To Be Called For* was imprinted on the lower left hand corner, with another, in large red letters saying, *Forward to,* and here in neat hand-printing, *Try Cristobal*. He looked at the other envelopes; they all had similar red stamps.

Bill climbed back onto his bunk and, now fully committed, removed the letter from the tattered envelope with the oldest postmark, and read:

> *My dearest Eric, it seems like ages since we were together, how could it only be two weeks since you held me in your arms?*
> *I'm glad you're not here to see me at the moment, I look like a whale. Doctor says all is well with the baby and no change with the due date. Hope you get to Hamburg in time to fly home for the birth. I'm not sleeping well though. The bed's just too big for one, although that's not quite correct, is it? Oh how I wish you were here.*

Bill felt guilty reading what was a letter from Larsen's wife and without reading further, folded the single sheet neatly on the creases and returned it to its envelope.

Not quite satisfied though, he withdrew the letter from the next envelope; it had a similar address, except this time the city was Cristobal, the other end of the canal. He remembered that from looking at the charts of the Caribbean.

> *My dearest Eric, how are you? Missing me as much as I miss you? The weather is still hot; it hit 105 in Redwood City yesterday, a record for this time of the year.*

Bill skimmed down the letter then turned it over.

> *The baby is busy, woke me twice last night; kept poking me in the ribs, just like someone else I know. Talked to the doctor about the indigestion pains I'm getting. My friend Lottie says they are normal, all pregnant women get them; I prefer to wait for the results of the doctor's tests.*
> *I tried to call you last night, but apparently your sat phone isn't working at the moment. Write soon, love from Samantha and soon to be Stephanie.*

Curiosity had really got hold of him, so Bill pulled the letter from the third envelope. This one displayed a port address in Houston Texas. He noticed the handwriting had changed.

> *Dear Eric, I'm sorry to be the bringer of bad news, Samantha has had to go into hospital for tests. The doctor thinks it might be some kind of intestinal infection. They are unable to give her any pain medication, because of the baby. The doctor has sedated her instead. He says she should be over it by the time you reach Southampton. Regards Lottie.*

Bill picked up the next to last letter, this envelope said,

> *To be hand delivered to Captain Larsen, MV Sargasso, c/o the Port Captain Southampton.* Someone had scrawled across the front, *Left port, try Hamburg.*

All these letters – and he'd never received any of them till he reached Hamburg. With trembling hands Bill removed the last letter and noticed immediately how tear-stained it was. The handwriting had changed and the return address wasn't San Francisco, it was an address in Portland, Oregon.

> *Dear Eric, I am not sure where you'll be when you get this letter, please call us as soon as you do.*
> *Samantha had not been well for several weeks. At first she thought it was just indigestion and was taking antacid medication. The doctor agreed with her treatment but last week she was admitted to hospital. At first he thought it was an intestinal infection, unfortunately it was worse, a severe case of peritonitis due to a ruptured appendix. I'm so sorry, Eric; they weren't able to save Samantha.*
> *You do have a wonderful daughter though. Initially we have called her Stephanie, that's the name Samantha had said she was thinking off when Rose talked to her last week.*
> *As soon as we realised how sick Samantha was we tried to contact your ship via sat phone, but no one in the San Francisco office could find the right number to call you on.*
> *Samantha's mother and I love you very much and look forward to hearing from you, remember there's always a room for you here at home,*
> *Andrew.*

Bill folded the letter and returned it to its envelope. On the page of the Bible where the letters had been stored, one verse had been underlined, it read,

> *And whenever you pray, if you are angry with anyone, forgive them, from your heart, that God the Father, who sees and knows all things and who also is the creator of all living beings, may forgive you your anger.*

Bill, not being a Bible reader, wondered why Larsen would have chosen this particular verse to read. Then he noticed an asterisk beside the verse directing the reader to a footnote on the following page, it read.

> *Anger, like fear and worry, is a negative emotion that debilitates the mind from thinking rationally, constructively and productively. We were not created to be destructive with our emotions; rather the message from day one of creation is that we are to build up, create, and reproduce what God has started.*
>
> *Your anger may not just be limited to being angry with others, you can be angry with yourself. For instance you may have some habit that you can't overcome, or others around you may have an annoying habit that winds you up, or even simple things, like your spouse, loved one, or friend always forgetting something that they promised to do. Start now and forgive yourself your own failings, and see how your world changes.*
>
> *Being angry will not repair broken relationships, only the selfless act of forgiving the aggrieving party, regardless if they intended their act or not can do that. For further information on forgiveness, see Word of Wisdom for Luke 23v 34 on page 1632.*

Bill stood and re-read the footnote; despite how much he tried to deny the fact, it was correct. He had many times in his life been angry with himself and those around him, especially his parents, when his little brother had died, for shutting him out of their grief. He sniffled and tried not to cry when he thought about his drinking and the car accident.

He read the footnote again: *only the selfless act of forgiving the aggrieving party*. But how did one forgive oneself? He thought for a moment, found a pencil, tore a sheet of paper out of his notebook and wrote,

Bill, I am so sorry for what I've put you through all these years. I've blamed you for all the problems, please accept my apology, and forgive me. Please tell Mum and Dad that I'm sorry for blaming them for shutting me out of their grief.
Me.

Taking a deep breath he looked at the note and read it. Nothing had changed. He read it again, same, no change. A third time, same result. This time he tore the note off and with a piece of sticky tape fastened it to the mirror.

He looked at the note, memorised it, then staring straight into his eyes in the reflection he spoke out what he had written; then repeated it, this time with more feeling; then again, this time louder and again, shouting out the words.

Larsen knocked on the door and entered, 'Edward, what's wrong?'

Bill turned to him, 'Oh, Captain, I've been such an ass. All these years I've blamed everyone for my problems when I should have looked in the mirror.'

'Wait a minute, slow down. Take a deep breath and tell me what are you talking about.'

'I read your letters.'

'What letters?'

'The ones your wife wrote.'

'Where are they?'

'Don't you know?'

Larsen shrugged, shook his head, and said, 'No, I've looked for them for years. I had begun to think they were lost forever. Where did you find them?'

'In your Bible, it fell from the bookshelf when you gave me the other book to read.'

'Of course, why didn't I think of looking there?' said Larsen.

'Did you underline the verse?'

'Which one?' he said picking up the Bible from the bunk.

'Here, where the letters are,' Bill said, turning the pages and pointing to the underlined verse.

Larsen read it quietly then looked up at Bill and nodded. 'When we tied up in Hamburg, my mail was delivered to me by a Mission to Seafarers chaplain. The company thought the news would be better received from someone experienced in that type of matter.'

'Was he able to help?'

'It was a long time ago, but yes, he was helpful. It was he who suggested the Bible verse. I circled it and almost read the words off the page.'

'Why the verse about anger?'

'You said you read my letters; you tell me?'

'I skimmed through them; I didn't read all of them.'

'Try the first one.'

Bill picked up the letters from the bunk and, pulling the letter from the first envelope, read past the part he had read earlier.

He finished reading and looked up at Larsen. 'You two had an argument before you left and she wrote to apologise, but you didn't get the letter.'

Larsen shook his head slowly. 'The one great sorrow of my life was, I was never able to say I was sorry and ask her to forgive me. I knew the baby was due in a few weeks and instead of taking leave I reasoned I would have enough time to get the ship to port in Hamburg and fly back in time for the birth. I drove the ship and men hard and was two days ahead of the schedule all the way. That's why the mail never caught up with me till I reached Hamburg.'

'What about the sat phone?'

'The old one died on the way down to San Diego, so I had it replaced before we left. I was so busy and focused on getting to Hamburg early, I didn't have time to have the number transferred to the new phone and I simply forgot to let the office know what the new number was.'

'So you were angry at yourself?'

'Myself, the company, I was angry with the whole damned world. I flew home as soon as I could and said goodbye to Samantha at the graveside while holding my daughter.'

'What did you do next?'

'I fell to pieces. I gave up the sea and tried working ashore, but was never able to settle and eventually turned to drink. My in-laws took Stephanie and raised her. In the end I went back to sea, where I belong.'

'And Stephanie?'

'We sort of keep in touch, usually end up arguing.'

'What's she doing?'

'I thought I told you, she's at Stanford University. She's studying law, hopes to work for the FBI.'

'Of course you did, I forgot. She sounds like quite a young woman, just like her dad. At least she's got a future, unlike me.'

'You could have one as well. You realise that now, don't you?'

Bill looked at him, thought for a moment, and then nodded.

Larsen picked up his Bible and the letters, leaving Bill staring at the note on the mirror as Larsen shut the door quietly.

Something had definitely changed, although he couldn't quite put his finger on it. There was a feeling of elation. Then a memory of something that happened when he and Ruth were first married. It was the weekend of their fifth anniversary; the girls were staying with their grandparents. Ruth had gone out with a friend the evening before and came home at two in the morning, the worse for drink. They'd had a blazing row and he'd sulked off to the spare room. He'd slept in till eleven, long after she'd gone into town to do some shopping. When he finally woke, he felt guilty, and spent the rest of the day tidying up the house. He prepared Ruth's favourite dinner; she showed up at the door with a tub of toffee popcorn and a DVD. They hugged, she apologised for what she'd done, and he apologised for shouting at her. It was one of the best evenings they had ever had together. Pity he'd never have another one.

The note on the mirror gave him an idea – he would write to the family and apologise, asking them to forgive him for what he had done. Of course he would never know if they would or not, it just felt right to do it. He'd write the letter and post it when they got to the Azores.

39
The Azores

It was their first and only morning in the Azores. Larsen said they would stay just long enough to re-provision before setting off for the uphill run to the UK. Kaufmann voiced his approval of this announcement at breakfast.

It was going to be a busy day for Bill. The letter had to be posted, fresh vegetables and fruit had to be purchased from the market, and there would be a mandatory stop at the Café Sport. Larsen had said not to bother with any meat. The last time they'd bought some in the Azores it was too tough, something to do with not aging the meat long enough. John and Stephen were going to take care of the water and fuel, so as soon as all the chores were done, they could leave, although not until the *Leviathan's* name had been painted on the sea wall.

Dropping the letter in the post-box was the final act of saying goodbye. He was now truly free of any obligations to his past and could get on with the rest of his life. The thought of spending the winter on the *Leviathan* while it was prepared for the new season on the Med sounded good to him. Maybe he could work in the *Admiral* and live aboard. Or a spell working with Betty in the marina restaurant had its appeal. Either way, he would have to discuss it with Larsen if he was going to live aboard.

Looking north as he walked down the pier past the yachts, he could see the green hills of the island rising behind the town. Yes, he thought, it will be good to get back home to England and my new life.

It was a long walk to the marina reception and the post box and he was glad to have Elijah and Marcel with him to help carry the provisions back. On the way they stopped at Café Sport for a drink. Bill had a coffee while Elijah stuck a small *Leviathan* flag on the wall to commemorate their visit.

'Where are our guests?' Bill asked Stephen as he passed the last bag of oranges down the companionway.

'In their cabins sleeping off one beer too many,' said Stephen, 'except Kaufmann. He's gone ashore. Captain has told him we are sailing at six, whether he's here or not.'

'And the Captain?'

'He and John have gone to paint *Leviathan*'s name on the sea wall, should be back within the hour.'

Bill went below with an idea, something that had been brewing in his mind since they left Bermuda. Leaving the oranges on the counter he headed for Kaufmann's cabin. He opened the door and went in, climbed the steps and opened the hatch; he didn't want to be caught in Kaufmann's cabin when he returned.

He tried the locker under his bunk first and found to his dismay it was locked. Then he methodically went through the drawers under the dressing table mirror, but all they contained were clothes. Next was the hanging locker; just jackets, coats and a hat. Last were the small bedside lockers against the hull. To reach them he had to climb up on the bunk. He reached over and pulled the doors open, another blank, only some well-thumbed top shelf magazines. He returned them and rolled back over the bunk. As he did, he felt something hard under the pillow; reaching under it, he withdrew a hand-held sat phone.

'I see you've found it,' said Marcel.

'Marcel! You made me jump! I thought it was Kaufmann.'

'Just as well it wasn't, we've seen what company he keeps. Just what are you hoping to accomplish by searching his cabin?'

'He's up to no good; I thought I could find out what. Look at this, a sat phone, why did he have to go ashore in Bermuda to use a phone when he had one of his own?'

'An excellent question, Herr Cook,' said Kaufmann, pushing his way past Marcel. 'And I will answer it. If you knew anything about sat phones you would know that certain phones do not work in all areas of the world. This model only receives service in Europe, not the mid or eastern Atlantic. Now, if there aren't any other questions, I would like to get ready for dinner.'

'Did you look under the bunk?' said Marcel, when they were back at the galley and out of earshot.

'No, it was locked, and I didn't have time to get the spare key. Why?'

'Doesn't matter, just wondered what he had under the bunk.'

'He told me he was importing native artwork, some charity thing he was organising.'

'And the moon is made of cheese,' said Marcel, as Bill continued stuffing the fresh oranges in the hanging fruit net.

'Ready to go to sea, Edward?' said Larsen, as he came down the companionway.

'Yes and no. I've just put the last of the provisions away but I need some time to have Marcel trim my hair. Since I am planning to make a clean start when we reach England, keeping my hair cut short is part of the plan. Oh, also, do I need to make soup?'

This had become his way of asking what the weather would be like over the next three days.

'Winds, southerly or south westerly, veering westerly or north westerly later, five to seven, occasionally four in south.' Larsen intoned in his best BBC Radio voice. 'Sea state – rough or very rough – becoming moderate or rough in the south later.'

'OK, it's soup then,' he laughed. He liked Larsen, as did all the crew; they were like one big, happy family. Then he realised for the first time he was a part of it. Pity about the quality of the guests, but at least they'd be gone in a few days. He wondered if they'd leave when they reached Falmouth or stay on till they reached Poole; he hoped it would be Falmouth; he couldn't wait for them to be gone.

'I'm going ashore for the clearance paperwork, be back shortly,' said Larsen.

As Larsen stepped out on to the deck, Kaufmann exited his cabin. 'Where's the captain, I need to see him,' said Kaufmann.

'You've just missed him. He's gone ashore, but said he'll be back shortly, were getting ready to depart.'

'Good, I want to talk to him about our passage. Tell him I must see him as soon as he returns.'

Ja vol Herr Commandant,' Bill whispered quietly to himself. He shook his head at Kaufmann's arrogance, and then returned to preparing the galley for going to sea.

Larsen returned a few minutes later and gave the order to get underway. The sound of the engine starting brought Kaufmann from his cabin.

'Where's the Captain?' he demanded again.

'On deck, where he belongs when we leave harbour,' said Bill.

'I'll wait for him down here; I don't want to get in the way,'

Bill got on with his preparations for lunch and watched Kaufmann. His face slowly turned white as the boat left the still water of the harbour and headed out into the Atlantic.

The atmosphere on the boat had definitely changed. At first Bill put it down to his rant in the mirror the previous week, but it wasn't just him. For the first three days after leaving Horta, Kaufmann, instead of living in his cabin as he had done for most of the time at sea, spent a good deal of the time up on deck pacing from one end of the boat to the other. He even convinced Davis and Jones to do a bit of recreational pacing with him, although, Bill noticed, he never saw all three of them on deck together at one time.

Normality was resumed on the fourth day as they reached 45 degrees north and ran straight into a westerly that lasted three days. By late evening on day five the sea had moderated and Kaufmann emerged to resume his pacing, though this time alone.

'Fresh air does wonders for your sea legs, Doctor,' said Larsen.

'Ja, I do believe you're correct, Captain. Tell me, Captain; how far from land are we just now?'

'Not planning to swim ashore are you, Doctor?'

'Nein, nein, Captain, just curious. You said yesterday that sometimes when the weather gets really bad you have to run before it.'

'Nearest land is about 90 miles to the south-east. When we crossed the Bay of Biscay it ranged up to approximately 300 miles.'

'What will be the closest we get to land?'

'I expect we will pass about 60 miles from the French coast.'

'And when will that be?'

'For a man that doesn't like sailing Doctor, you are asking a lot of peculiar questions.'

'Just interested, that's all. And if I may be permitted to ask one last question, when will we be off of the coast of France?'

'If this wind stays as it is then we should be off of Ushant just after midnight.'

'Ah, that is what I thought. Thank you, Captain. I'm going below now, too much fresh air for a man who spends most of his day indoors.'

Larsen followed Kaufmann below, went into the chartroom, and sat trying to figure out why Kaufmann was suddenly so active and curious about where they were. Normally he would be in his cabin, sleeping. What did it matter to Kaufmann where they were or how far from the coast? Surely, he didn't want to go ashore? They were less than two days from Falmouth.

Larsen heard the clock strike six bells, one hour to go till midnight and the change of watch. It was a puzzle. Why would Kaufmann want all that information about their position and yet not show any interest in when they would reach port? A thought came to him; he turned on the radar and went to the galley.

'Not sleepy, Edward?'

'No, just making sure the soup and hot water are ready for the night watch then I'm turning in. Tomorrow I plan to start getting ready for our arrival in Falmouth, got lots to do.'

'Good. It will be great to get back into port. This trip is tiring. Where are the others?'

'John just went forward to get his coat; he's on watch next after Stephen. Marcel has turned in for the night and Elijah is snoozing on the settee. He's going to sit up for a while with John when he goes on watch.'

'OK, I'll be in the chart room. Tell John when he comes back I need to have a quiet word with him, and Elijah as well. Is there any coffee on the go?'

'Just made a fresh pot, I'll bring you a cup.'

'Thanks, make some for the crew as well. I think they're going to need it.'

'You wanted to see us, Captain?'

'Yes. Elijah, go wake Marcel and ask him to spell Stephen at the wheel. I need him down here.'

'Sure thing, Captain.'

Bill stood outside to listen. There wasn't enough room for the whole crew inside the chart room.

Larsen said, 'I had a weird conversation half hour ago with Kaufmann; he kept asking how close we were to land. I want to know why.' He turned to John who was in front of the screen. 'See anything, John?'

'All I can see is a small blip about three miles away off our stern. On the port bow a large ship heading south, nothing else.'

'Is the small blip following us?'

'I certainly hope so,' interrupted the voice from the main saloon.

'Kaufmann! What the hell?' exclaimed Larsen.

'Yes, Captain, this is a gun I have pointed at the head of our cook. Now if you and your men will file out of the chart room, and sit down at the saloon table, Mr Davis will keep an eye on you all. Slowly, Captain, no tricks, or you'll need a new cook.'

They filed out of the chart room and sat at the saloon table while Kaufmann continued to hold his gun to Bill's head.

'Davis, Jones' said Kaufmann, handing Jones small pistol he took from his jacket pocket, 'keep an eye on them.'

Kaufmann let go of Bill and handed his pistol to Davis and intimated that Bill join the rest of the crew at the table, then headed into the chart room.

Immediately, Kaufmann could be heard talking on the VHF radio in Spanish. He came out of the chart room, a big smile on his face.

'Captain, my friends will be alongside in a few minutes and I want your word that you and your men will not try and prevent us leaving with our cargo. If you try to resist,' he turned to look at Bill, and drew his finger across his throat, 'you understand?'

'Yes, Doctor, that is if you are really a doctor, we understand,' said Larsen. 'But Doctor Kaufmann, answer me one question, please.'

'Certainly, Captain, we have plenty of time and, since you asked, I attained my doctorate in philosophy at the London School of Economics.'

'Why the facade about researching the rainfall on the river, won't UNESCO want their money back?'

'I doubt it. I'll just say I lost two of my team during an altercation with illegal loggers and I had no choice but to return.'

'Why the delay?' said Elijah. 'Why not show up, collect the drugs, then leave?'

'Ah, Colonel Gates, you have too honest a mind. The cartel weren't going to deliver my goods till they were paid.'

'And the uncut diamonds had to be valued first,' said Bill.

'Oh, Captain,' said Kaufmann, 'if only you and your crew worked for me. I'd make you all rich beyond your wildest imagination. But it's not to be.'

They were interrupted by the arrival of Marcel at the top of the companionway. 'Captain, there's a large Spanish trawler trying to come alongside, they want us to head up into the wind.'

'Ah, Señor Galan,' said Kaufmann, 'please return to your post, we can't have an accident at this stage of the voyage.' He turned to Larsen, 'Captain, have two of your men go on deck and do what is necessary.'

Larsen nodded to Elijah and Stephen. 'You heard the doctor, start the engine and drop the sails, and tell Marcel to run down the trough parallel to our visitor.'

'Thank you, Captain,' said Kaufmann.

The *Leviathan* slowed to five knots and hit a wave, causing one of the Thermoses to fly across the galley.

Bill stood up.

'Sit down,' said Davis.

'I need to pick up the Thermos, that's all.'

'OK,' said Davis, waving him over to the galley with his pistol.

The Spanish crew had obviously done this before. Bill watched them launch a rigid-hull inflatable with a crew of five; two had machine guns hanging from their shoulders. They motored over to the *Leviathan*, climbed aboard, and came below.

Kaufmann directed them to his cabin and showed them where to find his cargo. They immediately set to work transferring the contents from under his bunk to the inflatable. Fifty minutes later Kaufmann and his men took their leave of the *Leviathan* and were gone.

'Elijah,' said Larsen, 'go with Stephen and escort Señor Galan down here. He has a lot of explaining to do.'

Marcel came over to the table and sat down; Larsen and the crew sat either side, trapping him.

'Captain, if I may be permitted to speak,' said Marcel, 'before your men throw me over the side to the fish.'

'Go on.'

'Please be patient, I will explain.' Marcel took in a deep breath then slowly exhaled. 'When I left school, I joined the Spanish Navy. Just before I had served my time I was asked if I would like to continue working for my government as a civilian in the Foreign Office. I spent the first few years being posted to several embassies around the Mediterranean. Two years ago I was transferred to our embassy in Venezuela. That's where I came across the name of Señor Plata.'

'Yes, we already know that,' said Larsen, testily. 'What's that got to do with you working for Kaufmann?'

'Please, Captain – I will explain.'

Bill came over to the table with a fresh pot of coffee and sat down facing Marcel.

'I suppose that story about you being a hairdresser was all a fabrication?'

'No, that was all true, but please, be patient.'

'Let's hear it, then,' said Larsen.

'For several years the American and European governments have been quite successful in intercepting the import of super quantities of cocaine. In 2005 it was decided, at an intergovernmental meeting, that an international effort had to be made to reduce the demand while at the same time reducing the availability of illicit drugs. Consequently the smugglers have become more adept at circumventing these attempts. Some have even gone as far as building their own submarines. For some time we had suspicions that quantities of drugs, mainly cocaine, were being hand carried on the cross channel ferries to the UK. It looked like someone was trying to set up a new distribution network and were testing UK customs defences. Our break came when we intercepted a shipment last year.' He looked at Bill. 'Your hairdresser,

Isabelle, remember she wasn't available for your appointment, Edward? And I did your hair instead. You said she was bringing you something back from Spain, something special, I seem to remember you saying?'

Bill's face turned red with anger. 'And you thought I was dealing in drugs! How could you? You knew nothing about me.'

'Exactly,' said Marcel. 'But I was only doing my job, following the leads. When you suddenly disappeared, I was doubly curious.'

'So how did you make the connection?' asked Larsen.

'We felt our time was short and that South America was too large an area to investigate, so we concentrated on the possible landing sites in Europe between Gibraltar and Cuxhaven.'

'Where's Cuxhaven?' queried Bill.

'It's a coastal town on the North Sea in Northern Germany,' said Stephen.

Marcel continued, 'As I was saying, the coast was divided up into sections. Mine was from Saint Nazaire to Dieppe. We were despairing that no leads were forthcoming, till the incident at the ferry with your hairdresser – Isabelle.'

'I remember only too well,' said Bill.

'Isabelle didn't fit the profile of a drug smuggler; she was angry at being duped, and only too eager to help us. Her story was that while wandering through a street market she got talking to one of the street traders. They told her about an English lady who had purchased a valuable antique the previous day but, in the hurry, to catch the ferry had left her purse behind. Isabelle said the trader asked her if she would mind taking it with her and handing it to the lady who would be waiting for her when she arrived.'

'How could anyone be so gullible?' said Stephen.

'You'd be surprised how gullible people can be,' said Larsen. 'There are thousands of people, just like Isabelle, rotting in far-flung jails.'

'Because of the work of ETA,' Marcel continued, 'Spain now has many security measures in place, including a plethora of CCTV cameras in public places. We found one of the cameras at the market had recorded the transaction.'

'So Isabel was in the clear, you let her go,' said Bill.

'For the sake of the investigation, Isabelle agreed to stay out of sight while the investigation was ongoing. It was a very nice hotel, she said afterwards. We kept the stall under 24 hour surveillance and tried to identify anyone who looked like they may be part of the supply chain.

After a few false starts we worked our way back to the front door of Doctor Kaufmann.'

'Sounds like you've got quite a team,' said Larsen.

'It was quite a surprise for us,' continued Marcel. 'Kaufmann is a well-respected member of society, a champion of the global warming crowd. He even has connections in high places in the USA global warming movement, though I doubt they have any idea of his nefarious activities. The thing that attracted our interest was the fact that he was putting together an expedition to the Amazon to study the effects of low rainfall and illegal logging.'

'But how did you come to work as part of Kaufmann's team on the *Leviathan*?' asked Larsen.

Marcel poured himself another coffee then went on with his story. 'We now had a suspect and a good idea of what his plans were, we just didn't know how or when. My task was to infiltrate the operation and somehow get that information. Kaufmann is a very busy man; I followed him about from port to port. Apparently he was trying to charter an ocean-going fishing boat, without any success. We thought he was nuts. Sure, an ocean-going trawler would take them safely across the Atlantic and even up the Amazon, but would simply attract too much attention, now we knew what it was for. A few days later he headed for England and Poole. As it turned out he went there to check on his English contacts, probably hand deliver the lost consignment. That's where Martinez and crew come into the picture.'

'Couldn't you have arrested him at Customs?' said Bill.

'Yes, that could have been arranged, but we wanted to find out the extent of his operation. Arresting him would have scuppered that prospect.'

'Makes sense now you explain it,' said Bill.

'I think it was when he arrived in Poole and saw all the boats in the harbour that he got the idea to charter one from the UK. That gave us an idea; I made contact with my man in England.'

'Not the elusive Mr Smith was it?' said Larsen.

'The very same.'

'I suggested that if he could find a suitable vessel we might be able to get Kaufmann to take the bait.'

'So, the *Leviathan* was bait for Kaufmann's plan, is that it?' said Larsen.

'We didn't know you at the time, but you did fit the bill and the *Leviathan* did need work being done on it.'

'So I'm now a fugitive wanted for smuggling cocaine. Thanks a lot!'

'Wait a moment, Captain. Who said you've been smuggling cocaine? Let me finish my story, and then you'll understand. Once we got Kaufmann settled on the idea of the *Leviathan*, my next task was to get included on the team.'

'How did you do that?' said John. 'No one believed that cock and bull story you told earlier.'

'All I could think of at that moment. Kaufmann had his team; obviously, from observing them, they all knew each other. We ran background checks and found one of them had a warrant out for some GBH offence. It was a simple job for me to pretend to be drunk and pick a fight with him. I made enough of a ruckus that the police were called and we were both arrested, I tried to make a suitable impression by putting up a struggle and swearing at the police in several languages. As soon as the police found out there was an outstanding arrest warrant for him, he was out of the gang and it was a relatively simple job to get him locked up for the duration. Kaufmann was now one person short and I managed to talk my way in to his confidence and that, as they say, was that. Although I don't think he ever really trusted me.'

'But the cocaine?' said Larsen.

'You recall the story Plata told you, about what he was up to on the Amazon?' said Marcel.

'He said something about a business deal.'

'I suppose you could call it that. He told me one of his Columbian friends contacted him about a shipment of cocaine that was going to be transported down the Amazon River. The smugglers are always looking for new ways to beat the drug squads.'

'You mean the police?'

'Yes, and to quote the good Senior Plata,

Police, Army, Federales; what's in a name? They are all working for one goal, the elimination of this insipid disease that our modern hedonistic society calls freedom of choice.'

'Quite a man.'

'Anyway, he said it was an easy task for him to get his river friends to help intercept this particular shipment.'

'Did he manage to destroy it?' asked Larsen.

'In a way, one evening they intercepted the smugglers while they were camped by the river. Plata and his friends pretended to be fishermen. He said it was easy to get them drunk and by the time the fourth bottle was opened the drug-runners didn't taste the sleeping draft. While they slept, Plata and friends had the raw cocaine substituted with a mix of boric acid and chalk dust.'

'Surely they would have noticed when they woke?'

'No. Drug wrapping is not very sophisticated; just lots of clear plastic and aluminium foil to keep the cocaine dry. Plata's only regret was he wasn't able to swap out the sample package; that had been opened and would have aroused suspicion if anyone tasted its contents.'

'You mean Kaufmann's just imported a load of chalk dust?' said Larsen.

'The very same,' said Marcel.

'Oh he's going to be so angry when he finds out,' laughed Larsen. 'Serves him right, wouldn't want to be in his shoes when his backers find out what a screw-up he's made.'

'Has anyone noticed how ridiculous the situation is?' said Bill.

'This whole voyage has been ridiculous,' said Stephen.

'No, that's not what Edward means,' said Larsen. 'Is it, Edward?'

He shook his head, 'Don't you see how strange it is? Kaufmann hires a yacht, full of crew to sail to the Amazon, bring back a load of cocaine, and then just says good-bye. It doesn't add up. Why would Kaufmann leave us here, with the perfect way to make port and turn him in?'

'Right,' said Larsen, 'I want the boat searched from bow to stern. We may only have a few minutes, although I imagine Kaufmann will want to be far enough away that he cannot be considered a suspect.'

'A suspect in what?' said Edward.

'Something that goes *tick tock*,' said John.

'You mean a bomb?' Bill said, his eyes opening wide.

'When you find it, don't touch it, that's John's task. Right, let's get going.'

Fifteen minutes later they reassembled in the main saloon.

'There just has to be a bomb,' said Larsen. 'Are you all sure you've searched everywhere possible?'

'Did anyone search my cabin?' asked Bill.

Everyone shook their heads. 'We thought you did,' said Elijah.

'No, I searched the galley.'

'Quick,' said Larsen, 'lifejackets on, and up on deck. Marcel, Stephen, get the dinghy over the side, ship the outboard and get ready to get off the boat. John, Elijah, this is your area of expertise, how can I help?'

'By getting the hell out of here,' said Elijah, 'in case there is a bomb and it goes off.'

'No way,' interrupted Larsen, 'this is my boat, I'm staying,'

'Probable location is under the bunk,' said Elijah, 'he didn't have enough time to get sophisticated with where to leave it.'

John carefully opened the door under Bill's bunk and found what they were looking for, two pounds of fused semtex and a digital timer.

'What do you think, John?' asked Elijah.

'Quite professional,' said John, picking it up.

'Careful,' said Larsen, taking a deep breath.

'Not to worry; there's no trip wire or movement sensors. Otherwise it would have gone off as soon as he armed it. It is on a timer and if it's accurate I'd say we have about twenty minutes. I'll take it up top and throw it over the side.'

'No, wait a minute,' said Larsen, 'I've got an idea. If you throw it over the side it will be 500 feet down before it explodes and Kaufmann might get curious and return. Take it up on deck and place it in the dinghy.'

John carefully carried the bomb up on deck and did as instructed.

'Stephen,' said Larsen, 'get a couple of jerry cans, make sure they're full of diesel and put them either side of the bomb, pack it with some cushions, I want the diesel to ignite when the bomb goes off, should make a nice big ball of flame.'

They stood on deck and watched the glow of the explosion on the horizon.

'Pity about the dinghy,' said Larsen.

40

Picknick on the Watercress

'Are you awake, Rachael?'

'Yes. Can't you sleep either? What time is it?'

Hannah felt around for her phone.

'It's four-thirty; happy birthday, Sis.'

'Happy birthday to you, too,' said Rachael.

'I wish Bill was here,' said Hannah. 'I really do miss him. I wonder what happened to him. I still think it was my fault. If only I had been better behaved.'

'I feel the same way, too. I had that nightmare again last night. You know what I mean? the one about Bill being in a car that crashes into a river and he's not able to escape,' said Rachael, starting to sniffle.

'Mine is different. I see him washed overboard from a cruise ship and he tries to shout for help, but no one hears him. He keeps swimming after the boat but is never able to catch it. It's horrible, makes me cry.'

'I'm glad there's no school today,' said Rachael. 'What shall we do?'

'How about a picnic, just the two of us? We don't want Abigail, she'll just spoil it.'

'We can make sandwiches and cut some of the cake Grandma made on Sunday,' said Rachael.

'But where can we go? It's supposed to rain later today.'

'I know,' said Hannah, 'remember the film *The Railway Children?* We'll go into town to the Watercress line and pretend to be the girls. We can get cups of tea at the station and spend the day riding up and down the railway. I think they have steam trains running at this time of the year.'

'Brilliant! But how will we get there? Mum can't take us.'

'Simple, we'll just cycle into town. We'll tell Gran we're going to see some friends in town and be back in the afternoon. After all, it's not any further than the shops and we do that on Saturdays when we go to see Sophie.'

They woke again at nine-fifty.

'Rachael, it's almost ten, we must have fallen back to sleep.'

'Still want to go for a picnic?' said Hannah. 'Gran's probably gone shopping with Mum. We'll have to ask Abigail.'

'She'll probably say no, you know how she likes to spoil our fun. Let's not tell her.'

'OK, fine by me.'

They got dressed and went downstairs to make their sandwiches.

'Where's Abigail?'

'Isn't she in her bedroom?'

'No, I looked. Her bed is made, as usual, but there's no sign of her.'

'Must be a note somewhere, check the table?'

'Yep, here it is: *Gone to the farm for eggs, back by one, Abigail.* And she's left her phone behind.'

'Well, that solves our problem,' said Rachael. 'There's no one here to say no. We can't text her, so we'll just leave her a note. See how she likes it. You remember what Uncle Harry says?'

'It's always better to say you're sorry than ask permission and be told no,' said Hannah, laughing. 'What time is the first train?'

'I think there's usually one just before noon. I seem to remember it takes about an hour to get to Alton. We can get off for an hour, have our picnic, and then catch a later one back.'

'Good, hope it doesn't rain on us. Do you remember what the fare is?'

'Probably the same as last time, I'm sure I've got enough in my purse.'

'Where's the cake? It's not in the tin?' said Rachael.

'If it's not in the tin then Gran must have taken it with her.'

'Doesn't matter, I'll grab some biscuits instead.'

Sandwiches made and packed they set off into town on their bicycles.

At the station they chained their bikes to the bike-rack, and purchased two returns to Alton.

'C'mon, let's find a compartment that's empty,' said Hannah.

Climbing on board, they slammed the door and found an empty compartment with a small table. Hannah slid the door closed while Rachael placed their backpacks containing their picnic on the table.

The compartment smelled of age, damp and long since smoked cigarettes. The heating had just come on and the element under the seat creaked from the flow of fresh steam from the engine.

'Look, it's starting to rain,' said Hannah, head halfway out of the small ventilation window, 'and we forgot the tea.'

'That's OK; we can get some from the buffet car and have our picnic on the train. Let's wait for the train to get going and I will go have a look.'

They didn't have to wait long. With a shrill scream from its whistle *Lord Nelson* let out a blast of steam and smoke from its chimney, spun its massive driving wheels and set out on the 40-minute run to Alton.

'Hannah, watch the backpacks, I'll be right back with the teas.'

The train was quiet. Rachael didn't have to wait long to be served and was soon back in the compartment with Hannah.

'It's not the same without Bill, is it?' said Hannah wistfully, as they finished their tea.

'Hmm, I know what you mean. If he was here just now he would be making up some sort of story about us being spies on the Orient Express or something.'

'And be getting out the cards. I'm sure he was a better player than he let on, I think he let us win more than we should,'

'I guessed that much. What are we going to do, then?'

'Remember what Mrs Smallwood, the counsellor, said to do when we felt unhappy?'

'Yes, I've got a note pad, do you have a pen?'

'I'm sure I do,' Hannah said, rummaging in her backpack.

They cleared a space on the small table and got ready to write.

'In *The Railway Children*, they wrote a letter and asked the station porter to give it to the old gentleman on the train, remember?' said Hannah.

'That wouldn't work,' said Rachael. 'We just can't go up to any old gentleman and give him a letter.'

'Anyway, let's write down what we feel,' said Hannah.

'You start,' said Rachael. 'I'm not sure how to say what I feel.'

Hannah started writing,

> *Dear Dad,*
> *We all miss you, especially Mum. We are having the day off school today and celebrating our birthday on the train. Lord Nelson is in steam today and we should be in Alton in a few minutes. We stopped and fed the ducks on the way to the station, don't worry, we didn't get wet. Abigail has gone for eggs and Gran has gone to see Mum.*
> *We're sorry if we made you angry and you don't like us anymore. We all wish you'd come home. Rachael and I promise to be good and make our beds every morning without being asked, and keep*

our room tidy. We also promise not to pick on Abigail and make her angry, at least we'll try. We've washed your car and cleaned out all the rubbish so it's now ready for the school-run when you return. Love Rachael and Hannah.

'Now what will we do with the letter if we are not going to give it to an old gentleman?' said Rachael, as the train came to a halt in Alton station.

'I've been thinking about that. Remember what we do at Christmas with our letter to Santa?'

'We can't post it up the chimney,' said Rachael. 'There's no fire at home this time of the year. It would just lie in the grate and Abigail would read it and tell us off for being soft.'

'Grab your backpack and follow me. I have an idea,' said Hannah as the train pulled into the station.

They got off the train and walked up the platform to where the *Lord Nelson* was being readied for its run back down to Alresford.

They stopped by the cab of the engine and Hannah said, 'Do you see what I see, Rachael?'

'I get you, there's the fire and that thing sticking up at the front is definitely a chimney. But how do we do it? They're not going to just let us climb up into the cab and shove the letter into the fire, are they?'

The answer came from an unexpected source. The driver, who had been chatting to the fireman, shouted down to the girls, 'On a school trip, ladies?'

Rachael said, 'No, we've got the day off. It's our birthday and we are having a party on the train.'

'Where's your friends?' asked the driver.

'It's just us,' replied Hannah.

'Shame, birthday party and no friends to share it with,' said the fireman, who by now had climbed down out of the cab and was rubbing the painted number of the engine with an oily rag.

'You like steam trains?' asked the driver.

'Yes,' the girls replied.

'So do my grandchildren,' he said. 'Would you like to climb up onto the footplate?'

Rachael and Hannah stared at each other for a moment then turned and said, 'Yes, please.'

'Richard,' said the driver, 'help the young ladies up before you uncouple, would you?'

'Sure thing, Bert.'

Within minutes the girls were standing in the cab, staring at the plethora of levers and valves above the blazing fire within the firebox.

'I'm afraid you can't ride on the engine back to Alresford, ladies,' said Bert looking at their faces.

'Thanks, we do understand, but we were wondering if we could ask another favour?' said Hannah.

'What would that be?' asked Bert.

Hannah looked at Rachael then turned to Bert and explained about the letter.

'No problem,' said Bert. 'If it will help you feel better, Richard and I would be delighted to help. Richard, the shovel please. We can't have these ladies put their hands near the fire, now can we?'

Richard reached over and opened the doors to the fire box; a blast of hot air emanated from it.

'Right, ladies, pass me your letter, then both of you hold onto the handle of the shovel.'

Puzzled, Hannah passed the letter to Bert. The girls held on to the shovel handle, and then he placed the letter on the blade.

'Now, carefully place the end of the shovel inside the fire and tip the letter off.'

Before the letter touched the glowing coals it had burst into flames and disappeared into the innards of the firebox. They quickly pulled the shovel back from the intense heat and Richard closed the firebox doors.

♦

'What a lovely day it's been,' said Rachael, as they put their bikes in the garage.

'And just where have you two been?' asked Abigail.

'We left you a note,' said Hannah.

'You're not supposed to leave the house without telling me, you know the rules.'

'Well, maybe you should follow them yourself,' said Rachael.

'I was doing something important, we needed eggs,' said Abigail, as she stormed off into the kitchen.

'Bet she went to see Timmy Horton,' said Rachael.

'I told you – *his name is Timothy*,' shouted Abigail.

As the twins headed for the front room, they heard the sound of the post being delivered.

'I'll get it,' said Hannah. 'You go turn on the telly and find us a movie to watch.' She was quickly back, a puzzled look on her face.

'What's up?' said Rachael. 'You look like you've seen a ghost.'

'Rachael, something weird has happened. I think it's a letter from Dad.'

'What's that?' said Abigail, as she came into the room rolling up the cord on the Dyson.

'I said, it might be a letter from Dad,' said Hannah. 'It looks like his handwriting.'

'Here, let me have a look,' said Abigail, reaching to grab it.

'Leave it alone, I saw it first, he's my dad too,' said a defiant Hannah.

'All right, keep the letter; we'll see what Mum has to say about it. I'm going to call her right now. She'll tell you to give it to me.'

'Can I see it?' asked Rachael, as Abigail went out to the hall-phone.

She returned a few minutes later and said, 'Mum says she'll be straight home and not to open it till she gets here. She also said Grandma and Grandpa are coming over.'

Hannah made a rude face at Abigail and, clutching the letter, sat down on the settee with Rachael to wait for their mum.

♦

They assembled in the living room and waited while Ruth opened the letter; it was addressed to "The Drysdale Family." She looked at the stamp and saw it was posted in The Azores. She quickly scanned the letter before reading it out loud.

> *Dear everyone,*
> *I felt I have to write and apologise and ask for your forgiveness for the pain I have caused you. I see now what I did was wrong. Since so much time has passed I felt that I owed you this letter. I am very sorry for what I have done to you all and don't deserve your forgiveness. I have done something terrible and I need to start a new life. I will not bother you again. I just wanted you to know that I see things much clearer now.*
> *Bill*

Ruth looked up from the letter to see five pairs of tear-filled eyes.

'He's not coming home,' sobbed Hannah, hugging Rachael.

No one spoke. Tears were wiped, and noses blown. It was the girls' grandmother who spoke first. 'At least he's all right, sounds like he's taking care of himself. Always was the practical one – our only one,' she said, breaking down into floods of tears.

Ruth said, sniffing, 'That's it, then. He's made a new life for himself; I suppose we'll have to do the same.'

Agnes stood up and walked over to Ruth, 'are you all right?'

'Yes, just need to catch my breath, bit of a shock, the letter.'

'Do you want a glass of water?'

'No thanks; just let me rest for a minute.'

'If you're sure, in the meantime life must go on, and it's half past five, anyone hungry?'

No one spoke, so she said, 'We must keep up our strength, I'll make us something.'

'Oh, gosh,' said Ruth. 'Rachael and Hannah, I forgot it's your birthday today. Uncle Harry is coming to dinner tonight. It was supposed to be a surprise for you both since he couldn't make it to your party on Saturday.'

'Wonderful,' said Hannah.

'Shouldn't be a problem,' said Agnes. 'Just what we need, someone to cheer us up. What shall I make for him?'

'I'll help Grandma, mum you need to rest more,' said Abigail. 'We have a large piece of roast beef in the fridge. We've plenty of vegetables and we could make rhubarb crumble for pudding, I picked some rhubarb this morning.'

'Thank you dear,' said Agnes. 'Let's get started then, shall we.'

'I'll set the table,' said Ruth getting up out of her chair.

'No that's all right mum, we'll take care of the table, you rest; you've had a big shock,' said Hannah.

'For goodness sake girls, I'm not an invalid, I'll set the table. In the meantime, Rachael, Hannah, whatever you were doing today needs to be washed off of your faces, just what have you been up to?'

'We went for a ride on the Watercress line,' said Hannah. 'We had a birthday picnic on the train and we wrote – ' she stopped and looked at Rachael. 'Rachael, do you realise what's happened?' she said, with a look of awe on her face.

Rachael nodded solemnly.

'What are you talking about?' asked Ruth.

Hannah and Rachael told their mum all about the trip on the train, the writing of the letter, and posting it into the firebox on the engine.

'So, you wrote and posted a letter to your dad and he replies the same day? Not even the Royal Mail is that fast. That's got to be the weirdest thing I've ever heard. Wonder what your Uncle Harry will think of that? Now off you go and get cleaned up.'

The doorbell rang at seven-thirty. 'I'll get it,' shouted Ruth as she went to the front door.

'Evening, Harry.'

'Good evening Ruth, you look well.'

'Thanks, I've felt better. Welcome to the house of chaos.'

'Thanks. I've brought this gift for the twins; hope they'll like it. Saw it in a games shop a week ago.'

'Sounds great, whatever it is. You'll have to excuse us this evening, Harry, we're a bit preoccupied. We've had a letter from Bill.'

'What does he say? Is he all right?'

'Not much, and yes, but come on through. Dinner is about to go on the table, you can read the letter while you eat, it's a short one.'

Afterwards, as the table was being cleared, Hannah asked, 'Uncle Harry, is there anything we can do to find Dad? Now we know he's in the Azores.'

'Was, you mean,' said Abigail.

Ignoring her sister's interruption, Hannah said, 'Can't we just ask the police on the island to look for him?'

Harry breathed out, thought for a moment, and picked up the envelope. 'It's not quite that easy, the island is big and full of lots of tourists at this time of the year. Lots of cruise liners call there. He could have been working on one of them and now left. Also, the postmark is five days ago. He could have been on the island on holiday and has now flown somewhere else, back to where he is now living. I'm sorry, girls; we would need more information than just a letter.'

'What sort of information?' asked Rachael.

'Well in, say, a bank robbery, we would interview witnesses, check for CCTV footage also we might look through the records to see if we had any known criminals living in the area.'

'Would you look for fingerprints?' asked Rachael.

'Sometimes, but if it were a public building there would already be many fingerprints and it would be too time-consuming to find the criminal's amongst everyone else's.'

'Suppose the only fingerprints were the criminal's? What would you do then?'

'We would run them through the PND.'

'What's a PND, Uncle Harry?' said Rachael.

'Sorry, so used to using acronyms. It stands for Police National Database. If someone has been fingerprinted, then their details will be on file.'

'Did you do that when Dad went missing?' asked Rachael.

'No, it wouldn't have served any purpose; your Dad wasn't a criminal.'

'Wait a minute,' said Hannah, 'tourists have to give their fingerprints when they enter a country; we did that last year when we went to Florida.'

'That would work if your Dad was here to give his fingerprints,' said Harry.

'But then there would be no need to, silly,' said Abigail, while collecting the dirty dishes.

'No, wait a minute,' said Harry. 'What are you suggesting, Hannah?'

'You said that Dad might be on the island as a tourist or even working on a cruise ship. If he was, then somewhere he would have to have had his fingerprints taken, if so, that might help us to track him down.'

'There's still the problem of not having a copy of his fingerprints to start with,' said Harry.

'What about the envelope?' asked Ruth.

'Same scenario as the bank I mentioned earlier,' said Harry, 'too many people will have handled the letter, how would we know which ones are your dad's? Besides, looking at the paper it's written on, many hands have probably handled the notebook the letter has been torn from. No, to use fingerprints to attempt to trace your dad, we would require a known set, ones that could only be his, something only your dad has touched.'

Hannah said, 'If we could find that something, what would you do?'

'Humour them, Harry, it's their birthday.' said Ruth.

'Well, if you had an object that only your dad had handled, we could dust it for prints then run it through the computer and see if he has been printed at some time, like when you went to Florida.'

'Dad didn't go with us, he had the flu,' said Abigail.

'Would you all like to go through to the living room?' suggested Agnes. 'The fire's lit and I'll bring the coffee through in a minute.'

Ruth sat in the wingback by the fire and put her feet up on the footstool.

'Does your back still ache, Mum? Would you like another cushion?' asked Abigail.

'Yes please.'

'Uncle Harry,' said Rachael, 'I think we know where there's an object that only Dad has touched. Shall we get it?'

'Ruth,' said Harry, looking uncomfortable.

'You've got centre stage, I'm intrigued. OK girls, what is it you have to show your Uncle Harry?'

Rachael and Hannah got up from the settee and picking up the other footstool between them they walked over to the bookcase.

'It's behind the book on the history of cultivating roses, Hannah,' said Rachael steadying her sister, who was on her tiptoes.

Hannah pulled the thick volume from its resting place and handed it down to Rachael. Steadying herself, she reached into the cavity with her free hand and with her fingertips extracted a half full bottle of Jack Daniels.

'Will this do, Uncle Harry?' asked Rachael.

Harry stepped over to the bookcase and removed a handkerchief from his pocket and carefully took the bottle by the top of the neck.

'Can you see any fingerprints, Rachael?' asked Hannah.

'No, can you?'

'Me neither.' They turned to their uncle. 'Can you see any?'

'I'm afraid fingerprints don't just show up, like a label. They have to be brought out by scientific methods.'

'Like dusting with soot?' asked Hannah.

'Not quite, there are many methods used, depending on the circumstances,' he replied. 'It's a job for the SOCO team; they're specially trained to look for fingerprints.'

'What does SOCO mean?' asked Rachael.

'It stands for Scene Of Crime Officer, although they are now called CSI's, and yes I do, we have a team based in the local headquarters.'

'Could you ask them to look at this bottle and see if Dad's prints are on it?'

'Girls, it's past your bedtime,' said Abigail, 'you've got school tomorrow and besides, Uncle Harry has a lot more important things to do than dust an old bottle at this time of night.'

Harry looked at two saddened faces that had just found, only to have taken away from them, the last hope of finding their dad.

'I'll tell you what, girls, since it's your birthday; I'll put in a call to central control and see if anyone is available to look at the bottle, but please don't get your hopes up. We have been very busy lately.'

'Tonight, now?' said Hannah.

'Well, no, that's not quite what I meant. Unfortunately, it can take up to a week to get a CSI team to the scene.'

'But Dad could be miles away by then,' said Hannah, tears filling her eyes.

'Oh why not, give me a minute; I'll see what I can do.' He removed his mobile phone from his jacket pocket and scrolled through the directory before pressing one of the keys.

Two faces watched the phone, listening to it ringing, willing it to be answered.

The ringing stopped, 'Who's that? Ted its DCI Greyson. Are you by any chance available to lift a couple of prints? Yes, I realise you've been on duty since six this morning, and you haven't had a day off for two weeks. It's a missing person investigation. Remember that missing father back in February – yes, I know that was months ago. We may have a lead but time is something we don't have, you will, good, here's the address.'

After giving directions to their house, he turned to the girls. 'You're very fortunate. That was Ted Barker; he's just finishing at a scene of crime in the town and will be here in ten minutes.'

Ted was there in seven; Harry showed him into the lounge and introduced him to the family. 'This is Sergeant Barker; he's with the CSI team.' He nodded, 'Over to you Ted.'

Forty excited minutes later, a full set of prints from Bill's right hand were on display on a Home Office fingerprint card.

Harry showed Ted out to his van, and then returned to the house to be met by six pairs of expectant eyes staring at him.

'What's next, Uncle Harry?'

'Bed, that's what's next,' said Abigail, before Harry could reply, 'you've had a busy day and you've got school in the morning.'

'Mum,' pleaded Rachael. 'We're not done yet.'

'What more is there to do?' she asked.

'Uncle Harry still has to check the files to see if Dad's fingerprints show up.'

Ruth turned to Harry. 'Is that possible?'

'Sure, all I need to do is to go into the office. We've all the equipment needed there. After all, Bill's disappearance is still an open case.'

'I'll get our coats,' said an excited Hannah.

'Oops,' said Harry, 'sorry, Ruth, I meant tomorrow when I got into the office.'

The look on the twins' faces made him change this mind. 'Well, it actually might be better if we do it this evening. I can be very busy during the day and might not be able to get to it for quite some time.'

'I'll still get the coats,' said Hannah.

'Well, if you're going to play Sherlock Holmes, Grandpa and I are off to do the dishes,' said Agnes.

'I'll help,' said Abigail.

Rachael sneered and stuck out her tongue at Abigail.

'Wait for me girls,' said Ruth.

'You're not going out at this time of night in your condition, Mum, are you?' said Abigail.

'Of course I am, I want to see what your Uncle Harry can find out. Besides you know what sort of mischief your sisters can get into when they're on their own.'

It only took a few moments to scan in Bill's fingerprints.

They waited for the results to appear on the screen. A sigh of disappointment went up when the only result was from when Bill had been arrested for his DUI offence.

'That's just for the UK, isn't it?' asked Ruth.

'Yes.'

'Can you do a global search?'

'Not from here. There are various agencies to go through.'

'Like Interpol?' asked Hannah.

'That would do for Europe, and in the USA we would contact their Border Control.'

'How does it work?' asked Ruth.

'Being the SIO in the case I'd send a request through to my boss. She would send it up the line to the Foreign Office. They in turn would get in touch with their counterpart in the respective countries. If they deemed the case important enough, they'd respond with the information. That's if there was any information.'

'How long would that take?' asked Ruth.

'How long is a piece of string? I'm afraid we're stumped.'

'Wait a minute,' said Ruth. 'I think I know someone who might be able to help. Can I use your phone?'

'Sure, press nine for an outside line.'

Two pairs of eyes watched as Ruth dialled.

'Kenneth, it's Ruth Drysdale – no, not time yet. How are you? – Listen, I'm sorry to disturb you at home—oh, you're working, thought you'd retired – yes I know what that's like – No, this is not a business call; I need some help. Please say no if I'm putting you on the spot.'

Ruth recounted the story of Bill's disappearance up to the arrival of the letter and the subsequent fingerprints.

'Harry, Kenneth would like to speak to you,' said Ruth, handing him the phone.

They talked for a while then Harry hung up. 'Hmm. Wish I had your contacts,' he said.

'What'd he say?'

'He'd look into it and get back to me.'

'Did he say how long?'

'Short string, he's got my email address and will send through what he finds. In the meantime, it's going to be a long night. There's a drinks machine in the canteen. The desk sergeant can show you where it is. Ask him to show you round the station. He likes to show it off.'

When they returned, Harry was reading a report that he had just printed.

'Reply already?' said Ruth.

'Yes, remarkable result. Apparently, it does pay to know the right people.'

'What does it say?'

'It says Bill's fingerprints have turned up in the Homeland Security database in the USA.'

'Oh dear,' said Hannah. 'Dad's in trouble.'

'He was,' said Harry, 'but not now. Your dad has been very busy. This is a report from the Captain of the US Coastguard Cutter USS *Alviso*. In it he says that a fingerprint match identified the purser as one Edward Cook. He was apprehended on suspicion of a homicide on board the British sailing vessel *Leviathan*. The case was investigated, and he was exonerated, no further action required.'

'Wow,' was all the twins could say.

Ruth fainted back into Harry's chair.

'Mum, are you all right?' asked Rachael.

'Yes – I'm fine. Not sure I wanted to hear that about your Dad.'

'I'll drive you all back,' said Harry. 'Then I'm off for home before tonight becomes tomorrow.'

Ruth waved goodbye to Harry at the door and went through into the living room to break the news.

'So that's what he meant by he had done something terrible,' said Agnes. 'My poor baby, what must he be going through?'

'Have the twins gone to bed, Mum?' said Abigail.

'No, they said they have some homework to do for tomorrow. They're on my computer in my study.'

'That's new, not doing their homework has been the norm for them lately,' said Abigail, getting up to go and send the twins to bed.

'Leave them, they've had a shock this evening, maybe some good will come from it. I'll send them off to bed when I go up.'

Ruth said goodnight to Agnes and Arthur and went into her study. Rachael and Hannah were busy on the computer.

'Time to go to bed, girls,' she said.

'We're almost done, Mum. A few more minutes, that's all.'

'OK, just make sure you turn off the computer and the lights when you're finished.'

♦

When Ruth came down in the morning she found her desk covered with faxes, emails, photos of sailboats under sail, photos of luxury yacht interiors, all downloaded from the internet. Stuck to the wall opposite her desk were the old newspaper clippings of Bill's disappearance.

Out of habit she clicked on the email button. She didn't just have one email; there were ten of them from various places around the world.

She scrolled down to the first; it was an email from a US coastguard giving contact details of the USS *Alviso*. Next on the list was a reply from the Captain of the *Alviso* to a question about the incident on the island of St Kitts. Ruth read the reply; it corroborated the information Harry had gleaned the previous evening, didn't mention Bill by name.

Next was an email from the port captain in Bermuda. The yacht *Leviathan* had taken on board fuel, provisions, and water and departed for the Azores. On down the list next was a short email from the port captain at Horta: *Leviathan* departed, unknown destination. The next emails were from various ports on the Iberian Peninsula: no sign of the *Leviathan*.

She was about to turn off her computer but was now curious about what else the girls had been looking at. The YouTube tab caught her interest; the girls had apparently found a video of what looked like a boxing match on the USS *Alviso*. How clever her girls were. She just wished they would apply themselves in the same way at school.

Boxing had never held much interest for her, so she was about to close the tab when she saw something that stopped her dead. It was one lone figure in the crowd watching and cheering the boxing match. A tall sailor who could have been her Bill, except this sailor had shorter hair, looked well-tanned, taller, and more muscular; all the same he did look like Bill.

Just then Abigail came into the room and said, 'I wish you wouldn't let the twins stay up so late, it's difficult enough to get them out of bed in the morning. There's not a peep from their room, I'll have to go wake them.'

Ruth looked at the clock on the study wall. 'Give them another half an hour; I'll drive you all to school this morning.'

'Mum, you spoil them too much,' said Abigail, slamming the door of the study.

Ruth was distracted by the sound of raised voices from the kitchen. Entering it, she got a big surprise; the twins were just finishing their breakfast.

'Morning Mum, we've got a big surprise for you.'

'What's that? You've got out of bed early, tidied your room, and made up your beds?' said Abigail sneering at them.

'No,' Hannah replied, 'we've seen Dad on the internet.'

'You mean, that video, you think that's your Dad?' said their mother.

'Sure,' said Rachael, 'he's lost a lot of weight, and cut his hair shorter than usual. He looks great! We're sure that's Dad.'

'You're right, he does look great,' agreed Ruth.

41
Home again

Bill made a mug of hot chocolate as the familiar profile of the chain ferry came into view. He retired to his cabin and climbed up onto his bunk to think.

Would Beryl and Dot still be at the *Admiral*? It would be good to catch up with them. He was sure they would love to hear about his adventures and just maybe they could help him find a job. Or maybe the elusive Mr Smith might help. He'd have to talk to Larsen about that. No matter what, the *Leviathan* would be in Poole Harbour for the winter and there wouldn't be any work for him while it was in the yard being worked on.

Larsen had radioed ahead, and arrangements had been made for them to tie up at the same dock they had occupied before they left for the Amazon. Customs wouldn't be a problem, especially since Kaufmann, his cargo and his team were gone.

Immigration took some explaining, but after a long interview, the *Leviathan's* crew were cleared to go ashore, and Bill went across the road to the *Admiral Aubrey*.

'Are Beryl or Dot around?' he asked the bartender.

'No, they won't be back till later in the day. Can I get you something to drink?'

'Black tea, please.'

He smiled to himself, here he was in a pub and only wanted a cup of tea.

At four-thirty, he heard Beryl's unmistakable voice coming from the kitchen. Not being able to wait any longer, he stood up and went through.

'Edward! You're back, what a lovely surprise,' said Beryl. 'I saw the masts and knew you wouldn't be far away.'

'Wow, I wouldn't have recognised you,' said Dot. 'You look fantastic!'

'Thanks,' said a surprised Bill. 'Hadn't realised I've changed that much, maybe a little weight off the middle, but it's still me.'

'This calls for a celebration,' said Beryl, 'Dot, the champagne—not the stuff we serve in the bar, the good stuff.'

Bill put up his hand and said, 'No thanks, Beryl. Just a good cup of tea and a chat will do.'

'Not even a tiny glass?' said Dot.

'You can, but I don't drink.'

'You poor dear,' said Dot, muttering to herself as she went off to put the kettle on.

Three hours and many cups later Bill returned to the *Leviathan* to think. Beryl had said he could work in the hotel if he wanted. Michelle was getting married in a few weeks and there would be a vacancy. But was it what he wanted? The long hours wouldn't be a problem, after all that's what the last months had been, long days with interrupted sleep. But, of course, there was the adventure. He decided to sleep on it and make up his mind in the morning, but first he needed to get ready for dinner.

Much to his surprise and delight, Beryl had invited the crew of the *Leviathan,* plus Betty, Mrs Philip, her daughter Sandra with husband and dad Terry, along with Bob, John, Dave, and Pete from the boatyard.

Dot had made a roast dinner for them with trifle for desert. After months of shipboard food Bill smiled to himself as he watched the crew eat as though they hadn't eaten for months. He didn't mind though; it was good to be back and away from the cruising diet.

Bill stayed on after the meal to help clear up. He might as well get used to the hotel life he thought, realising he had subconsciously made his mind up to take the job.

'Beryl, could I stay here as part of my pay? I'm not sure I will be able to stay on board while the yard works on the *Leviathan*?'

'Certainly, dear, you could have room seven if you wanted. Does that mean you've made up your mind?'

'Yes, but right now I just need to go to bed and get some sleep.'

'OK dear, we'll see you in the morning.'

'Night Dot, Beryl,' he said, as he left the *Admiral,* the door closing softly behind him. He ambled across the road and stopped at the edge of the quayside and looked up at the clear night sky. The song, *when you wish upon a star* floated through his consciousness. If only, he shrugged and climbed down the ladder onto the *Leviathan's* deck.

Larsen was sitting at the saloon table reading.

'Evening Edward, all washed up?'

'Dishes yes, me no. Captain I have question, I would like to work for Beryl and Dot in the hotel till the *Leviathan* is ready to go to sea again, that is if you won't need me on board during the overhaul?'

'That's fine by me. The yard can't take us for a couple of weeks and there is several weeks of work to do on her. Will need you back on board after that.'

'Great, I think I'll turn in, got an early start in the morning, good night.'

'Good night Edward.'

At a quarter to six in the morning he was back in the *Admiral's* kitchen. Beryl and Dot were in full swing, preparing breakfasts for the early morning risers.

'Beryl,' said Bill, 'do you think it would be wise for me to go and have a look at my old house? Not to knock on the door or anything like that, just to have one last look? For all I know, they could have sold up and moved somewhere else.'

'Is that what you really want to do dear? Or is there a deeper reason?'

'I suppose I want to know they're alright.'

'Suppose your wife has a new man – your girls a new father?'

'I'd deserve that. As long as they're happy, that's all that's important.'

'Well, if you're sure. Will you take the train?'

Bill shook his head. 'There aren't any trains to Alresford anymore.' Then, remembering the Watercress line and the day trips with the girls, he smiled and sniffed.

'You all right?'

'Yes, just some memories coming back. I thought of asking Terry to drive me if he's still around.'

'Not sure, shall I call him for you?'

♦

Terry stopped his taxi in the bus lay-by. 'I'll be back in an half an hour to pick you up. Are you sure you don't want me to stay with you? I could park the taxi a way down the road and walk back.'

'No, thanks, this is something I need to do alone. See you in half an hour,' Bill said, shutting the door.

The bus lay-by was directly in front of the driveway. He stepped back into the shadows of the rickety bus shelter, leaned on the wall and stared up the driveway at the house, trying to still his racing heartbeat.

Nothing had changed. The house looked just like he remembered it. The garage door was partially open, and he saw what looked like Ruth's car. His watch said it was ten-fifteen. Ruth should have already gone to work. What had happened?

Bill stared intently at the front door, expecting to see her run out the house and jump in the car. Nothing happened. All was still until an eight-seater taxi turned into the driveway and drew up at the door.

The driver got out and rang the bell. Bill watched, hands trembling, wondering who would answer the door. He was disappointed. It was his mother. She said something to the driver then shut the door. The driver returned to the taxi and sat in the driver's seat waiting, but for whom? A few minutes later the garage door closed, the front door opened and out charged the twins, followed by Abigail and Bill's mother and father.

The taxi headed down the driveway towards Bill and the main road. It slowed, then stopped at the end of the driveway. For a moment Bill wanted to run out into the road and call, 'Here I am, I'm back!' But before he could say or do anything the taxi accelerated out of the driveway and went off in the direction of town.

Leaving the sanctuary of the bus shelter, Bill walked across the road and up the driveway. The noise of the gravel under foot made him nervous. He stepped onto the grass verge until he got to the front of the house. Would his key still fit the lock? To his surprise it turned easily and he was standing in the reception hall. It was as though he had just popped out to the shops for some groceries. It all looked just the same. Then why shouldn't it look the same? It was probably still the same Mrs Parker who kept it tidy.

He closed the door behind him, and then froze. He felt more trapped now than when he and Marcel had been locked in the Indian shack in the jungle. Not wanting to go forward in fear of what he might find, or back and never to know the truth. Suppose Ruth had a new man and he was in the kitchen or, worse still, in bed upstairs?

Nothing ventured, nothing gained, he said to himself. He slipped off his shoes and placed them on the doormat. Almost on tiptoes he walked forward to the kitchen, pushing the door open and peered inside, there was no sign of life. The table was tidy, breakfast dishes drying in the rack beside the sink, counters clear and clean. He relaxed a little and walked over to the sink and looked out onto the garden.

Next was the dining room. He saw, with joy, the mahogany dining table shining as though it was fresh out of the cabinet maker's workshop. The glass-fronted dresser that had been left to him by his grandmother was still full of his steeplechase trophies.

The front room was different. New carpet, settee and the old analogue television was gone, and a new, very large flat screen unit now hung from the wall. The fireplace, still with smouldering ashes and spark grill in place, brought back memories of when he, Ruth, and the girls used to toast marshmallows together.

Time to take the bull by the horns, he turned and retraced his steps to the bottom of the staircase. Taking a deep breath, he began to creep up the stairs, ready at the first sound to turn tail and run for the front door.

The first room on the right was Abigail's. Gently pushing the door open he looked in; surely no child lived here? Tidy and neat, her desk with bookshelf above showed signs of serious study having taken place. Out of curiosity Bill went over to Abigail's wardrobe and looked inside. Gone was the child, gone were the bright, cheerful, childhood dresses, now replaced by sober clothes that wouldn't look out of place on an office junior working in the city.

Sadness descended on him and he went out into the hall and down to the twins' room. Surely they hadn't changed? He smiled when he saw the sure signs of rebellion against order. Although the blankets were in place, they hadn't been tucked in all the way round, socks hung from drawer fronts, also it looked as though the soft toys had been having a battle and had fallen where they lay.

A little more contented, he took a deep breath and walked to the end of the corridor and the master bedroom. With trepidation Bill pushed the door open and entered. He was overjoyed to see the bed was not made and the covers were thrown back on Ruth's side. There was no one else.

He went into the room and lay down on the bed. He pulled the bedclothes over him, buried his head in her pillow, and breathed in deeply. The story of Goldilocks flooded into his mind, in a panic he threw back the bed clothes and got off the bed. He looked into the adjoining box room and saw that Ruth must be having a clear out. The twin's old bassinets were sitting in the middle of the small room and piles of baby clothes festooned the top of the small chest of drawers. As he walked back into the master bedroom he glanced at the bedside clock and realised Terry would be back in a few minutes to collect him. One last look at the bedroom, a shrug of his shoulders, and he started down the stairs realising this would have to be goodbye. They had got on well without him and would probably be better off without him complicating their lives by returning.

At the bottom of the stairs he noticed the study door was partially open and decided there was just enough time to go in and see what Ruth had been up to.

He walked in and looked out of the window at the back garden and the neatly tended flower beds, how did Ruth ever find the time to keep them so tidy?

He turned to leave, then stopped. There in front of him, covering the whole wall, were newspaper clippings, printed emails and maps. At first glance it looked like a mishmash of information, perhaps some project the twins were working on for school, then, when he looked more closely, he saw the wall had been laid out chronologically by date. This wasn't some school project; they had been trying to locate him.

There were even photographs of the USS *Alviso*, with its rigid hull inflatable racing in a circle, a huge rooster tail following behind. Most amazing of all was a whole set of photos of the *Leviathan*, including the interior, with his galley prominently placed in the middle. He got up and walked over to look closer at the photos.

All the way up, on the right-hand side, behind the door, were newspaper clippings. The oldest was from the local *Poole Echo*, then national papers, followed by police reports of his accident then subsequent disappearance. Some of the redtops were insinuating that Ruth had done away with him. How could they think that?

There were clippings telling of a broadcast by Ruth asking for help in finding him. Beside them were photocopies of police reports from airports and seaports. No sign of him, he had managed to disappear completely.

Then he saw his letter; it was right in the middle, tear-stained and crumpled. He tried to read it, but his tears wouldn't let him focus on the handwriting.

He pulled a handkerchief from his pocket and wiped his eyes. Right beside his letter was a police notice with his name, address and what looked like a fingerprint. There followed copies of official police and Immigration Office emails. They had still been looking for him up till a few days ago.

What he saw next stunned him. An email from the USA Homeland Security Service stating that a Edward Cook with these fingerprints was apprehended and released after questioning on the US Coastguard cutter, the USS *Alviso*. Next was a reply to an email from Captain

Delaware of the *Alviso*, stating that a Edward Cook had been questioned while working as crew on the SV *Leviathan*.

There were stacks of emails from cruising boats that had seen the *Leviathan*. There were also emails from port captains in Bermuda and The Azores stating when the *Leviathan* had arrived and departed; although nothing about recent sightings from Falmouth. His head started to swim, he felt trapped. Time to leave he thought, he definitely didn't want to be caught in the house.

This time he walked briskly down the path and arrived at the gate as Terry drove up.

'All as expected?' Terry asked as Bill closed the door and fastened his seat belt.

'If only.'

'What'd you mean?'

'I went to the house expecting them to have started a new life I – I assumed they would be getting along fine without me – now I don't know what to think'

'Shall I turn back?'

'No, it's too late for that.'

♦

'Your back,' said Beryl. 'You're just in time for lunch. How was it?'

'Fine, they seem to be doing Ok without me.'

'Disappointed?'

'Yes and no.'

'All right mister ambiguity, tell Beryl what the yes and no are?'

'The yes is, I was right, they don't need me.'

'And the no?'

'The no is – is, I just don't know. I had a look in the box room beside the main bedroom and saw Ruth was clearing out all the twins' baby things. Made me realise it's too late for me Beryl, I've lost the best thing I ever had and – and I'll never get it back.'

'Edward, I'm sure some day you'll settle down. Don't worry I'm sure it will all work out for the best.'

'How can it? Ruth and the girls were the only family I was ever likely to have, and now it's too late. I've lost them forever, and I thought.'

'You thought what?'

'My dream's back, well at least the latest version is.'

'What do you mean? The latest version, all dreams are different; usually something to do with what we were thinking about before we go to sleep.'

'In my dream I was back on the grassy slope by the river. Two young boys, they looked like they were brothers, about six and four years old, walked out of the woods on the far side. They sat down on the grass and stared at me, just smiling. Then as in my previous dreams the four-year-old stood up and started to walk towards the river. He stopped at the edge of the river, turned, and looked at the older boy and waved, the older boy waved back. I watched as the four-year old took a step onto the first of the steppingstones that led across the river

'Progress was slow; he had to negotiate the gaps between the steppingstones. Sometimes he stepped and other times he did a little jump. For the first time ever, he reached the far bank and walked slowly up the grassy slope towards me. He stepped into my embrace, curled up on my lap and fell asleep.'

'That why you wanted to see the house, hoped the family would still be there?'

Bill shrugged his shoulders and said, 'who knows. I'd thought I was all done with the dreams, looks like I'm stuck with them.'

'By the sounds of it they've changed, wouldn't you say?'

'Maybe, after all the others I thought this one might have been, a premonition of things to come, but I suppose not, just a variation on an old theme.'

'Well I suppose it is.'

'What do you mean?'

'You've held down a job for these last several months, cooked and cleaned for the crew and guests, had a fantastic adventure and you're now back waiting for the next adventure to start.'

'Beryl,' Bill said exhaling slowly, 'there was a time when that would have set my pulse racing, but now.'

'But now – what do you mean by, now?'

'Now it just sounds like a lot of sleepless nights and dishes to wash. I'd willingly give it all up to have a normal family life, no matter how many dishes there were too wash.'

'Here's my phone,' she said offering Bill her mobile. 'Give them a call, I sure they'd love to hear from you.'

'It's no use Beryl, I just couldn't. I walked out on them.'

'Edward, let's take one thing at a time. Tell me, and be honest with yourself, do you or don't you want to see your family again?'

'I – I suppose I do, but it's no good Beryl, they'll never take me back. Oh, I suppose the twins would be happy, but Ruth and Abigail will never want me back.'

'You just told me you wanted children.'

'My own is what I meant.'
'I thought you adopted Ruth's girls?'
'I did, but they never accepted me as their dad, I was just someone to keep the house tidy and run after them.'
'That's an old record you're playing Bill, time you sang a new song.'
'Huh, don't really feel like singing just now.'
'Edward, what would you do if Ruth walked in right now?'
'There's no chance that's going to happen.'
'Humour me, suppose she did, what would you do?'
'I'd – I'd probably faint.'
'Really?'
'Oh, I suppose I'd ask her to forgive me and ask if we could start again.
'Look, it'll be dinner time soon. We've a private function on this evening so I need you at your best. Why don't you go for a walk, get some fresh air; clear out the cobwebs.'
'Ok, see you later.'

♦

'Dot,' said Bill walking into the kitchen. 'I thought Beryl said we were going to have a full restaurant this evening?'
'We do. It's a private function, family reunion.'
'Oh – where's Beryl?'
'She's in the flat. She's on the phone, be here to help in a minute.'
'Ok, I'll nip upstairs and change.'

♦

'Is he back, Dot?' asked Beryl as she closed the door to their flat behind her.
'Just gone upstairs to change; are our guests here yet?' said Dot looking at the kitchen clock.
'No. Just talked with the taxi company, the taxi's stuck in a traffic jam in Ringwood. The dispatcher thinks they will be about another fifteen minutes.'
'It's so exciting Dot, just love parties, helps to.'
'I know Beryl, broken families are.'
'Are what Dot?' interrupted Bill as he walked into the kitchen.
'Oh—you know, are.'
'Are better off together,' interrupted Beryl.
'That's easy for you to say,' said Bill.
'Bill,' admonished Beryl. 'Remember Dot lost her children and it wasn't by choice either.'
'Sorry Dot, I forgot.'

'That's Ok. I understand what you must be feeling.'

'Edward,' said Beryl, 'can you go through to the laundry room and take the tablecloths and napkins out of the dryer. We'll need them tomorrow.'

'Beryl waited for Bill to leave then said to Dot. 'I'm going out to reception to wait for our guests. Make sure you keep Bill in here till I return, I don't want him wandering into the restaurant till we are ready.'

♦

'Dot, where's Beryl?'

'She's seating the guests. She said for you to get the starters on the trays, ready to take out,' replied Dot.

'Oh wonderful,' said Bill as the sound of crying babies could be heard coming from the restaurant. 'Great party this is going to be. What is it Dot, I've never seen you look so nervous?'

'It's nothing really; family gatherings are always difficult for me.'

'Oh sorry, short memory.'

'That's Ok.'

'Right,' said Beryl as she returned. The first our guests are seated, let's take the starters through. Edward, you first, please.'

Bill picked up his tray and walked blithely through into the restaurant and promptly dropped his tray.

The End.

Lightning Source UK Ltd.
Milton Keynes UK
UKHW050425240820
368570UK00002BA/25/J